JACK SHEPPARD

Contemplating his escape while chained and padlocked to the floor of a strong dungeon in Newgate.—Page 423.

LONDON :

JOHN WILLIAMS, 44, PATERNOSTER ROW.

1840.

THE
HISTORY
OF
JACK SHEPPARD:

HIS

WONDERFUL EXPLOITS AND ESCAPES.

A Romance,
FOUNDED ON FACTS.

WITH ORIGINAL ILLUSTRATIONS,
FROM DRAWINGS BY JACK SKETCH.

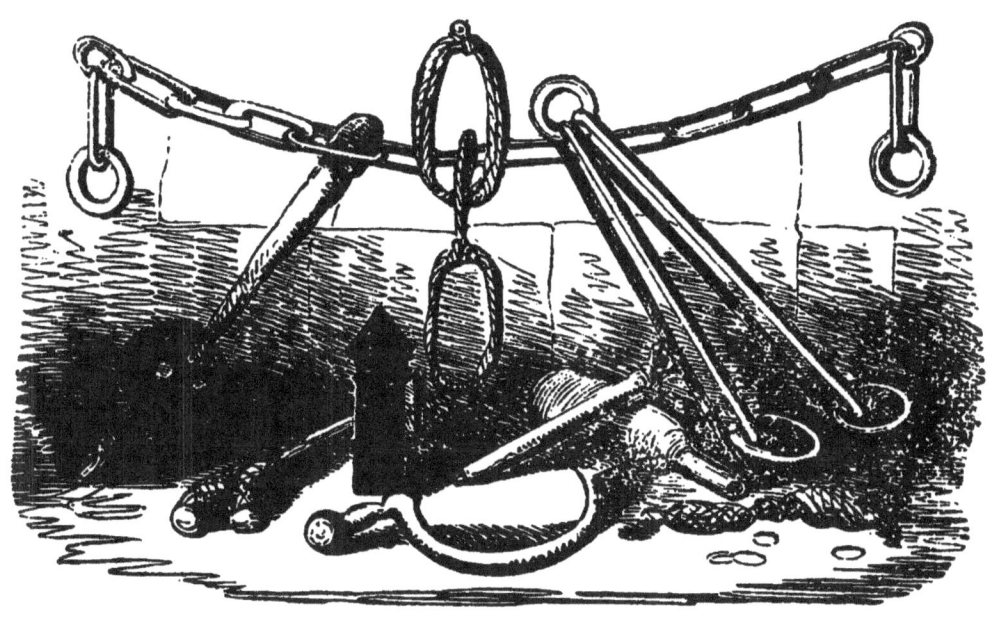

" TRUTH is stranger than *Fiction.*"

LONDON:

JOHN WILLIAMS, 44. PATERNOSTER-ROW,
AND 43. ALDERSGATE-STREET.
1840.

THE INTRODUCTION.

Newgate.

THE turnkeys bowed as a visiter entered the lodge of Old Newgate, Tuesday, November the 17th, 1724, the morning after the memorable execution of Jack Sheppard, and slipping a two-guinea piece into the hand of the head gaoler, Mr. Austin, requested to know if he could not be indulged with the sight of the building, particularly those portions of it that had been the scene of the wonderful escapes of this notorious and daring individual.

"Certainly, sir," answered that officer, respectfully touching his hat, and pocketing the money: " we don't show Newgate to every body that don't come here exactly on business; but to a gentleman like you, sir, as wants to inform your mind, or what not, why the case is different —it's always a pleasure then. We were just going our rounds, to see that our flock arn't in want of any thing, so you can't have a better opportunity."

" You have lost your most remarkable lodger," said the visiter.

A 2

" Oh! what Captain Sheppard?" answered the gaoler; "yes, he's gone, poor fellow, to our loss and his own too — why, we used to take a matter of thirty pound a day, sometimes, by the quality coming to see him! — Jack was an astonishing fellow, sir, a very astonishing fellow — he played me two or three scurvy tricks, certainly, plague on him; but I can't help being sorry we were obliged to part with him. It was in this very lodge that he made his first escape from these walls, before our identical eyes. — Newgate lost her invincibility that day, if she never did before. Yes, our honour received a tarnish then, that will require all our future vigilance to rub off."

" I am acquainted with the circumstance," said the visiter, " and am not sorry to have an opportunity of actually observing the scene of this remarkable proof of hardihood and dexterity."

He made a minute survey of the place, and wrote down some memoranda in a small pocket-book which he had brought for that purpose. After having been shown the relics usually exhibited in the lodge to visiters at that period, such as the spike which Sheppard had broken off the hatch when he forced his way through it; the knife with which Blueskin had attempted to cut the throat of Mr. Jonathan Wild; a nosegay which had been given by a duchess to Claude

Du Vall, and the irons of the far-famed Captain Hinde, &c., he proceeded, with Mr. Austin and the two other turnkeys, Langley and Revel, to the condemned hold. Here he satisfied his curiosity with the complete inspection of this last abode of crime, and read the names its different tenants had, at various times, scratched on its dreary walls.

" There are some fine bold hands there, sir," remarked Mr. Austin, alluding to the writing, " and some very curious ones, too: that name you are looking at now, which is in German text, or some other outlandish hand, was written there by its owner, Jack Meff, the weaver, the very last morning he left us. Poor Jack was a striking proof of the truth of the old proverb, that he who is born to be hanged will never be drowned."

" How was that?" inquired the visiter, a tall thin man, dressed in black, with high boots, a somewhat small cocked hat, a two-tailed wig, a rather stiffly starched neckcloth, and a very investigating look.—" I shall be thankful to be informed of any remarkable particulars not generally known, that may have happened to have come under your cognisance."

"Bless your soul, sir," said the turnkey, " I'm a man full of remarkable particulars. Meff was first ordered to be hanged for milling a ken, that is, breaking open a house ; but as he was going to Tyburn, just as they were stopping to give him his last draught out of Sir Giles's bowl, hang me if Jack Ketch wasn't arrested for debt. It was said it was a sham arrest, and that Meff was at the bottom of it ; but be that as it may, they were obliged to bring him back again here ; and, to make amends for his disappointment, his majesty ordered him to be lagged to Virginny : well, on their voyage a terrible storm arose, the ship was run ashore, and more than one half of the crew were lost ; but, as I said, those who are born to be hanged will never be drowned. Meff escaped, and some years afterwards took the liberty of returning without leave to the Hundreds of Drury again, where he carried on business as brisk as ever ; but as the devil would have it, hang me if he wasn't cotched one day by a fellow who knew him : he was brought back to his old quarters, tried for returning from transportation, and took a second airing in the cart. Jack Ketch didn't happen to have any debts to pay this time, so poor Meff——"

" Paid the last debt of nature, I suppose," said the stranger, faintly smiling.

" Just so, sir ; he was topped at Tyburn, after all his escapes.—That name you are looking at there, sir, is the writing of Lewis Houssart, the French barber, a sad fellow, sir — cut his wife's throat with one of his master's razors. He was the favourite companion of Jack Sheppard, during the time they were confined together, here, before Jack's first escape."

"Ha!" said the visiter eagerly, "how so?"

"Lord bless you, sir," returned Mr. Austin, "there's no telling you the rigs they put upon the other prisoners."

"Sheppard was a lively fellow, then?"

"Lively!" said Mr. Austin — "hang me, if I ever saw his like — why, before his second escape, just because I happened to observe to him, as I was stapling him down in the castle-room with three hundred weight of iron, that I'd give him leave to get away if he could, hang me if he didn't take me at my word; and then had the impudence to send me a letter, through Mr. Applebee, the publisher of the dying speeches, which he took there himself, dressed as a porter, and in which he begged my pardon for not stopping to take leave of me, and also apologised for taking the irons with him, which he said he should not have done if I hadn't given them to him; assuring me he would very gladly have left them behind him, if it hadn't been extremely inconvenient to him. The fellow then concluded with some poetry — perhaps you don't deal much in poetry, sir; it aint to your taste?"

"A little," dryly returned the visiter; "but,

I must confess, I am not over fond of it — I find it rather a drug."

"Well, Jack's is not very good, sir, as far as I'm a judge, so I won't trouble you with it. I should have told you, that, along with my letter, he sent a very jeering one to Mr. Applebee, himself — to be sure I believe these publishers, as they calls themselves, are very queer gentry, and deals in all manner of lies;" the visiter winced a little; "but I don't think Jack ought to have served him in that way — but come, sir, I'll now conduct you to the castle, our great show room."

"I am anxious to see it," said the visiter.

Passing across the lodge at the end of a long passage, there advanced from one of the wards, in which there were several untried prisoners, a man whose remarkable appearance caught the visiter's attention; his throat was enveloped in a huge roll of neckcloth, and his frontispiece seemed to have been much battered.

"That's the celebrated Mr. Wild," whispered the turnkey, observing his companion's attention drawn towards him; "an extraordinary character, sir, a very extraordinary character; it is to him that the country is indebted for getting rid of Jack Sheppard and Blueskin."

"I have heard as much," significantly answered the other.

" Yes, sir, he has hung as many men as Jack Ketch himself: it was he that brought Thurland, Dun, Ray, and the other rogues, to the nubbing Cheat * for the murder of Mrs. Knapp; and lagged Bob Parrot for robbing the Bishop of Norwich's Crib; and lifted Bill Rigelsden and Bess Shirley for breaking into the Banqueting House, Whitehall, and holding communion with the sacrament plate : he's a fearful man — hang me if I care to speak of him within his hearing ; nobody's life is safe with him ; but he's gone now. You saw those marks on his canister: they were cracks he got in capturing his different victims; was forced to get trepanned himself through trepanning others, ha! ha! But if I was to tell you one half of the terrible stories that are told of him, why they'd fill up a volume, and turn you into a jelly."

" I should be glad to hear them, nevertheless," quickly returned the visiter, "and will pay handsomely for the information."

" Then, I'm just the man to furnish you with it," returned the gaoler; "and if your honour will only step down here to the lodge any one of these evenings after locking-up time, hang me, if, over a bowl of punch, you shan't be made

* The gallows.

B

acquainted with all I've known and heard, and that's not saying a little."

" Agreed," said the visiter, " I'll take you at your word; but let us onwards to the castle."

In the castle, a strong room, the scene of Jack Sheppard's far-famed last escape, the party were joined by the Reverend Mr. Thomas Purney, at that time Ordinary of Newgate. The massive staple and enormous padlock by which Jack had been fastened to the floor, together with his feet-locks and handcuffs, were here exhibited; but out of respect to the presence of the Ordinary, and in compliment to the gentlemanly appearance and liberality of the visiter, the usual custom of persuading the curious stranger to suffer the irons to be fastened on him in order to see if *he* could release himself from them, and then making him pay a considerable sum for his liberation, was omitted. The old nail with which Jack had picked the padlock, the iron bar he had wrested from the chimney, and the chimney itself, were all objects of keen investigation.

" You seem greatly interested," observed the Ordinary to the visiter, " in the transactions and fate of that unfortunate criminal, Sheppard."

" I am more than ordinarily so," returned the visiter.

" He was, indeed, a striking example of the folly of men," observed the Ordinary, " as I had occasion to remark in a late sermon. What a melancholy consideration it is that men should show so much regard for the preservation of a poor perishing body, that can remain at most but a few years, and at the same time be so unaccountably negligent of a precious soul which must continue through the ages of eternity. What amazing difficulties did the notorious malefactor, Jack Sheppard, overcome! Oh, that mankind were all Jack Sheppards!"

The visiter started.

" Don't mistake me," exclaimed the reverend gentleman, " I don't mean in a carnal, but in a spiritual sense. I would exhort the world to open the locks of their hearts with the nail of repentance; burst asunder the fetters of their lusts; mount the chimney of hope, take from thence the bar of good resolution, break through the stone wall of despair, and all the strongholds of the dark entry of the valley of the shadow of death; raise themselves to the leads of divine meditation; fix the blanket of faith with the spike of the church; let themselves down to the turner's house of resignation, and descend the stairs of humility, so that they may come to the door of deliverance from the prison of iniquity, and escape the clutches of that old executioner, the devil."

Here the reverend minister had entirely exhausted himself by the force of his own eloquence, and suddenly stopped.

" The world has been much misled concerning the true history of this daring offender, Jack Sheppard," remarked the visiter, after a pause; " his parentage has been belied; he has been associated with many persons who never had existence: the public have been led to form a very wrong idea of him: I would fain obtain a true history of his eventful life and transactions."

" That, Sir," answered the Ordinary, confidentially, " can only be obtained from myself. In addition to the criminal's own confession, which I obtained by virtue of my holy office, I have procured many particulars, equally as worthy of notice as they are veracious, and which, I am persuaded, would be very acceptable to the world at large, but the cares of my flock do not allow me leisure to bestow on them the necessary form of a continuous narrative. I should be happy to commit my materials into the hands of any ingenious gentleman, whose talents and time might permit of his rendering to the actions of this great criminal that justice, after death, which, in his lifetime, so signally conducted him to the halter."

" If you would entrust these manuscripts to my care," said the visiter, eagerly, his eyes glistening with pleasure and satisfaction, " I would take care that an 'eminent hand,' whom I have in my pay, should render them their full literary deserts. It was in search of such documents and testimonies that I came here, and my gratitude shall evince itself beyond bare words. Fifty guineas — I speak without offence, reverend sir, — shall gladly be at your acceptance for their use."

" Inasmuch as they will enable me to do, I trust, a considerable worldly good," gravely answered the Ordinary, " I will accept your offer. My narrative attends the wretched sufferer from his very cradle, through all the events of his boyhood to his last solemn exit. Many circum-stances have come to my knowledge which have escaped all others, the truth of which will be borne out, in all their more important points, by the various imperfect accounts that have hitherto been published. The narrative will, indeed, be as interesting as it will be authentic and com-plete.

" Ah, sir! let the idle and frivolous seek for excitement in the pages of the poet, and the wild fictions of the romance writer, as they will; if they would really stir up their jaded feelings, they should resort to the terrible realities so often to be found within these walls: all that imagination can conceive to interest the fancy, and hold attention breathless, will fall short of the every-day occurrences it is but too constantly my painful duty to witness."

" I doubt it not, reverend sir; I doubt it not," replied the visiter; " the eagerness the public have ever manifested to become acquainted with those whose crimes have rendered them notorious, the sympathy that is extended to their sufferings, the varied feelings and emotions, their exploits, escapes, and ultimate fate awaken, strikingly attest the truth of your observations.   The adventures of the desperado have ever possessed more charms for the multitude than those even of the hero.   In all ages, the lives of the rogue, the pirate, the burglar, the highwayman, and the murderer, have had their attractions for the general reader.   The most gentle natures are often those that peruse, with the greatest avidity, the actions of the most daring and ferocious; their appetite becoming greater in proportion to the amount of turpitude presented to it."

" Exactly so," said the Ordinary, " else wherefore the throng of the weaker sex that invariably crowd our courts to catch a glimpse of any criminal of more than ordinary hardihood; would not one naturally suppose they would shrink with abhorrence from such exhibitions? but no, the greater the offender the greater is their — what shall I term it? — I will give it its mildest name, curiosity."

" It is a thorough knowledge of this fact that has led me here this day," remarked the visiter. " I despair not to see the time, reverend sir, when the poet, the dramatist, the romance-writer, and the novelist, shall all draw the materials of their various works from the calendar of crime produced within these walls; when genius, as priestcraft has done before it, shall canonise the memory of the malefactor, and make the saint the greater, the more he has been the sinner. Punishment will appear martyrdom when a halo is thrown round the guilt for which it was endured."

The Ordinary winced slightly at the observation of the stranger reflecting on the priesthood; he however said nothing, comforting himself with the thought, that the priestcraft alluded to did not belong to *his* church.

" I will take an early opportunity of calling on you for the manuscripts, reverend sir, and will not, at the same time, forget the coin," resumed the visiter, who, it may here be mentioned, was a distinguished Bookseller of that day.

He kept his word: a day or two afterwards he paid his promised visit to the Ordinary, and obtained the precious memoranda in question. From him he proceeded to Mr. Austin in the lodge, of whom he gained much information of the most astounding and exciting nature re-

lative to Mr. Jonathan Wild.   It is from these
combined materials, the eminent hand alluded to
by the publisher, and who was a poor author
whom he occasionally employed, prepared the
narrative which, for reasons not necessary to
explain, will here, for the first time, be given to
the world, and which will form its own comment.
Suffice it, that it will be found to be the only
correct detail hitherto published, among the many
that have appeared, of the life, transactions, and
escapes of the renowned house and prison
breaker, the redoubtable JACK SHEPPARD.

JACK SHEPPARD.

BOOK THE FIRST.

THE PREDICTION.

CHAPTER THE FIRST.

INFANCY OF JACK SHEPPARD.

HOW OUR HERO HAPPENED TO BE BORN. — LOVE IN THE CRADLE. — THE GIPSY'S PREDICTION.

It was the month of March, in the year of our Lord 1702. The time-honoured bells of Stepney old church, celebrated for its monumental "Fyshe and Rynge," were ringing one of their merriest peals. A bullock, given to the populace by the liberal authorities of that no less liberal parish, which, as is well known, extends its guardian registration to all such offspring of wayfaring English subjects as may have the misfortune to be born on, or beyond, the seas, was roasting whole upon the village green, where an immense bonfire had been kindled, in the ashes of which several sacks of potatoes were embedded,

to form an appropriate garniture to the masti-
cation of the noble animal then in the progress
of the culinary art.   Several barrels of strong
beer, the joint benefaction of the just mentioned
generous churchwardens and Messrs. Tapmen
and Hopkins, of the "Crown," and "Marlborough's Head," two worthy publicans and sin-
ners, who had grown rich by administering to
the necessities of the draught-loving topers of
Stepney, were judiciously placed under the care
of Mr. Burley, the respected beadle of the place,
in order to be ready for distribution to the loyal
inhabitants of Stepney, when the completion of
the cookery should require their accompaniment.
Mr. Burley was assisted in his important and arduous trust by a strong body-guard of stout
paupers, with pitchforks, or it might have proved
no easy task to have kept off the thirsty and
eager crowd.   The royal standard of England
was proudly floating on the ancient church
tower, courteously waving to the vibrations of
the joyous bells beneath it.   The moon, which
had risen full and high in the heavens immediately above, was brightly and complacently
shining as if in approbation of what was passing
within its view, pouring a rich flood of splendour
on all around, its calm and silvery beams con-
trasting strikingly with the fierce and glaring
flames of the bonfire.   Squibs were flying, and

crackers were bursting, in all directions. Men were hurrahing, boys were hallooing, and children were screaming, all half frantic with delight and expectation; nearly the whole population of Stepney were assembled, from helpless infancy to tottering age. The auspicious event which had congregated this multitude, and called forth these rejoicings, was no other than the accession to the throne of merry England of Anne of Denmark, afterwards called "Good Queen Anne," though she is now more generally remembered for the supposed rarity of her farthing, than for any recorded virtue or authenticated public good. Nevertheless, at this period her accession had inspired the whole nation with universal joy; all parties, Whig, Tory, and intermediate, coalesced together to hail the commencement of a reign, under which they expected to see the power of France humbled still more effectually abroad, and the Protestant religion established still more firmly at home.

It was at this precise juncture that, in a neat though poor cottage in one of the by-lanes of that then picturesque village, tenanted by one Robert Sheppard, a rural carpenter, the front part of which served as his workshop, while the room behind formed the dormitory and general meeting place of the family, that the renowned hero of this memorable history first saw the light.

The worthy carpenter, not dreaming that an addition to his family was so suddenly to have been made, for Mrs. Sheppard's calculations, and the received period for the occurrence of such events had not led them to look for it for at least two months to come, had gone to join the general throng who rushed forth to hail the happy advent of the time, and partake of the good cheer provided, as has been premised, on the green, leaving his helpmate, whose interesting situation, and rather delicate health just then, did not make it seem prudent that she should accompany him, under the surveillance of their eldest daughter, a child of about ten or twelve years of age.   Some time had elapsed since his departure when the sudden firing of several old pieces of musketry, joined to the loud clamour of the rustic crowd, and the glaring light from the huge bonfire that made its way through the attice of their little dwelling, so alarmed the good matron, that her cries speedily drove the child into the lane to look for assistance; but their few neighbours, the inhabitants of the scattered hovels that here and there rose above the hedges that skirted the lane on either side, had departed for the general festivity, and the child was perfectly in despair, when, to her great joy, she saw emerging from a clump of hazels, towards the top of the lane, a female, whose garb and manners at once pointed her out as one of those wandering race known in this country by the name of gipsy. With one arm she bore an infant, while with the other she guided her steps by the assistance of a long thin straggling wand or stick, cleft at the top, formed of the stripped branch of a tree; her figure was tall, erect, and commanding, even though she was partially in tatters, and strongly reminded the spectator of that mixture of masculine strength and feminine beauty which is found in the females of many of the southern parts of Ireland. Her features were earnest, but somewhat stern, and careworn; she was enveloped in a long mantle, or cloak: a species of wallet bag was fastened to her waist; her only head-dress, which was partially covered by the hood of her mantle, was a sort of toque, formed of a twisted handkerchief, similar to that worn by the French peasantry, beneath which her long raven hair hung wildly over her shoulders; the usual gay 'kerchief of the gipsy females covered her neck, nor were their customary profusion of rings and brooches wanting. To her the little girl made known her story — she was a gipsy, outcast, and wandering, hunted and lawless, scorned and revengeful — but she was woman! To hasten to the cottage was the work of a moment; she laid the infant she bore in a cradle, which stood in one part of the room, and speedily rendered to the suffering matron those attentions which only woman can, or ought to render. Her skill and care, made familiar to her by the practice of her tribe, soon enabled her to relieve at once all Mrs. Sheppard's pains and fears by bringing safely into the world a healthy boy. At the moment of his birth a still merrier peal than before burst from the village bells. "This should be an omen," muttered the gipsy, in the wild Romanee jargon of her nation, "but whether of future private joy or public notoriety I know not." The infant was soon completely wrapped in some clothes that had *not* been provided for him, but which had served the same office for two or three brothers and sisters before him. As he seemed inclined to sleep, the gipsy laid him down in the cradle by the side of the infant she had previously placed there, whose exceeding fairness so greatly at variance with her own swarthy hue, forbade any one for a moment supposing it was hers; for in her arms it, indeed, seemed like some pure pearl upon an Ethiope's breast; while she turned to administer some necessary cordial to the now happy mother. Gaining strength, Mrs. Sheppard proceeded to return her grateful thanks to the gipsy for the timely aid she had rendered her, and to express

her surprise that she should have been found
absent from the festivities then going forward.
" What is the new queen to me?" muttered the
gipsy. " I owe her no allegiance, and what are
these rejoicings? I cannot sympathise in their
wild tumult: my thoughts should rather be of
one as highly born, as justly, too, entitled to
dominion, — one fugitive and beggared — her
only canopy the forest bough, her only roof the
spaceless sky above her, — one from the burning
East — one to whom, albeit born of the royal
race of Pharaoh, and mated with the dukes of
Lesser Egypt, no one now bends the knee — her
sceptre but this worthless hazel wand, her
realms but those all may at pleasure drive her
from." The gipsy's dark eye flashed as she
spoke these words, which, had they not been
uttered in the mystic language of her race,
would in any other have been equally unintelligible to the wondering matron. " Yes," continued the gipsy, " but Zara shall avenge her
wrongs. Ring on, ring on, ye empty, senseless
flatterers! the homage of the world, e'en when
not less loud, is not less hollow, nor less fleet-
ing! — ring on, ring on! I 'll war upon the
world — the base, the ingrate world, that so
has wronged, despoiled, and scorned me; already my first hostage has been taken, this
poor child Bess!" At this instant the bells

suddenly ceased their jovial clamour, and for a
few moments a dead silence pervaded the air,
when the iron tongue of midnight slowly knelled
forth that witching hour.   The gipsy started —
again a deafening shout in the distance rent the
sky, and a fiercer glare gleamed in at the casement window, and streamed full upon the cradle,
in which, side by side, lay reposing the two in-
fants.   The cradle was placed immediately under
the casement which looked into the cottage
garden, the head of it touched the wall at that
side the apartment, on which, just above it, was
pasted a favourite ballad of that period, describing the life and exploits of the " Ladies' highwayman," the celebrated CLAUDE DU VAL.   On the
top of this ballad was a rude wood-cut of a
gibbet, to which the handsome gallant was seen
suspended.   As the gipsy's eye fell, on turning
round, upon the cradle, she started at perceiving
that the infant she had borne had moved from
the position in which she had placed it, and
nestling itself more closely to the new-born boy,
had thrown its little arm in fondness round his
neck, but so tightly as almost to strangle him.
" Mighty Pharaoh!" she exclaimed, extricating
the poor babe from the unconscious jeopardy
in which the tenderness of his companion had
placed him, " what dread portent is this?
Ah! that blood-red glare — how fierce it gleams

upon that picture gibbet, this mark of love akin to death, too. Quick! let me examine the firmament, my only horoscope." As swift as lightning her eagle eye was turned to the heavens. "What is this I see?" she shrieked, gazing with painful earnestness on two planets that shone brightly out from amidst the myriad of stars that twinkled round them. " VENUS and SATURN in conjunction — strange! Venus! it is her natal star — poor Bess, yes, luckless wench! fair as that orb, thy lot will own its sway, thy fate will feel its influence. Love! love! will be thine all, thy joy, thy sorrow. Saturn—ah! 't is a fearful planet, moody and malignant. Why hurried this poor babe to life to own its influence? It rose upon him at his birth; I marked its aspect; it is his natal, ruling star! what will be their fate? my Art impels me — I must, although I fain would not, foretell it." The gipsy then in a wild and low, but solemn chant, muttered in a species of ROMANEE doggerel some lines, of which the following is the substance : —

The Prediction.

By the power to me that's given,
What matters if from hell or heaven,
From star or planet, charm or spell,
    From card or omen, angel, fiend,
The fates of mortals to foretell,
    And trace their course, and point their end,

As through this vale of tears they go,
Their pains and pleasures, weal and woe?
I must, though fain I would be dumb,
Their fortune show, for it *will* come!
Yes, yes! I feel within me burning
Words, that for utterance are yearning;
A secret knowledge that *will* speak,
Howe'er the prophecy I'd check.
Yes, I the fortunes *must* unfold —
Sad secret! but it will be told!
Of those who lie unconscious here
Of all but life — who hope, and fear,
And joy and woe know not as yet,
Nor nurse the sad wish to *forget!*
The baleful light through the casement pane
That redly glares on the infant twain —
What does that baleful light proclaim
But guilt and anguish, sin and shame?
Dim SATURN sadly shines afar,
This new-born infant's *natal star!*
VENUS, the loveliest gem of eve,
Seems o'er its subject-babe to grieve —
What does their strange *conjunction* mean?
In vain I would the knowledge skreen: —
That arm around the new-born thrown! —
What of their destiny is shown?
A fatal love allied to death:
Through her, alas! he'll yield his breath!
Closer than sister's to a brother
Their fates are wound with one another:
Howe'er removed, they still will join —
In rapture, and in anguish twine.

The Power impels me, I must on,
Ere yet the witching hour is gone !
The Gibbet that now frowns above,
Sad emblem of their end will prove !
I 'll read no more ; — unhappy mother !
'T were well for thee, though thou 'dst no other,
Thy babe in birth had breath'd its last.
The words are said — the power has pass'd!

The gipsy ceased.   It was fortunate the good
matron had all this time been in a sound but
gentle slumber, or the wild exclamations of the
sibyl might have alarmed her more than might
have been safe for one in her peculiar situation.
The little girl who had been ministering to her
mother, as occasion required, affrighted by the
mysterious gestures and deep tones of her
strange companion, had cowered fearfully behind
the bed-curtains, from which at intervals, as her
courage permitted her, she anxiously watched
all that was going on.   Recovering herself after
a short pause, the gipsy resumed her mutter-
ings.   "Their destinies linked unto each other,
there then should be within their palms the line
of marriage ; — let me convince myself : — yes,"
taking up, and examining the hand of the infant
girl, "'tis here parallel with the line of life. —
Now for the boy."   The hand of the new-born
infant was here subjected to a similar scrutiny.
"Plagues of Egypt!" exclaimed the fortune-

teller, "the palm is smooth! he'll die unwedded;
so much the worse for thee, poor girl, so much
the worse; — but here's a line, the line of death,
— where does it run to? I trace it from the hand
across the palm, and up the arm, until it joins
this vein, and here 't is lost. — What vein is this?
Powers of darkness! again the omen — the fatal
one, the *jugular.*" Here the door of the humble
apartment was suddenly opened, and honest
Robert Sheppard, the owner of the mansion, in
a most happy state of intoxication, was led in by
Mr. Burley, the beadle. "Huzzah! Long live
the Queen! Long live her Majesty," hiccupped
the carpenter. The gipsy started; but honest
Sheppard, though he saw double, did not at
the moment see her. "Huzza! dam'me if ever
she shall want money to buy a pot of strong drink
while Bob Sheppard has got sixpence left in
the world. But where's my better half, Kate?"
calling her. His boisterous vociferation here
awakened the sleeping infant, who set up a loud
cry, which in turn awoke the mother. "Halloo!" said the carpenter, almost sobered with
surprise, "why, what the devil's this? My
wife in the straw, and a couple of children in the
basket?" "No, only one child, dear Robert,"
murmured Mrs. Sheppard affectionately. "Then
I must be seeing double, as you say, Mr. Burley
for curse me if there aint two; but how come

it all about, Mrs. Sheppard, and why didn't you wait till I came home, before you suffered this to happen?" "The event certainly was rather unexpected," said Mrs. Sheppard, smiling, perceiving the condition of her husband; "and but for this good woman's timely skill and solicitude, I know not what would have been the result." Here the attention both of the carpenter and the beadle was turned to the gipsy. "Eh! This good woman?" hiccupped the carpenter. "Ah! a gipsy!" roared the beadle, as his eyes encountered hers. "Oh! the baggage—the witch — the vagrant! See that you have your spoons safe, Master Sheppard, and that none of the poultry necks have been twisted off in the hen-roost. I must exercise my official authority here — this woman must go to the cage." "Mercy!" shrieked the gipsy, catching up the child she had brought with her, and pressing it to her bosom. "Punish me not for having been the means, through heaven, of preserving, perhaps, two lives." "Nay, nay, touch her not — harm her not, Mr. Burley, I entreat, I implore you!" supplicated Mrs. Sheppard. The parish functionary stood irresolute. "Answer me one question, hussy," hiccupped the carpenter. "Are you going to take that second child away with you?" "I am," returned the gipsy. "Is it yours?" "It is." "Then on that account I'll forgive you;

but if my family had been increased, through
you, by two children instead of one, to the cage
you should have gone ; nothing should have
saved you.   You must let her walk off scot-free,
Mr. Burley, though I dare say she's a terrible
offender ; but if she's deprived me of a chicken
or two, she's given me another chicken, this
child! so it's tantamount—tit for tat; therefore we
must let her go." " This is a very onerous piece
of business, Mr. Sheppard," gravely observed
the cock'd-hatted authority.   " But stop, now I
think of it, this being the accession of her most
gracious Majesty, God bless her! an act of am-
nesty has passed, letting loose all felons and other
prisoners ; so I think I may let her loose. But
stop, stop ! what am I doing?— the act does not
extend to criminals guilty of murder; and how
do I know but this woman has been murdering
some of your cocks and hens?" " No, no," indignantly exclaimed the gipsy. " I will stake my
life on her innocence," said Mrs. Sheppard.
" Well, well, on that consideration, and with the
understanding that you take all the responsibility
upon yourself, friend Sheppard, I shall even let
her go about her business ; so vanish, woman !
quick ! trudge!" Placing the lips of the infant
she bore to those of the new-born offspring of
the carpenter, and ejaculating in a sad but
solemn tone, " You'll meet again, ill-starred ones!

naught can resist the force of destiny. Farewell, good mistress; Heaven shield you and your offspring in your dark hour's peril — farewell!" The gipsy walked with an air, possessing much of innate dignity, out of the apartment, and plunging with her little charge into the lane, was speedily lost in its darkest shades.

No sooner was the cottage relieved from her presence than the carpenter began to examine the new subject that had that night been born, to own the sway of good Queen Anne. The little fellow crowed, as the father, more gently than was usual with him, patted his infant cheek. " Odds my life!" he exclaimed, " he'll be a fine boy! — in a devilish hurry to see the world, though — no fear of his pushing his way any where — nothing will stop him. Well, bless his little round poll! I shall make a carpenter of him like myself; he'll be a rare one to handle a chisel, a saw, and a centre-bit, I'll warrant him." Mr. Burley, the beadle, now in his turn advanced to examine the little stranger, but no sooner did he stoop down, than the infant manifested the utmost dislike and terror at his appearance — squalling, kicking, and struggling to get away, with all his might and main. " It must be my cocked hat and staff that frightens him," said the beadle, drawing away somewhat disconcerted: " they certainly are the terror of all offenders; but this little rogue has done nothing as yet to make him alarmed at them. But come, friend Robert; I see Mrs. Sheppard can well dispense with our presence, so I'll go and get neighbour Diggins's wife to sit up the remainder of the night with her, and get you a shake down at the 'Marlborough's Head:' they will open their doors to me at any hour; and there, over a cool tankard, I'll tell you what are the Duke's plans in the next campaign with the allies against the French. I have it official: we in authority know these things; therefore come. Good night, or good morning rather, Mrs. Sheppard." Taking leave of his wife and new-born son and heir, the carpenter departed with the beadle, who speedily got a nurse for Mrs. Sheppard, a bed for her husband, and a foaming tankard of nut-brown ale for himself; in the enjoyment of which we will for the present beg to leave him.

CHAPTER THE SECOND.

THE CHRISTENING.

EARLY INDICATIONS. — " 𝔗𝔥𝔢 𝔣𝔞𝔪𝔬𝔲𝔰 𝔅𝔞𝔩𝔩𝔞𝔡𝔢 𝔬𝔣 𝔠𝔩𝔞𝔲𝔡𝔢 𝔡𝔲
𝔘𝔞𝔩𝔩."— THE DEPARTURE FROM STEPNEY.

THE little urchin, the future hero of our history, throve, his premature birth, though it rendered him somewhat diminutive and delicate in appearance, not interfering with his future growth and strength. His mother, who had all along been, as the gossips call it, as well as could be expected, got about again earlier than usual, and in due course of time a day was fixed for our hero's christening. It was settled that he should be called JOHN ; Mr. BURLEY, the beadle, who bore that name, having consented to do him the honour of standing sponsor to him; but on the day appointed, the clergyman of the parish, the Reverend Mr. Muggerage, who was a bachelor, and a wag, and withal an Oxford man (one of the conditions on which the living is bestowed, which is in the gift of Brazen Nose College, and a very valuable one, being, that the incumbent shall in all cases be a bachelor); the aforesaid reverend gentleman, we repeat, by what spirit inspired we know not, but we will

charitably set it down to his innocent desire of
passing a joke on his official, the beadle! chose
to make that important functionary's intention
of giving our hero his name, somewhat imperfect, by facetiously christening him JACK, instead of *John*. The gravest men will joke at
times; and when they do, their inferiors are spe-
cially bound to laugh at them: accordingly, the
whole affair was passed over as a most excellent
jest, betraying a vast deal of wit in the reverend
fellow from BRAZEN NOSE; though there were
times when the beadle did not scruple in private
to express his opinion that our hero would come
to *no good* from the *misnomer*, it sounding to
him very much like an *alias!*

Little Jack was an uncommonly good-tem-
pered child, like others, when he was pleased;
but he liked to have his own way, and discovered
at times a headstrong obstinacy and wilfulness
that somewhat alarmed his good mother: he
was also subject to gusts of passion, but was
always pacified whenever his mother sang to him
the good old "Ballade of Claude du Vall, the
Ladies' Highwayman," which had, ever since
the exit of that worthy, been an especial favourite
with all cantatrices in the middle and lower walks
of life. As this "Ballade" may be considered,
even at that early age, to have had some effect
in biassing our hero's future course and charac-

ter, we shall, having been favoured with an exclusive copy of it, present it to our readers.

𝕿𝖍𝖊 𝖋𝖆𝖒𝖔𝖚𝖘 𝕭𝖆𝖑𝖑𝖆𝖉𝖊 𝖔𝖋 𝕮𝖑𝖆𝖚𝖉𝖊 𝖉𝖚 𝖁𝖆𝖑𝖑,*

THE LADIES' HIGHWAYMAN.

1.

OF ROBIN HOOD, that *outlaw* good,
   Our forest songs may tell;
A gentle thief, he once was chief,
   And bore from all the bell !

* This celebrated highwayman was by birth a Frenchman, having been born at Domfront, in Normandy, in the year 1648. His father was a miller, and he himself having run away from his home, was for some time a footman in Paris. He came to England on the restoration of Charles the Second in 1660. Being very gay and extravagant, his excesses soon forced him to take to the highway, where he became so celebrated, that he had the honour of being named first in a proclamation for the capture of several notorious malefactors; on which he decamped to France for safety, but soon returned and resumed his lawless practices. The anecdotes recorded of him in the ballad, are, with many others of a similar nature, detailed by most of his biographers. He was the most accomplished, polished, handsome, and well dressed thief, gallant, and gambler, of which we have any record; and was a prodigious favourite, as might be expected, with the ladies. His career, after some years, was at length cut short by his being arrested while drunk at the " Hole-in-the-Wall," Chandos Street, Covent Garden. While he lay in the condemned hold in Newgate, he was visited by myriads of ladies of the first quality, all anxious to have a *safe* peep at the handsome highwayman; though they by no means grudged to pay for peeping, such was his attraction. Great intercession was made to save him, but in vain; he was ex-

While GILDEROY was *Scotland's* joy,
  Though bound in prison thrall;
But all must yield, I ween, the field
  To gallant CLAUDE DU VALL!
Oh, rare DU VALL! oh, brave DU VALL!
  All hearts did he trepan,
Wherever seen, so fair his mien —
  The Ladies' Highwayman!

2.

From sunny *France*, with song and dance,
  He came to steal all hearts;
His graceful air won all the fair;
  His eyes were Cupid's darts!
So blythe and bold, none could prove cold,
  But freely gave up all;
With ruin pleased, if he but seized, —
  The gallant CLAUDE DU VALL!
Oh, rare DU VALL! oh, bold DU VALL!
  To rifle was his plan,
Both young and old, of love and gold, —
  The Ladies' Highwayman!

---

ecuted at Tyburn on the 21st of January, 1670, when he had
barely reached the age of twenty-seven, amidst the universal
tears of crowds of handsome females. The immortal author
of Hudibras honoured his memory with some lines on that
occasion. A house called Du Vall's house, situated in Du
Vall's Lane, or Devil's Lane, as it has been vulgarised, at
Islington, leading to Hornsey Wood, is still pointed out to
the curious as having been the comely highwayman's retreat.
Full accounts of Du Vall are to be found in the Harleian
Miscellany, his Life by Dr. Pope, Johnson's Lives of the
Highwaymen, Leigh Hunt's Indicator, and Chambers's
Journal for 1838.

3.

When he cried " Stand !" throughout the land
 Was none that could resist :
All found they lost, were to their cost ;
 For he his aim ne'er missed !
Full many a maid he stript, 't is said,
 Young, handsome, short, and tall ;
Such plundering guile was in his smile,
 The gallant, gay Du VALL !
Oh, rare Du VALL ! unmatched Du VALL !
 Since first the world began,
On plain or green, such ne'er was seen, —
 The Ladies' Highwayman !

4.

Their hidden wealth, his prize by stealth ;
 Young minion of the moon !
Such grace they thought ne'er dearly bought,
 Though paying to some tune.
While husbands, lovers, owned his might,
 Invited to a ball,
And yielded many a sturdy wight
 To gallant, gay Du VALL.
Oh, rare Du VALL ! oh, stout Du VALL !
 Ne'er foiled by sword or fan ;
The joy of maids, the fear of blades, —
 The Ladies' Highwayman !

5.

One day a coach he saw approach,
 In which a lady sat,

Who sweetly played; — he rode, and said,
 While doffing low his hat : —
" My country, France, with you to dance,
 A favour deem I shall !"
" Thanks, sir," said she, " I'll partner be
 To gallant, gay DU VALL."
Oh, rare DU VALL ! oh, gay DU VALL !
 Thy equal find who can ?
All joy'd to be robbed, if by *thee*,
 The Ladies' Highwayman !

6.

He took her hand, a saraband
 They danced upon the heath ;
Her spouse, the knight, gazed with delight,
 And laughed till out of breath.
Quoth CLAUDE, " I pray, the *music pay*,"
 And sung a madrigal.
The knight then found a hundred pound
 For gallant CLAUDE DU VALL.
Oh, brave DU VALL ! polite DU VALL !
 Still first in Cupid's van ;
Who danced so gay a purse away, —
 The Ladies' Highwayman !

7.

In France, we are told, a JESUIT old
 Could not his art resist ;
But gave his gold, to have tenfold
 Made by our *alchymist !*
This he in *lead*, through the old fool's head,
 Returned with a pistol ball !

" I 've oft, of old, turned *lead* to GOLD ! "
  Quoth the gallant gay DU VALL.
Oh, rare DU VALL ! jocose DU VALL !
  In the flashing of a pan
The money came, and went the same,
  With the Ladies' Highwayman!

8.

A COMRADE once, an arrant dunce,
  From a *child* its CORAL bore;
A lady fair, with many a prayer,
  Begg'd he would it restore,
In vain; till CLAUDE, at point of sword,
  Cried, " Yield it up you shall !
Though you 're not *weaned* yet, or you 'd ne'er forget
  The *manners* of CLAUDE DU VALL !"
Oh, rare DU VALL ! genteel DU VALL !
  No chariot or sedan
More gallant load took on the road
  Than *the Ladies' Highwayman!*

9.

But WINE did what the world could not:
  DU VALL was snared at last;
He was seized and tried, and, till he died,
  Was in Newgate's dungeons cast.
At *Tyburn*, he, graced the triple tree,
  And none in park or mall
Dimm'd more bright eyes, woke more fond sighs,
  Than the gallant CLAUDE DU VALL !

D

Oh, rare Du Vall! ill-starred Du Vall!
  Such race none else e'er ran,
Bewept his fall, and loved by all, —
  The Ladies' Highwayman!

The recital of this "Veritable Ballad," for
which our hero, little Jack, was always extremely
eager, invariably produced some very remarkable
effects in him. Even when at so tender an age
that he could scarcely be expected to penetrate
the meaning of what he heard, the recital of the
gallant highwayman's exploits with the knight's
lady and the old jesuit never failed to excite in
him the greatest mirth, nearly convulsing him at
times with laughter; while at the mention of poor
Claude's being betrayed when in wine, and conducted to Newgate, his brow assumed an angry
expression, and he was often seen to double his
little fist, and shake it with indignation: the recital of the hero's fate on the Tyburn triple tree
brought tears into his little eyes, and required
all his mother's blandishments to restore him
once more to good humour. Time flew on with
its usual heeding, but unheeded, pace: the
infant became a child; pap gave way to more
substantial food; long coats dwindled into short
coats; speech succeeded to motion, and little
Jack's tongue and legs were soon engaged in a
very serious struggle which should run the fastest:
as usual, there were times when each gained the

mastery. Speech, which is but action in sound, or, as the Chinese call it, vocal painting, was however the last of the two great gifts of childhood which little Jack acquired in full perfection.

Nothing more had been seen or heard of the mysterious gipsy, and her little charge, whose fate, according to the prediction, was so strangely mixed up with that of our hero. The worthy carpenter, or honest Bob Sheppard, as he was generally called by his neighbours and acquaintances, unfortunately about this time possessed himself with a very good excuse for visiting the public-house, by acquiring a taste for politics. The fact was, Bob was a very sociable, well-meaning fellow; but strong drinks, had strong attractions for him, and so as he fancied by the attention he paid to it, had the policy of the then existing government; and accordingly at the "Marlborough's Head," he regularly twice a day with the assistance of the *Farthing Post*, conned over all the measures of the ministers GODOLPHIN and NOTTINGHAM, and examined into the expediency of the military movements of the great duke and his allies against the GRANDE MONARQUE! But a working man can seldom attend much to public affairs, without neglecting his own private affairs; and poor Sheppard soon began to com-

plain that he found his business deserting him:
whereas the truth was, 'twas he that was deserting his business; but be this as it may, the
result was a determination on the part of honest
Bob, to quit Stepney, where he had resided for so
many years, and take up his quarters in London,
where he imagined he should not only get more
business, but have a better opportunity of ex-
ercising his political talents. Accordingly about
five years after the commencement of this history, just before little Jack had achieved that
first and most anxious honour of boyhood — the
being breeched, the family left the cottage in
which they had passed so many happy hours,
and took their departure to a small house and
shop in one of the by streets of the then po-
pulous and thriving neighbourhood of Spitalfields, which the kind advances of a patron had
enabled them to take: this person was a Mr.
WILLIAM KNEEBONE, a substantial woollen draper
living in the Strand at the sign of *The Fleece
and Shears*, near St. Clement's church. In his
family Mrs. Sheppard had passed her early years,
more as a companion than a servant, having
been god-daughter to the woollen draper's mother, and married her first love, honest Robert,
(whom she met at a tea gardens in Clerkenwell) from the woollen draper's house. As the
matron with little Jack hanging by her gown

turned at the top of the lane to quit the village, she cast one last glance at the home of her love. The little cottage had been erected on a shelving bank on one side of the lane, between a profusion of wild briar bushes, hazels, and woodbine. The ascent to it was by the means of some rude stones, intended for steps, which the care of the matron had rendered of dazzling whiteness; its neatly thatched roof, 'neath which two or three robins had found a refuge; its clean whitewashed front, covered with honeysuckles; the little casement in which had been exhibited the emblems of the carpenter's occupation,— all awoke remembrances, now more sad, in proportion as the sources of them had formerly been pleasing. The good-natured carpenter witnessed the evident heaviness of heart with which his spouse surveyed the scene; and gently taking her arm to remove her from the spot, endeavoured to cheer her, by jokingly remarking that in leaving Stepney for Spitalfields they were getting a step nearer to the object of their ambition, — a humble but comfortable independence. Yielding to his wishes, she brushed the tear from her eye, and taking little Jack by one hand, while her husband led him by the other, followed by their daughter, they quitted White-thorn Lane — for so the place of their residence was named —for ever.

CHAPTER THE THIRD.

JACK'S FIRST SCHOOLING.

MR. GARRET THE SCHOOLMASTER.—TEACHING "THE YOUNG
IDEAS HOW TO SHOOT" IN 1708. — MASTER BLAKE. —
INITIATORY PILFERING.

No sooner were the carpenter and his family settled in their new habitation in Spitalfields than
Mrs. Sheppard turned her thoughts to the education of her son, little Jack, which honest Bob
said must be particularly attended to, inasmuch
as he meant to bring him up to his own honourable trade of a carpenter, which, he affirmed
was one of the most ancient and important of all,
belonging to the three originally practised by
our general ancestor, Adam, on his departure
from Eden, maintaining that the first master-
crafts in the world were the primeval ones of
tailor, carpenter, and gardener: Adam having
first made himself clothes of the fig leaves, then
constructed a habitation, and then cultivated the
earth for sustenance.   Accordingly, Mrs. Sheppard selected a day-school, in some repute, in
St. Helen's, Bishopsgate, the master of which
was a Mr. Garret.

If the masters of day schools at that period did not commit the same atrocities as the masters of Yorkshire and other boarding schools, they were not, generally speaking, less ignorant and incompetent : the profession of schoolmaster being too usually considered by the idle, improvident, and unfortunate, like the situation, in our own days, of check or money-taker at a theatre — an unfailing refuge for the destitute. The office of schoolmaster was, in truth, too often considered as the only one for which no regular apprenticeship was necessary — those engaged in it too frequently conceiving the arduous task of educating youth to be one requiring no education at all. Another inducement to become a schoolmaster was, the very little stock that was requisite to commence business. An old desk and stool, a few wooden forms, a bundle of goose-quills, half a dozen leaden inkstands, with some slates, spelling and copy books, procured as wanted, and generally paid for by scholars in advance, together with a cane and rod, being quite adequate to meet the exigencies of any diurnal seminary or scholastic establishment of the like nature, — though a figured stuff gown and velvet cap, if they could at all be conveniently procured, were deemed very imposing additions, being regarded — like the wig and gown of the counsellor, the band and surplice of the clergyman, the sword and sash of the soldier, and the hat and cane of the doctor—as the insignia and diplomas of proficiency. The daily pedagogues of the metropolis, at the beginning of the last century, were generally composed of men previously of unsettled habits and no certain occupation, and who might formerly have served as lawyers' drudges, kept book stalls, acted as supernumerary gaugers, or filled other desultory situations, till decayed or discarded, they gravely settled down into schoolmasters. Testimonials were easy. The intimation, affixed as a nota-bene to the cards or bills, which announced that youth were liberally instructed in all the branches of reading, writing, and arithmetic; giving the assurance to anxious parents, that mathematics, algebra, mensuration, navigation, and land surveying, with all other extras, were taught, if required, on moderate terms, was sufficient to stamp the master as a prodigy of learning; such intimation being always given in the very neighbourhood where the acquisition of these accomplishments was never very likely to be required. If, in addition to this, the schoolmaster, by dint of practice, was enabled to flourish an outline of a goose, after the manner of that great artist of the quill, Mr. JOSEPH CHAMPION, " Professor of Caligraphy," his abilities as a writing-master could not be doubted. " That eminent hand, out of

gratitude to the *capitol* bird, with whose feathers
he had imped the wings of his fame," having,
in his " ORNAMENTAL WRITING " handed down
its effigies to posterity in a variety of ingenious
upper strokes, under strokes, curves, meander-
ings, and zigzags, truly marvellous to behold, and
forming the accredited test of excellence in "the
noble science of penmanship!" As for arithmetic, the works of WINGATE, LEYBOURN, and the
renowned EDWARD COCKER, PHILOMATH! furnished explanations sufficient to enable the tutor
to puzzle the most calculating inquirers.

Mr. Garret, from his height, dilapidated appearance, and the very scanty manner in which
his upper story was furnished, did not very in-
aptly personify his name. He was a lank, spare
man, bearing evident traces of debility from
former dissipation, with wiry iron grey hair, and
a rather severe look, arising from the indulgence of an habitual ill-humour at his own impro-
vidence and its consequences, which expression
never gave way, save to a look of sinister cunning
when compassing any favourite project, his satisfaction being always marked with a tinge of
malevolence; this, with a constant affectation of
superior consequence, rendered him quite una-
miable enough for the office he held. He always
wore high, creaking shoes, and exercised his
lungs in a species of important cough, that had

E

grown into a fixed habit with him, becoming, as
habits often do, completely second nature. From
some expectation in early life, a weak mother
had suffered him to pass into manhood with a
neglected education, and no permanent employment. The little money he had on coming of age
he soon squandered in dissipation, and then, for
subsistence, pursued a variety of loose occupa-
tions for which but slender acquirements were
requisite. At one time he had figured as tapster
to an alehouse, then had officiated as clerk and
master of the ceremonies to a skittle ground;
but finding the *nine* in this case, as in others,
more literary, did not adequately remunerate his
exertions, he amused his leisure by copying noti-
ces for a proctor, served copies of writs for a
bailiff, with occasional engagements of polling-
clerk at elections, — but all with very scanty
success, till the happy thought struck him of
turning schoolmaster. He soon acquired the
art of striking, as it was termed, the aforesaid
Mr. Joseph Champion's goose, which he often
did so flatteringly as to cause it to be sometimes taken for a swan, and even an eagle; in
truth, it was as like one as the other. Then he
had managed to procure insertion for a doggerel rebus, and a rhythmical answer to an
arithmetical question in the *Ladies' Diary*, fully
proving his accomplishments in the polite art of

literature;—no wonder, then, that he was thought in his immediate neighbourhood, a complete *rara avis.* The usual routine of day-school tuition for the youthful mind at this period consisted in the " young idea" being regularly set to go through the first six chapters in Genesis, as reading lessons; and in order to induct them into all the difficulties of spelling, to commit to memory a collection of words, progressing from one to seven syllables in the spelling books of those worthies, Dr. Thomas Dilworth and Mr. John Dyche —Vyse not having at that period, as he since has, revised and superseded their labours,—finishing by the pupil, after a long probation of pot-hooks and hangers, being plunged into all the mysteries of writing, by copying the approved correct texts of Mr. Champion, consisting of pithy, if not very appropriate, words and sentences, such as "Abomination," "Honour among thieves," &c. &c.

A cold gleam of satisfaction played over the sharp nose and chalky visage of Mr. Garret, when our hero was first introduced to him as a scholar; and a frosty twinkle for a moment shone in his small grey eyes, from beneath their shaggy lids, as the full charge for reading, writing, and arithmetic, was agreed upon. Jack did not prove a very apt scholar: his mind was decidedly too mechanical; and he had too great a disposition to wish to acquire things at once, to allow of his making much progress in the paths of Priscian. though there were times when he evinced an obstinate perseverance and determined patience that augured well for his surmounting, if he had so chosen, the greatest difficulties. The information touching the genealogy, age, and death of the patriarchs from Adam unto Noah, telling how " Methuselah lived an hundred eighty and seven years, and begat Lamech," and how " all the days of Methuselah were nine hundred sixty and nine years," with other astounding records of a like nature, puzzled our little hero exceedingly ; nor could he be brought to see the utility of learning to spell such " Scripture proper names of four syllables," as " A-na-ni-ah," " He-ze-ki-ah," " Je-re-mi-ah," and " Za-cha-ri-ah." The tempting apples that hung so abundantly on the pictured tree of knowledge, prefixed as a frontispiece to the Rev. Thomas Dilworth's spelling book, and with which the scholars were seen, by the aid of a convenient ladder, filling their satchels so plentifully, looked all nice enough ; but by what species of allegory the aforesaid reading and spelling lessons could be typified into apples, Jack could not, for the life of him, understand ; however, he managed to master the alphabet, both in reading and writing, but not until after many long and painful lessons,

— still he did master them, thanks to the attractions of his first Christmas piece, which portrayed, in a series of glaringly-coloured cuts, "THE NOTABLE AND MERRY EXPLOITS OF ROBIN HOOD AND HIS MEN," including his "slaying the fifteen foresters," his robbing "the proud bishop and his company," his "cozening the sheriff of Nottingham in Sherwood Forest," his "rescuing the three squires from Nottingham gallows," and other memorable feats of this celebrated outlaw, — all which served still further to sway Jack's future progress.

Among the scholars with whom our hero early formed a friendship, were Masters William Blewit and Joseph Blake, though they were considerably older than himself. School friendships do not usually survive till manhood; but as in this case they continued till death, and as the latter young gentleman is destined to cut a very conspicuous figure in these pages, the reader must pardon us if we record, somewhat minutely, the progress of this intimacy. Master William Blewit was a dogged, sullen, mischievous boy, one of those still streams that run deepest, while Master Joseph Blake, or Blueskin*, as he was

* Blueness of skin, amounting in some cases almost to the darkness of a mulatto, is not of such rare occurrence as may be imagined; it is sometimes born with persons, as in the case of Master *Blake*, and then is caused as we have been

nicknamed by the other boys, from the peculiar
purple hue of his complexion, — a nickname he
retained, and in which he acquired such an unen-
viable notoriety in after-life,—was of a more lively
turn. He was a stout-built thick-set lad of about
twelve years of age, with hard, but not unplea-
sant, features ; a spice of cunning roguery con-
tinually mingling with the sterner expression.
He first won Jack's unqualified admiration by
the dexterity with which — having committed
some fault that required punishment, upon being
ordered by Mr. Garret to hold out his hand to
receive certain cuts with a leathern strap which the
pedagogue always carried in his coat pocket for
that purpose — he managed to pick the master's
pocket of the aforesaid leathern strap with one
hand, and pass it to Blewit, while, with apparent
fear and trembling, he held out the other.   This

---

assured by an eminent surgeon and anatomist, by some interior disorganisation of the blood-vessels. In other cases
it is owing to a sudden revulsion of the blood, arising from
fright or other strong excitement; while, in other cases, it
may arise from an over-dose of some mineral poison, such as
nitrate of silver, as in the instance of a lady at Highgate,
known by the name of the Blue *Lady*, whose disfiguration
proceeded from her taking poison, happily ineffectually, on
being disappointed in a love affair : also in the person of a
popular comic actress on the Surry side of the water, whose
good looks, however, were not materially spoiled by it,
though she considered it necessary afterwards to resort to a
Vale, which she constantly retained.

trait of genius tickled Jack amazingly : genius
is always acquisitive in its outset. A predilection
for taking that which does not belong to it,
being almost the first impulse that developes
itself in the infant mind; though what is vulgarly
called thieving in some, through a different
manifestation, is often termed a thirst for knowledge — a praiseworthy ambition — a daring love
of enterprise, with a hundred similar fine names
in others ; but, however they may be diverted
in after life, their original source is the same, —
an innate love of acquisitiveness. We all know
those learned *phrenologists*, Messrs. GALL and
SPURZHEIM, have declared the organ for forming good dramatic plots, and that of acquisitiveness, or plunder, to be one and the same,—a fact
strikingly proved in our own day, most of the
present race of playwrights, from Bulwer to Mon-
crieff, doing nothing but steal ! steal ! steal !

To Master Blake and his companion William
Blewit, though in a lesser degree to the latter,
little Jack very soon attached himself; and it
was not long before an incident occurred, which
had the effect of cementing his connection with
the former young gentleman, more or less, during the rest of his life. One day, after their
school hours, Master Blake — having a very fine
collection of "taws" and "alleys," which, with
other inferior marbles, he had Elgin-like acquired,

wherever he had found them, without being at all particular about the means, was indulging in the well-known game of " Lagging out." When little Jack came up and began to gaze very wistfully at his stores, and the manner in which he was increasing them ; — Master Blake immediately invited him to join in their game.

" I cannot," answered our hero, in a disconcerted tone. " I have no marbles."

" That's one reason, certainly," answered his companion ; " but you've got some money to buy some, have'nt you ?" Our hero reluctantly confessed that he had not. " Neither money nor marbles!" continued Master Blake ; " that is a blue look out, certainly ; I'm thinking little Arthur Chambers* wouldn't have been long

* This prince of prigs was the most dexterous pickpocket of his own or any other day. He was of low extraction, and, according to Captain Charles Johnson, commenced pilfering even while he was in petticoats. He was a perfect master of slang in all its varieties, from the maunders, or beggars, cant, to the *romanee*, or gipsy patter, and Newgate flash of the light-fingered gentry. Many curious stories are related by Johnson of Arthur's proficiency as a cheat : one in which he got himself conveyed into his own lodgings as a dead man, and in the character of a ghost contrived during the night to rifle the house, is really dramatic, and might almost form a farce. After a long career of roguery in all the lower walks of his profession, for Arthur never aspired to the dignity of a housebreaker or highwayman, and being confined in Bridewell and many other prisons, he was detected in a street robbery, found guilty, and, some time before the birth of our hero, suffered the usual fate of such offenders at Tyburn.

without money, or marbles either, before he was half your age, if he'd been in your situation." "And who was little Arthur Chambers?" asked little Jack. "Not know who Arthur Chambers was!" exclaimed Master Blake in surprise; "well, that is a go! why, Arthur Chambers was the very prince of prigs; the downiest diver, the rummest pad, the kiddiest scamp, the prettiest cheat, and most dexterous filch upon town; but I'll tell you what Arthur Chambers was, my blade, ay, and in his own words, too."

Here he began singing a well known song, which had formerly been a great favourite with little Arthur, and was generally supposed to have been composed by himself. It ran as follows: —

The Song of the Young Prig.

My mother ⚫ dwelt in Dyott's isle, [1]
 One of the canting crew [2], sirs;
And if you'd know my father's style,
 He was the LORD *Knows-who*, sirs!

[1] "Dyott's isle:" St. Giles's; so called from Sir Edward Dyott, a celebrated judge, having a mansion there in a street named after him, Dyott Street; and which has since been desecrated to the purposes of a twopenny lodging-house, better known by the name of the *Rookery*.
[2] "Canting crew:" beggars.

I first held horses in the street,
  But being found defaulter,
Turned rumbler's flunky[3] for my meat,
  So was brought up to the halter,
Frisk the cly[4], and fork the rag,[5]
  Draw the fogles plummy,[6]
Speak to the tatler[7], bag the swag,[8]
  And finely hunt the dummy.[9]

2.

My name they say is young BIRDLIME,
  My fingers are fish hooks, sirs;
And I my reading learnt betime,
  From studying pocket-books[10], sirs.
I have a sweet eye for a plant,[11]
  And graceful as I amble,
Fine-draw a coat tail sure I can't,
  So kiddy is my famble.[12]
    Frisk the cly, &c.

[3] "Rumbler's flunky:" a cad, or footman, to hackney coaches to water the horses, &c.

[4] "Frisk the cly:" to pick a pocket.

[5] "Fork the rag:" lay hold of the notes or money.

[6] "Fogles plummy:" draw out the handkerchiefs dexterously.

[7] "Speak to the tatler:" steal a watch.

[8] "Bag the swag:" pocket the chain and seals.

[9] "Finely hunt the dummy:" adroitly search for a pocket-book.

[10] Pocket books are called "readers."

[11] "Plant:" an intended robbery.

[12] "Kiddy famble:" having a practical and skilful hand.

3.

Oh, I 'm the boy to fake away, [13]
 In spite of trap [14] or beak [15], sirs,
To go out on the morning lay, [16]
 Upon the area sneak [17], sirs.
For cupboard love, so rare my parts,
 Welcome as rose in June, sirs:
I slily steal the slaveys' [18] hearts,
 Along with their masters' spoons, sirs.
  Frisk the cly, &c.

4.

Turn feather merchant on the hop, [19]
 Or peckers [20], if there 's not any:
Hedge draper [21], open a sky shop, [22]
 And practise moonlight botany; [23]
But when more attic rigs I 'd ply, [24]
 My skill much higher raising,

[13] " Fake away :" to follow one's occupation.

[14] " Trap :" police officer.

[15] " Beak :" justice.

[16] Prowling about in the early part of the day to pick up any thing that may present itself.

[17] " Area sneak :" a fellow who watches opportunities to sneak down areas when the door is left open, to pilfer plate, and other " unconsidered trifles."

[18] " Slaveys :" maid servants.

[19] A fellow who robs hen roosts, &c.   [20] Fowls.

[21] A fellow who steals linen from bushes, &c.

[22] The fields and public roads.

[23] Robbing gardens by night.

[24] Try something higher.

I swiftly the blue pigeon fly,[25]
    And go at night star gazing.
        Frisk the cly, &c.

5.

Or scout it on the milky beat,[26]
    Where walking pap feeds[27] rove, sirs:
Turn lully prigger[28], for a cheat,
    Awake to every move, sirs.
Smash brummy benders[29], bobs[30], coach wheels,[31]
    None can the change ring faster,
Trip in a ramp[32] some old cove's heels.
    And fly away his castor.[33]
        Frisk the cly, &c.

6.

The fences[34] all smile soft on me,
    For fogle, tatler, reader;
And ogle clearers[35], when they 'd see
    Gilt-cove's screens[36], and nose-feeder.[37]
And when in booze-ken[38] I 'd delight
    With dells[39] to sport and play, sirs,

[25] Stealing lead from gutters.
[26] The Spring Garden quarter of St. James's Park, formerly the great resort of nursery maids.
[27] Nurses.
[28] A thief who robs children of their bread and butter, &c.
[29] To pass counterfeit sixpences.   [30] Shillings.
[31] Crown pieces.   [32] To hustle in a pretended fight.
[33] Run off with his hat.
[34] Receivers of stolen goods.
[35] Spectacles.   [36] Goldsmiths' notes.   [37] Snuff-box.
[38] A public-house.   [39] Women of bad character.

I steal a few hours from the night
 And add them to the day, sirs.
  Frisk the cly, &c.

7.

A night bird[40] oft I 'm in the cage,[41]
 But my rum chants ne'er fail, sirs;
The dubsman's[42] senses to engage,
 While I tip him leg-bail[43], sirs.
There 's not, for picking, to be had,
 A lad so light and larky,[44]
The cleanest angler on the pad,[45]
 In daylight or the darky.[46]
  Frisk the cly, &c.

8.

And though I do n't work capital,[47]
 And do not weigh my weight[48], sirs,
Who knows but that in time I shall,
 For there 's no queering fate, sirs.
If I 'm not lagged to Virgin-nee,[49]
 I may a Tyburn show be,[50]
Perhaps a tip-top cracksman[51] be,
 Or go on the high toby.[52]
  Frisk the cly, &c.

---

[40] A disorderly vagabond.   [41] The round-house.
[42] Gaoler.   [43] Running away.
[44] Frolicsome.   [45] Expert street robber.
[46] The night.
[47] Commit any offence punishable with death.
[48] The 40*l*. payable on capital conviction.
[49] Transported.   [50] Hanged.   [51] House-breaker.
[52] Turn highwayman.

The greater part of this pious chanson being perfect Greek to Jack, Master Joseph Blake, who was thoroughly initiated in the language of the modern Greeks, or slang, as it is termed, undertook to explain it to him, which he did to Jack's great edification, making him wish most devoutly that he could emulate the accomplishments of "young Birdlime," to get him out of the dilemma in which he was at that moment placed.

"That you can easily do," said Master Joseph Blake. "Has your mother got any jewels?" Jack had never heard the word. "Well, that is a rum start! Here, Bill Blewit, here's this young kid, Jack Sheppard, do n't know what jewels is! Well, then, has she got any trinkets?" Jack was equally as ignorant in this particular. "Well, then, has she got any rings, or brooches, or pins —— ?"

"Yes, she's got some pins," said Jack, very innocently; "I bought her a ha'porth this morning."

"Psha!" said his companion, laughing at his simplicity; "I mean has she got any lockets — things with sparkling stones set in gold, with a tongue at the back to fasten them to the breast, that we could speak to, or a gold chain to hang them round the neck with? — though hanging round the neck ain't exactly the rabbit."

"Mother had a good many rings and them sort of things once," said Jack; " but since father has had so little work, and has been so busy with the political club down at the " Blue Posts," I arn't seen any of them; they have all disappeared; she never wears them now: there's only one, — it's a white glass heart, with father's name at the back; it's got gold all round it, and a pretty chain that it is fastened to. I know where she keeps it; it's in one of her drawers: it's locked up, but I can easily push back the lock with a knife."

"That will do capitally," exclaimed Master Blake, rubbing his hands with much satisfaction. "Only you get that, without anybody seeing you, and bring it to me, without anybody knowing it, and I'll take it to my friend Levy Laurence, the Jew, who keeps a fence in Mop Alley, Rosemary Lane, and you shall soon have marbles, and money too, my trump. Lipey arn't particular; he'll take any thing."

Jack promised to comply with his wishes, and, returning home, committed his first robbery that very evening, by skilfully forcing open the lock of his mother's drawer, and taking out the only ornament that remained to her of her former days of prosperity. It was a treasured one; she had struggled hard to retain it, had wrestled sorely with want and necessity, but she had kept it —

kept it to be stolen by her child, her darling, to whom she looked for future comfort and support.

The next morning Jack conveyed his ill-gotten spoil to Master Blake, who conveyed it equally as speedily to honest Levy, or Lipey, as he was more usually called. The worthy Israelite declared upon his conscience that the heart, which was of the purest crystal, was only composed of imitation glass, while the setting and chain, both which were virgin gold, was, he affirmed, " coppersh, vasht over with a little gilt, and not vorth more at the outside than a shilling." Master Blake doubting the veracity of this statement, the Jew called upon several solemn evidences, not to be treated lightly, to bear witness to his truth and integrity; Master Blake therefore told him to hand over the bob, which, in less than half an hour afterwards was expended in sweetmeats, marbles, &c., and divided equally between the two juvenile culprits.

Some days elapsed before Mrs. Sheppard missed her locket; when she did, and found her drawer had been forced open, her suspicions immediately rested on our hero, who had for some time before manifested an extreme degree of ingenuity and perseverance in getting corks and stopples out of bottles, untying difficult knots, and other works of handicraft. She had only been led very reluctantly to seek the ornament, to extricate her from a situation of urgent need ; and her disappointment at its disappearance was doubly bitter. She immediately taxed her son, for she knew no one else could have taken it, with the theft, threatening to punish him in the most dreadful way if he did not instantly make a full confession.

It is amazing how very terrible the threats of really fond mothers are, their anger always appearing more violent than that of others. Mrs. Sheppard assured her son, that if he did not immediately tell her what he had done with the locket, she would tear him limb from limb, be the death of him — with many other dreadful denunciations of vengeance of a similar kind ; — to all which Jack, after giving a determined denial of any knowledge of the theft, listened with sullen silence. After many other equally fruitless efforts to extort the truth, the poor woman gave up the attempt in despair.

" It was the last of my ornaments," she exclaimed, with bitter sadness, "the last remembrance of my former days of happiness and comfort. I had preserved it through every exigence — poverty had sought to deprive me of it in vain. I had resisted even the sharp promptings of hunger, and now to lose it thus!" The tears stole into her eyes. " My poor, misguided husband ! "

she continued; "it was his first and dearest gift —
that with which he declared his passion for me :
never shall I forget that time!   It was a lovely
summer's eve — we left the busy town at Clerkenwell, and wandered through the pleasant
meadows towards Islington by the banks of the
rapid Fleet, which then flowed brightly onwards :
all nature seemed to welcome us.   Then it was,
while the evening breeze breathed wooingly,
that he cast the chain around my neck, and heart
met heart : a crystal heart, and set in virgin gold,
bearing his name upon it, as mine still does his
image — pure, precious, bright ; showing — how
truly ! — our then happy state.   Alas! what is it
now ?   Sullied, despoiled, and wretched ! the
last link of my former happiness is gone, and
only misery and anguish now remain."   Here
she burst into an agony of grief, and gave vent
to her feelings in a flood of tears.

Jack, who had heard all this with an apparent
apathy, could resist no longer. " Mother, dear
mother," he exclaimed, " I don't want not to be
punished, but I can't bear to see you cry : I did
take the locket ; I did force open the drawer,
and I'll tell you who I gave it to, and where it is.
I gave it to Joe Blake, my schoolfellow, and he
sold it to Levy Laurence, the Jew ; and now
beat me ; do what you like with me ; I can bear
it all."

This was a harrowing confession for a doting mother to hear; her darling son a thief, and at so tender an age too! But her anguish was somewhat alleviated by the openness of the disclosure, and the generosity of the feeling that had prompted it: then there was the prospect of recovering the cherished token. Casting a look of sad reproach at her guilty son, which touched him more deeply than would have done the keenest invective, her first step was to repair to the nondescript residence of the Jew Levy, a forbidding looking dwelling, the lower part of which would have been described by an Irishman as composed of four halves, half cellar, half parlour, half shop, and half warehouse. As there was no law then in force for the punishment of the receiver of stolen goods, the conscientious Lipey immediately confessed having bought the article in question, describing it in the most frank and unblushing manner, but declaring as before that the crystal was glass, and the gold copper. He was offered ten times what he had given for its return, but this was impossible: the article, as is usual in those cases, had been broken up; but the Jew commiseratingly assured her she should have the remains for "half de monish." They were brought: the gold, and chain were gone; the name had been effaced from the crystal; and the heart was broken.

"It is my fate," said the stricken woman, with a heavy sigh, as she gazed on the fragments. "The gold and chain are gone, the name no longer dwells within the heart; the heart is broken."

CHAPTER THE FOURTH.

JACK'S SCHOOLING CONTINUED.

PRECOCIOUS EVASIVENESS. — THE PUBLIC GOOD NOT ALWAYS PRIVATE BENEFIT. — DEATH OF ROBERT SHEPPARD.

ON the discovery of the robbery of Mrs. Sheppard's locket being made known at the school the next day, the discipline of the birch was, by particular desire of Master Blake's parents, administered to that exemplary young gentleman, for his participation in it, by Mr. Garret himself, and had the effect of materially changing the colour of his skin during the sittings for some time afterwards, though, in the progress of its infliction, he had only thrust his tongue in his cheek, and made other unseemly grimaces. Mrs. Sheppard's tenderness would not suffer her to expose her son to the corporal mercies of the preceptor; she therefore determined on taking his punishment into her own hands. Accordingly, conveying him to a garret at the top of the house, she locked him up in a large spare closet which happened to be empty, expressing her intention of keeping him prisoner there with-

out victuals during the whole of the day. Our
hero neither expressed contrition, nor besought
pardon, but yielded to his fate with a passive
unconcern that awakened in his mother's breast
many a sad foreboding.   Not content with lock-
ing him up in the cupboard, she, for greater
security, bolted, on the outside, the door of the
garret in which the cupboard was situated. She
was no sooner out of hearing than Jack began to
whistle the well-known tune of " Lillibullero,"
and instantly set his little wits to work to devise
some means of escape.   Searching the shelves of
the closet in which he was confined, he found an
old broken fork with only one prong; with this
prong he very soon managed to force back the
lock of his prison door, and was the next moment at liberty in the middle of the room.   He
had then the outer door to force: with the same
implement, by working the prong through the
crevice of the door, which was an old, and consequently a crazy one, he managed to shoot back
the bolt, and was in an instant on the landing
place. As he did not dare to venture down
stairs, the only access to the street being through
the two lower apartments — for the luxury of a
passage was then rarely known in the houses
of mechanics, — and he must inevitably have
been seen by one of his parents, he boldly
passed through the staircase window into a gut-

ter, skirted by a small parapet that ran along the front of the whole of the houses in that side the street. He crawled along this gutter like a cat, at the imminent hazard of his neck, till he came to a house, the inhabitants of which he knew would, at that time, be absent; and procuring an entrance from the roof through a small trap-door into a species of cockloft, made his way down the various stories, and through the different rooms, securely into the street, committing no other offence in his progress than the entire destruction of a whole pot of preserves, which a maiden lady had with great pains prepared for the purpose of furnishing the contents of a series of roll puddings, during the ensuing winter. This was Jack's first escape — a precocious one, certainly, but strongly foretelling what might afterwards be expected of him.

Mrs. Sheppard had, meanwhile, with much heaviness of heart, proceeded to Spitalfields market to provide the dinner of the day; but though she had mentally resolved that her son should not dine with her, but rather with Duke Humphry, and might have dispensed with at least half a pound of the meat she usually provided, she had somehow contrived, by accident of course, to buy half a pound more. Returning homewards, her maternal bosom filled with a thousand anxious visions of the dismal situation to which she had consigned her peccant son, what was her surprise, in crossing Spitalfields Square, to behold the supposed prisoner very joyously engaged, playing at "knuckle down," with a parcel of other boys. She could scarcely believe her eyes. "Why, goodness gracious! you little villain!" she exclaimed, "who can possibly have let you out? tell me this moment or I'll tear you to pieces, I will! — your father, I dare say; for since he's taken to drinking that strong bubb, and puzzling his poor weak head with politics, he's grown foolish enough for any thing."

"Nobody didn't let me out," said Jack boldly.

"Then how did you get out?"

"I got out by myself," coolly returned the boy.

"What, when I locked and bolted you in?" said his mother.

"Yes," sturdily replied Jack, "and would if you had locked and bolted me in ten times as much."

"Why, you incorrigible little scoundrel!" screamed his mother, almost choking with rage.

"I don't care," said Jack; "no locks nor bolts, neither, shall keep me in. I won't be shut up for any body, and so I tell you."

"I am petrified!" said his mother.

"Well no more I won't," repeated Jack in a still louder and firmer tone.

"Can I believe my ears?" ejaculated the astonished Mrs. Sheppard. "Jack Jack! you'll come to no good; I can plainly perceive that: but if there's a stick to be had for love or money, your back shall pay for this, sir. Only wait till I get you home."

"Only wait till you catch me," said Jack, with a laugh, snatching up his marbles, and running off with a celerity that took him out of sight in a minute, leaving his astonished mother perfectly thunderstruck at his hardihood and audacity.

"He is lost!" she exclaimed, "ruined—hardened! punishment will have no effect on him; I must try and reclaim him by kindness. — Yes! I will not let any one know of this dissolute conduct of his, lest they should suppose that he is past amending. I will reason with him by ourselves. Ah! if his father — if Robert Sheppard were but true to himself — to his family—to me, how easily might all this be remedied; but that fatal 'Blue Posts' — those endless politics! No, no! there is no hope."

It must now be premised, that from the moment the Sheppards settled in Spitalfields, honest Bob had plunged more deeply into politics, and porter, or strong bubb, as it was then called, than ever. Some parish *quid nuncs* had, a short time previously to Bob's arrival there, formed themselves into a sort of political club, or society,

at the " Blue Posts," a house noted for the
strength of its liquors, into which he got immediately admitted. One of the overseers of Spitalfields, a somewhat wealthy weaver, with the
parish clerk — who also held the office of sexton,
which he under-let — a jobbing attorney the ex-
ciseman of the district, and a disbanded lieutenant, advocated the Tory cause, and were of the
high-church and state party, vigorously supporting the pretensions of Harley, afterwards Earl
of Oxford, and Mr. St. John, who subsequently
became Lord Bolingbroke, lauding the influence of Mrs. Masham with the Queen, and
speaking with greater respect than became
good subjects of the Pretender, the Duke of
Berwick, or James the Third as he styled himself: Bob, on the contrary, backed by the foreman of a silk manufactory, a distiller's clerk,
a rider to a Manchester house in the City, and
a half crazy barber, were of the Whig party,
and strenuously espoused the Marlborough
administration, regularly regulating the plan of
attack for the Duke and his allies at the opening of every fresh campaign in Flanders. Great
were the calculations in the financial department,
that Bob made for the ministers Somers and
Godolphin, totally regardless, poor fellow! of his
own finances; but while he was busy in voting
fifty thousand here, and raising a hundred thou-

sand there, how could he be expected to cast a thought upon such paltry considerations as shillings and sixpences at home? His rejoicings at every fresh victory of the great Duke were unbounded : he had foreseen them—he had marked them out. The Duke was not more indebted to the confederation of Prince Eugene and the States, than to him (Bob), for the zeal with which he backed all his movements, in Spitalfields ; and as the Tory faction now began to gain ground to the prejudice of the hero of Blenheim and Ramillies, — the idol of Holland and glory of England, — fervently did Bob execrate Mrs. Masham as a meddling, underhanded ——, we must not mention what, to " ears polite." As the star of his hero waned in the ascendant, and the Court faction became more powerful, Bob's indignation increased. The names of the great men of the age were as familiar in his mouth as "household words;" and nothing was to be heard from morning till night but Marshal Villars, the Elector of Bavaria, the Emperor of Austria, the King of Spain, &c. Continued talking produced continued thirst, and the butts of the landlord of the " Blue Posts " were in constant requisition.

To public difficulties now began to be added pecuniary embarrassments at home. The critical position of national affairs from the intrigues of the opposition party, the rapidly increasing de-

cline of the Duke's power and favour, with the
necessity of checking the triumph of the weaving
overseer and parish clerk, and their party, so
preyed upon poor Bob's weak mind, joined to
his own personal troubles, that he began at last
to sink under them. Vainly were his *ebbing*
spirits attempted to be rallied by the eloquence
of his friend the barber, and the strong drinks of
the potentate of the " Blue Posts :" — Bob took
to his bed.   A distress was unfortunately at this
period put into his house for rent ; the tide of
adversity flowed in full upon him ; Mrs. Sheppard courageously strove to stem it, and might
have succeeded, but for a public event which just
then occurred, and not only settled the destinies
of Europe for the time being, but sealed the
fate of poor Bob for ever.

We have said that he was reduced to his bed :
a distress for rent was in his house. The man
in possession sat like an evil genius — a goule —
a nightmare, in the little room at the back of the
shop, in which the family lived. They had let
the other part of the house, with the exception of the aforesaid garret in which little
Jack slept. An order had just been received
for the shell of some parish pauper. The overseer at the " Blue Posts," though opposed to Bob
in politics, honouring the zeal he evinced for his
party, and anxious to assist him, the order was

given to be executed to Bob's only journeyman, who was then busily engaged upon it.

Mrs. Sheppard had procured the daily Journal for her husband, the more to amuse his mind, which, to say the truth, had for some time previously betrayed symptoms of being wandering, and unsettled. She was speaking to him of the expediency of paying their unwelcome and ill-boding inmate his daily half-crown, that their goods might not be sold, until at least they had made an effort to save them.

" Yes," faintly murmured Bob, "we must pay him — we must pay him. Ah! what is this?" he said, his eye catching a paragraph in the paper, announcing the signing the memorable treaty of Utrecht. " What is this?" glancing his eye rapidly over it; "the Tories have triumphed! our queen has been betrayed — sold! The lustre of England's crown is sullied!"

" But the man, dear Robert, the man," whispered Mrs. Sheppard, seeing how much he had become excited, and wishing to divert his attention.

" True, true," groaned Bob, much agitated; "pay him the half-crown; we must get rid of him. There are villains in the cabinet — the confederation is broken up — they must not sell our goods, you will go to our landlord, love? — the French king has been too much for us—we

are lost — the balance of power — the distress—
what am I talking of? my senses wander—they
must not turn you out into the streets, poor
wench!—the troops—the taxes—ruin!—I could
have saved all — strong measures — no, no —
would I had never gone to that fatal public-
house!—but all shall be well yet.—I grow
weaker — give me your hand, Kate—God bless
Old England!—take care of our boy—watch over
little Jack—let him be a carpenter.—The cabinet
will be broken up — the duke — the queen —my
eyes grow dim — let Thomas finish the shell —
good-bye — good ——"

Poor Bob let the fatal paper fall from his grasp
and sank upon his pillow. The martyr to public
good, for private ill, had fallen to rise no more.
The nation still went on as usual—but Mrs.
Sheppard was a widow, and little Jack was
fatherless.

CHAPTER THE FIFTH.

JACK'S SCHOOLING COMPLETED.

JACK ADOPTED BY MR. KNEEBONE. — THE OLD BAILEY
SESSIONS OF 1712. — THE GIPSY'S WARNING.

THE death of Robert Sheppard soon brought all his friends and acquaintances around his widow : — death is a stern and uncompromising moralist, and often teaches their duty to many, who would listen to no other schoolmaster. We fear him, and dare not treat him with disrespect. Numbers who had for months preceding deserted Bob in his poverty, now that he no longer needed their aid, came to offer their assistance — it is remarkable how ostentatious and gratuitous is one half of the charity of the world — but their attendance had the effect of procuring the poor carpenter a respectable funeral. The political club, his attention to which had cost him so dear, paid him the last mark of respect, both parties mingling in peace and good will together at his grave. But amongst all the friends this calamity had rallied round her, none were more sympathising, more serviceable to the poor widow, than her old acquaintance Mr. Kneebone, the woollen-draper, the son, it may be remembered, of her former protectress, when she was happy and unmarried. Now that poor Bob is dead, we may venture to disclose a secret which, during his lifetime, might have savoured somewhat of scandal. The worthy woollen-draper had early felt a very ardent passion for his mother's comely god-daughter—for comely she then was: she was the first love of his heart; and he had earnestly looked forward to an union, but the Fates had ordered it otherwise — the amiable angel, whose gentle task it is, according to received belief, to make marriages in Heaven, having been induced by poor Bob's apparent fervour and sincerity in his addresses to Kate to link their fates together. We may wonder at the number of mistakes committed by this sweet spirit in paring mortals together; but when the thousand arts and "perjuries of lovers, at which Jove laughs," are considered, we can easily conceive why he should be so often deceived in the course of his delicate and important registration.

Mr. Kneebone's first step was to clear the poor widow's house of every species of distress, save that caused by her bereavement, by kicking out the man in possession, and satisfying the various claims on poor Bob's insolvent estate. As there was a very considerable custom at-

tached to the shop, which would be easily
executed by a foreman, and was capable of providing a very comfortable subsistence for Mrs.
Sheppard, it was agreed that she should still
carry on the business. As for little Jack, Mr.
Kneebone declared his intention of wholly taking
the future care of providing for him upon himself. It is almost needless to remark how grateful the poor widow was for all this real kindness.
Jack was immediately removed from Mr. Garret's, where he had learnt little but roguery,—for
Mr. Garret had not, as before mentioned, much
to teach: he invariably, when his acquirements
were brought to a stand still, getting out of the
dilemma by flogging the boy whose superior
knowledge had got him into it,—an approved
method with London Orbiliuses even to this day.
Little Jack left Mr. Garret without regret.

Master Joseph Blake had previously been ex-
pelled the school for having, in concert with
Master William Blewit, stolen the pedagogue's
best silver snuff-box, and got it converted into a
white soap* for their joint benefit, by worthy
Lipey Laurence. Accordingly, leaving the
widow as comfortable as she could be, under
the circumstances, Mr. Kneebone conveyed little Jack to his own residence in the Strand,
which, as mentioned before, was at the sign of

* Melted.

I

the "Fleece and Shears," situated near the Old
Angel Inn, in a row of houses long since pulled
down, and which faced one side of St. Clement's Church, looking into the churchyard,
according to the strange fancy at that period of
mingling the living and the dead in the closest
neighbourhood.

Mr. Kneebone had, it would seem, proved
constant to his first love, for he was still unmarried, his domestic arrangements being super-
intended by a dear, good, unconscious old creature, a widow of the name of Partington.   Mrs.
Partington, without being deficient in common
sense, natural shrewdness, and even judgment,
was the most simple soul imaginable.   She had
passed through life smoothly, and had experienced none of those trials, which, like the
rough stones of the cutler, serve to sharpen us
as we are brought in contact with them.   She
had never known the want of money, and could
not, therefore, have any idea of the struggles
required in its acquisition, or of its real value;
for the value given to money in the common
arithmetical tables of our ciphering books, that
twelve pence make a shilling, and twenty shillings a pound, but little conveys an idea of its
real worth when wanted.   How different is the
pound acquired by inheritance, gift, or the labours of others, to that which has to be bor-

rowed or worked for. The offspring of parents
in comfortable circumstances, with an easy temper, and perpetual good humour, she had married early in life without experiencing any of
the pangs of previous passion, to a thriving
suitor, who, after some years of childless wedlock
died, leaving her a widow with what, if well
managed, would have proved a snug compe-
tency for her life. But poor Mrs. Partington,
guileless herself, never suspected guile in others:
she took every thing literally, and thought all
she heard was what it purported to be — all she
saw what it appeared to be; and it was only
when she had got rid of almost all that had
been left her, that she found out her mistake.
Luckily for her, the death of Mr. Kneebone's
mother at this juncture, by rendering it necessary that he should have some one to preside
over his domestic arrangements, not too young
to excite scandal, nor too old to prevent the
duly attending to his comforts, provided her
with a home not inferior to either of those she
had enjoyed with her parents and with her
husband. Poor Mrs. Partington! — so long as she
did not know the want of a shilling, she was
perfectly ready to believe the streets were paved
with gold; and yet she was notable in her occu-
pations, and an admirable manager in all that
required her superintendence. But extreme sim-

plicity is very often to be found united to the very highest qualities of the mind. Fontaine, Gay, and our inimitable Goldsmith, all, in wit were men, but children in simplicity. She received Jack very kindly, and when Mr. Knee-bone told her she must be a mother to him, earnestly promised to be so, and in a short time really almost imagined that she was so. Mr. Kneebone's house was substantial, and well fur-nished; he had a flourishing business, and but for an habitual gravity, the cause of which, whether it arose from the disappointment in his early love affair, a natural tendency, or any other source, was quite a mystery, might have been considered a completely happy man: his temper was equable, his habits regular, and his wishes moderate. Faithful to the trust he had taken upon himself, he immediately commenced com-pleting Jack's education; he set him, as our hero afterwards gratefully confessed, copies with his own hand, and took a delight in hearing him read from any book or printed paper that pre-sented itself.

One day as they were sitting behind the counter, the beadle of St. Clement's entered with a jury paper, in which Mr. Kneebone was sum-moned to attend the sessions then holding in the Old Bailey. Little Jack was very curious to know all the particulars of this duty, asking many questions touching the functions of the judge, and what juries were for, and what was the meaning of counsel, with other pertinent interrogatories; also what sort of a place Newgate was, and how persons fared who were transported either to Virginia, or Maryland, — to which colonies convicts were usually transported at that period, — whether they were nice places or not; — to all which questions the goodnatured Mr. Kneebone, seeing the deep interest Jack took in them, answered as well as he could, promising further particulars the first opportunity. When the day arrived for Mr. Kneebone's attendance at the court, Jack was very eager, on his return, to know all that had passed; and Mr. Kneebone could only get rid of some very puzzling importunities, by promising at the end of the sessions he would bring him a printed " report of all the trials, with the sentences of the prisoners, &c." and would hear him read out of that, instead of the Bible, which they had then nearly got half-way through. The sessions soon terminated, and Mr. Kneebone proved as good as his word : he brought Jack the official account of the various trials that had taken place, which Jack immediately proceeded to spell out with great avidity. The principal trial was that of a highwayman ! one

John Hawkins, who subsequently became very notorious, and was some years afterwards executed at Tyburn for robbing the Bristol mail.* He was accused of stopping Justice Blenkinsop in his carriage on Hounslow Heath, and taking from his person twenty guineas, a silk nightgown, a new tie-wig, a pinchbeck family watch, and a shagreen spectacle case. Thomas Biddlecombe, the coachman, a Mr. Whiffin, who was in the carriage at the time, and several other witnesses swore positively to the fact. Hawkins' defence was an *alibi*. He brought one Solomon Shabner, who kept a lodging-house in Knave's Acre, London, to swear that he was at his house at the very time the robbery was committed, in proof of which Shabner produced a receipt of thirty shillings for a pair of leather breeches, which he affirmed had been given him at that very time by Hawkins; but the judge having examined the receipt, and finding that the body of it was written with ink of a different colour to that with which the name at the bottom was signed, told the jury, he did not think Shabner's evidence was entitled to any credit, and they were about to bring in a verdict of guilty, when an acquaintance of the prisoner, who said his name

* He was hung with his accomplice, James Simpson, after an extraordinary career of villany, on the 21st of May, 1722.

was Stephen Quigley, happening to look over
the notes of Mr. Cuttlemuck, the short hand-
writer to the court, perceived, that by dipping
his pen into an inkstand, the ink in which was
thick and muddy at the bottom, and watery at
the top, part of his writing was pale, while the
other was more than usually dark, snatched it
out of his possession, and handed it to the foreman of the jury, a Mr. Puddledock, who, with
his brother jurors, was so staggered by this testimony to the truth of Shabner's evidence, that
in spite of all the other witnesses, they immediately allowed the *alibi*, and acquitted the
prisoner.

Jack was overjoyed at this result, declared
that he thought an *alibi* was a capital thing, and
was what he should always procure if ever he was
tried; and when told by Mr. Kneebone that in
a case of doubtful evidence, where he wished to
acquit the offender, he had remained locked up
with his brother jurors for more than two hours
past his dinner time, until fairly worn out by
famine — having had only his usual lunch — he
was obliged to give in, Jack expressed his determination, if ever he was on a jury, to die of
hunger before he'd find a single prisoner guilty.
Mr. Kneebone goodnaturedly set down these
sentiments as proofs of the simplicity and tenderness of Jack's heart. The next trial which

attracted Jack's attention was of one Thomas Donnikin, for housebreaking. It appeared this prisoner had burglariously attempted to enter the dwelling-house of a Mr. Lammiman, a ladies' tailor, and had been caught in the fact, through the bungling manner in which he had gone to work. In forcing open a shutter he had awkwardly broken a window, which had alarmed a cat that was asleep in the room, who suddenly jumping up, had in her fright overturned a large glass globe, filled with gold and silver fish; this had aroused Mrs. Lammiman's poodle, who having aroused Mr. Lammiman, he immediately awakened his wife, she in her turn summoned the apprentices, and they called the attention of the watch. Donnikin was taken in the act of running away; he was found guilty, and sentenced to be transported. This, Jack said, he was very glad of, for that Donnikin quite deserved it; that he ought to have taken a centre-bit and a knife, or a small saw, and cut a pannel of the shutter out, when he could have put in his hand, slipped back the bolts, opened the window, and got in without any noise.

Mr. Kneebone admired the love of justice manifested in his *protégé*'s approbation at the conviction of this man, and was also pleased at the workmanlike knowledge displayed in his pointing out the proper way by which the shutter ought to have been opened.

" Jack must be a carpenter," he exclaimed :
" his poor father was right; and however much
I may wish to bring him up to my own trade of
a woollen-draper, his natural genius must have
its way."

The last trial of the sessions was one which,
when he came to it, so surprised and confused our little hero, as to render him perfectly unintelligible when he attempted to read
it. It was the trial of William Blewit and
Joseph Blake, two youths about fifteen years
of age, for picking the pocket of the Rev.
Ebenezah Spooner, a dissenting minister, of a
silver tobacco-stopper, a gilt toothpick, an old
linen handkerchief, a leathern pocket-book,
containing some valuable notes for an intended
charity sermon, a list of subscriptions for the
New Bethesda Chapel, together with four-pence
in copper. A Mrs. Ogle and one Peter Winks,
two passers-by, with several other respectable
witnesses, deposed to seeing the prisoners—who
appeared very hardened—hustle the reverend
prosecutor, though they managed by their audacity to escape at the time; but Mr. Jonathan
Wild coming forward, stated that, being employed to restore the stolen property by the
reverend gentleman's congregation, he had occasion to know that it was taken by one Tit
Blundell, who was then out of the way. He

further spoke to the good character of the two prisoners; and it appearing, on his cross-examination, that the two guineas reward paid for the recovery of the property being all swallowed up in expenses, he would only accept of the prayers of his pious employer, as he was actuated solely for the public good, the prisoners were acquitted, though the judge expressed very strong doubts of their innocence.

"And well he might," said Mr. Kneebone. "I never saw two such ill-looking young scoundrels in my life; they must have been brought up in a very bad school."

Here Jack, who had a tender recollection at his back of sundry visitations of Mr. Garret's cane, said he was certain it *was* a very bad school; and immediately began making some inquiries respecting Mr. Jonathan Wild, through whose evidence the prisoners had so fortunately got off.

"Whoso toucheth pitch, shall be defiled," answered Mr. Kneebone; "all I know of him is, that he keeps an office in the Old Bailey for restoring stolen goods to their proper owners, on consideration of an adequate reward being given, and 'no questions asked;' and from his success in his vocation he must be acquainted with almost every thief in London. He passes for a person of probity and credit; but there's an old saying, 'birds of a feather flock together;' and for my part," continued Mr. Kneebone, "the saints . preserve me from his coop, say I. I should expect to be pretty well plucked if ever I got in his clutches, as my opinion is, that he rather encourages and protects the thieves by his proceedings than any thing else."

Jack greedily swallowed this information. "They must have been my old schoolfellows, Will Blewit and Joe Blake," thought he to himself—"the names and age are the same;" but all doubt was removed from his mind by his protector's next observation.

" If they'd had a grain of modesty in their compositions," said Mr. Kneebone, " they must have been moved when the reverend prosecutor so pathetically admonished them to restore his manuscript notes, which it appeared had not been recovered with the other valuables; — but I forgot — it was impossible to make one of them blush, for his face was as blue as a bilberry: indeed one of the constables deposed that he was well known among the young prigs of Moorfields by the nickname of Blueskin."

This was enough; Jack did not venture to betray his acquaintance with them by any further remarks, but dropped the subject; — still the memory of this occurrence incessantly haunted his imagination : in his sleep he was with his former companions lightening the Reverend Ebenezah

of his worldly load, and sharing with them his
four-pence in copper, under the protection of
the charitable Mr. Wild.   Some time after this,
our hero, discovering that it was rather inconvenient at times to be without a supply of ready
cash to purchase cakes, fruit, and other luxuries
that might occasionally present themselves, bethought himself of Levy Laurence, as a probable
banker; but as it was necessary honest Levy
should have assets in hand, ere he would answer
any demands upon him, Jack looked about to
see if there was any valuable that had not been
properly put away, as it were, and wanted to be
taken care of. He was not long before he discovered a piece of negligence that he thought required being made an example of.   Mrs. Partington had a large gold seal ring, which had belonged
to her grandfather, and which she prized very
much, and only wore on high days and holidays.
It was of amazing consistency, and bore, on a
large red cornelian that stood out like a nutmeg,
the device of a pair of scissors, with a motto,
" We only part to meet again."   This ring she
had taken off, one summer's evening, and placed
on her prayer-book in the window-seat of the
dining-room, it was deeply embayed, intending to
carry it up stairs with her, when she should retire to bed.   This ring Jack found next morning,
though she did not,—albeit she searched diligently

for it, which was more than he had done. The
suspicion that any one in the house had taken it,
much less that little Jack had done so, never
entered Mrs. Partington's innocent imagination:
she only knew that she had lost it; and as she
set great store by it, she determined to employ
every means in her power to recover it.

Before Jack had an opportunity of visiting his
friend Lipey, in Houndsditch, her resolution
was taken. "If I could but see the dumb man
at Westminster, that answers all sorts of difficult
questions," she exclaimed, "he would tell me
in a moment; but unfortunately he is in Bridewell for breaking the peace in a night-brawl.
Then there's Mrs. Bunce, the cunning woman of
the maze in Southwark, that tells fortunes, but
she's picking oakum in the New Prison for not
being able to account for a pair of sheets and
some silver spoons that was to be used by her
as a charm. Never mind, I shall find somebody."

Mrs. Partington was not wrong in her supposition: that very afternoon, a wandering gipsy,
who was going about from house to house,
covertly soliciting the females to become acquainted with the secrets of futurity, peeped in
at Mr. Kneebone's door. To convey her, unobserved, to the kitchen where little Jack was
most unconsciously sitting, was the work of only
a few moments. Jack was humming to himself

the burden of Arthur Chambers's "Lay of the Prince of Prigs,"* — which our readers will remember had been sung to him by Master Blake previously to the robbery of his mother's locket— and which he had represented to Mrs. Partington, when she inquired its meaning, to be Latin; an assertion the good woman firmly believed. As the gipsy's dark shadow fell upon him, on her entrance, he started up in some surprise. Her appearance was in truth somewhat wild and striking; which the reader will readily believe, when informed she was the very identical gipsy who had some years previously assisted at Jack's birth in the little cottage at Stepney. Jack's surprise almost changed to terror, when he heard Mrs. Partington immediately afterwards proceed to explain to the gipsy the business on which she wanted her.

"I know, my good woman," said the worthy dame, "that you gipsies can tell every thing, discover hidden treasures, point out the thief,

---

* See page 41. We omitted to give the name of the particular tune to which this "most choice chant," was originally sung, and in compliance with the wishes of several of our readers, will now supply the desideratum. The tune, which was composed for the purpose, was long used as an old English morris dance, and is known in our own time by being associated with the words of a popular comic song called the "Literary Dustman," written by that son of mirth, BOB GLINDON.

when any robbery has been committed, and
reveal the place where any thing that is lost
may be found."

Jack's colour changed at these words—the
gipsy fixed her piercing eye full upon him, which
had not the effect of materially lessening his ap-
prehensions.

" I *can* point out the thief," said she in a
deep, but hollow tone, " I *can* reveal where the
lost property may be found. Nothing is unknown
to me — nothing can be concealed from me : the
planets are my servants, and the stars hold secret
council with me."

Jack trembled in every limb.

" Ay, ay, I know that," rejoined Mrs.
Partington, " I know that very well. Why I've
heard that you gipsies can read the stars as well
as we do our A B C — Lord bless me ! that
you are as intimate with Venus and Mercury,
and Gemini, and Jupiter, and all the other
planets, as if you had been brought up with
them,—that you are visited at night by the Great
Bear, and the Dog-star ; and that you can ride
on the Dragon's tail. Now, you must understand, that I have lost a very valuable ring.
There is no occasion to describe it to you, for I
dare say you are perfectly well acquainted with
it, though you have never seen it, mercy on me !

" I am well acquainted with it," said the

gipsy confidently, glancing at the same time very significantly at Jack.   " It was lost ——"

" In this house," said Mrs. Partington.

" I knew it," returned the gipsy.   " You must cross my hand with a piece of silver, and then leave me. Do not be alarmed," she continued, observing the good dame's hesitating look; " leave me with this boy — he will be my guarantee, that while your ring is found, nothing shall be missing: the owner of the lost property must not be present during the potent incantations necessary to be performed in order to effect its restoration."

Jack felt a strange species of fear and awe steal over him at the prospect of being left alone with the mysterious stranger.   We have remarked the singleness and simplicity of Mrs. Partington's character,—though superstition was no predominant feature in her nature — for superstition implies a degree of fear and weakness which did not exactly belong to her—yet she implicitly believed in fortune-tellers, dreams, charms, prognostics, &c. ; accordingly she without hesitation crossed the gipsy's hand with a shilling ; and saying that she would wait in the back kitchen during the performance of the mystic ceremonies, and that the gipsy was to cry " hem!" when she had finished, as a signal for her return, she retired in full confidence as to the result, promising the further reward of a silver crown if it should prove to be a successful one.

"Never fear," cried the gipsy, as she closed the door after her; "my art has never failed me yet." She then advanced slowly towards Jack, and stopping directly before him, gazed at him full in the face with a searching look under which he quailed, while she muttered the following lines, probably part of the formula of her profession :—

The Gipsy's Chant.

1.

THINK'ST thou the gipsy's art is vain,
And does but dwell in Fancy's brain;
That o'er the earth a wanderer driven,
No mystic power to her is given
The secrets of the past to read,
And tell the present's hidden deed,
With all, the future shall bestow,
Of good and bad, of joy and woe?
  False is thy thought, by sign and spell
  The gipsy every thing can tell.

2.

Think'st thou the spheres exist alone;
That earth and sky no kindred own;
That 'tween the stars which people heaven
And man, no sympathy is given;

That planets roll above our earth,
And beam upon each infant's birth;
Nor own an influence o'er its fate,
To sway its future love and hate?
  False is thy thought, by their weird spell,
  The gipsy every thing can tell.

3.

Sprung from the East, where wisdom reign'd,
Why is the gipsy's skill disdain'd?
Her power is in her being shown,—
Unmix'd she lives — apart — alone.
Seek, if in others thou canst trace,
One feature of the gipsy race;
Mark the dark words she, only, speaks;
See the warm glow that stains her cheeks;
  And slight her not, by sign and spell —
  The gipsy every thing can tell.

4.

To her each hidden secret 's known;
To her the future still is shown:
She in the teacup's dregs can read
Whate'er the Fates may have decreed;
Can in the lines which cross the palm,
Trace future welfare, future harm;
The hidden and the lost unfold;
Point out the thief, yield back the gold.
  Scorn not her words, but mark them well —
  The gipsy every thing can tell.

Absolutely terrified at the solemnity of the gipsy's tones, the mystic import of her words, and the angry glaring of her eye, without staying for any question, Jack's hand instinctively sought his breeches pocket, from which he tremblingly drew forth the lost ring.

"I found it, ma'am," he faltered forth, "and was going to give it back, only I didn't know exactly who it belonged to. Indeed I did not steal it: I only took it. Pray don't tell Mrs. Partington,—she'll give you twice as much if she thinks you found it all of yourself, and nobody told you."

" Peace, boy!" said the gipsy, sternly, taking the ring; "you begin by times.—Your hand—let me peruse its palm — your left hand, imp! — the lines run deepest there—ah! what is this? What see I on the plain of Mars?—a crooked line, crossing the table line: — that should betoken sudden death. — The sister line is broken too, — the line of fate!—that looks not well; this line which runs across the wrist, and there is lost in blood — have I not read this palm before? Let me regard thee — that mole upon the neck, on the left side—ah! I remember now, when I removed her infant hand which shadowed it — then first I saw it. — Thy name, boy?"

" Sheppard, Jack Sheppard," faltered Jack.

" Thy parents came from Stepney?"

" Yes."

" It is the hand of fate that brought me here !" exclaimed the gipsy ; and immediately set herself about drawing a planetary configuration on the floor with the by-forked hazel wand she had in her hand, and with which she guided her steps. " Strange, strange," she continued, as she gazed on the figures, and began to cast their relative positions to each other. " This house which seeming chance has brought me to, has reference to both their future fates ; there's a dark secret wound with it in which they both have part. What has this house to do with *her* nativity ? Strange that I should meet this boy again, and here !" She fell into a deep and sad abstraction. After a few moments, recovering from her musing, she turned to Jack, and with looks and words that partook more of sorrow than of anger, thus addressed him : — " Listen to me, boy !—a baleful star gleams over thee, betokening a shameful end : if thou'dst not die a felon's death, withdraw thee from its influence—forsake thy present course ; I'll not betray thy confidence, moved by some previous knowledge ;—but beware ! and let this present mercy induce repentance, where punishment perchance had hardened.—Shun evil ways — theft, and the counsel of the wicked ; but, above all, should there e'er cross thy path one fair as morning, with eyes mild as the unclouded blue that veils the heaven of a summer's eve, and tresses golden as the grain that ripens in autumnal suns, one wearing thine own age, and bearing on her neck a spot impressed by art, a counterpart of that which nature, for thy warning, so ominously hath planted upon thine; —should such e'er cross thee, avoid her— fly her, ay, as thou would'st a scorpion, or aught more foul. Though promising elysium, she'll prove destruction to thee : thy seeming bliss will be thy certain bane. Treasure my words — how shall I show thee farther ? "

Here she began again to make various planetary and zodiacal signs upon the floor. " What's this ? Ah ! Leo—the Lion ! Though gentle as the breath of noon in spring, far better 'twere that thou should'st meet a lioness: her love will be thy doom — avoid her — fly her — she bears a royal virgin's name.   I may not tell the more — avoid her — fly her, ay, as thou would'st the hangman : but should'st thou disregard me — ah ! what then ?—aid me my art ! — In thy dark hour of peril,"—and she again resorted to her mystic characters on the floor — "once may'st thou escape, twice may'st thou escape — ay, when the doom is said, the coffin made, and the grave dug, and — Magi ! what see I ! By the twelve plagues that overspread our land, by the ensanguined sea that overwhelmed our might, e'en though the hemp be twined, the beam be raised, the priest be ready, *thrice*, THRICE, shalt thou escape; but then — ah! there's a blank: all's dark — dark as eternity. I've warned thee, boy: beware the third time — beware the temptress.— Let me away!— but first this ring." She coughed thrice.

Jack was mute and motionless with terror. He understood but half of what had been addressed to him, but that half was enough: his spirit was checked, his blood ran cold in his veins, and a determined resolution of future honesty took full possession of his mind. All expectation and apprehension, Mrs. Partington was not long in making her appearance.

"Well, my good mother," she asked, with much eagerness, "have your conjurations proved successful."

"They have, mistress," said the gipsy, solemnly.

"Shall I recover my ring?"

"You will."

Mrs. Partington was overjoyed.

"Bring hither a bible and a key, a plate of salt, and a clean napkin, together with a garter you wore the day on which the article was lost."

"Mercy on me!" said Mrs. Partington, "this is wonderful; but I have heard of such things before:" and retiring for a minute or two, she returned, bringing with her all that the gipsy had required.

" 'Tis well," said the sibyl, beginning to mutter some unintelligible words, which Mrs. Partington had no difficulty in believing was a very powerful charm; she then placed a portion of the salt in the napkin, which she folded up in a very peculiar and mystic manner, very much after the fashion of what are called puzzle purses; then binding the key and bible together with the garter, she suspended them from her fore-finger over the cloth, making them perform a number of gyrations, muttering all the time a variety of uncouth sentences in an unknown tongue, which had the effect of greatly adding to the imposing nature of the proceedings. The ceremonies being at length concluded, and appa-rently to her satisfaction, " It is enough," she said. " Take this napkin, bury it where no living eye can see—no human voice can tell; let it re-main inurned three days: on the morning of the third day go, fasting and in secret, dig it up, re-peating thrice the words, ' In the name of Egypt, I charge thee, O ring, appear!' and the bauble will be restored to you."

" Wonderful!" exclaimed the unsuspecting matron, at the same time gratefully thrusting a five shilling piece into the gipsy's hand. " I 'll not fail, depend upon it."

"Good. Farewell mistress," returned the gipsy. — "Remember. And you, boy," she added, casting an expressive glance at Jack, "do not *you* forget:" saying which, she mysteriously departed.

CHAPTER THE SIXTH.

JACK'S APPRENTICESHIP.

MR. WOOD, THE CARPENTER. — JACK'S APPRENTICESHIP.
— MADAM WOOD. — JACK'S WELCOME.

IT is almost needless to observe that Mrs. Partington most religiously obeyed the gipsy's injunctions. Secretly digging up the buried napkin on the morning of the third day, in the manner directed, she had the inexpressible satisfaction of finding her lost ring duly preserved in the salt. " It is really astonishing," she exclaimed, " but I knew it would be so. What disinterested and praiseworthy creatures these gipsies must be, not to find every thing that is lost for themselves! Well, I shall never be at any trouble for any thing that is missing after this."

As for Jack, he had received so complete a lesson by the narrow escape from detection which he had experienced, that he thought it best to say as little as possible on the subject. He resolved to think no more about his former companion Master Blake, or of honest Levy Laurence, but to keep his fingers to himself. The gipsy's warning had made a deep impression

M

upon him, — perhaps the more so from the greater part being unintelligible to him. He was confirmed in his belief of her supernatural powers by a conversation with Mrs. Partington, some time afterwards, to which he artfully led, and in which that good lady, in answer to Jack's remarks on the credibility of the gipsy's skill, took occasion to observe, that the restoration of the ring was nothing ; that she had known many things much more remarkable ; particularly one, where some plate having been mislaid, by a gentlewoman of her acquaintance, a gipsy was called in, who, with nothing more than a pack of cards, found out that the whole of the plate had been sent away, by mistake, of course, along with some foul linen to the butler's own mother.   She also related another circumstance, where a second gentlewoman of her acquaintance, in order to obtain a prize in the lottery, had consulted a celebrated fortune-teller, who advised her, by way of charm, to bury a silver teapot, with a snail in it, in her garden for nine days, when she would find the lucky number, traced by the snail at the bottom of the pot ; but that forgetting one of the many ceremonies she was enjoined to observe during this transaction, when she came to dig up the pot, she only found a brickbat buried in its place : consequently, instead of getting the 20,000*l.*

prize, when she bought a ticket she only drew a blank. These instances made a deep impression on Jack's mind; and it is but justice to say, that for the two years afterwards — the period of time which he spent at Mr. Kneebone's house before he was apprenticed — his honesty was perfectly unimpeachable. But becoming now a well-grown boy, having reached the age of thirteen, and having learned as much in the way of reading, writing, and arithmetic, from Mr. Kneebone's tuition as it seemed probable he ever would learn, — for we have before remarked Jack's parts were not remarkably bright in these particulars, — the worthy woollen draper looked about to find some proper person, following the profitable trade of carpenter, with whom he could apprentice Jack, agreeably to his father's last request, and the boy's own express wish on the subject. He was not long before an eligible opportunity presented itself, in the person of a Mr. Owen Wood, a substantial carpenter, residing at the sign of "The Ark" in Wych Street, Drury Lane. Mr. Kneebone had formed an acquaintance with this individual in his occasional evening visits to a tavern in the neighbourhood of Clare Market, known by the name of the "Black Jack," from the ale being usually served up in large leathern measures called jacks, or rather, from their co-

M 2

lour, black jacks. Mr. Kneebone was accustomed to visit this house of an evening, to recreate himself after the labours of the day with the company of some of his brother tradesmen in the immediate neighbourhood, amongst whom was Mr. Wood. The house had also the additional recommendation of being frequented by Mr. Miller, the well known comedian, who at that time performed at the theatre royal, Drury Lane, and who was more distinguished by a certain taciturnity and dryness of manner, than by any remarkable brilliancy of wit, though a collection of jests was, after his death, printed under his name, for the benefit of his widow, which have since formed a foundling hospital for every stray witticism and fatherless joke that has been uttered for the last century: nevertheless, as his tombstone in the adjacent ground informs us, Mr. Miller was an honest man; to which we may add, he was a convivial one.

Mr. Owen Wood was by birth a Cambro-Briton, being a native of Caernarvon. He was an honest but somewhat irascible man, like most of the descendants of St. David. He was about the middle stature, strongly built, but not over bulky; his features had rather a frosty and furrowed appearance, wearing somewhat of an expression of fretful pettishness, not at all compromised by a very sober bob wig. He wore a waistcoat of grey stuff with large flaps; a stiff skirted coat of brown cloth, with brass buttons about the size of a crown piece; black velvet breeches, the knees of which were concealed by the grey ribbed hose which rolled over them, according to the fashion of the time, and very high shoes with enormous silver buckles.

It so happened that about this time an acquaintance and customer of Mr. Kneebone had commenced building a house at Hampstead, being a gentleman of independent fortune.—He had contracted for the brickwork and masonry, but had not settled with any one to execute the woodwork of the intended edifice. This Mr. Kneebone knew; and as he had great interest with the gentleman, it struck him as affording him a favourable opportunity for accomplishing his wishes as respected Jack; he therefore proposed at once to the honest Cambro-Briton to procure him the contract for the carpenters' work of the building, which could not fail to prove highly lucrative, on condition that he, Mr. Wood, should take Jack as his apprentice for the term of seven years, without requiring any other premium. This was gladly agreed to; and accordingly, very soon afterwards, on a day fixed, Mr. Kneebone and Mr. Wood took little Jack before the chamberlain at Guildhall, where the indentures were formally signed and sealed ; Mr. Kneebone contracting, on his part, that little Jack should not, during his apprenticeship, commit matrimony, or any other improper act ; while Mr. Wood, on the other hand, agreed to supply him for the said term with all proper and necessary food, lodging, and raiment, and, further, to induct him completely into the noble art and mystery of his own trade of a carpenter.

Apprenticeships were treated at that time as much more solemn, important, and binding engagements than they are now. After a suitable discourse from the chamberlain, embracing much conventional advice and admonition, the parties retired to partake of an entertainment provided by Mrs. Partington at Mr. Kneebone's house, previously to Jack's leaving it in the afternoon for his new quarters. The plum pudding, and other delicacies, somewhat reconciled Jack to entering upon his noviciate ; for his master had taken him without trial on the strength of the contract.

A copious supply of the strongest ale had been procured for the occasion from the " Black Jack," with which Mr. Wood indulged himself until a genial flush had completely thawed the usual frostiness of his puckered features ; and he descanted to Jack very largely on the dignity and utility of the master-craft to which he was about to be brought up, which he described as first having been brought to perfection by the patriarch Noah in the construction of the ark, the sign of his shop. He spoke of the handiworks of Hiram the builder; of the rare joinery and precious wood employed by Solomon to augment the magnificence of his temple, with much other edifying matter of a like nature. He then went on to descant on the virtues of the rule and compasses, the plane and line, and the difficulties that might be accomplished by the judicious use of the centre-bit, the chisel, the saw, together with the hammer and gimlet, and other implements of the trade. Jack knew already what might be done with some of these tools, perhaps even better than the worthy carpenter himself; for though he had scrupulously abstained for some time from all dishonest courses, yet when Mr. Kneebone had innocently exchanged the bible for the Old Bailey Calendar in Jack's reading lessons, from that moment unfortunately did that fatal calendar become Jack's only gospel.

After the honest Cambro-Briton had taken as much ale as he could conveniently carry, and was becoming, if the truth must be spoken, somewhat quarrelsome, Mr. Kneebone thought it advisable Jack should depart to his new home. A new prayer-book, bought for the occasion, in which his name was written, and a large plum cake, was given to him, with some tears and a

quantity of goodly advice, by the kind-hearted
Mrs. Partington, to which Mr. Kneebone added
a complete change of new wearing apparel, and
a handsomely bound copy of " The Carpenter's
Guide and Joiner's Assistant," with a bran span
new half-crown, with some hearty wishes that he
might turn out a good boy, mind what his master
said to him, and make a bright man.　A shake
of the hand from Mr. Kneebone, a few motherly
kisses from Mrs. Partington, and taking his little
bundles under his arm, Jack, conducted by Mr.
Wood, commenced his journey from his kind
protector's house, adjoining " The Angel," to his
master's shop in the adjacent Wych Street, — a
short journey, certainly, but how important a one
to Jack !

Arriving at the door of Mr. Wood's shop,
which was by this time shut up, a resolute
though rather staggering knock of its master
summoned to their admittance a dirty servant
girl.　Ascertaining from this handmaid that Mrs.
Wood was up stairs in the best room, the carpenter was about to conduct Jack thither to introduce him to his future mistress, when with a
prodigious rustle, and sweep of silk and brocade,
Mrs. Wood encountered them at the foot of the
stairs.　She was a lady of what is usually termed
"a certain age," which, by the by, is generally
the most uncertain age we know of.　A prodi-

gious high cap, embellished with a profusion of ribands, and having long lappets, was stuck upon a large mass of turned up hair thickly powdered; her stomacher, which was high and ample, was liberally ornamented with lace and jewellery; added to these were a stiffly starched muslin apron, a festooned hoop petticoat, and large flowered damask silk gown, with a negative species of train; — she had worked mittens on her hands, and an embroidered kerchief over her shoulders, pinned carefully down; a large mock pearl necklace was round her throat, two or three beauty spots of black Taffeta, or *mouches*, as they were called, diversified her face, which, from excitement or some other cause, very strongly, at that moment, resembled a full blown peony: a large fan, on which was represented the various scenes in Mr. Dryden's improvement on Shakspeare, " The Enchanted Island," hung suspended from her right wrist; a shagreen cased watch, about the diameter of a saucer, dangled from her girdle at the left side: high red-heeled shoes with paste buckles, completed the picture.

" A pretty hour this is to come home," she exclaimed, looking fiercely at Mr. Wood, and then casting a disdainful glance at Jack, " when you knew I wished to visit the Duke's Theatre. Every person of any consideration has been to

N

see Mr. Otway's new tragedy of 'Venice Preserved;' and how could I possibly go to Lincoln's Inn Field without having somebody to
walk by the side of my chair. You know, independently of other respects, there has been a
great many robberies in that quarter lately."

"Fery true, Mrs. Woot, my lofe," answered
the carpenter in a rather conciliatory tone;
"fery true; but what coult I do? You know I
was opliged to stay out; I had to pind the poy."

"And I suppose the chamberlain kept you
till this time," answered Mrs. Wood disdainfully,
"and that you have been entertained in the
Guildhall with spiced wines and other potations,
instead of swilling your ale at that filthy Black
Jack;—a likely matter indeed!—If I had
gone, such a thing might have happened. They
would have known how to have paid a proper
respect to one whose cousin has passed the
chair, and who has received the honour of knighthood from her Majesty's own gracious hands."

It must here be remarked that Mrs. Wood, or
Madam Wood as she was universally called by
the neighbours, on account of her lofty deport-
ment and high pretensions, was originally a small
city heiress, a distant relation of an eminent tallow chandler who had arrived at the dignity of
mayor, and having to carry up an address of
congratulation on one of Marlborough's victo-

ries to good Queen Anne, in St. James's palace, had received the honour of knighthood with Prince George's own sword. By one of those mistakes which the amiable angel we have before alluded to so often makes, the heiress had early in life been destined for Mr. Wood, then only a journeyman carpenter; though no one could discover the reasons for this match, except that there was no very great disparity of age between them, nor overpowering predominance of beauty on either side : — to be sure Mr. Wood traced his pedigree through the line of Cadwallader considerably beyond Caractacus, which assimilated in some measure with the gentility of Mrs. Wood's condition, and her relationship to the ex-mayor before alluded to, Sir Timothy Gutteridge. Then Mrs. Wood's money had helped to set Mr. Wood up in business on his own account. Thus far they seemed suited to each other, but in no other respect. Mr. Wood was choleric and Mrs. Wood was haughty; and that peculiar variety of married life, known by the name of " cat and dog," was the continual and perpetual consequence.

" I say, Sir," said Mrs. Wood after a short pause, in which the carpenter was either trying to keep his spirit down or to work himself up, it was not very clear or material which,—" I say, Sir," she exclaimed in a louder tone, " it is shameful that an heiress in her own right, as I was before I had the misfortune to marry you, one with the offers that I had — there was the bridgemaster's son and the city remembrancer's nephew — should be neglected in the manner I am. If my cousin Sir Timothy——"

Here the worthy Cambro-Briton could contain himself no longer — his anger burst out with full force. "Look you, Mrs. Woot, Got's poty! hur will hafe no more of this. What if you had a thousant pounts from your uncle, the tide-waiter, tidn't you marry a gentleman by pirth and plood? When you think of your city re-memprancers, look you, do not forget that. What though your cousin Sir Timothy, the tallow chantler, fas Lort Mayor when hur father the squires was married, look you, hur had no less than twelve cooks at her fedding, though that vag, Mr. Joseph Millers, said it was because every man toasted his own cheese; but it vas not: hur has not tallow in hur veins, Mrs. Woot; do not forget that, I pray you."

" Why you pitiful, ignorant, leek-eating fellow!" said Mrs. Wood, growing greatly enraged; "wouldn't you have been running bare-legged over the mountains, after your own ill-savoured goats, at this very time, if it hadn't been for me? Would you ever have tasted any thing beyond the luxury of the toasted cheese you speak of,

but for my money? I that demeaned myself, by
marrying such an uncultivated barbarian ; but I
am rightly served." Here she thought proper to
go into hysterics, which Mr. Wood seemed to
regard as a matter of course, though Jack was
very frightened.

"Let her alone, poy," said the choleric carpenter; "she vill gife ofer vhen she's tired. Get
to your garrets, look you; you vill find it ven you
hafe cot to the top of the house as far as you can
go. See that you are up early in the morning,
that hur may set you to work. You vill not vant
a light—there is the moons, look you. Your
mistress will hafe plenty of time to come to her
senses, while hur is taking her onion and salt in
the kitchens with the mait."

"I shall not wait for that, you wretch!" said
Mrs. Wood, suddenly recovering. "You'll eat
no onion if you mean to come near me, I can tell
you that. What are you standing staring for there,
boy?" turning to Jack, who was gazing at her,
with his eyes and mouth open to their utmost
extent. "I'll make *you* treat me with respect, at
all events, if other people don't. Take that, and
get to bed directly, sirrah! leave your pretty
master to sober himself as he can." Here, giving
Jack a hearty slap of the face by way of supper,
she flounced into her bed-room, the door of which
she immediately locked after her, resorting for

consolation to a flask of *rosa solis*, which she invariably kept filled for such occasions. "Tam her for a cantankerous tefel!" muttered Mr. Wood, as she departed; "but hur is glad she is gone. Get to ped, poy, get to ped. Here, Taffleen!" calling to the servant girl, "get hur onions and salt reaty, and go to the Plack Lion for a quart of ale, look you. Hur will be comfortable yet, py the plessings of Got, though she is one great pig primstone Jezepel; tat is the fact, and hur does not care if she knows it." With these words he staggered down stairs, and Jack crawled his way up, not over-elated at the prospect that had opened itself before him; but a slice of his plumcake, which he fortunately had with him, reconciled him to his bare garret, and the hard truckle bed he found in it, and he soon fell asleep to awake on the morrow to a new life.

CHAPTER THE SEVENTH.

JACK'S APPRENTICESHIP, CONTINUED.

MR. WOOD'S FAMILY.—THE WRITING ON THE BEAM.—
MEETING AN OLD ACQUAINTANCE.—THE BLACK LION.

NEW servants rise early: Jack was up betimes to commence his apprenticeship. He found Mr. Wood somewhat clouded from the events of the previous day. Madam Wood did not show herself till the afternoon. Mr. Wood soon set him to work, and was both surprised and pleased with the quickness and aptitude he evinced.

The carpenter had no family of his own, which was to be lamented, as the want of those conjugal peace-makers, children, rather augmented that tendency to cat-and-dogism so evident in him and his sleeping partner. His household consisted of Taffleen, a Welsh orphan girl, who officiated in the character of servant of all work, and Griffith Thomas, also a native of the Principality, the fellow apprentice to Jack. Taffleen was a slatternly, fiery, but not ill-tempered wench: the misfortune of having a fine mistress greatly contributed to her being so untidy a maid. Griffith Thomas, or Thomas, as he was always called,—for Griffith is an awkward word in any

but a Welsh mouth—was a wooden-headed youth
well suited for the performance of the practical
part of the trade to which he was bound : he did
what he was put to with a staid punctuality that
rendered him very dependable. Had steam
machines been in fashion in those days, and the
carpenter had had one in human shape to perform
certain duties, it would have been much of the
same value. Thomas could do nothing without
being duly fed, no more than a steam engine
can; and a certain portion of received morality,
that had been early implanted in him, served as
a sort of safety valve to prevent mischievous ex-
plosions. Jack was very different; there was no
regulating him: he worked by impulse, very frequently with six-boy power, though often, when
the steam was not up, he would not work at all,
—he either wanted no telling, or telling ten
times over. Yet he suited very well with Thomas,
supplying mind to his body and skill to his labour; and Mr. Wood was well pleased. If there
was a fault to be found with Jack's new situation,
it was that he had rather too much his own way.
Madam Wood was too fine a lady to trouble
herself with her husband's apprentices, and poor
Mr. Wood was too glad to get out of the sound
of his wife's alarum, to remain longer at home at
any time than was absolutely necessary. The
worthy Cambro-Briton was very much addicted

to the practice of pennillion singing*, according
to the custom of his country, and in which, by
the by, he was very skilful ; this he pursued
with the greater gusto, as it gave him frequent
opportunities of indulging in invectives against
the sex, those pleasant compositions being by no
means sparing in their sarcasms at married life,
and the frailties of the weaker vessel.

It was Mr. Wood's wont to resort, two or three
times a week, to the different houses in the metropolis where his countrymen congregated, to
pursue, with the assistance of a native harper, this
national pastime. Though Madam and Mr. Wood

---

* Pennillion singing is a convivial custom of some anti-
quity practised by the Welsh, which, after having long fallen
into disuse, is now again being brought into fashion. It con-
sists of a party meeting together, attended by a harper, when
Pennills — a name given to a variety of stanzas on different
subjects in the ancient Welsh tongue, handed down by oral record from father to son—are sung, either attached or detached, and of different lengths of metre, to any tune the harper
may happen to play ; for it is irregular, and, in fact, not
allowable for any particular one to be chosen. One person
commences, after two or three bars have been played, with as
many pennills as will fill out the melody ; adapting them to the
air as he goes on, he is joined, as he proceeds, by as many others
as choose, which has a very social and inspiring effect, as the
company can sing or not as they please. The pennills are
mostly in praise of the harp, Wales, the Welsh tongue, and
other national subjects. Among other societies existing
now in London, that of the " UNDEB CYMRY," or United
Welshmen, is the most prominent.

regularly attended church every Sunday, —
Madam Wood for the real purpose of showing off
the fashions of St. James's in her own person, to
the envying gaze of the congregation, and Mr.
Wood for the no less praiseworthy motive of
gaining the character of a worshipful tradesman
with the parishioners and his neighbours, — they
cared little how the Lord's day was passed by
their household. The domestic drudge employed
the day in the exercise of the dishclout, and .
other equally commendable services : Thomas,
on the contrary, sought the organ-loft at St. Clement Danes, where he carefully noted down
the text, and slept during the whole of its com-
mentary. Jack, under pretext of visiting Mr.
Kneebone, listlessly lounged away the day in
rambling about the metropolis, joining whatever
idle boys he met, and indulging in all sorts of
desultory ways of passing the time, never omit-
ting, however, to give worthy Mrs. Partington a
call some time before he went home at night, for
the double purpose of keeping up appearances,
and getting the lumps of pudding and other tit
bits she had stored up for him during the week,
— he relishing these much more than the good
advice with which they were accompanied.

Bitterly did Jack regret, in after life, this two
great laxity. " I am far from presuming to say,"
he observed in his last sad confession, when

speaking of his apprenticeship to Mr. Wood, " that I was one of the best of servants; but I believe, if less liberty had been allowed me then, I should scarce have had so much sorrow and confinement after."* In truth, this unrestrained liberty paved the way for a host of future evils: he acquired habits he could not shake off, and made acquaintances he could not forget.

When the contract for the carpenter's work of the house at Hampstead, which had led to his apprenticeship, was required to be executed, the proficiency Jack had then made, though the period of time had been so short, rendered him of the greatest service to his master: the panneling, flooring, doors, windows, &c.—all engaged his especial attention, and were much indebted for their completeness to his adroitness and handiwork. His skill was rewarded by his master even more liberally than was prudent. It is as bad for a boy to have too much money as it is to have too little: excess is encouraged by the one, while temptation gains force by the other.

Thus two or three years passed away. Jack became an able but self-willed workman. No serious quarrel, however, had as yet arisen between him and his master, who, though naturally choleric and testy, had, to say the truth, suf-

* Vide Confession, Appendix.

ficient to employ him in the way of dispute with Madam Wood, to allow of his being over anxious for any contest with other people.   With Madam Wood herself the case was somewhat different. Jack could never bring himself to pay her the homage she required; execrating her in his heart as a fantastical and affected old duchess, he took a delight in slighting her injunctions.   To take madam down a peg, as he called it, was the height of gratification to him; and in this, as candid historians, we are bound to confess he was often secretly encouraged by Mr. Wood himself.   But the period was approaching when this good understanding between master and man — for such Jack now thought himself — was to be materially disturbed.

One day, having taken a holiday on his own account, which was not unusual to him when business happened to be rather slack, Jack paid a visit to the Tower of London for the purpose of seeing the curiosities there.   He was first shown the lions, after the customary joke had been passed on him of being asked if he would not rather stay and see them washed.   The presence of these noble animals did not excite such admiration in him as might have been expected, — in fact he rather expressed a contempt for them, that, with their strength and powers of offence, they should suffer themselves to remain in such insignificant cages as those within which they were shut up. Passing over the horse and foot armoury, he then visited the Jewel Office. The sight of the Regalia perfectly made his mouth water ; and he listened with breathless attention to the warden's account of Colonel Blood's daring attempt to steal the crown, &c. during the reign of Charles II., lamenting the unexpected arrival of the then keeper's nephew from sea, which had had the effect of detecting and frustrating the plot. His last step was to visit the different dungeons and apartments, &c. kept for the reception of state prisoners, all of which he examined very minutely. In the room which had so long served as the prison of the illustrious Sir Walter Raleigh, he was shown the name of that celebrated man scratched by himself on one of the walls. He surveyed it with deep interest : a noble ambition seemed to inspire him.

" I will do something," he mentally resolved, " to make my name memorable. Yes ! I won't be a common man — I won't die and be forgotten: people shall think of me after I am dead ; and I 'll carve my name, the first thing when I go home, on one of the beams in old Wood's shop, that the world may hereafter have a record, under his own hand, to gaze at of Jack Sheppard." Filled with this heroic determination he immediately returned to Wych Street, and, the coast being clear, entered the workshop, where, with a large clasp knife he proceeded to cut his name in very legible characters on one of the principal beams, as may be seen to this day, the autograph being much more durable than elegant. He was interrupted in this choice employment by the entrance of Mr. Wood.

" God's poty!" exclaimed the Cambrian, " what toings is here ? 'T is your pusiness, look you, to repair the woot works of puildings, and not testroy them. What the tefil are you writing your name up there for ? "

" Nobody has a better right," answered Jack rather surlily, " for nobody does so much business here as I do."

" Pusiness, pusiness! you hafe no pusiness to do tat, you idle tog!" said Mr. Wood, getting greatly incensed.

" Well, I have done it, at all events," said Jack; "and as I don't see what particular harm there is in it, I should like to see who will dare to deface it. My name is as good as any body else's."

" What is tat you say ? " exclaimed the angry Welshman. " Do you presume to say tat your name is as goot as mine, sirrah! dat has tescentet through fifty generations, look you, from the Ap Shenkinses to the Ap Watkinses, and from the Ap Watkinses to the Griffithes, the Davises, the Williamses, the Thomases, the Philipses, the Lloyds, the Llewellyns, the Wynnes, and the Woots, look you? Passion of our pody! what intignities is this! Put I will get you sent to Pridewell, to teach you petter manners, sirrah! The champerlain shall learn you how to pehave to your master, Owen Woot. Do you forget that Matam Woot is cousin to Sir Timothy Cutteridge, dat was Lort Mayor, and kissed the Queen's own hant?"

"If I do," muttered Jack, "there's no fear that you'll forget it; you have it dinned into your ears too often for that."

"Passion of hur heart!" spluttered Mr. Wood, almost choking with rage, "what to you mean by tat, you young villain? Hur will teach you dat hur has no occasion to look to Madam Woot's for hur respectability, tat hur own father was a squire, tat hur own grantfather hat a harper, and tat hur own self in hur own country is a shentlemans porn, and hur will not hafe hur work neglected and hur timper wastet. Hur toes not feet and clothe you to testroy hur property: the Typurn peam will preserve your name petter than any peam here, and so I tells you, — you will tie like a tog."

"So long as I am not forgotten like a dog," said Jack sturdily, "I should not much care for that; but there's no occasion to make such a fuss about your paltry rafter. A day may come when you may be proud to have my name there, when it may be more famous than all your pedigree put together — with old St. David at the head of them."

Mr. Wood could contain no longer; this depreciation of his patron saint and his illustrious ancestors was not to be borne with. Seizing Jack by the leg, and getting his heel in his mouth to the dislodgment of a couple of his teeth, he pulled him from off the bench on which he was standing, for the better execution of his autograph, he began to cuff him about his head and ears with all his might and main — uttering at the same time a profusion of maledictions in Welsh.

Jack did not venture to fight again, though his wrath had risen to a height very nearly equal to his master's: he, however, extricated himself as swiftly as he could, and made his escape into the street.

The offended Welshman, who had beat himself with his own passion, was glad to sit down and attempt the recovery of his lost breath. "Plessings on hur forpearance!" he muttered; " it is Got's mercies that hur has not killed the villain. Compare himself with St. Tavit, and hur ancestor Catwallader!—it was not to be entured! Hur is only glat hur has not quite peat his

prains out. Hur must get some salt and try to
fasten hur two teeth in again, or what will become of hur penillion singing? Here, Taffleen,
Taffleen! pring the salt-pox. Hur is glat no one
fos here to see hur.—Mercy of Got! if hur has
not swallowed one of hur own teeth! Hur is
ruined! Here, Taffleen, Taffleen!"

The poor carpenter ran into the kitchen to
concert measures for the recovery of his lost
tooth, where we will for the present leave him,
and proceed to Jack, who was making his way
down Wych Street in no very enviable mood
of mind, smarting under the blows he had received, and burning with indignation at the injustice of them. He was going blindly along, too
much occupied with his own thoughts to regard
any thing else, when, passing the door of the
" Black Lion" alehouse, which we have before
mentioned, and which had the reputation of
being a low species of flash ken, or a receptacle
for loose characters, he ran violently against a person who was at that moment rather hastily issuing from it,—a concussion which had the effect
of sending one party sprawling into the kennel,
and the other against the bar window, where
his elbow perforated a pane of glass, and materially damaged a china punch-bowl which was
placed there as a token that good punch was

made within.   Getting up somewhat alarmed for
the consequences, but resolved to brazen them
out, and turning to his opponent, Jack was
greatly astonished at recognising his old schoolfellow, Master Joseph Blake, or Blueskin, as we
shall henceforth call him, now presenting the
appearance of a sturdy young man.

"What, Jack—Jonny Sheppard!" roared
out that exemplary person. "Well, strike me
lucky! but this is a go. Who'd have thought of
meeting you in this manner? Is this the way
you welcome your old acquaintances—knocking them down and making them mill the
glaze?"

Here the landlord, whose attention had been
attracted by the fracture of the pane, suddenly
joined them.   "Halloa! my covies! said he;
"what's this? you are not going to frisk the crib
on the run, are you?"

"All right, Master Hind," said Blueskin, tip-
ping him the wink,—"merely an accidental
smash; I'll shell out the pewter."

"There's the best punch-bowl chipped, Master Blueskin," said Hind.

"Get it filled with a quart of the reg'lar: I'll
make it all right."

"Oh! what, you're breeched," returned the
landlord.

"Yes, in Tip Street, thanks to a bunch of

onions* I grabbed last night, which Mr. Wild has been so kind as to say he'll get made into a brown stew, and has advanced a quid on."

"Oh, that's another thing," returned Mr. Hind, beginning to sing part of an old song.

" Punch cures the gout, the cholic, and the phthisic,
 And is for all men the very best of physic."

" I'll get you your rum slim † ready directly, gentlemen."

"Do, and let it be stiffish, — do you hear?" returned Blueskin. "This kinchin's an old pal."

" A young one, I should rather think," muttered Mr. Hind in a low tone. " Why, blow me, if it is n't one of old Wood the carpenter's lads, down the street! Well, this is a turn up. You shall have your suck before you know where you are." So saying Mr. Hind retired into the bar to prepare the punch as ordered, while Blueskin conveyed our wondering hero into a snug little back parlour, which happened at that time to have no one in it. Sitting down, Jack was about to ask half a hundred questions, when he was stopped by his companion.

Wait till we get the booze†, Jack, and then

---

* Watch, chain, and seals.
† Punch.   ‡ Drink.

I will tell you all about it." The liquor was not long before it made its appearance, Mr. Hind bringing it in, humming part of Iago's song to Cassio:—

> " Let us the cannikin clink, brave boys,
>   And let us the cannikin clink."

It must be observed that Mr. Hind was a universal vocalist, and accompanied every thing he did with a snatch of some appropriate ditty, always singing most intently when any mischief was going on. Filling himself a glass, in order to ascertain whether it was brewed *secundem artem*, and drinking to our hero's better acquaintance, Mr. Hind tossed it off, and, declaring it imperial, left the room humming part of the old catch,—

> " Nose, nose, and who gave thee that jolly red nose ?
>   Nutmeg, and ginger, and cinnamon, and cloves ;
>   And they gave me this jolly red nose."

The moment his back was turned, the two young gentlemen, after ascertaining that he had spoken the truth, by each draining a brimming glass of the generous fluid to the bottom, proceeded to relate their various adventures since they last parted. Mr. Blueskin intimated, that finding he had no genius for the trade to which his father had destined him, he had one night suddenly left that revered person, and had set up in business on his own account, having become acquainted with Mr. Jonathan Wild, by whose advice, and under whose patronage, he had chosen a very light and lucrative profession. He did not exactly mention the precise nature of his employment, but Jack was at no loss to understand it. Jack, in his turn, recounted the circumstances of his adoption by Mr. Kneebone, together with his apprenticeship to Mr. Wood, finishing by detailing the particulars of the affray that had that day occurred between them.

Mr. Blueskin pathetically damned Mr. Wood for an old hunks; and grasping Jack's hand with great fervour and sincerity, swore by the living jingo, that it should go hard if they did n't, before long, make the old Welshman skip like one of his own goats, and smoke him as they would a piece of toasted cheese. This declaration, which was pledged bumper deep, afforded Jack great satisfaction.

As they penetrated deeper into the contents of the bowl, the two friends became more confidential. Jack hinted at his knowledge of that transaction in the Old Bailey Calendar, in which his schoolfellow's name had appeared conjointly with Master William Blewitt's, and made many inquiries respecting Mr. Wild.

" He's the primest trump in town," exclaimed

Blueskin with enthusiasm, "and will glory in doing a good turn for a lad of spirit like you."

"Jack said he should be happy to make his acquaintance."

"You shall," said Blueskin energetically; "I'll introduce you myself." The bowl was drained on this assurance; and Blueskin having settled the reckoning, and paid the damage which had caused their meeting, which Mr. Hind received, humming the appropriate song of —

"Sing tantarantara rogues all, rogues all,"

the *nobile fratrum* departed, — Mr. Blueskin to attend a little appointment he had in the dusk on the pavement in Fleet Street, and Jack, punch valiant, to encounter his master, Mr. Wood. The worthy Cambrian had, however, fortunately gone to join in a penillion meeting at the "Goat in Boots," in Little Britain. Our hero, therefore, retired to his truckle bed without any farther quarrel, and passed the night in dreaming of the promised meeting with Mr. Wild.

CHAPTER THE EIGHTH.

JACK'S APPRENTICESHIP, CONTINUED.

SAINT DAVID'S DAY IN 1715.— WELSH PENNILLS.—JACK
SHEPPARD'S FIRST MEETING WITH JONATHAN WILD.

WHEN Jack and his master met the next morning, their meeting, as may be imagined, was any
thing but a cordial one. Mr. Wood was alternately
short, sharp, sullen, and silent; though he had
swallowed his own tooth, he could not swallow
the affront that had been put upon his ancestors,
and his patron saint, St. David, by Jack's hinting at the probability of his name one day eclips-
ing theirs. Jack was, on the other hand, dogged,
morose, and gloomy, brooding over the blows he
had received, and, in fancy, planning, with the
assistance of his former schoolfellow, Blueskin, a
variety of schemes to revenge his wrongs. Mr.
Wood, at times, gave vent to his feelings in
sundry muttered sentences; but, as they all happened to be in the Welsh tongue, Jack did not
think it necessary to notice them. Before he
had left Blueskin on the previous evening, he had
made an appointment with that exemplary young
man to meet him at the "Black Lion" on the
evening of the following Thursday, for the pur-

pose of being introduced, as promised, to Mr. Wild, when Jack determined not to stick upon niceties any longer. Since the affair of Mrs. Partington's ring, he had religiously obeyed the laws of *meum* and *tuum*; but now that it was to avenge his own wrongs, the observance of the strict bounds of honesty appeared a very different thing; and he determined that the carpenter should literally pay for the injuries which, as he conceived, that Cambro-Briton had inflicted upon him.

It happened that the Thursday appointed for the interview with Mr. Wild was St. David's Day, a day, which the reader need scarcely be told, is a very memorable one with all true Welshmen: then do leeks become flowers, while toasted cheese is provided as a bait in various " mousetraps of a larger growth." Every honest Cambrian skips and rejoices, like one of his own native goats; the glories of the Principality are sung and said by a thousand tongues; the heroic actions of that church militant, St. David, are recounted; pedigrees are traced, and draughts of the lusty *cwrw* go round to the inspiring sounds of the harp, and the cheering sentiments of the national *Pennill*.

It was the custom of Madam Wood, who took no interest in the patriotic enthusiasm of her lord and master, on this auspicious day, to withdraw herself to the house of some friend, that she might neither sanction nor thwart by her presence the enjoyments in which her husband might think fit to indulge; she had accordingly set out very early in the morning to the country house of her great relation, Sir Timothy Gutteridge, the ex-mayor, at Hogsden, from whence she did not propose to return till very late.

It is not to be supposed that so staunch an ancient Briton as Mr. Wood would suffer any work to be done in his house on so memorable a day as St. David's. It was his custom to make it a holiday with his whole household: he did not depart from this custom on the present occasion, but gave Jack and his fellow apprentice, Griffith Thomas, full liberty to do what they pleased with themselves, but enjoined them very particularly to return in the afternoon, as their presence would be required on an occasion that could not be neglected. As he was always wont to make them some little present on this day, they naturally enough supposed, from his significant winks, and smirking nods, that something very agreeable was forthcoming.

Jack, having his appointment in the evening to attend to, did not stroll very far from home, and was in waiting on the carpenter very shortly after the usual dinner hour. He was somewhat surprised to find his master sitting over a spacious bowl, dressed in his best clothes, with a huge leek stuck, by way of nosegay, in his bosom; an immense two-handed sword, nearly as long as a spit, which had been formerly the property of one of his ancestors, was buckled, with a broad leathern strap round his waist, to the imminent danger of tripping him up whenever he attempted to move; a large sandy-coloured tie perriwig ornamented his sconce, in lieu of the usual bob, on the top of which, though he was in the house, was stuck a very fierce three-cornered cocked hat, bearing, by way of cockade, another large leek; a few sprigs of olive, which accompanied this latter, somewhat neutralised by their peaceful character the alarm this military display might otherwise have created. The good-natured Welshman (for, like all hasty people, he was at the core really good-natured), had provided from mine host of the "Black Jack," several quarts of his strongest ale, which he had spiced with his own hand. Taffleen had prepared a proportionate quantity of toast: pippins and cheese were not wanting; and for the first time since their quarrel, Jack was received by his master, on his entrance, with a welcoming smile. Several circumstances had conspired to put the worthy Cambrian into a more than usual good humour. On this particular First of March, anno Domini 1715, it being the birthday of the then Princess of Wales, Wilhelmina Carolina, as well as the anniversary of the Cambrian tutelar saint, the Honourable and Loyal Society of Ancient Britons had been instituted, at once in compliment to the Princess and in celebration of the saint.

A dinner had been given at Haberdashers' Hall, at which an ode, written by Hughes, the poet, and set to music by the celebrated Dr. Pepusch, was sung by Madame Margaretta and Madame Barbier. The well-known Tom Durfey, the dramatist and song writer, had also volunteered, and given one of his comical chants. This alone was cause sufficient for excitement; but there was added to it the exhilaration induced by the various tastings the worthy carpenter had had occasion to make of the ale while in the process of preparing it, and, lastly, though not least, there was the absence of Madam Wood!

" Come in, Jack, you tog," said he, as his eye fell on our hero, "and take a seat. This is Saint Davit's tay, a glorious Saint Davit's tay! ant py the plessings of Got, we must forget all crievances; though you fos wrong, fery wrong, look you, to tisparage St. Davit and hur ancestors. St. Davit fos a great saint, — he could fight as well as he could pray, and he suptued the heathen as well with his sword as his pible :

you must drink a cup of ale in honour of St. Davit!" To this ceremony Jack was nothing loath, and a bumper was speedily drained.

"Wales is a great country, look you," continued the carpenter with true national enthusiasm — "a fery great country! there is not hur equal! and hur county, Gaernarfon, is the paradise of Wales! You must drink success to Wales, and hur native place, Gaernarfon, Jack." Handing Jack another glass of ale, the carpenter began to sing the well-known pennill in praise of Caernarvon, beginning with, "*Wyf ofalus (a phaham) o hiraeth am Gaernarfon.*" To the tune of "*Anhawdd Ymadael,*" or "Loath to part;" a rude translation of which, for the further delectation of our readers, we shall here attempt: —

THE PRAISE OF CAERNARVON.

1.

" My heart is sad when to my mind
    Spring thoughts of sweet Caernarvon! —
    What woe was Adam's, forced through Eve,
    His native Paradise to leave —
    Such woe is mine, to leave behind
    My paradise, Caernarvon!

2.

" Oh ! still in smiles, ye gentle skies,
  Look down on sweet Caernarvon ;
  Its pleasant vales, the rose of health,
  Yields each maid's cheek her dearest wealth ;
  Then still shall wake my fondest sighs
  For Wales and for Caernarvon !"

They were here joined by Griffith Thomas, who was forced by the carpenter to do honour to the two toasts which had been drank in his absence.   As the ale circulated, so did the *amor patria* of Mr. Wood grow stronger.   " Jack, Jack, you tog ! " he burst forth, " you fos wrong, fery wrong, to say any thing against hur ancestors or hur country.   Caractacus fos a fine prince, so fos Cadwallater, ant Matoc, and Llewelen, and so is the Lort Pishop of Pangor, look you ! hur language is a fine language,—it fos the one spoken by Atem ant Eve pefore their fall in the Garten of Eten, and fos the only one safed from the confusion of tongues in the tower of Papel, it is like puttermilk in the mouth, all eloquence and honey.   Oh ! it is a nople tongues, the Welsh!" — Here he sung to the air of " *Yr Eos lais*," or "The Nightingale's Voice," the well known pennill, in praise of the Welsh language, commencing, " *Iaith wiw lan i'r gan hib goll*," and which may be thus paraphrased : —

THE PRAISE OF THE WELSH TONGUE.

1.

" As sweet as sugar in the mouth,
Mild as the breezes of the south,
Soft as the cooings of the dove,
Steals on the ear the speech I love ;
The angel-tongue, to song most dear,
Which warrior, sage, delight to hear :
The speech that best the heart can move,
The words of Wales, the speech of love.

2.

" He only sings, in Welsh who sings,
For Welsh alone the harp has strings ;
No bard is he who cannot write
In Welsh—the muses' best delight.
He has no learning who's unskill'd
In Welsh, with all of wisdom filled.
Still shall its praise by men be sung,
My native Welsh, my mother tongue.

3.

" Its accents, like some pleasant tune,
Or ripplings of a brook in June,
Dear to the throat, as mead or wine, —
Well for its love may echo pine ;
While there is water in the sea,
Or air in heaven, beloved shall be
Thy language, Wales, which still shall last,
'Till earth has into chaos passed."

The softness, sweetness, copiousness, and energy of the Welsh language celebrated in this last pennill, or rather pennills — for it was composed of a series of three — might have been more credited if delivered in any other language; as it was, the loss of Mr. Wood's two teeth might have been very well ascribed to the force of the crack-jaw words with which the panegyric was pronounced. Warming with the subject, though he still could not help reverting to what had passed, —

" Jack, Jack, you tog!" he continued, replenishing the glasses, "you should not have said any thing in tisparagement of the ancient Pritons, look you; they are the original people of the earth, ant can trace their ancestors further pack than any other nations! I myself am tescended from a collataral pranch of Uther Pentragon! put let that rest — it is nothings; I have seen much higher tescents tan tat, though I do not go so far as my joking friend Mr. Joseph Millers, at the " Black Jack," who says he saw a petigree of a Welsh gentleman, in the middle of which was written, " Apout this time the world was created." I do not go so far as to say that, put the Welsh are an original people; and py the plessing of Got, and the great teed of this tay, we shall flourish. You hafe peen wrong, Jack, fery wrong! you shoult hafe learnt wistom from the goat, look you.   To you not see, when two goats meet on a narrow pridge, and neither can pass without pushing the other into the water, that one goat will lie town, and let the other goat walk over him : so it shoult pe with you. You shoult supmit,— yes, we shoult all be goats. Ah! the goat is a wise animal; look at his peard!"

"And his horns," said Jack, the sullen resentment he had preserved since their quarrel gradually giving way before the good humour of his master. "But come, Sir," he continued, rather maliciously, "with your permission I will give a toast : here's the health of our mistress, Madam Wood."

Mr. Wood made a wry face, and drank it in Welsh, Jack shrewdly suspected with some variation ; we shall not presume to conjecture what, but it appeared to want some washing down, as he drained two or three copious draughts after it, and rather inarticulately hiccupped out another pennill, the not very gallant one, "*Tri pheth ni saif yn llonydd,*" "The Husband's Experience," which he sung to the tune of "*Ar hyd y Nos,*" or "All night long," and which may be thus rendered :—

THE HUSBAND'S EXPERIENCE.

" Three things that ne'er stand still I sing:
A pig whose hind leg's in a string,

A snail that crawls the walls along,
And Mrs. Wood's confounded tongue.
Three things there are, most puzzling to man,
The wind, the weather, and a woman :
The wind 's uncertain, so the weather,
And Mrs. W. more than either."

Having apparently relieved himself by this last ebullition of feeling, Mr. Wood took from his pocket two new silver crown-pieces, and gave one to each of his apprentices, requesting they might be kept in commemoration of the day, " which, though you have kicked out two of my teeth, Got help me, Jack," he said, " does great credit to the ancient Pritons, whom you would have tisparaged, look you. We have this tay founded an institution py which many a poor lat shall be snatche thenceforth like a fireprant from the flame, and be rentered an honoraple memper of society, taking them from the paths of temptation, and teaching them virtue and sopriety, — a great thing, look you, for a Welshman to hafe tone — follow hur example, poys." Here, seizing the bowl, he did not stop till he had completely drained it of its contents, which had such an effect upon him, that, after attempting to sing another pennill in praise of the maids of Merioneth, to the tune of " *Megen a Gollodd ci gardas,*" or " Peggy that lost her Garter," the lads thought it prudent to carry him to bed,

R

which they did, he singing very good humouredly
all the way as they were proceeding with him up
stairs, the fine old melody, " Of a noble Race
was Shenkin," leaving them in undisturbed possession of an immense pipkin of leek porridge,
which had been made for his supper.

The hour for Jack's meeting with Blueskin
had arrived; but so much had his master's good
nature, kindness, and the few exhortations arising
out of the events of the day affected him, that he
half repented his appointment, and more than
once resolved to break it.   But on what trifling
things hinge the fates of mortals!   The thought
that Blueskin had paid for him at the previous
meeting, and that he should appear shabby, if he
did not return it on this occasion, overcame all
his virtuous resolutions, and, shutting up the
shop, he slipped out of the back door, through
the yard, and was in a few moments at the
" Black Lion."

Mr. Blueskin was punctual to his appointment, and welcomed Jack with apparent delight, cordially shaking him by the hand, and
assuring him he was a trump and a half, good
weight, and a pen'north over. " The governor,"
said he, with a significant look, " is here; all's
right; he's only settling a small account of dues
and regulars for some odd fogles and fawnies,
with Okey, Simon Jacobs, Levi, and a few

other coves of the right sort, in the *sanctum*, behind the bar; the moment he's done with them I'll introduce you. His usher of the big stick, Mr. Quilt Arnold, Esquire, has been in attendance these two hours, so come along, and I'll get the governor to enter your name on his book, and take you under his own especial thumb, in no time. I have got a rare bowl of Hucklemybuff ready for us in the parlour."

Jack had half made up his mind to back out of the association, but there was no withdrawing after this. He did venture to stammer out he was afraid he had not money enough to pay for his entrance.

" Why, you precious soft," said Mr. Blue-skin, " there's nothing to tip; the governor will tip you; he always stands Sam at first: he'll give you a retaining fee, by way of earnest, and then you will consider yourself bound to him. Lord bless you, we do business on the most liberalest terms here." The conversation was here interrupted by the arrival of Mr. Wild's first satellite, the aforesaid Mr. Quilt Arnold, Esquire, as he was usually called by Wild's men, for such was the name by which the gang who flourished under Jonathan's protection styled themselves. Jack was duly introduced to this worthy, and received from him the encouraging assurance that he had no doubt he would do in time.

"Do! to be sure he will," said Blueskin; "he's just the one to do. Look at him; why he could worm himself through a mouse hole. Then there's a hand! why, it seems made for a pocket! If he minds what he's at, he'll make as pretty a pad, and kiddy a diver, as any on town. But come, where's the cove of the ken? here, landlord! Joe Hind, why don't you show three gentlemen in, Mister?

"Beg your pardon, my noble," said Joe, suddenly appearing. "This way;" and he began humming the, at that time, popular air of

"Come unto these yellow sands,"—

whether in allusion to the newly sanded floor of the back parlour we cannot say; but to that apartment he ushered them. Here they found a foaming bowl of Hucklemybuff, ready prepared, consisting of beer, brandy, sugar, eggs, spice, &c. which Jack insisted upon paying for. After a little demur on the part of Blueskin, his wish was acceded to. Mr. Joe Hind was desired to name the figure. "I am not mercenary," said he, singing the gallant Lovelace's song of

"My mind to me a kingdom is;"

"so you may give me a crown." Mr. Wood's

present, in commemoration of the day, was instantly put into his hand, and was as instantly conveyed into his pocket.

Filling a large bumper of the Hucklemybuff, and inviting his companions to follow his example, Mr. Quilt Arnold, Esquire, now pronounced a high eulogium on the liberality, power, and other good qualities of Mr. Jonathan Wild, and concluded by proposing his health, which was drank with enthusiasm. A door in the passage opening at this moment attracted the attention of Joe Hind.

"Hark! hark! the watch dog's bark,"

sung that gentleman, "the culls are mizzling, and the governor's coming. — You're a lucky kinchin, young fellow," continued he, addressing Jack, "to be taken by the hand by Mr. Wild so early; there's no knowing to what height he may raise you."

Mr. Hind's reflections were cut short by the entrance of a red-headed, blear-eyed, dirty-bearded Jew, in a loose shambling dress, another of Mr. Wild's satellites, who came to announce his master. Abraham, or Abraham Mendez — for that was the Jew's name — dropped on one side, and the great man entered. Jack and the others rose to receive him. He was a grave-looking man, dressed in a rather sober suit, but under

the assumed frankness and general benevolence
of his appearance, an acute observer could not
have failed to remark a determination and cunning that sufficiently explained his character. He
wore a small cocked hat, and had a rather genteel
sword by his side : a few ornaments of jewellery
adorned his person, more intended to indicate
his responsibility and rank in society than for
any purpose of embellishment.

"This is the kinchin cove I spoke to you
about, governor," said Blueskin, pointing to
Jack ; "you'll find him the thing, depend on't."
Mr. Hind began humming Carew's song —

> " Ask me why I send you here,
>   This firstling of the infant year."

"Peace, landlord!" said Mr. Wild, benevo-
lently. "Be seated, friends ; I am glad to meet
you, young gentleman ; your schoolfellow has
spoken favourably of you : you are inexperienced,
it appears, and require a guide — I love youth,
and would be a parent to you ——"

> " Full fathom five, thy father lies,"

sung Mr. Hind. "Peace, landlord!" cried Mr.
Wild, rather angrily ; "go, and replenish this
bowl."

> " I'm gone, sir, but anon, sir,
>   I'll be with you in a trice,"

hummed Mr. Hind, vanishing. Jonathan resumed his observations. " You will remain
here, Abraham, and you, too, Quilt," he remarked, " in order to do honour to the inaugu-
ration of our young friend."

" I shall do dat, governor," said the Jew, who
generally went by the name of the patriarch,
" and so will Mr. Quilt Arnold, Esquire, here."
How this latter gentleman had acquired this
form of address, we don't know, except that it
might be from his always wearing an immense
cocked hat, very like a footman's, with broad
lace, and his being dressed in a large faded silk
coat, with huge cuffs, and vast skirts, trimmed
with a quantity of tarnished gold binding, an
embroidered silk waistcoat, with extensive flaps,
which was very much soiled and worn, a singular
profusion of dirty neckcloth, a very swaggering
sword, and a quantity of mock jewellery, — the
whole presenting a very tawdry appearance.

" Youths," said Mr. Wild, impressively, " are
too apt to commit themselves, and get into
trouble ; youth is the season of inexperience, and
subject to a thousand temptations, and, more
than any other, particularly requires the protection of some one whose age and observation may
render him capable of shielding it from the consequences of those little ebullitions and extravagances natural to that buoyant age. For my

part," continued Mr. Wild, " I'm not for checking those playful eccentricities which lead the
juvenile mind to scorn the severer restraints of
society, and neglect the vulgar observance of
those limits which a musty prudence and twad-
dling morality may have prescribed for the guid-
ance of the uninformed."

" Jist my sentiments," roared out one of the
satellites, the aforesaid Mr. Quilt Arnold, Esquire.
" Good, damned good!" emphatically observed
Blueskin ; " the governor speaks like an angel!"

" I love youth, promising youth," continued
Jonathan, "and willingly extend to them my
protection and advice. I regard them as my
children, and expect from them, in return, the
obedience and reverence due to a father. A
monarchy must naturally be despotic; and having constituted myself king of the whole fraternity, from the lully prigger to the high spice toby
gloak, I expect implicit obedience from my subjects."

" Exactly my sentiments!" ejaculated the satellite. " Damned good!" said Mr. Blueskin.

" Yes," said Jonathan, sentimentally, " constituted as human nature is, what is called robbery must inevitably form a part and parcel of
the commonwealth; and it is my aim to render
it respectable, and put it upon an established
foundation."

" Jist my sentiments ! " again re-echoed the satellite ; and " Damned good ! " again rejoined Mr. Blueskin.

" It is but just," continued Mr. Wild, "that people who lose their property through careless-ness should have it restored to them on an ade-quate remuneration being made. I like fair play in every thing, and am a stickler for my word : ho-nour is my foible. I would not act dishonestly, even if I were dealing with the devil himself—there is no occasion for one to behave meanly or dishonourably, even in what the world calls vice."

" Beautiful, by G—! " bellowed out the satel-lite, giving the table a knock with his fist that made the glasses dance again. " Oh, superfine, smother me ! " said Mr. Blueskin.

" With these views then, it is," said Mr. Wild, " that I am willing to take you under my pro-tection, young gentleman ; you will henceforth belong to me : I will enter you down in my book, and regard you as a child ; you will form one of the great family of which I am the head and arbiter : all that I shall require from you in return is frankness and confidence. I shall not presume to direct your actions, but shall leave you to the free exercise of your own natural genius. You will follow the unrestrained bent of your inclinations : no evil consequences shall accrue from any action of which there may be

a full avowal made to me. Whatever is confided to my care, shall be liberally, and punctu-
ally accounted for, without fear of detection;
but, I again repeat, confidence I expect,—there
must be no secrets: I must know every thing;—
this observed, the law is impotent, and Justice,
may pursue her efforts in vain."

"Equitable to a hair!" roared out the satellite.
"The Governor could not say more, if he was
his own flesh and blood."

"Oh, damned equitable – damned equitable!"
said Mr. Blueskin.

"If you do any thing in the fullness of your
fancy," continued Mr. Wild, not regarding the
interruption, "that may expose you to awkward
results, confide the evidences of your indiscre-
tion to me: I will protect you —give you the full
value of whatever you may have hazarded your
liberty to obtain, and ensure you a continuance
of your efforts with freedom and impunity."
With this edifying assurance, which was very
grateful to Jack, and which Mr. Blueskin swore
"curse him, was infernally correct, and such as
no gemman could possibly object to," Jonathan
concluded his harangue.

He then entered Jack's name in his fatal book,
who, on his part, went through a sort of formula,
attested by the attendant satellites and Blueskin, pledging himself wholly to Jonathan, and

was duly admitted into the fraternity; Jonathan presenting him with a guinea as the final part of the compact. Not more surely does the urchin who, in exchange for a halfpenny, receives from the baker in return a roll of the same value, — not more surely, we repeat, does that urchin pur- chase that roll, than did Jonathan Wild with that guinea purchase the life-blood of the unsuspect- ing victim before him. Shutting his book, which he was accustomed to call his Poll-book, Jona- than summoned the landlord to produce the second bowl of Hucklemybuff, in which to drink Jack's enlistment.

" Where the devil is that fellow ?" said Blue- skin.

" Where the bee sucks, there lurk I,"

sung Mr. Hind from the cellar.

" But we want you to suck here," rejoined Blueskin, violently agitating the tinkler.

" In a cowslip's bell I lie,"

answered Mr. Hind, who had by this time re- gained his bar. " Yes, and every where else," said Mr. Blueskin. " I'll pound you for that, Master Joe !" The bowl was brought in, and paid for by Mr. Wild, who told Jack he should be very happy to see him in the Old Bailey whenever he might come that way, and receive any little proofs he might choose to bring him of his aptitude for the profession, on the noviciate of which he was about to enter. Mr. Wild further, in reply to Jack's wish that he might one day have an opportunity of visiting Newgate, cordially assured him that his desire should be gratified. With a variety of pleasant matter of this description the bowl was emptied, and the meeting broke up: Mr. Wild and his satellites departing for the Old Bailey, Blueskin taking a dive into the hundreds of Drury, and Jack, with Jonathan Wild's guinea in his pocket, stealing cautiously to his truckle bed in the garret of Mr. Wood.

CHAPTER THE NINTH.

JACK'S APPRENTICESHIP, CONTINUED.

JACK'S FIRST PUBLIC ROBBERY. — EARLY LIFE AND TRANSACTIONS OF MR. JONATHAN WILD. — JACK'S FIRST VISIT TO NEWGATE.

ALL the next day, and for many succeeding days, Jonathan Wild's guinea nearly burnt a hole in Jack's pocket; he dared not spend it, and yet felt almost afraid to keep it. At length, mustering up his resolution, he laid it out in the purchase of an old pair of pistols, which he saw exposed for sale in the shop window of the "Four Balls," a pawnbroker's in Holywell Street. The price of blood was thus appropriately expended in purchasing the instruments of destruction. Mr. Wood's good nature, however, —for he had soon totally forgotten their quarrel —so wrought upon Jack from this time, that, notwithstanding his compact with Jonathan Wild, he shrank from all thoughts of premeditated depredation; he, however, constantly visited the "Black Lion," where his nightly association with Mr. Blueskin, and other gentlemen of a similar stamp, sapped by degrees the few remaining virtuous resolutions he had managed to pre-

serve; and at the repeated instigation of Blueskin, who took every opportunity of reminding
him that Jonathan Wild would expect some
proof that he had not improperly been admitted
a member of the fraternity, he determined to
try his skill by laying hands on the first loose
articles that presented themselves.   He was not
long without an opportunity, very soon afterwards having to execute some jobs, in the way
of his trade, at the " Rummer Tavern," Charing Cross, amongst other repairs, he was set
to make a cupboard secure in one of the store-
rooms.   Jack performed his task to a miracle;
but as tinkers generally make two holes where
they mend one, Jack, while making this depo-
sitary safe, managed to pick the lock of another
in the same room, where he found a couple of
apostle spoons, or " gossips," as they were called
in the slang of the day, from a dozen, or set, of
them being the received present of respectable
sponsors at every christening.   These spoons,
which were rather larger than the dessert spoons
of the present day, were formed of solid silver,
and had the effigies of the Twelve Apostles chased
on the tops of the handles; the bowls were generally gilt.   Their ostensible purpose was, to be
used in drinking that most maternal potation,
caudle, though they were afterwards devoted to
general service.   The two spoons that so tempt-

ingly met the eyes of Jack bore the effigies of
St. Peter and St. Thomas. These two saints
were very speedily enshrined in Jack's breeches
pocket; a species of canonisation which, in this
instance, happened to go off very well, for,
dexterously shooting the lock back again, so as
to leave the cupboard as he found it, Jack got
clear off with his booty. This was his first
robbery.

The articles were not missed for two or three
days; and then, as Jack afterwards learnt from
the columns of the "Daily Post," suspicion
having fallen on a Jew who had visited the premises in the pursuit of his vocation, he was
traced to his residence, which being searched, a
quantity of broken silver was found, which not
being very satisfactorily accounted for, he was
point-blank charged with the robbery. St. Peter
did not more lustily deny his Master than did
the Jew forswear all knowledge of that saint
or his spoon. The landlord, however, proved
as unbelieving as St. Thomas himself. The
poor Israelite was dragged before Mr. Justice
Page, who, as the robbery could not be clearly
brought home, answered the ends of justice by
mulcting the Jew, on suspicion, in three times
the value of the stolen property; in addition to
which, the descendant of Abraham was on his
way home put under the pump, to gratify the

virtuous indignation of the populace, and was otherwise much maltreated.

Making the best of his way with his plunder to the office of his patron, Jonathan Wild, in the Old Bailey, Jack found that useful and amiable member of society deeply engaged in consultation with an old lady touching the possibility of the recovery of a snuff-box set in brilliants, that had been abstracted from her in her way to court at the last drawing-room, and which, just at that moment, happened to be most identically contained in Mr. Wild's waistcoat pocket. Jonathan was very particular in taking down a most minute description of the article in question, with the whole of the circumstances attending its abduction, and having ascertained that Lady Nosworthy — for such was the name of its owner — would willingly give a reward of twenty guineas for its return — rather more than its full value — he most commiseratingly requested her ladyship would do him the favour to look in upon him again in the course of a week, during which period he would, in consideration of its being a family relic, and the love he had of public justice, set such inquiries on foot, as he had no doubt would lead to some agreeable information as to " its whereabout." Being requested by the good old lady to name what he would expect for his disinterestedness, he very conscientiously turned up the whites of his eyes, and refused to accept a single farthing, declaring that her ladyship's prayers and his own innate satisfaction would more than repay him.   After entertaining the dowager with some affecting remarks on the calumnies with which he had been assailed both in public and in private, particularly the libels contained in a pamphlet entitled " The Regulator ; or a Discovery of Thieving and Thief-takers," written by Charles Hitchin, the city marshal, a brother thief-taker and rival in iniquity, and pointing out the injustice of supposing that the act of parliament just then passed, subjecting all persons receiving goods, knowing them to be stolen, to fourteen years transportation, was levelled at him, he drew from her ladyship five shillings as a retaining fee, took down her name and address with all the particulars in his office-book, and another customer coming in, very politely bowed her out, Jack standing meanwhile a silent spectator of all that had passed.

The second visitor was a Mr. Obadiah Woolfree, a traveller to a manufacturing house in Birmingham, who had had his pocket picked of several samples of jewellery, with the particulars of which he had previously made Jonathan acquainted, and now came, according to direction, to know if any information had been procured.

Jonathan, assuming the most friendly look

T

imaginable, told him that he had found out, by mere chance, that some suspected goods had been stopped by a very honest man, a broker, with whom he was acquainted, and that if the lost goods fortunately should happen to be those in the hands of his friend, restitution should be made; that of course his friend would expect to be remunerated; and that it must be perfectly understood that no evil consequences should accrue to him from his having imprudently neglected to apprehend the offenders. This Obadiah, rather than encounter the trouble and expense of a prosecution, readily consented to, the more especially as the goods had been lost in a place, and under circumstances, that might have savoured of ill fame to his employers.

The next applicant was Mr. Peter Entwistle, a gentleman who had been robbed of a pocket-book, containing a great number of very valuable memoranda, of no use to any body but the owner; he received the same answer that Obadiah had done, but was not equally satisfied with it. Being a limb of the law, Mr. Entwistle very pertinaciously put some questions, very like cross questions, as to the particular manner in which his property had been discovered, &c. Upon this Jonathan immediately ascended the high ropes, and pretended to be very much offended that his honour should be called in question.

" The only motive I have," said he, "is to afford all the service in my power to persons who may have been plundered; but since my intentions are received in so ungracious a manner, and it is thought necessary to interrogate me in so suspicious a way, I have nothing further to say on the subject. I have my own conscience to satisfy me, and that is enough; the name of Jonathan Wild need not shrink from any investigation." The legal gentleman was here convinced he had been too hasty; he therefore apologised to Jonathan, and offered him an additional reward — on which the good man became somewhat pacified; and a time and place were fixed for the restoration of the property.

To a fourth party, Mr. Jonah Strugnell, a drysalter, who had been hustled under Gray's Inn wall, and almost stripped to the skin, Jonathan answered he had received some information respecting his (Mr. Strugnell's) lost cocked hat, perriwig, coat, sword, and silver buckles, but that the agent he had employed had informed him that the thieves pretended they could raise more money by pawning the property than by returning it for the proposed reward; "but," added Jonathan, " if I can by any means procure an interview with the villains, whom I earnestly implore heaven to punish, I shall, I doubt not, be able to settle matters agreeably to the terms proposed;" though he artfully insinuated the most safe, expeditious, and prudent method would be to make a small addition to the reward. Poor Jonah, on hearing this, eagerly agreed to give an extra ten shillings, when Jonathan, with a benevolent air, told him to call the next day at three o'clock, when his confidential assistant, Mr. Mendez, the patriarch before alluded to, should accompany him to a certain post in Kent Street, where a gentleman in a smock-frock and dustman's slouched hat would, on receiving the reward, return the lost property — "no questions being asked." Jonah departed delighted, fancying himself once more in his own coat, perriwig, &c.

Wild next despatched his satellite, Quilt Arnold, to Miss Virginia Withers, an elderly spinster, who, by the cutting away of her pocket in the New Jerusalem Chapel, had been robbed of "The whole Duty of Man," a large silver smelling bottle, which by mistake had been filled with strong waters, and a silk purse containing a note of hand, of the Reverend Simon Cunnington, together with some loose silver, desiring him to inform the bereaved lady, that she could have her smelling bottle, note of hand, and "Whole Duty of Man" back again, on payment of a certain sum; but that the strong waters and loose silver were missing. He then beckoned our hero into a little back room, and assuming a bland air, most encouragingly inquired the nature of his communication.

Previously to entering upon this, however, as Mr. Jonathan Wild will henceforth be one of the principal persons that figure in this very memorable and eventful history, it may be necessary to give the readers, for the better understanding our pages, some account of this great personage's " birth, parentage, and education," together with his "life, character, and behaviour," up to this precise period.

This extraordinary man, according to all ordinary accounts, was born at Wolverhampton, in Staffordshire, about the year 1682. Posterity have to lament that the precise day of the birth of this distinguished man has not been ascertained with sufficient accuracy to allow us, as conscientious historians, to record it with any confidence. His parents were somewhat humble, but extremely respectable; he was their eldest son, their first-born, as may well be imagined from the strength of character he afterwards displayed. At a proper age they put him to an established day-school, which he continued to attend till he had gained sufficient knowledge in reading, writing, and accounts, for general purposes; his father intended to have brought him up to his own trade, but afterwards changed his mind;

and when his son was about fifteen put him apprentice for seven years to a buckle-maker in Birmingham ; this, at that time, was a flourishing business. Upon the expiration of his apprenticeship Jonathan returned to Wolverhampton, and soon feeling the soft infection of love, married a young woman possessing both virtue and comeliness, and for some time earned a tolerable livelihood by following his business in the minor degree of journeyman. But a mechanical life possessed few charms for Jonathan : his spirit aspired to higher things ; and after two years passed in buckle-making, during which time his consort had presented him with a son and heir, he, one fine morning, to gratify his love of change, and give some scope to his wish for distinction and command, showed his beautiful wife and lovely offspring a fair pair of heels, and unceremoniously left them, to repair to London, where he imagined his talents would meet with proper encouragement. In the great metropolis he soon procured employment, and for some time supported himself by his trade ; but being, in addition to his ambition, of a very lively turn, and above prejudices, and having, withal, very original ideas touching the correct disposition of property, it is not to be wondered at that he should soon have got into debt, still less so, that, getting into debt, he should have got into the hands of the lawyers, and after that, have got into gaol. The fact was, that very few months after his arrival in London he was arrested, and thrown into Wood Street compter, where he remained a prisoner for debt upwards of four years.

At that time, contrary to the present practice, their was no classification in our prisons; and debtors and felons mixed indiscriminately together during the day, and very often at night. Neither was the modern poor-law system of separating the sexes in vogue; consequently Mr. Wild soon became acquainted with most of the reigning depredators of that period : he was admitted into their privy council, — became acquainted with all the secrets of their several states, — learnt how they levied contributions on the public, imposed exactions, raised supplies, made war on their neighbours, and replenished their exhausted treasuries. The city marshal, the notorious Charles Hitchin *, was, at that time, lord paramount of all the thieves in the kingdom. Jonathan soon began to envy the sway this man

* This consummate miscreant, who was undoubtedly Jonathan Wild's master in the peculiar profession which he subsequently pursued with so much notoriety, was overtaken by the arm of justice for a gross misdemeanor, and dying soon afterwards, left Wild in undisputed possession of the field. It is hard to say which was the greatest scoundrel of the two : but Wild was the more artful and specious one.

exercised. During his confinement, he formed an acquaintance with a fair nymph of Venus, known on the *pavé* by the name of Mary Milliner, the most redoubtable purloiner of hearts and handkerchiefs that then occasionally illumined his majesty's gaols. Naturally inflammable, Jonathan soon formed a tender *penchant* for this vestal, and the usual *liaison* was the consequence. She had escaped the penalties attendant on sundry larcenies; but the liberality of her disposition was too great to shield her from the inexorable hands of John Doe and Richard Roe.

Obtaining their joint freedom, after a short period, this congenial pair availed themselves of the independent facility afforded by a sultatory movement over a broomstick, to appear to the world's eye as man and wife. The adroitness of the fair Mary in the way of her vocation, and the knowledge Jonathan had acquired while in " durance vile," soon enabled them to raise sufficient money to take a small public house in Cripplegate, where Jonathan commenced his well-known trade of restoring stolen property. For some time his house was a regular loch, or receptacle for plunder of every description; but on the passing of the act against receivers, he called all the thieves together, and constituting himself their head and arbiter, entered into a compact with them, that all articles stolen should be committed to his custody, for which he would regularly pay more than they could procure from the pawnbrokers, and without any risk to them, trusting to reimburse himself by the rewards obtained from their owners, to whom he might restore them. His success was great — he contested the palm of sovereignty with the then king of the thieves, the arch-villain Hitchin. These worthies at first attacked each other in pamphlets, and tried which could prove his rival to be the greater rascal; but finding, that by their opposition they were cutting each other's throats, they joined in partnership together. Hitchin, who had lost his situation as marshal, acting as master, and our *ci-devant* buckle-maker, Jonathan Wild, officiating as man. This union did not long continue. The towering genius of Jonathan soon crushed all the pretensions of the ex-marshal, notwithstanding there was no act of villany, however great or daring, from which the latter shrunk. Jonathan was soon left master of the field, and reigned alone; he gave up his public house, and opened a public office, at the house of a Mrs. Sego, in the Old Bailey, where his fame became so great, that scarcely any thing was lost but application was made to him for its recovery: not a prig dared practise his profession without having first received a diploma from his

U

hand.   Mill-kens * and Bridle-culls †, alike trembled at his nod,—in a word, he reigned undisputed king of the thieves ; but though terrible to his own immediate subjects, whose lives he held in his hands, to the public at large he was plausible and pious — as sleek and fair to appearance as the serpent of the deserts, but not less venomous and deadly.   Such was Jonathan Wild's position and history at the time that Jack brought him the first fruits of his deviation from the paths of honesty.

"What is your business with me, my son ?" said he, addressing Jack with an air of parental kindness. "Any little outbreak, eh?—Well, well, youth will be lively : we cannot put old heads upon young shoulders."

Jack produced the two spoons.   "Ah, ha! a couple of *Godfathers!*" said he. "Good, good ; these give you a *name* that fully entitles you to be received among my children; no reward will be offered for these. Here, Abraham !" said he, summoning the patriarch.

"Yesh, Mishter Vild, shur," answered that worthy, suddenly appearing from behind an immensely ugly bushy beard. "Any tings de mattersh ?"

"No, Nab," answered the potentate. "Is the white broth on ?"

* Housebreakers.   † Highwaymen.

" Jusht on, Mr. Vild."

" That's right; stir it up with those two spoons then, Nab," — tossing them to him. The Jew grinned horribly a ghastly smile at the thoughts of crucibleing the good saints.

" Dey shall be in de pot directly, Mishter Vild," said he; and disappeared with them in a twinkling.

" As old silver, they may fetch five shillings," said Jonathan, handing Jack the money : the value of them was at least a guinea. " Now relate to me the particulars of their capture."

Jack related the account of the robbery with a commendable modesty. Mr. Wild bestowed much praise on the cleanness of his workmanship, and assured him there was no doubt but that in time he would become a great artist, encouraging him to pursue the path upon which he had so auspiciously entered. Then desiring the patriarch to step over with Jack to Newgate, and request Mr. Revel, the under turnkey, to afford him the high treat of a thorough inspection of that celebrated mansion — that last "retreat of the unfortunate *brave*," Mr. Wild shook hands with him, and bade him good bye, hoping very shortly to see him again.

The inspection of Newgate very deeply interested Jack; there was no part of it on which he did not, as if by some secret prescience, bestow the

most minute attention, an attention which proved
of singular use to him in after life.   He asked
Mr. Revel a thousand questions, and appeared so
interested as to excite the patriarch's attention.

" Vy, you seems quite sthruck vith the plaishe,
my kinchin," said that worthy. " Vell, it is a
nishe plaishe, quite out of the way of the coaches.
You musht treat him vell, Mishter Revel, if ever
he comes here for a short time, as who knows
vot may happen : give him one of your best
berths."

" Ay, ay, we'll accommodate him," said the
dubster.

" Much obliged to you," returned Jack. " I
may look in upon you one of these days."

" But come," said the patriarch, " you musht
make haste, youngster, for I'm in a hurry. Vhy,
hang me, if I don't think you'd like to stay here
altogether, you seem so fond of the plaishe."

" You will be hanged, then," said Jack, " for
I should'nt like to stay here at all, and, what's
more, I would'nt. — What do you call these
things ?" said he, examining some fetters and
handcuffs that were hanging up ready for use.

" Vot, the darbies and the ruffles ?" said the
Jew. " Oh! you'll know all in goot time, you
may depend upon dat."

" Shall I ! I thank you for the information.
They must be made a little stronger than these

to last long with me. Why, I should wear a suit
out in no time."

" Ve shall see, ve shall see !" said the Jew.
" But come, you've staid quite long enough ; so
make your bow to the gentlemans, and bowl dish
vay."

" I'll not detain you," said Jack; "nobody
shall ever complain of my wanting to stay too
long, whenever I happen to come here."

" Dat's very goot," chuckled the Jew. " But
come, I've got to go to Newtoner's Lane, so I'll
see you safe out here, and valk vith you as far
as Vych Street ; so goot morning, Mishter
Revel, goot morning, shur, thanking you vastly
for gratifying my young friend here."

" Shall be happy to see him at any time,"
growled out Mr. Revel : " he seems a promising
bird."

" Don't you wish you may get me ?" laughed
Jack ; " but your's are snug quarters, I must
say : when I want to learn a trick or two, I don't
know that I can come to a better college."

Jack and the Jew then departed, — the patriarch to Newtoner's Lane, and Jack to the shop
of his master.

CHAPTER THE TENTH.

JACK'S APPRENTICESHIP, CONTINUED.

MAY-DAY IN 1716. — THE MILK MAID'S GARLAND. — JACK'S FIRST LOVE.

A TWELVEMONTH rolled away, during the whole of which period our hero did not once attempt to repeat his handiwork of the spoons; though tender inquiries how he went on were made from time to time by Mr. Wild, through the medium of Blueskin, who assured Jack that the governor took a great interest in him, and hoped he would'nt disappoint that gentleman's expectations, nor disgrace his, Mr. Blueskin's recommendation. Jack replied, it was all in good time, and that he should wait and see how things turned out.

At length time brought the first of May, 1716, and a glorious first of May it was—bright, balmy, warm, and inspiring — not one of the first of Mays we have been used to have since the great M. N. S. Murphy has meddled with the weather; but one recalling images of joy and beauty, and awakening thoughts of repose and love. The skies were without a cloud — the hawthorn and early fruit trees presented, with their gay profusion of blossoms, the appearance of gigantic nosegays — the air was as vocal as it was fragrant: it seemed as if both birds and flowers, in gratitude for their being, were rendering back to heaven the sweet breath they inhaled from it in love and honour — the one in incense and the other in song. The waters, as they glistened in the sunbeams, looked bright and pure, yielding those ideas of comfortable coolness and grateful refreshment that only belong to the limpid element in summer. Jack's heart felt the delicious exhilaration of the season, and was attuned to the reception of tenderness and pleasure.

He was conveying, with a bounding step and buoyant bosom, a packing — not a law — case to the chambers of Counsellor Jay, in the Temple, when crossing through one of the leading streets in the Strand, his notice was attracted by the sounds of a pipe and tabor, to what was then the usual exhibition of May-day, but which has long since given way to a less pleasing pageant: the cleanly milkmaid having been superseded in her appeals to the public generosity at this vernal season by the sooty sweep. "Ah, ah! the milkmaid's garland!" said Jack. "I must see this; it seems one of the gayest and grandest I have witnessed yet." Making his way through the crowd which had gathered round it, Jack soon got a clear view of this, then, very innocent and

pleasing sight. A pyramid of some six or eight
feet in height, covered with fine damask, was
erected on a sort of stand, which a couple of
bearers carried, by means of two horizontal poles,
similar to those of a sedan chair. This pyramid
was ornamented on each side from top to bottom,
with a great number of real silver salvers, spoons,
jugs, watches, teapots, cream ewers, dishes, &c.,
surmounted at the top by an elegant tea or coffee
urn,— the whole borrowed for the day from the
various customers of the milkman, with some
occasional loans from pawnbrokers, who let out
plate on security for the purpose. The various
pieces were tastefully and profusely decorated
with bunches of ribands of different colours, the
articles being so disposed as to form many fanci-
ful devices. A man playing on the fife and tabor
headed the procession, and a number of milkmaids in their best Sunday boddices and kirtles,
trimmed with bunches of ribands, and their neat
straw hats, adorned with flowers, danced around
the pyramid at the several places where it rested,
which was generally before the doors of their
customers whose contributions they solicited as
well as those of the spectators. The sight of
so much valuable plate, and so many watches,
considerably excited Jack's interest, and awoke
sundry speculations in his mind of a nature which
we shall not here allude to further,—suffice it "he

looked and longed, and longed and looked again;" but all at once, his eye glancing by chance from the pyramid and its treasures his vision fell upon an object which from that moment was never afterwards erased from his memory.

Before the pyramid, in the centre of the other maidens, he beheld a young girl dancing, whose surpassing grace and loveliness immediately made the ribands look dull, and the plate seem valueless. She appeared about fifteen years of age : the bud of girlhood was just expanding into the first blossom of woman ; her skin was of a warm dazzling whiteness, exhibiting a rich purity which could only be compared with that of the water lily, and which made the milk she vended look cold and chalky, when coming in contact with it, as it would have done snow, and many other substances to which poets have delighted to compare the outward texture of their mistresses. Her eyes were of that clear blue, in which as you gaze, you seem, as when gazing on the heavens, to lose all thoughts of mortality, and only receive glimpses of peace and delight. Her mouth was small, with ripe rosy lips compressed, as if withdrawing into their own odorous bower, and gave, perhaps, a stronger promise of innocence and modesty than was conveyed even by her retiring look, and somewhat downcast

X

lids : clusters of flaxen ringlets fell beneath her
straw hat, over her shoulders, on either side her
face.   Her figure was *petite*, and seemingly fragile, but exquisitely moulded, and of the most perfect symmetry.   A bystander might have thought
it wonderful that such a world of beauty and
enchantment could have been enshrined in so
small a compass.   Her dress was elegantly simple ; but had it been that of a queen, it would
have obtained no regard opposed to such attractions of person as those with which it was
united.   In her hand she held a wreath, or garland of flowers, which, in conjunction with a
companion with whom she danced, she was
twining into a number of graceful figures.   Jack
stood entranced, gazing at her in stupid wonder.
Though he had walked abroad all his life amid
a world of female beauty, this was the first time a
consciousness of its existence had crossed his mind.
All the charms that he had ever individually seen
in the thousand lovely creatures he had at times
beheld were here concentrated into one, and
seemed to unite their hitherto separated force to
overpower and enslave him.   On a sudden the
maiden stopped in her dance, and curtseying to
the multitude, sung, in a somewhat tremulous
but unusually clear and melodious voice, the customary "*Milkmaid's May-day Carol*," with a copy
of which we have been favoured, taken down from

the recitation of an old lady of our acquaintance, and which we here present to our readers.

The Milkmaid's May-day Carol.

1.

THE skies shine bright, the meads look gay, and streams
    run soft and clear,
And bees and flowers proclaim 't is May, the sweet
    time of the year;
And lowing kine, where hawthorns twine, the luscious
    draught supply—
A drink divine, like generous wine, fit for the gods
    on high.
The fount of innocence and love, it cheers both young
    and old;
And erst, the care of princess fair! was, in the age of
    gold.
Then pretty maids above, below, as you our carol hear,
Remember the poor milkmaid in the sweet time of
    the year.

2.

We bring our garlands to your doors, with rose and
    lily twined,
To call alike your beauty and your purity to mind.
With silver tankard, ewer, cup, your memories to rub
Of curds and whey, and custard, and the fragrant
    sillabub.

Without our aid, ah! what would all your foreign
　　luxuries be;
Our milk it is gives relish to your coffee and your
　　tea.
Then pretty maids, above, below, as you our carol
　　hear,
Remember the poor milkmaid in the sweet time of
　　the year.

3.

Think how, when wintry rains fall deep, and howls
　　the dreary wind,
While to your cheerful fires you creep, and warmth
　　and comfort find,
Think how we go through frost and snow, ere morn
　　begins to gleam,
To fold and field, to you to yield new milk and clouted
　　cream.
Regardless both of toil and care, of anguish and of
　　ease,
So we, our merry masters and mistresses but please.
Then pretty maids, above, below, as you our carol
　　hear,
Remember the poor milkmaid in the sweet time of
　　the year.

She ceased. A shower of pieces of money
from copper to silver rewarded her skill. Jack
drank in every word, as he had done every look,
and was only aroused from his dream of light
and joy by a deep voice muttering — "That

"Ach lindchen . Was macht . dir den ?"

Kinchin! he is mine! I have him *now:*" when turning round, he beheld with surprise Jonathan Wild, regarding him with sinister satisfaction. By Jonathan's side stood a gaunt-looking fellow, somewhat rudely attired, with a companion of the same stamp, significantly pointing with his finger to the various valuable articles of plate suspended on the pyramid. Jack was somewhat alarmed as well as surprised at this sudden appearance of Wild; and more so, when continuing his gaze around, he discovered the exemplary Mr. Blueskin and some gipsy friends of his of rather equivocal character, that he had met occasionally at the "Black Lion." At this moment, the fair girl with whom he had been so struck suddenly rested her attention upon him. A glance was exchanged between them which seemed to have some electrical power, for a sympathetic thrill in each was its immediate result. A feeling of sadness passed for a moment over Jack's mind; his fancy conjured up a thousand images — he became once more wrapped, his eyes fixed on the enchanting vision before him; and it was not till jostled by the retiring crowd, that he discovered that he was gazing on vacancy, and that the fairy-like creature who had so deeply spelled his senses had imperceptibly glided away, and that with her had vanished the garland, Jonathan Wild, Mr. Blueskin and his companions, with the numerous persons by which it was accompanied. Arousing himself from his reverie, though he still continued to behold in fancy the bright object of his enchantment — the mind's eye retaining the impression of particular images long after they have departed — Jack repaired with the case to Counsellor Jay's.

After some time, his suspicions began to direct themselves to the motives that had brought Jonathan Wild and his friend Blueskin in attendance upon the garland; and he remembered, among the plate which was affixed to the pyramid, there were some massive salvers, bearing the well-known arms of Mr. Kneebone, which consisted of three legs and thighs, so connected together at the femoral extremities as to form a species of radius; and that there were also the well-known Sunday tea-urn of Madam Wood, and her state set of spoons, which had been presented to her on her marriage by no less a person than her relation the ex-mayor, Sir Timothy Gutteridge himself: there was also Mr. Wood's great family turnip-shaped watch, with its imposing appendages; and it now occurred to Jack that the leader of the procession, the man who played the pipe and tabor, and carried the money-box, was Mr. Wood's and Mr. Kneebone's own milkman, David Lloyd, a countryman of Mr.

Wood, proprietor of the principal milk-walk in that quarter, and an extensive cow-keeper. The truth now flashed upon him that some mischief was intended, though he recoiled at the idea that the fair damsel who had so intensely interested him was either knowingly or willingly a party to it. Mr. Kneebone's plate he had no doubt had been borrowed by the milkman of the goodnatured Mrs. Partington; and national predilection satisfactorily accounted for the possession of Mr. Wood's time-teller, and other property. He felt half inclined to go and warn both his protector and his master. Jonathan Wild, Blueskin, and their associates were, he was convinced, only lurking about the valuables for the purposes of plunder; but he was restrained by the thought that he might, by disclosing his suspicions, unintentionally get the lovely milkmaid into trouble; he therefore returned to his work, though not with that alacrity with which he usually pursued it: he was thoughtful and moody, and could not help reverting to the scene that had so lately passed. Again was the form of the beautiful milkmaid dancing before his eyes — again were her melodious accents ringing in his ears. He saw the malignant looks of Jonathan, the furtive glances of Blueskin and his companions, and he anxiously awaited for some intelligence. The afternoon had scarcely well set in, when his worst

fears were confirmed by the sudden entrance of
Mr. Wood.

"Mercies of Got!" exclaimed that gentleman, "here is calamities, look you! hur is
ruined! hur great family watch that had tesented
to hur from father to son pefore watchmaking
was known, and hat peen worn by Calwallater
himself, with hur great seal of the leek, is gone,
look you! Put that is not the worst: Matam
Woot's pest tea-urn, ant all her Suntay tea-spoons
tat was given her py her relation, Sir Timothy
Gutteridge, that was lort mayor, ant which hur hat
lent tat villain Tavit Lloyt, without her knowletge,
is gone too. Some scountrels have run away with
the garlant, plate and all. Hur is ruinet! hur is
ruinet! That villain, Tavit Lloyt, passion of hur
heart! but he shall give hur satisfaction for hur
losses, which hur shall never hear the last of from
hur laty, Madam Woot."

The unfortunate Welshman here applied for
consolation to a huge jug of cwrw, which happened, luckily, to have been just brought in, to
be in readiness for the family supper. It produced a momentary calm, during which Jack
managed, adroitly enough, to extract from his
master, without exciting any suspicion, the information, that a gang of desperadoes had attacked
the garland as it was proceeding through a place
near the top of the Strand, then known by the

name of Porridge Island, and was of somewhat doubtful character: that after violently beating the bearers of it, knocking down, and otherwise ill treating its owner, the aforesaid David Lloyd, and frightening away the milkmaids in all directions, they had got clear off with their booty, leaving no trace behind them by which they could be discovered. Leaving Mr. Wood at one moment mourning over his loss, and the next burning with indignation at the authors of it, Jack repaired in the evening, as usual, to the " Black Lion." It was some time before he was joined by any of the company that regularly resorted there; their absence did not particularly surprise him : he had long settled, in his own mind, who were the persons that had so daringly carried off the May-day treasures, and felt a proportionate degree of anxiety to learn the fate of the beautiful milkmaid. He was not long left in doubt. About ten o'clock Mr. Blueskin, with his gipsy companions before mentioned, entered the room ; they were immediately followed by Jonathan Wild.

" Cleanly done enough, that I must own," said that great man to Blueskin. " Rather unlucky, though:" and here he fixed a marked look on Jack, " rather unlucky that pretty Bess should be nabbed : the gang must shift their quarters for a while in case she should squeak."

Jack's blood flew to his cheeks, and his heart throbbed violently — she was, then, a prisoner. " Where have they caged our little singing bird ?" continued Mr. Wild.

" In old St. Giles's roundhouse," answered Blueskin.

" Ah, there !" said the potentate. " Not much of a ken that: a lad of any spirit might get her out in no time. Old Guffin, the keeper, wouldn't stand the kick of a fly's leg. If the little beauty had but a fancy man, now ——" here he fixed another glance of peculiar meaning on our hero.

Jack stopped to hear no more ; he rushed out of the " Black Lion," and hastily bent his steps towards St. Giles's, resolving either to rescue the beautiful milkmaid, or remain and suffer with her.

CHAPTER THE ELEVENTH.

JACK SHEPPARD A PRISON-BREAKER.

ST. GILES'S ROUNDHOUSE.— RESCUE OF EDGWORTH BESS.
— VISIT TO NORWOOD.

WHIRLED along by the impetuosity of his feelings, and scarcely knowing which path he took, Jack made his way up Drury Lane, across Long Acre, and through the maze of streets that constitute the Seven Dials, till he came to St.Giles's roundhouse, then a square building of two stories, forming a sort of postern, situated on one side of St.Giles's churchyard, having the church and churchyard in its rear, with a street in front. Arriving at this official structure, he, without any settled purpose, or fixed plan, save that of rescuing the pretty milkmaid by any means that presented themselves, knocked violently at the door ; it was speedily opened by Mr. Hannibal Guffin, the parish beadle, and keeper of the roundhouse.

" Hey-day!" said that functionary, who had exchanged his cocked hat and official wig for a comfortable thrum cap, in which he meant to enjoy a pleasant sleep in the parochial night-chair, though he still retained the imposing blue great-coat, with huge red collar and broad gold binding, which marked his rank and authority — "Hey-day! what night bird have we here? why one would think the whole parish were at the door by the noise—you couldn't be in a greater hurry if you were Mr. Head Churchwarden himself."

"You have a young girl here," interrupted Jack, "unjustly charged on suspicion of being concerned in a daring robbery."

"What! Edgworth Bess? for so some of the villains were heard to call her, or plain Bess, as she styled herself, though the jade is pretty enough for that matter, but that was the only name she'd give. The baggage pretended, before the justice, that she never knew she had another. What do you want with her? If you have any thing good to give her, let me have it; I'll take care it's properly delivered."

"I must see her," exclaimed Jack, "and that instantly; she is innocent: I am ready to swear it — to stake my life upon it. She has been entrapped—betrayed," he continued passionately.

"Hoity-toity!" exclaimed the dignitary of the roundhouse—"here's a young bantem *must see her!* What, then, have you got an order from Justice Page, my fine fellow?"

"No," said Jack, energetically; "but I repeat I must and will see her. Where is she?"

" Out of your reach, young Pickle. What, I
suppose you are one of the gang, are you ? Well,
you're beginning betimes, at all events. But
come, take yourself off, and thank your stars that
I haven't my Sunday service cane at hand, or I
might mark such a pretty backgammon board, of
red and black stripes on your back, as you
wouldn't forget in a hurry. Come, tramp,
tramp !"

" Not before I have seen this poor luckless
girl," returned Jack, with a determined air.
" Where is she, I ask you ? "

" Halloa !" said the astonished functionary,
" do you know who you are speaking to,
scoundrel ? Do you know that I am Mr. Hannibal Guffin, the *locum tenens* of their worships
the overseers, and keeper of the roundhouse ? "

" If you were ten thousand beadles," said
Jack, losing all command of himself, " you *shall*
let me see your ill-used victim."

" I am petrified !" roared out the astonished
Mr. Hannibal. " This language to me ! St. Giles's
is certainly coming to a chaos; but I 'll make
short work of it. The hussy you speak of is
there, in that cage," pointing to the door of a
small cell at the back of the apartment, " safely
cooped up, and if you don't instantly show me
a fair pair of heels, I'll make you her companion,
by clapping you into the fellow-cage to it."

"Scoundrel!" cried Jack, enraged; "but I'll hesitate no longer: the coast is clear—I have a fair opportunity, so here goes."

With these words he snatched up a stout watchman's bill, which happened to be lying on a table, before which the beadle had been sitting, and directed it at the functionary's skull with such good will, that not having any hat or wig as protection, it instantly stretched him senseless on the floor. His next step was to force open, with the beadle's own staff, the door of the cell which had been pointed out as containing the fair prisoner. The poor girl was sitting on a bundle of straw, suffused in tears, and looking, if possible, even lovelier in her tears than when Jack saw her, all life and joy, in the morning. She arose in surprise and alarm.

" Oh! for mercy's sake!" she exclaimed, with a faint shriek, "spare me, spare me! indeed I am innocent — I knew not what I did."

" Compose yourself, dear girl," said Jack; " I am come to save you; but we must not lose a moment — quick! let us fly, then."

" Ah, at liberty?" said the amazed girl, suddenly brightening up. " To whom do I owe my deliverance? Oh, let my thanks, my gratitude——"

" It matters not who I am," said Jack; " it is sufficient I have rescued you: hereafter we may know each other better. But come, damsel, let us complete your escape while we can."

It was fortunate that the respectable Mr. Hannibal Guffin and pretty Bess were the only inmates of the roundhouse at the period of Jack's visit. The nightly watch had been set, and those worthy guardians of the rest of his Majesty's subjects had departed on their several beats, and the hour had not arrived when the usual nocturnal visiters of the roundhouse were generally installed in it, or Jack's exploit might have been one of somewhat more difficulty.

Taking the fair maiden's hand, who, to say the truth, was nothing loath, and bestowing a hearty kick on the prostrate carcass of the senseless beadle as he passed him, Jack hastened with his precious prize into the street, carefully shutting the door of the roundhouse after him. Hurrying onwards in the direction of Drury Lane, neither feeling inclined, till perfectly out of danger, to indulge in conversation, they were stopped at the corner of Monmouth Street, by encountering the tall and muffled figure of a woman, which Jack immediately recognised as that of the gipsy who had discovered the pilfering of Mrs. Partington's ring at Mr. Kneebone's.

"Ah, my mother!" said the little maiden, springing joyfully towards her. "Welcome, welcome! Why did you ever leave me? That terrible black Martin—I have been betrayed, dear mother, accused of theft — dragged through the streets a prisoner—thrust in a dungeon, and but for this good youth——" here her emotions completely overpowered her; her spirit, which had borne her up till this moment, now suddenly appeared to fail her; the remembrance of all she had suffered flashed across her. It was too much for one so tender, so timid; and she sunk fainting on Jack's shoulder.

" Ah!" said the gipsy, as if struck by an electric shock, and flashing her dark eye on Jack. "And is it with you, boy, I thus meet her; is it by your hand she's been rescued from her peril? Then I foretold too truly. Did I not warn you to avoid her—did I not tell you those flaxen ringlets would prove chains to you; that beneath those now closed lids beamed fires whose brilliancy, like the lightnings, would blight thee?"

Jack was startled, and listened with silent wonder to the vehemence of the hag. " See, " she continued, removing a necklace, and pointing out a counter mole on the throat of the insensible girl — " see that fatal mark, twin to the one thou bearest. Did I not name it to thee, and charge thee, boy, to fly its bearer? By Satan, we are but willing puppets of the Fates, and lend ourselves to our own destinies;

then what avails our prescience — what avails
the gipsy's warning—what imports the foreknow-
ledge drawn from star and planet?"

"Indeed," said Jack, who almost quailed beneath the gipsy's hollow tones and mystic words,
and vainly tried to shrink from her searching
glances, which seemed to have the deadly fascination of the serpent's, "Indeed I meant no
harm, I thought no harm ; but I couldn't bear
that such a pretty creature should be shut up in
a prison for what I was sure she had not done.
If she had really stolen the things, it wouldn't
have been so bad ; so I determined to get her
out ; and I have. I knocked the old beadle on
the head.— Don't be frightened,—I did not kill
him, bless you ! — his skull's too thick for that ;
and now where's the harm ?"

"Unconscious instrument of destiny and ill,"
exclaimed the gipsy, "who shall explain to thee
the dark riddles of futurity? Time is the only
certain solver—he unravels all things : let Time,
then, answer thee ; I cannot —will not. But let
me revive this child of revenge and misfortune.
Poor wench ! this day she has turned o'er the
first page of her book of woe. How many are
there ere the volume close ? 'Tis a black-lettered
tome : its leaves illumined with characters of
blood ;—'twould sear my eyeballs did I seek to read
them !" She here applied a powerful essence

to the senses of her *protegée*, who was still enclosed in Jack's arms : it speedily revived her.

"Where am I ? " said the poor girl. " In that horrid cell, dragged by those fearful men ? No, no,—free, and with her I love ! Yes, I remember all."

"You must away, Bess," said the gipsy sternly. " Take leave of your deliverer."

"Ah ! " said Jack, "must we then part so soon ? But we shall meet again — you 'll surely not deny me that ? "

"Oh yes, yes ! " tenderly ejaculated the poor girl, as the gipsy withdrew her from Jack's embrace, "often, very often ,— that is, I hope — perhaps — shall we not, mother ? " observing the severe look of the gipsy.

"You must part, child," returned the gipsy solemnly, " with my consent never to meet again. What the stars will, they will ; I may not change their bidding : my rule is but of earth — and how brief that — how wretched ! A wandering race, an outcast tribe, the thicket, and the ruin. When will the curse upon our nation leave us ? But come, there's danger in our tarrying here : — night wears, the alarm ere now is doubtless given, and we may be surprised. Say farewell, Bess, to your preserver."

"Good bye, good bye ! and thank you," sobbed the poor girl, gratefully pressing Jack's hand.

"I may not disobey the bidding of my mother. Good bye, God bless you! You have my thanks —my prayers."

Ere Jack could sufficiently rally his thoughts to answer her, the gipsy had withdrawn her from the spot, and both had vanished.

Recovering from the surprise of their disappearance, Jack turned his steps back again to the domicile of the tuneful Mr. Hind. He found the vocal landlord of the sable monarch of the woods in close attendance on Mr. Wild, Mr. Blueskin, and the gipsy gentlemen of their acquaintance. A significant glance successively passed from one to the other of the whole of these interesting persons.

> " Drink to me only with thine eyes,
>   And I will pledge with mine,"

hummed Mr. Hind, emptying a glass of punch that happened to be standing just then before him, and leering with an expression of peculiar meaning from Jack to the company around him. "Or leave a kiss, tol lol de diddle doll!" — he did not conclude Ben Jonson's well known song.

For a moment there was a deep pause, which was at length broken by the bland tones of Jonathan.

"Why, you left us all in a hurry, Jack," said he encouragingly.

" Yes, there was no time to be lost," answered Jack.

" Something particular, eh ?" said Wild, in an insinuating tone.

" Yes," said Jack. " I thought the sooner the poor girl was released from her unjust confinement the better."

" What, then, is she free ?" said Wild, exultingly. — " All's safe boys," he muttered aside to his companions. " But you surely haven't committed any violence ?"

" I have only broken open the door of her dungeon," said Jack, " and given old Guffin, the beadle, a rap on the mazzard — that's all."

" Your hand," said Jonathan ; " you have proved yourself one of the right sort, Jack ; and whenever you choose regularly to enter the service, you shan't want a commission : I'll appoint you one of my lieutenants the very first thing."

" Ve'll drink the lieutenant's goot healths," said the patriarch, who happened to be present.

" With all my heart," returned Blueskin, " if it was a mile to the bottom   I always said Jack was a regular court card, and that whoever turned him up would find he'd turned up his nob."

> " It was a lover and his lass,"

sang Mr. Hind.

"But where is the wench?" inquired Jonathan of Jack.

"With one we met upon our way; one she called mother."

"Tall, and in tatters?" asked Jonathan.

"The same," answered Jack.

"Ah! the witch, Zara," said the monarch of the thieving fraternity; "that is unlucky: the baggage, Bess, may slip through our fingers; and I have further business for her. But we will not think of that now. Landlord! bring in a double crown bowl of punch, and let us drink to the hero of the night, the champion of love and beauty. You must all pledge me in this toast, gentlemen."

"To be sure we will," said Mr. Hind.

"We'll drink, and we'll never have done, boys!"

He soon produced a foaming bowl; bumpers were filled all round; and Jonathan proposed the health of their staunch colleague, Jack Sheppard, which, it is needless to say, was drunk with loud acclamations. Mr. Blueskin was affected even to tears at the proof Jack had given of his gallantry and courage, and hiccupped out something about his having been the first to discover his friend's great genius. Jack returned thanks in an appropriate speech. The health of pretty

Bess was then drunk — Mr. Hind singing the beautiful song of—

"Oh! happy happy fair,
  Thine eyes are lode-stars, and thy breath sweet air."

Other toasts followed in rapid succession, till one of the watchmen of St. Clement's was heard proclaiming the hour of midnight.

"Hark! the lark at heaven's gate sings,"

sang Mr. Hind.

"The bowl is out, and it is time we should break up, gentlemen," said Jonathan. "There is much business to be done to-morrow. No doubt numerous applications will be made at my office for the recovery of the stolen plate. We must be on the alert. The girl having so fortunately effected her escape, thanks to the bravery and genius of our young friend, Sheppard, there is no clue to the authors of the abstraction; so we may expect to make a pretty market. Let all betake themselves in peace to their retreats. Good night, good night! Come, Abraham."

"Ay, ay," said Mr. Hind, "good night:" and observing two or three of the company in a very blissful state of intoxication, he sung part of the witches' chorus in Macbeth, which he waggishly altered for the occasion, and which ran thus : —

"We fly by night with *lots of spirits*."

A general leave-taking here ensued; the party retired to their several abiding places—the major part to dream over fresh schemes of plunder, while Jack stole to his garret, to enjoy once more in sleep the vision of the enchanting milkmaid.

The news of Bess's escape from the round-house was early spread abroad the following day, and excited much surprise and chagrin. Suspicion had fallen on her, in consequence of her having been seen in frequent communication with the villains who had afterwards so severely beaten Mr. David Lloyd, and carried off the plate; and it was ascertained, on inquiry, that the written recommendation of a lady at Norwood, upon the faith of which she had been engaged in the milkman's service, was a false one, no such lady being known at Norwood, or any of the adjacent villages. Fortunately for Jack, Mr. Hannibal Guffin's regard for his own character as a man of valour and discretion did not permit him to give a very correct version of his prisoner's escape; consequently detection was out of the question. The beadle affirming that Bess had been rescued by two or three powerful men armed with bludgeons, with whom he had held a fearful combat of nearly half an hour, much to their damage, before he sank under the force of numbers, he was handsomely rewarded by the parish board for his courage and sufferings; and there being thus no trace, the affair of the escape speedily died away.

As Jonathan foretold, applications were immediately made at his office for the recovery of the stolen property. Mr. Wood, Mrs. Partington, and David Lloyd, the poor milkman, all met there at one time; and a very ludicrous scene of lamentation and reproach was the consequence. The poor milkman, whose cows had been impounded by the pawnbroker, to whom he had given bond to secure the value of the plate that had been borrowed from him, and who had been threatened with what he called actions "*of clover*," from the different customers who had lent their property to him, particularly his countryman Mr. Wood, and Mrs. Partington, was very nigh having the coat torn off his back by the latter amiable persons.   Jonathan, however, interfered with his usual philanthropy, and, on the promise of adequate rewards being paid, assured them he had but little doubt of tracing the horrid villains who had perpetrated the robbery; that Mrs. Wood should have her civic tea-pot and spoons returned; that the pawnbroker's property should be redeemed, though he did not exactly pledge himself to this; and that Mr. Kneebone's plate should be restored, without a leg having been removed from his escutcheon. This latter assurance particularly gratified Mrs.

Partington, though she observed she knew very well it would be the case; for a gipsy man in her neighbourhood, whom she had accidentally met coming out of the " Black Lion," had assured her, on consulting him, that if she applied at the respectable office of Mr. Jonathan Wild, in the Old Bailey, she would be certain, through his means, of having the property restored to her; that the gipsies never told wrong.

Weeks passed away — the property was of course regained on being paid for; but from the moment that Jack saw the beautiful Bess, his value as a good and industrious apprentice was gone: he could think of nothing, pin himself down to nothing in the way of business — his mind was wholly absorbed with her image. Mr. Wood's irritability was roused by Jack's negligence, and frequent quarrels were the consequence, from which he invariably retired for refuge to the back parlour of the hospitable and harmonious Mr. Hind. Blueskin was not long in obtaining the secret of Jack's heart, and readily promised his good offices to find out, if possible, where the beautiful milkmaid had been conveyed to after her escape with Jack. He was as good as his word. Not long after Jack had disclosed his love, this true friend one day sought him with a look of unusual exultation.

A A

" Tip us your daddle, my covey," said he;
" it's all as right as a trivet; I've found her
out."

" Who — who ?" eagerly asked Jack.

" Why the pretty bit of goods who helped us
to speak to the garland last May-day."

" Ah !" exclaimed Jack, transported, " the
beauteous creature I rescued from the roundhouse ?"

" Herself, my Trojan," returned Mr. Blueskin; " and, what's more, all ready to jump into
your arms; I can tell you that."

" Delightful, delightful !" cried Jack, in ec-
stacy. " Blueskin, you are a trump! But where
is the charmer ?"

" Ah, where is she," slily echoed Blueskin;
" that's the secret,"—and here he winked very
significantly, — " and a secret worth knowing,
too."

" Do not trifle with an old pal, I conjure
you !" earnestly exclaimed Jack. " For heaven's
sake, if you really do know where she is to be
found disclose it instantly. I have never known
a moment's rest since I saw her — she has been
my dream by night, my thought by day."

" And now she may be your dozey by night
and your dell by day, if you only play your cards
rightly," said Blueskin. " Listen to me;—but you
must stand a dram for my giving you the office."

" Any thing, even to my soul's salvation ! — only tell me !" exclaimed Jack, in an impassioned manner.

" Well, well," said Blueskin, apparently moved by his earnestness, " not to keep you in suspense, then, I happened to have a little business with one of our gentlemen to speak to a ken [1] at Norwood the other day. It was a put up affair [2] ; and it being rather necessary we should go cautiously to work, as the old cove of the castle was known to keep barking irons all ready fed [3] in his snooze [4], and did not want for pluck to give them tongue [5] whenever there should be occasion for it, we were obliged to lie snug in the neighbourhood till the Johnny Raw [6], who was our pal, and was to go regulars [7], nosed [8] to us when the coast was clear. So, by way of passing the time in a gentlemanly manner, we thought we'd amuse ourselves with a little shooting in some of the preserves round the neighbourhood, bag a few short ones [9], and wire a long one [10] for a friend in Romeville. [11] So, rambling about the

---

[1] Break open a house.
[2] A planned robbery in which the servants are concerned.
[3] Loaded pistols.
[4] Bedroom.
[5] Fire them.
[6] Footman.
[7] Share in the booty.
[8] Gave information.
[9] Partridges.
[10] Snare a hare.
[11] London.

woods, who the old one should we fall in with but Black Martin's gang of Romoners."

" Romoners!" cried Jack, not as yet wholly understanding Mr. Blueskin's mystic Cabala; " and who the plague are they ?"

" What! don't you know ? well you are an innocent! Why gipsies, to be sure—the palming tribe.   Being " the season of the year," there they were, all of them, Ben Morts[1], and Ubram men[2], mixed together under the bushes as gay as larks, and as merry as sand boys.   Of course it was all Oli Compoli[3], with lads of the right stamp like us.   The Dimber Dambers[4] were as pleased as so many trouts to see us, and invited us to a boozing bout, when Oliver whiddled[5], in their leaf palace down in the three-tree dingle.   You may be sure we did not fail to join company,—we'd too good a taste for the stock pot; we knew too well what Pharaoh's lean kine was, to do that.   When, never trust me, among the Autem Morts[6], and Dimber Dells[7], who should we clap our ogles on, the very first thing, but your pretty milkmaid. Yes, there she was, all amongst the tawny ones, looking for all the world like a lily among so

[1] Fine girls,
[2] Impostors.
[3] All right.
[4] Pretty fellows.

[5] Moonlight.
[6] Married women
[7] Pretty girls.

many marigolds, and, what's more, there she is still."

Jack was overjoyed at this information; he expended his last farthing in a bowl of punch on the strength of it; and asked a thousand questions respecting his charmer—who she was, what she did there, how she had become mixed up with the robbery, when he could see her, &c.; to all which Mr. Blueskin answered with becoming frankness and friendship: from which Jack gathered, that she was an orphan, under the protection of Zara, the queen of the gipsies, and was known among the gang by the name of Edgworth Bess, from her having been born in Edgworth; that during the temporary absence of the queen, Black Martin, the generalissimo of the tribe, and potentate, in default of Zara, had, at the instigation of Jonathan Wild, procured her an engagement in the service of David Lloyd, the milkman, and had given her instructions by which she was unconsciously made the instrument of the robbery of that unfortunate Cambrian's May-day garland, her participation in which had thrown her into the confinement from whence Jack had rescued her. In answer to Jack's further interrogatories, as to when he could visit her, Blueskin pacified his impatience with the intelligence that they could never have a more favourable chance than presented itself at that very juncture; that the old queen, Zara, was then again absent, on some state business of her people, and that Black Martin would receive him with open arms.

"I care not for Black Martin," laughed Jack, "but pretty Bess. It is too late to set off for Norwood to night, but I will procure leave of absence from old Wood; or if he won't grant it me, take French leave, and start with you the first thing to-morrow morning."

"I am yours, to the back bone," said Mr. Blueskin. "To-morrow morning!—be it." Bess will be delighted to see you."

"I will die rather than fail," said Jack; and with this understanding, after draining the bowl, they parted company.

CHAPTER THE TWELFTH.

JACK SHEPPARD A HOUSEBREAKER.

LOVE AND DESPERATION.— THE GIPSY ENCAMPMENT.— ROBBERY OF MR. BAINS.

LONG before it was light the following morning —for he could not sleep, thinking of his charmer —Jack was up; and having procured a day's holiday from Mr. Wood, under pretence that he wanted to visit his mother, who was dangerously ill, and had sent for him, he repaired to the residence of Mr. Blueskin, which was, at that time, in the sanctuary of the Old Mint in the Borough, that gentleman honouring a back garret in the Maze with his particular sojourn, in company with another gentleman known by the name of Tom Trick Tyburn, from the dexterity with which he had, at various times, escaped conviction for capital offences. Routing out his friend, and procuring a morning dram at the flash house of the master of the Mint, they started for Norwood. It was a lovely summer's morning. Emerging from the murky recesses of the Mint, at that time the usual retreat of profligate debtors, suspected felons, and bad characters of every description, they were soon on the high road to their place of destination.

Jack's heart was unusually buoyant at the thoughts of so soon meeting the beautiful object of his affections: he laughed, sung, jumped, and committed a thousand extravagances. Blueskin, who was more phlegmatic, proceeded with greater prudence, cautiously peeped in at the doors of the different cottages as he passed along, having determined, if he found any of them without their tenants, to make them pay for their negligence by the abstraction of any little article that might present itself.

" There's nothing like reading them a practical lesson," said he : " words go for nothing ; but the loss of their property they never forget."

This was a maxim he had learnt from the judicious Mr. Wild.   They made their way across Kennington Common, and passed the gibbets where, to mark the civilisation of the country at that period, were suspended in irons the mouldering carcasses of two notorious footpads and murderers, who had been executed there some years previous, and whom they did not either of them affect to notice, till they came to the somewhat straggling village of Brixton, celebrated in our own time for the virtue of its mill, by which many disorders are often corrected, and old offenders comparatively ground young again. It had, then, no such blessing. Refreshing themselves with a cool tankard at a pleasant road-side alehouse, the only one Brixton then possessed, they pushed forward to the beautiful resort of Tulse Hill. Passing under the refreshing shade of its umbrageous trees, and catching glimpses as they went of two or three of those snug, comfortable looking boxes to which our wealthy citizens retire, that they may enjoy the fruits of their early industry in the pleasing leisure of age, and which seemed, as Blueskin emphatically remarked, only built on purpose to be *cracked* *, they reached at length the object of their wishes; the verdant vales, the bosky dingles, and gently rising slopes of Norwood unveiled themselves before them — we need not say to our hero's high content and gratification.

" Well, here we are at last, my Romeo," said Mr. Blueskin. " This is the favourite retreat of the sibyls; this is the spot to learn your fortunes in, and have the stars and planets read for you — the Fates can't keep any secrets here."

Jack was well aware the secret of his destiny would be here unravelled.

" But let us look out for the gipsy's standard," continued Mr. Blueskin. " Ah! there it is waving in the air, above that clump of trees, there; I twig it."

" I see no flag," impatiently returned Jack.

* Broken open.

B B

" Where are your ogles, then ?" retorted
Blueskin. " Don't you see that thin spiral column
of blue smoke, that's losing itself in the sky
there ? That's the gipsies' flag, my boy ; and
see, here's one of their advanced outposts,"—
pointing to a wiry-looking long-faced cur, with a
peculiar significance of countenance, that was
approaching towards them, his eye glistening
with satisfaction as he sniffed Blueskin, while
his tail was fastly wagging behind him in token
of amity. " We shall not be long now before we
stumble on a sentinel who will conduct us to the
camp," said he, returning the dog's caress with a
friendly pat. " Good boy, Fox, good boy ! It's all
right — he's a friend :" seeing the animal sniffing
Jack.   " On with you, Fox — he'll lead us into
the right path, Jack, never fear that ; but we are
not on a wrong scent, if I may trust my nose —
what a savoury odour ! almost makes one hungry
only smelling it.   Ah ! there's nothing like the
flesh pots of Egypt, my boy ; I am quite longing
for a glass of Usquebaugh, and a dive into the
general kettle : sure to bring up the thigh of a
partridge, the back of a hare, or the leg of some
barn-door rooster."

Jack's love had quite taken away his appetite,
and he did not enjoy in perspective the promised
delicacies so greatly as his companion.

The dog now bounded quickly before them,

barking, and tossing his head in the air, with unusual liveliness and vigour; and presently afterwards the hum of many voices was heard, and a man suddenly appeared at an opening in the thicket before them, as if to challenge their approach.

"Ah, by the Hookey, here's Black Martin himself," shouted Blueskin. "Welcome, Duke, welcome! His grace is duke of Lesser Egypt, Jack," said he in a side wind to our hero, "and a rum duke he is, too. I've brought a friend to visit you — one of the right sort — as jannock as steel."

"Welcome, young Sir," gruffly muttered out Black Martin, a tall bony man, of swarthy aspect, with matted black hair, and garments of very uncouth, but not unpicturesque, appearance. "You're welcome to Three-tree Dingle. Being a friend of Mr. Blueskin, you cannot but be a good one. — This way, this way."

Jack's heart throbbed quickly as they entered into the *sanctum sanctorum* of the tribe. His eye glanced with the rapidity of lightning over the motley crew that then presented themselves, and as quickly rested its gaze, with fixed intensity, on the lovely features of his inamorato. Yes, there she stood, looking in her little straw hat, her gay 'kerchief, neat stuff petticoat, and smart red cloak, if possible, still more bewitching than when tricked out, as he had last seen her, in all her May-day finery.

"Ah!" said she, recognising him in an instant, and blushing deeply as she encountered his enamoured gaze, "my preserver! my deliverer! Welcome, welcome!"

"What!" cried Martin, "is this the Ben Kinchin cove that delivered Bess from the Philistines, broke open her prison, let her out of limbo?—Why didn't you tell me this before, Blueskin? He shall have Freeman's key here, at all events." Encouraged by the gipsy chief's approbation of Jack's visit, Bess had by this time ventured to advance towards him, and cordially offered her hand: Jack covered it with a shower of kisses. Her example was followed by almost all the members of the swarthy race: men, women, and children, all greeted Jack with much warmth; and many a sparkling black eye, and clear brown cheek, beneath which the rich blood mantled, till it assumed the ripe blush of some mellow pear, slily smiled approbation on him for his gallantry and manhood in rescuing their companion. The chief declared that in honour of Jack's visit the day should be a holiday; and some patient donkeys that were browsing under the boughs, waiting to set forth on their usual foraging excursions, were immediately unpanniered—the fire under a huge kettle that was mystically suspended from three sticks in the centre of the hollow, or dingle, as it was termed, was replenished, a cloth of snowy whiteness was spread on the grass by Bess, cups of horn, some pewter platters, with knives and forks, and spoons, the latter of silver — probably the produce of plunder — were arranged in due order. Jack was invited to take a seat — which was assigned to him, out of compliment to his heroism — by the side of the fair creature he had rescued. It need hardly be said that he did not want to be asked twice to take it. Some flasks of Usquebaugh and a keg of humming ale were produced from a leathern budget, together with some brown bread; and the kettle, from which issued a rich steam of all savoury odours — capons, partridges, pheasants, hares, rabbits, celery, onions, thyme, sweet marjoram, and a few lumps of salted pork — was unhooked from its supporters, and separately borne round to all present, that each might help themselves to as much as they chose of its contents. Bess, whose experience in angling in this palatable caldron was greater, and her dexterity more perfect than could be expected of her companion, had soon supplied his plate with a delicious knuckle of ham, the breast of a pheasant, and the wings of a fine capon, with a proportionate quantity of the rich soup and its vegetable ingredients. But half her care was thrown away ; Jack could eat but little : he was too much occupied in feasting his eyes on her ever-varying beauties, and pouring into her ear, in rude but fervent terms, his admiration — his delight.   Perceiving how much they were occupied with each other, the chief forbore to task Jack's attention ; and the rest of the tribe, in conformity with their general rule never to spoil sport, turned their notice from the lovers — for such they had both by unconscious consent become, — and directed their cares to the Usquebaugh and ale, and some nuts and apples, which served to finish their repast.   A variety of gipsy songs, in praise of poaching, fortune-telling, and similar subjects, then went round, during which Jack found abundant opportunity to declare his passion for his beautiful companion, and receive her blushing avowal in return that he was not indifferent to her.   The afternoon advancing, an old fellow with a white beard, who had said grace at their banquet, and who, it appeared, was the PATRICO, or priest, of the beggar part of the tribe, produced from a bag a cracked fiddle. A general shout of " A dance ! a dance !" arose, the panniers were stowed away, the sward was cleared, the inspiring tones of *Money-musk* were struck up, and every toe was immediately in action.

Jack had, of course, for his partner his charming companion, Bess; and Mr. Blueskin was honoured with the brown hand of Mrs. Mary Maggot, an Amazonian Autem Mort of the tribe. Bess's grace and fascination in dancing has been before noticed; but on this occasion she outshone herself. As he whirled the lovely fair over the sward, Jack's brain grew giddy with rapture, and he felt a corresponding gloom steal over his mind when the advancing shades of night warned him it was time to bend his steps back again to town. He had enjoyed one perfect day of happiness — but happiness has more limited bounds than misery. There are infinite varieties of wretchedness and modes of sorrow; the pleasurable sensations are but few — love, fame, friendship, competence, parental affection, and religious contentment, make up the sum of worldly enjoyment. Jack had tasted transport and rapture, the fulfilment of hope, the nourishment of desire. He turned to bid farewell to his companions — his regret in doing so tempered by the remembrance of the pleasure he had experienced. The tribe accompanied him and Blueskin to the limits of the thicket in which their retreat was situated, Black Martin expressing his earnest wish that they might speedily see Jack again; and pretty Bess, as she tenderly pressed his hand, bedewing it with a tear, and, with a half-choked voice, affectionately bidding him farewell.

On their way to town, Blueskin fed Jack's fancy by repeated eulogiums on the beauty of Bess, adroitly drawing a picture of the happiness that might be enjoyed with so rare a creature, by any young fellow of spirit, who had the means and leisure to devote himself to her society: he then contrasted this by speculating upon the little chance there was of any one, in the station of a mechanic, arriving at such a blessing. His words, which were apparently uttered without intention, made a deep impression on Jack's mind, and he fell into a fit of profound abstraction. When they at length arrived in Wych Street, he declined visiting Mr. Hind's house that night, and immediately retired to rest, telling Mr. Wood, as he bade him good night, that he had found his mother better. He rose the next morning not much refreshed: his sleep had been thoughtful and troubled; and his dreams, if the truth must be told, though chiefly occupied with the angel semblance of the lovely milkmaid, were fraught, at least, with as much of bad as good.

The employment of his trade became henceforward more irksome to him than ever. It has been said that idleness is the nurse of love: it certainly is as much the offspring as the nurse. Jack's passion rendered him indolent and inattentive; he thought of nothing but the beautiful

Bess; and delighted to bask away the hours in alehouses, skittle-grounds, and similar retreats, musing on her image. Mr. Wood, who, not to speak it profanely, was like a great many of his countrymen, rather wooden-headed, and knew little of his craft beyond common jobbing, had long felt and acknowledged the superiority of his apprentice, confiding to his skill and vigour all work requiring any degree of dexterity and enterprise, and rewarding him with a liberal commission on the profits of his labours for his pains.

It was with no small degree of vexation and anger Mr. Wood all at once found his main prop failing him: complaints of negligence and carelessness became the order of the day; customers grew impatient and indignant; and business threatened to leave the honest Cambrian quite as quickly as it had, through Jack's exertions, increased. Frequent visits to Norwood left jobs unfinished and calls unanswered. For some time Jack accounted for the frequency of his absence, by saying it was necessary, in order to acquire a perfect knowledge of some of the finishing branches of the art, that he should work with experienced artisans, and that therefore he undertook various jobs in the country gratuitously, in order that he might get an insight into things. This did very well for some time.

" Put, passions of hur heart, Jack," one day

exclaimed honest Owen, " you neet not pe apsent all night; you cannot pe at work in your
sleep, though, Got's poty, you too often sleep
over your work. This must pe amentet, look
you. Hur is afrait it is some very improper
joinery you are apout when you are apsent.
Charity pegins at home, Jack; you shoult attent
to hur customers first; as to learning the craft,
Got pless hur, hur is afrait you know too much
of the craft, Jack. Hur will have hur work tone,
look you, or hur will know the reason why."

Jack took little heed of these remonstrances;
he had become a favourite guest with the gipsies,
and Bess's passion soon grew as ardent as his
own. This lovely creature was a singular instance
of unconscious purity existing in the very circle
of contagion; from her very infancy she had
been used to the details of acts of plunder and
deception, till she accounted them as matters of
course, as things of general practice, and listened
to them without either reprobation or surprise.
But though she passed over them so lightly in
others, there was a certain consciousness of right
and wrong within herself, that would have led her
to shrink from the slightest action contrary to the
strictest morality, — she was a gem, where all
around was dark and worthless—a well of hidden
waters in a desert, where all was blight and bar-
renness. As foul things shun the light, it seemed

as if vice and contagion, though moving continu-
ally around her, recoiled from her contact, and
left her pure and undefiled. In her communion,
the hours passed with Jack as moments; their
young love, as yet unstained, untroubled, was a
dream of golden sunshine; but the clouds were
gathering around them—the storm was lowering
in the distance.

On his return from one of these sweet, but
furtive, visits, he was summoned by Mr. Wood to
accompany him to Ball's Pond, in the neighbourhood of Islington, to execute some repairs in the
house of a customer, whose patience had been
nearly exhausted by Jack's repeated procrasti-
nation, and who came now peremptorily to de-
mand completion of his work, threatening, that
if any further delay took place, he should immediately employ some other person.

Mr. Wood was in a very ill-humour, which he
oddly enough manifested by a variety of guttural
sounds, which he persuaded himself was singing.
He growled out, in Welsh, a pennill in favour
of St. David's virtues, which he intermixed with
execrations on Jack's bad conduct. Jack's conscience smote him, and, gathering his tools together, he determined to make up, by extra
diligence, for his past misbehaviour. Repairing,
with his master and Griffith Thomas, to Ball's
Pond, he set to work in such good earnest, that,

long ere the afternoon was over, to the great
astonishment of the owner of the house, the
whole of the repairs, which would have occupied
an ordinary workman at least three days, were
completed in the most masterly and finished
manner. This should have been sufficient to
have restored harmony — but we have said that
Mr. Wood was in an ill-humour. By a strange
perversity of human nature, that which should
have destroyed his anger, only increased it. The
exhibition of what Jack could do, did but make
Mr. Wood the more angry that he had delayed
doing it so long, and did not even do more. He
retired, very grumpily, to a public house in Islington, kept by one Britt, and known by the
name of the Rising Sun; here, as they were all
in need of refreshment, he ordered Jack and
Griffith Thomas a pint of small drink, and a
halfpenny loaf each; while he solaced himself
with a quart of the strongest ale, accompanied
by some sea biscuits, which the landlord produced as a rarity, with a very respectable piece
of cheese and a good sized bunch of leeks.

Jack by no means relished the lenten entertainment that had been assigned to him; he,
however, said nothing, thinking that his master
would recover his good-humour in time. As for
the dolt Griffith Thomas, he would have been
satisfied if the small drink had only been water.

Dipping the head of a leek in some salt, and accompanying it with a large lump of cheese, Mr. Wood now commenced his meal, washing every mouthful down with a copious draught of ale, singing meanwhile, as if to cover his ill humour, the favourite pennill of the leek, which he did to the harmonious air known by the name of " Difyrwch-y-Frenhines," or " The Queen's Fancy," which ran thus : —

The Leek.

1.

" Of all that springs from mother earth,
    Commend me to the Leek:
  Nature gives nought more precious birth,
    Its praise Bards well may speak;
  In fruit, and flower, for rarer worth,
    Mankind will vainly seek.

2.

" Let England for her Red Rose shout,
    Scots o'er their Thistle grin,
  Ireland her Shamrock boast about,
    The Leek the prize will win;
  For 't is an ornament without,
    And *very good* WITHIN."

Mr. Wood suited the action to the word, by immediately engulphing one of his favourite leeks, which he did with an air of determination sufficiently marking his stifled choler. Finding nothing was to be got by silence, Jack plucked up resolution, and reminding Mr. Wood that he had had a hard day's work, and that the refreshment provided for him was not of a nature greatly calculated to recruit his exhausted strength, ventured to request that he would, as usual, allow him something, by way of commission for what he had done, that he might procure some better entertainment for himself.

"Got's ploot, you idle tog!" cried the aroused Cambrian, "allow you commission for what you have tone! Will you allow me commission for what you have not tone? look you, tell me tat: you are a goot for nothing fillain, ant go to your ale-houses, your Plack Lions, and other apominations, insteat of toing hur work; put hur will not put up with it." Here he began to sing something in praise of striking the harp, to which he added, in an under tone, something about his intention of striking Jack, if he did not speedily mend his manners.

Jack could hold out no longer, but resolved at once to break all squares with his master. "If I do neglect my business," said Jack, "aint it your fault? you are not able to teach it me: I am sure I work like a horse sometimes."

"Ant like an ass, look you, at other times," cried the enraged Cambrian. "Not teach you your pusiness! Put you are right, or you woult not talk to hur in this way, hur that is a shentleman porn and tescentet from the great Catwalladar himself: if hur hat taught you your pusiness properly, hur shoult have taught you petter manners, look you: put hur will speak to the Champerlain apout it; you shall be privately whipped, and publicly reprimanted for your insolences ant tisrespects."

"I don't care for you, nor the Chamberlain either," growled Jack surlily, "nor old Cadwalladar into the bargain, — some old Put, I dare say, like yourself, never satisfied with any thing."

"What!" screamed Mr. Wood, almost inarticulate with passion, "not care for Catwalladar, — old Put, — hur will make you rememper these plasphemies; look you; only let hur get at you!" Here darting suddenly on Jack, he caught him by the hair.

"Hold off," cried Jack fiercely, "or by the living God you shall repent it!"

"Ah! to you tare to threaten, tog?" roared out the Carpenter, pot-valiant; "take that." Here he aimed a smart cuff at Jack's dexter listener. Disengaging himself from his master's grasp, with

the velocity of lightning, Jack, aroused to a pitch
of fury, returned the blow with a force and good
will, that immediately stretched his opponent over
the chair, on the floor, where his sconce coming
in contact with the ale-can, that had fallen in the
scuffle, he was very near showing more of his
brains than was absolutely necessary to attest
his knowledge.

" Mercy of Got, hur is murteret—hur is murteret !" cried the prostrate Welchman: "put let
the villain pe securet ; hur will have him hanget
ant quarteret: striking a master is petty treason,
mark tat: hur will have his heat on Temple Par.
—Knock the scountrel town, Griffith Thomas,—
ton't let the villain escape.—Murter ! murter !"

Doubtful of the extent of the mischief he had
occasioned, Jack here thought it prudent to de-
camp: accordingly, jumping out of the window,—
(they were in the back parlour),— he made his
way across the skittle-ground, and over a ditch in
the rear of the premises, which conducted him to
some fields ; and very soon arrived, unpursued, in
London.　His first step was to see how the land
lay in the house of his master.　It may easily be
conceived, he was in no very amiable mood of
mind.　The first person he met with was Madam
Wood, who received him with a volley of matronly reproaches.　She had learnt from Taffleen,
that a young female had been that morning in-

quiring after Jack, and demanded how he dared
have any creatures come after him in a decent
respectable house like hers.

" By your indentures, sir," said she, " you are
bound to attend to no other female than your
mistress, who, being at years of discretion, and of
a proper age, knows how to treat young fellows
properly."

Jack muttered something, that she might be
the reverse of blessed, and proceeded to the
carpenter's yard at the side of the house, when
his passions were instantly aroused by the sudden
appearance of Bess.

" Oh! Jack, Jack!" she exclaimed, rushing
towards him, " save me! save me!"

" Explain yourself, dear girl," hastily cried
Jack; " what means this alarm?"

" They will tear me from you, dear Jack!"
answered the maiden. " Our queen has sent a
suitor."

" Ah! the hag Zara?" rejoined Jack, fiercely.

" Yes, my adopted mother; she would have
me wedded, Jack — wedded to another — a hateful man who follows, who pursues me. —Ah! he
is here!" she shrieked, suddenly seeing some
one. — " Save me! save me!" She threw herself
into Jack's arms.

Turning his eyes in the direction to which she

D D

had pointed, Jack now saw a young fellow in the undress of a foot soldier entering.

" So, I have you, Bess!" exclaimed he, exultingly ; " you won't escape me this time."

He was advancing towards the poor girl, when Jack, stung by rage and jealousy, having no other means of stopping him, restrained as he was by his fair burthen, hurled a small lath, which happened to be in his hand, at the intruder with all his force. Unfortunately, the soldier adroitly ducking down, the missile took effect on the portly person of Madam Wood, who was at that moment entering to see what was the matter, and grazing her left cheek in its passage gave occasion for the application of a beauty spot of rather more unseemly dimensions than those she usually wore. She hastily screamed out murder, at the very top of her voice, till the entrance of Taffleen allowed of her fainting in that maiden's arms, in a safe and dignified manner. Bess had extricated herself from Jack's embrace on the first alarm, and, with the swiftness of the affrighted dove, had made good her escape, while her lover and his rival were most affectionately engaged in ascertaining the exact diameter of each other's wind-pipes. It was not until there was some doubt which was the blackest, the face or the hat of the intruding soldier, that Jack unlocked his loving grasp, and suffered him to beat

a retreat; an example which he himself immediately followed, leaving Taffleen busily engaged
in singeing Madam Wood's nose with sundry fu-
migations of burnt feathers, brown paper, &c.

Unable to obtain any trace of the route of his
fair enslaver, Jack bent his steps in search of his
staunch friend and counsellor, Blueskin, and fortunately found him taking his siesta in Mr. Hind's
back parlour. From Blueskin, Jack obtained
confirmation of pretty Bess's tidings, that a suitor
had been sent by Zara, in the person of the
soldier, with a mandate to Black Martin, that he
should he received as her future husband: the
arrival of her Majesty herself to witness the con-
summation of the nuptials was daily expected.

" Things are all as queer as Dick's hatband,
Jack," continued Blueskin, "and, strike me funny,
if the wench won't slip through your fingers,
if you don't mind. You have only one chance,
and that is, to try the effect of a little oil of palm*
with the gang — make the girl your own at once:
fifteen or twenty quids† now might do the trick;
but where's that to be got?—I haven't a mag." ‡

Jack's brain was all on fire, his senses in a
whirl.

" Say no more," said he; " something shall be
done; but where is Bess?—Where can she have
fled to?"

* Bribery.   † Guineas.   ‡ Halfpenny.

"Oh! she's safe enough, never fear that. Poll Maggot was waiting for her, and she'll take care of her — she's a match for half a dozen such swaddies* as that rival of yours — no doubt they have returned to the camp."

"No doubt, no doubt!" said Jack, wildly; "will you promise me one thing, Blueskin?"

"What is it?" asked that worthy.

"That you will be ready to start with me to Norwood by day-break to-morrow morning."

"Why, what then have you resolved upon?" said Blueskin, with an air of affected carelessness."

"Ask me not, I know not!" answered Jack, desperately, "only say that you will meet me."

"I will — in the Mint," coolly replied Blueskin.

"Enough, enough!" said Jack, gratefully squeezing his hand. "Bess shall be mine to-morrow, if I swing for it the day afterwards."

With these words Jack rushed out of the room.

"Wheugh! Tol lol de diddle doll!" sung Blueskin.

"Buz quoth the blue fly, hum quoth the bee,"

sung Mr. Hind, entering at the moment; if that young fellow don't show his indentures a fair pair of heels, before he's four and twenty hours

* Footsoldiers.

older, I'm no conjuror." The gentlemen emptied a jug, on the strength of the prophecy, and parted.

Unable to resolve on any settled course, Jack wandered about, till he found himself in White Horse Yard, in Drury Lane, a narrow turning, secluded enough from observation, and chiefly occupied, as it is to this day, by piece-brokers, persons who deal in remnants of cloth, stuff, &c. Here it occurred to him, that he had a job to finish in the house of Mr. Baines, one of this fraternity; and without any precise intention he entered that gentleman's shop, and proceeded to accomplish his task : among other things he had to repair the shutters of the shop: whilst engaged in this employment, seeing the quantity of rolls of fustian, and other property that was scattered about the shop, and perceiving, on Mr. Baines casually unlocking the till, that it contained a quantity of money, the thought all at once flashed across him, that here would be an easy opportunity of effecting all his wishes. His resolution was instantly taken : minutely inspecting the premises, he soon saw in what way an entrance was best to be obtained; all the bars and fastenings of Mr. Baines's shop he purposely made more secure than ever, to that gentleman's great satisfaction.

" I 'll defy any scoundrel to break into my shop now," said that gentleman, " thanks to your skill and pains, my honest lad; there's a shilling for you to drink."

Jack's plan was laid.   Leaving the piece-broker, he loitered about the neighbourhood till twelve o'clock at night: during his rambles, he unnoticed heard some of the neighbours talking of the desperate attempt he had made to murder his master and mistress; he had the satisfaction, however, of finding that Mr. Wood had walked home, and retired to rest, and that Mrs. Wood had required nothing more from the doctor than a large piece of sticking-plaster and an extra bottle of sal volatile.

It was the night of the first of August, 1716!— As some other author has said before us,—we like to be particular in dates.   The hundreds of Drury were more than ordinarily peaceable, and notwithstanding the stars shone brightly, and there was a new moon, the narrowness of White Horse Yard, in which the shop was situated, kept the houses in partial gloom. Following the watchman to his box, and waiting till that functionary had comfortably composed himself to sleep in his nightcap, Jack stole to the scene of action : he knew that he should be uninterrupted for half an hour at least ; the coast was clear, all was dark and still. In the pavement, in front of Mr. Baines's shop, was a grating of wooden rails, forming a sort of area, which conducted to a cellar underneath the shop, from whence access could be obtained to any other part of the house. Jack's heart beat quickly as he surveyed it, and, stooping down, he was about to commence operations, when, just at that moment, the well-known chimes of St. Clement's announced the half hour after midnight, by ringing forth the solemn and beautiful melody of the Hundred and forty-ninth psalm, "Oh, praise ye the Lord!" As the sounds, borne on the night breeze, caught his ear, Jack started, and paused for a few moments, irresolute; he remembered the words of part of that psalm: —

> " With glory adorn'd,
> His people shall sing
> To God, who their beds
> With safety does shield."

He was about to abandon his sinful purpose when the chimes died away in the listening silence. — The thoughts of losing his pretty Bess, and the prospect of securing her for ever, flashed across his mind; his guardian Angel deserted him, and he resumed his intentions. With a chisel, the handle of which he muffled, and a muffled mallet, he proceeded softly and cautiously to loosen the wooden bars: he dexterously drew out the nails, and, as he was remarkably strong in the wrist, and skilful in the precise application of his tools, he had in ten minutes, witnout any disturbance, removed the bars, and obtained entrance into the house. Cautiously making his way up the cellar stairs, he found the back door of the shop locked: to shoot back the bolt, with one so skilful as himself, was but the work of a moment. A small skeleton key, a keepsake from Mr. Blueskin, on which he set great store, effected this last operation without noise or violence. Producing a light from a phosphorus box, he now proceeded to take stock of the shop. In the till, the lock of which soon yielded to his ingenuity, he found about seventeen pounds in money, which he was not long in conveying to a place of greater security : he then ransacked the stores and selected a variety of the choicest stuffs and best cloths as presents to the gang. Having loaded himself with as much as he could conveniently carry, he began to retrace his steps : shooting the bolts of the locks back again, he made his way through the cellar, leaving every thing in appearance exactly as he had found it. The wooden bars he replaced, and nailed down again in the most workmanlike manner, so that no one could perceive they had been removed ; and long before one o'clock, he by the aid of a latch key had made his way, undiscovered, to his truckle bed in the garret of Mr. Wood. This was Jack Sheppard's first burglary.

CHAPTER THE THIRTEENTH.

JACK A ROMONER.

REBELLION IN THE CAMP.—THE GIPSY MARRIAGE.— THE LION AND LIONESS.

DAY had scarcely begun to dawn, after the commission of the burglary at Mr. Baines's, when Jack arose : he had merely thrown himself across the bed, and was not over refreshed with his short and broken slumber. Dressing himself with unusual care, he proceeded to arrange and pack up his booty: placing a roll of fustian in his box, which he found inconvenient to carry with him, he made a compact parcel of the other articles, which he slung over his shoulders in the form of a knapsack ; then, without having aroused his fellow-apprentice, Griffith Thomas, he stole gently down stairs, and quitted his master's house, as it subsequently turned out, for ever.

It was not without some feeling of hesitation and regret that he closed the door of the house where he had passed the years of his boyhood, though he had formed no intention of not re-turning : an emotion of compunction stole over him ; he remembered Mr. Wood's simple-hearted good-nature and honesty of purpose, more than

E E

counterbalancing his national choler and occasional irascibility—but the die was cast. Endeavouring to persuade himself that he was ashamed of having given way to such weakness, he assumed an air of bravado, and with a more determined step than the occasion seemed to require, swaggered down the Strand, and made the best of his way to the Mint. He found Blueskin up and ready to receive him : their eyes met on his entrance ; a glance passed between them, which explained at once all that had occurred.

" Tip us your bunch of fives, Jack," said Blueskin, exultingly ; " I see it's all right, my trump—the wench shall be yours before the day's out ; I'll carry the swag for you. Well, I always said you'd turn out a good one — I told the governor so long ago, and he was quite of my opinion ;—but what have you got here ?" said he, eagerly undoing the parcel. " Stuffs — cloths !" and here his eyes glistened with the most unctuous expression of gratification. " Why, what dealer in rags, ken, have you been speaking to since I saw you last night ? — but no matter, I don't want to know — it's quite sufficient the trick's done. I suppose these are not the whole of the assets, are they ? You have got some rag of another sort as well, haven't you ? We shan't have to take these to a fence and smash for browns, shall we? There's our old friend, Levy Lawrence, hard by, you know."

"No, no!" said Jack, with a knowing air, "you don't find me such a soft as that; — look here, my boy!" and he produced a capacious leathern purse, which he had fully lined with the piece-broker's floating capital.

"Well, that is rummy!" said Mr. Blueskin, giving, at the same time, an extraordinary skip; —"fork us your famble again, Jack—why, there must be a matter of twenty quid there: — a fig for old Zara—Black Martin will soon give that young lobster, your rival, orders to march—yes, yes, he'll have his furlough in no time, be billetted on another town in a twinkling:—why, hang me if I don't lend him a ticket of leave with my own particular pedestal*; — if you don't make the dimber morts and dells' eyes twinkle to-day, why, there's no corn in Egypt, that's all; — but come along, come along."

Hurrying Jack from the cockloft he honoured with his residence, and spurring themselves on with sundry drams on the road, they reached the gipsy camp before the community had assembled to breakfast. Their early arrival created some surprise, but more pleasure. As Blueskin had prognosticated, Bess had, the evening before, returned to the camp, under the convoy of Poll

* Foot.

Maggot: she had been followed by the young
soldier, who, not expecting their quarters would
have been beat up so soon, did not then happen
to be on guard. Bess flew into Jack's arms ; and
while they were exchanging those endearments,
which can always be better imagined than described, Blueskin requested a private audience
with the gipsy regent, Black Martin.

This illustrious personage having conducted
his friend Indigo, as he familiarly termed Mr.
Blake, to a snug retreat, under cover of some
donkey-carts, a conference was immediately
opened. No sooner had Jack's plenipotentiary
expressed his friend's wishes, and the means he
possessed to pay for their accomplishment, than
Black Martin instantly declared himself a rebel
—damned his sovereign, Zara, for a hard-hearted
old hag, and said, that in five minutes the whole
camp should be in a state of mutiny. He proved
as good as his word.

Assembling the tribe, he briefly explained to
them Jack's views and resources, having previously instructed Blueskin to be prepared with
the subsidies. Jack's parcel was opened, the
cloths and stuffs were distributed, and the gang
at once declared themselves a commonwealth.
Never was a monarchy so easily overturned, or
treason more triumphant: in spite of the ordi-
nances of Queen Zara, it was settled Jack's

marriage should take place that very day. The patrico of the crew was summoned in, and ordered to hold himself in readiness for the solemnities, an order in which that reverend person expressed his perfect acquiescence.

" Fortunately," said he, " one of our forest ponies died last night : there is nothing, therefore, to forbid the banns ; it is a special licence."

A very few moments sufficed to prevail on the blushing Bess to consent to this arrangement : she knew it was her only chance of escape from the hateful union about to be forced on her, and easily yielded to Jack's impassioned solicitations. At this juncture her suitor, the soldier, appearing, without being aware of the mine about to spring up under his feet, Black Martin beckoned him towards him.

" We have just been holding a court-martial, my friend," said that chief ; " finding your presence here contrary to our articles of war, we have resolved that you shall be drummed out of our regiment without military honours : in fact, friend lobster, it is very plain to us you are a spy in our camp ; you have been quartered here by mistake, and must be sent to the right-about as soon as possible."

Before the astonished soldier had time to inquire into the cause of this sudden alteration in the sentiments of the gang, he was seized by

a couple of sturdy gentlemen, following the profession of tinkers, who, turning his coat inside
out, and clapping an old saucepan on his head,
by way of helmet, seated him on a donkey, with
his face towards the tail; and in this state they
conducted him, with much drumming and hallooing, beyond the boundaries of their encampment, warning him that martial law was proclaimed, and that, if he ever presumed to appear
again in their territories, he would have to run
the gauntlet of the whole gang, without any
further notice.   It was in vain the discomfited
soldier threatened these rebellious subjects with
the vengeance of their queen: they boldly declared they had thrown off their allegiance, and
dethroned her in favour of her *protégée* Bess,
to whom they vowed the utmost loyalty and
affection — as long as Jack's money lasted.
Finding all remonstrances perfectly useless, the
defeated son of Mars retired, to convey to her
tawney Majesty the tidings of the insurrection.

Having thus got rid of the enemy, without his
baggage, as Mr. Blueskin facetiously remarked,
the tribe returned to that part of their retreat
which formed their state place of assembly.
It was not the dingle before described, but
a smooth space, carpeted with verdant turf,
and surrounded on all sides with umbrageous
trees and gently rising hills, forming a species of

amphitheatre. A select orchestra had been instituted by some feathered vocalists in a clump
of trees on one side, which overhung a small
pool, or tiny lake, formed by the waters of two
or three rippling brooks which welled down
from the neighbouring hills, and met there, as in
a basin, or reservoir. That most loving bishop,
St. Valentine himself, could not have desired a
more hymeneal morning. The soft and vernal
sward seemed teeming with vegetation ; wild
flowers sprang up at every turn ; the air was that
warm and balmy air which invites while it pre-
disposes to abandonment, producing a pleasing
listlessness peculiarly amatory and favourable to
the saffron-robed deity. It was before the little
sylvan lake we have mentioned, as being backed
by the clump of overspreading trees in which
the forest choristers were accustomed to hold
their concerts, that the morning repast which
was to usher in the day's festivities was spread.
Black Martin had given orders, in consequence
of Jack's largess, that the stores of the tribe
should be thrown open for general use.

"Our granaries and wine-presses shall be
made public," he said, "on this auspicious occasion." A variety of delicacies had therefore
speedily been brought forward for the gipsy
breakfast, consisting of a cold game pie, which
had been baked in a turf oven, some savoury

smoked bacon, hot home-made bread, oaten cakes of peculiar sweetness, done on the ashes, butter and milk, a piece of new cheese, and a jug of clouted cream, abstracted from the dairy of a neighbouring farm-house: to these was added for those who chose it, a keg of cider and a flask of strong spirit, tasting very potently of the peat, and called mountain dew, to take off the rawness of the morning air.

It was by the side of the pellucid waters before-mentioned, which were as cool and refreshing with their gurgling sound to the ear as they were to the eye, that Jack and Bess threw themselves. We cannot as honest chroniclers undertake to state positively whether they indulged in any of the good cheer so liberally provided, or whether, as on a former occasion, their appetites were satisfied with the lighter food of love; in fact, we do not think they scarcely knew themselves, — Jack was so much employed in gazing into the blue depths of Bess's eyes, in which he discovered the faces of certain cherubs, bearing a strong infantine resemblance to himself; and Bess, we believe, was similarly occupied on her part: the birds seemed to enjoy the treat as much as the greater bipeds, and merrily carolled away in every possible variety of note; never was a happier set congregated together. They were only aroused from their morning repast by the very warm intimation of the sun, that the day had arrived at the maturity of noon, and the appearance of the patrico in his pontificals to make preparations for the ensuing nuptial ceremony. This primate of the canting and palming crew was arrayed for the occasion in a long canonical sort of robe, tied round with a wisp of straw by way of girdle; his long white beard had been carefully combed out with the teeth of an old garden rake, and a sort of mitre with asses' ears was on his head. "You have come well, patrico," said Black Martin, as he saw him advancing; "we have dallied too long: it is time, brother Romoners, that we should instal our new ally, Jack, into our ancient and honourable fraternity, by uniting him, according to our rites, with our pretty Bess, in virtue of which he will be entitled to the protection and privileges of our tribe. Let the altar be prepared forthwith : go some one to the next brook down in the valley, and form a rush ring for the bride ; turn the beasts out to pasture on the common; let them freely brouse where they will: we pronounce this a *fête* day for all, and excommunicate work of every description." A loud hurrah followed the delivery of this resolution.

The remains of the breakfast were immediately removed in obedience to Black Martin's injunc-

F F

tions.   The worshipful patrico set about preparing the altar, which was formed by the body
of the dead pony he had alluded to, placed
transversely on the turf, with its head towards
the east; the ceremony of marriage between
members of the canting and palming crew being
always performed over some dead animal — a
horse for preference, which may have given rise
to the common taunt of singing psalms over a
dead horse.   Poll Maggot, and two or three
other brown matrons, volunteered their services
as bridesmaids to Bess; whilst Mr. Blueskin
undertook to wait upon Jack.   In a short time
all was ready for the ceremony, and Jack and
Bess, with their attendants, were led in grand
procession to the upper part of the space, where
the venerable patrico, with his ministering as-
sistants, awaited them.   Jack and Bess, placing
themselves on either side of the dead poney,
with the patrico in the centre, that reverend
person's nose being immediately over the tail of
the defunct animal, the whole of the tribe, with
Black Martin at their head, formed themselves
into a semicircle around them; and the patrico
taking a tattered book in one hand, whilst he
held a glass of what he called "divine spirit"
in the other, proceeded to perform the marriage
rites, the form of which ran as follows : —

Romanee Marriage Ritual.

" Brothers, sisters, who together
 Here, in spite of wind and weather,
 Meet — a ranting roaring crew,—
 That nothing better have to do,
 Having first join'd hands and kiss'd
 To your autem bawler * list."

Here the males and females, with the exception of Jack and Bess, who were restrained by the barrier between them, having mutually saluted each other, the patrico kneeling down, and reverently paying homage at his altar, by pressing his lips to the latter end of the moribund beast that formed it, the whole crew joined hands, and the service continued.

" Why we 've met here, if you 'd know,
 Thus propounds your patrico :—
 Sheppard Jack, and Edgworth Bess,
 Wishing neither, nothing less —
 Denizen of Romeville he,
 She a dell of Romanee, —
 Cannot longer live alone,
 But would be one flesh and bone, —
 Ride one donkey, share one tent,
 Each on fun and frolic bent.
 Sheppard Jack vows he must wive,
 Or incontinently live.

* Parson, or patrico.

F F 2

Edgworth Bess says she must pair,
Or of harming beck * beware.
Both are young and form'd for sport,
Ben cove strong and dimber mort.
The hour is meet, and fit the spot,
   Say subjects then of Romanee,
Shall we make one this twain or not,
   On payment of the autem fee ? "

Here a loud shout of " *Rumrib Noozlem !* "
the gipsy term for "marry them," almost deafened
the air, which was increased to vociferation, as
Blueskin, by Jack's direction, distributed a large
handful of the piece-broker's coin amongst them.
Order was for a few moments totally destroyed
by a general scramble, in which the august
patrico unfortunately got more kicks than half-
pence. The authority of Black Martin, however,
at length restored decorum ; and the patrico,
addressing himself to our hero and Bess more
immediately, went on with the service : —

" Here, as none the bands forbid,
That you may do as Adam did,
Both must nimbly jump across
This dead beast we 'll call a horse ;
And till he starts alive again,
None shall presume to part you twain.
That mystic ceremony done,
You are now for ever one."

* Constable or beadle.

Patrico. "You are now for ever our."

Here Bess and Jack, by desire of their attendants, exchanged sides, by each lightly jumping over the body of the dead animal, over whom, turning round, they joined in a conjugal embrace, to the great gratification of the crew, who hailed their union with loud and prolonged shouts, increased as before by Jack's largess from the piece-broker's till, distributed by his trusty almoner Blueskin. It now only remained, the hymeneal beast evincing no disposition to divorce the happy pair by coming to life again, for the patrico to pronounce the bridal benediction, usual on the marriage of a ben cove and dimber dell, which he immediately did in these words, draining the glass of spirits he held in his hand with much apparent fervour : —

Bridal Benediction.

" By this glass of most pure spirit,
   The which within may you inherit,
   And by this mystic ring of rush,
      I now pronounce the autem tie,
   That you are free of every bush,
      And licensed 'neath one hedge to lie —
   Drink of one can, eat of one meal,
   In consort beg, in union steal,
   And peck and booze with kinchin store
   Your marriage bless till all is o'er."

The patrico threw the glass into the air over his left shoulder for luck, presented the rush ring and shut his book, the altar was removed, and the newly-wedded pair, conducted by their attendants, were led round to receive the congratulations of the whole assembly, among whom Black Martin was foremost. Blueskin nearly emptied Jack's treasury in a last distribution of his coin to the shouting crew, leaving our hero very little wherewith to meet the expences of the conjugal state. The ceremony of installing Jack a member of the tribe, and entitling him to all the privileges of Romanee, followed that of marriage, and was conducted with much state and solemnity. We have not room to particularize it; suffice, Jack received the freedom of the gang, which was impressed on his wrist by an old sybil of their number, with an indelible liquid, in some uncouth characters, which, he was informed, presented to the initiated the name of Pharaoh. The exhibition of this mystic signature was to secure in all cases the utmost assistance from any member of the gang he might chance to meet to whom it might be shown. Whatever was his peril, by that token he would command protection and assistance : thus did Jack become a ROMONER, a great degree in the profession of vagabondism.

It may here be proper to mention that, during

the time the marriage ceremony was performing, a person had suddenly appeared from one of the clumps of trees surrounding the space, who, un-observed by Blueskin, Jack, and Bess, remained for some time a silent spectator of all that passed. The few members of the gang whose attention he attracted seemed awed from all remark by a single look:—he departed as suddenly and mys-teriously as he had appeared. This person was Jonathan Wild.

It was settled that a tent should be raised for the special accommodation of the newly-married couple in a convenient nook of overhanging hazles, where, on a fragrant couch of some new-mown hay, the birds singing their epithalamium in the leafy shades around them, they could forget the cares of the world, and think only of love and rapture. These arrangements made, revelry became the order of the day.

Jack and Bess, with Blueskin as their prime minister, were elected, by acclamations, king and queen of the festivities. While Blueskin went to announce that every one might do as he pleased, the lovers retired from the heat of the sun to commune with each other, beneath a convenient canopy that had been formed by throwing a piece of canvas across the lower branches of a couple of trees. Here they sat on a sort of turf throne — recreation became general. The tribe divided

themselves into little knots : some smoked and
drank ; some played at cards ; others recounted
stories of the former power of their race ; while
others sang songs commemorating the history of
JOHNNY FAW, one of their kings, and his adventures with Earl Casilis's lady, when he " cast
the glamour o'er her."   In this blissful state of
things they were, when the attention of all was
roused by the sudden appearance of Fox, the
long-headed cur before-mentioned, who came
eagerly tearing into the enclosure, barking
with a vehemence betokening something extraordinary.

Black Martin was the first to start up.

" By the damnable waters of the Red Sea,"
said that chief, " this bodes no good : I know
that cur's bark well ; a surprise is at hand — it
may be the harming beck : we must be on our
guard ; — to your cudgels, lads ! "

The whole of the crew were on their feet in
an instant, and eagerly seized their sticks.

" Surely no traps, on account of the speak
last night," muttered Blueskin to Jack, coolly
cocking a pistol which he drew from his bosom.

Jack turned pale at this anticipation of discovery. Poor Bess, greatly alarmed, clung closely
to him. All at once Fox ceased his barking and
crouched down at Black Martin's feet ; and suspense and expectation were put an end to by the

appearance of Zara and the soldier, followed by half a dozen gipsies of peculiar height and ferocity of appearance, armed to the teeth with knife and pistol, as appeared when they threw open their long rough coats. Zara's black eyes flashed fire, the lightning of a dark night, as she indignantly surveyed the astonished group before her.

" What is this I see ? " she cried in a terrible voice ; " has my power then been set at nought— my orders disregarded ? Dog ! " and here before he could be aware of it, she felled Black Martin to the earth, with one blow of her powerful arm, and as suddenly drawing a knife from her girdle, would have plunged it in his heart, had she not been vigorously withheld by Blueskin, who, seeing the peril of the chief, by his sinewy grasp afforded him time to recover his legs. The daring promptness of their queen, and her meditated vengeance on their leader, struck terror to the souls of her rebellious subjects ; they instantly dropped their cudgels, which they had raised in attitudes of defence, and bent low before her, in token of submission and allegiance.

" Ah ! yield ye, rebel recreants ! " she cried, exultingly ; " why, this is well, but you shall not escape : look for our heaviest ban." The gang slunk back abashed. " For you, Black Martin,

traitor that you are, we thrust you out from our
community, remove you from our caste: no more
you are minister and chief—away!" Black
Martin sullenly withdrew, not daring to brave
an increase of anger by further disobedience.
"But for this guilty pair," she continued, pointing to Jack and Bess, who still remained together
closely united—"Yes, I will thwart the Fates in
their despite, mar the prediction, though it be with
blood: better it be by my hand than another's,
—there will be less of agony and shame.   Norman—Bernard! seize that reckless girl!" Two
of the six before-mentioned gipsies stepped forward.   "Gaspard and Luke, remove that ill-
starred fool her paramour, who'd rush upon his
fate."   Her orders were instantly obeyed; Jack
and the affrighted Bess were seized, and torn
from each other's arms.   Blueskin raised his
pistol in defence of his friend, but it was immediately struck from his hand by the soldier;
and he himself was seized by the two remaining
gipsies.   "Now hear my final orders," cried the
queen.   "Lyon," addressing the soldier, "bride-
groom of my adoption, hasten to your affianced,—
this night she shall be yours—remove those bold
intruders, trusty friends—convey them through
the bye-ways from whence they came, whilst we
strike tent, pannier our beasts, and in some distant quarter remove all trace of route and rescue.

—Away, your queen will be your leader!" In spite of Jack's imprecations, Blueskin's struggles. and Bess's heartfelt entreaties, the two former were instantly dragged one way, and the latter, under the direction of Rupert Lyon, for such it appeared was the soldier's name, and the lioness Zara, was dragged another. The encampment was struck, their moveables packed, the beasts caught and panniered, and long before Jack and Blueskin were released from custody by their swarthy guards, in a lonely cross lane near Camberwell, all vestige of the gipsies had effectually disappeared from the neighbourhood of Norwood.

CHAPTER THE FOURTEENTH.

JACK SHEPPARD SETS UP IN BUSINESS.

THE ROBBERY DISCOVERED. — SUBORNING THE EVIDENCE. — A MOTHER'S LOVE.

"DAMN that queen Zara for a cantankerous old hag," growled out Blueskin, on the departure of their escort, after a few moments' silence; "did ever any one come near such an incarnate devil." Jack groaned in bitterness of spirit: he was heartsick with hope deferred; disappointment had struck him to the very core: to lose his lovely prize in the very moment of possession was a thought of desperation; to make the matter worse, Blueskin, with the benevolent intention of condoling in his misfortune, only added to his tortures. "A pretty business we have made of it," said that cerulean gentleman — "lost our blunt and our baggage too."—Jack groaned more deeply.—" I wouldn't so much have minded if it had been only one of them," continued Blueskin, "but body and breeches! oh, damn it!" Jack groaned again. " Curse that Black Martin, for a cowardly hound!" resumed his companion, whiffing a short pipe, which he had managed to light, by means of a phosphorus box, that he always carried about with him. " I 'm almost half sorry now, that I didn't let the witch knife him, as she wanted to do : to think that he should have turned tail after all, and that scurvy gang, when I had given them every dump we had, and such a prime cargo of cloths and stuffs ! " Jack was roused almost to madness.

" Shall we not go back ? " said he violently.

" What would be the good of that ? " coolly asked Blueskin, " we shouldn't find them if we did ; they are all off on the grand hop, long before this time. Didn't you twig what a round-about way those gentlemen who handed us so politely along, brought us, on purpose, to give them time ? — no, no, we must e'en stump it to town, and see how the land lies there. We must let Mr. Wild know what has past — there must be no working under the rose with him ; for though he 's a very civil, pleasant-spoken gentleman, he 'd think no more of getting a fellow scragged, than I would of twisting the throat of a barn-door pecker — by the bye, said he, if there isn't a fine fat speckled hen, grubbing up the worms by the hedge-side there — well reminded, we shall want something for supper." The next minute the poor hen, with its neck tied in a knot, was safely deposited in his coat pocket, leaving a brood of half-fledged young ones to deplore her untimely end.

It was quite dusk when they arrived in town, which Jack was not sorry for, as he wished to learn what had passed in his absence before any one saw him.   Making their way unobserved to the back parlour of Mr. Hind, they learnt from that gentleman, as well as the snatches of song with which he interlarded his information would permit, that Griffith Thomas, who had turned out not to be quite so great a fool as he appeared to be, and had been awake while Jack supposed him sleeping, had seen the roll of fustian in Jack's box, and informed his master of it, who, on hearing of the robbery in the house of his customer, Mr. Baines, had suspected what was really the fact, that his runaway apprentice Jack was concerned in it, and had hastened to Mr. Baines to give him notice, when he found that gentleman busily employed in taking into cus-tody a poor widow woman, who rented his back garret, being convinced, as he said, that no one but some one in the house could have perpetrated the robbery, there being no marks of violence ; besides which there was the damning proof of the widow not having a thing in the world, which, as the piece-broker remarked, was positive evi-dence she had taken the property. Nevertheless, Mr. Baines thought, that in a case of so much loss, there was nothing like having two strings to his bow; so he got the widow locked up, and had issued out a warrant for the apprehension of Jack. A council of war was immediately held on this intelligence; and it was settled, by the advice of Mr. Hind, that, as there was only the roll of fustian to bring against Jack, he should, in the middle of the night, enter Mr. Wood's house, making his way from the roof of the Black Lion, over the tiles, to the garret of the carpenter—get in at the window and bring away, if it could be found, the unfortunate fustian that had thus become a witness against him.

" And if to this," said Blueskin, " you could only manage to rob yourself, Jack, and bring your own things away, why, you'll prove a thief of thieves."

" It shall be done," said Jack, becoming bold by the repeated bumpers of brandy he had taken to drown his chagrin for the loss of Bess — " it shall be done : as soon as St. Peter's witness sounds the first morning call on his clarion, I'll catterwaul it along the gutter, and bring off the booty."

" Bravo, bravo !" said Blueskin; " you must make it a *piece* offering to Mr. Wild; as you won't be able to go back to Old Chips after this, you'll have nobody else to look to now, you know."

" True, true," answered Jack, "that's to be
thought of; though if I do manage to bring off
the stuff, I am not going to put up so quietly
with their nonsense as you may think : a plan
has just occurred to me — but, mum — we'll
talk of that to-morrow : if I am to be a thief, I
won't be a half-and-half one — I'll be a bold one
or nothing.

" Well said," again roared Blueskin, giving
him a hearty slap on the back in token of approbation ; " but I always prognosticated it."

More brandy was ordered in upon these mutual
assurances ; and as soon as the cock announced
the first faint approach of day, and all the other
cocks around the neighbourhood had answered
the challenge, and telegraphed it to their re-
spective districts in token of their watchfulness,
Jack stole from Mr. Hind's cockloft, and, with
all the dexterity of a tom-cat, made his way over
the tiles to Mr. Wood's garret, obtained an entrance without arousing Griffith Thomas, and,
after ascertaining that he really was asleep, by
applying the flame of the candle to his nasal
organ, discovered that the roll of fustian was still
where he had deposited it, and bore it triumph-
antly off, with a few favourite articles, to the
Black Lion, retracing his steps by the same way
that he had come.

It was lucky Griffith Thomas really was asleep, for Jack's determination was, if discovered by him, to have stood on no repairs to have secured his silence. The fustian was conveyed, the first thing, to Mr. Wild, as a trifling offering from Jack, in proof of his allegiance, previously to entering regularly into his service. It may be mentioned that, among other things really belonging to Jack which he had brought away with the fustian from the garret of Mr. Wood, was the pair of pistols he had purchased with the retaining guinea he had received from Jonathan Wild on their first introduction to each other. As Jack handled these ill-omened weapons, the vein of daring and adventure which lay dormant in him was fully aroused; he felt himself the hero he afterwards proved.

" Yes," said he, " enterprise shall be my guiding star, resolution my companion. If fate will make me a highwayman, it shall not be said that she has fixed on one either unfit for, or unworthy of, the distinction she would assign him." He here cocked his pistols with an air of determination, and began singing a slang song in praise of taking the road, which had the reputation of having been a great favourite with the prince of highwaymen, the celebrated Captain Hind : —

" Of all gallants to frisk a gull,
　　My blessing on the bridal cull ;
　　So ranting, roaring, wild, and free,
　　On road or plain there 's none like he," &c. &c.

It was broad day-light ere Jack, on quitting the
case * of Mr. Hind, arrived at the Attic residence
of Blueskin, in the Mint, where he proposed to
rest during the short period till morning, and
then boldly to visit Mr. Bains, having secured
the only evidence against him, and, by means of
bullying, deter that gentleman from taking any
further steps for his apprehension. Accordingly, at nine o'clock, after having partaken of
a regular Mint breakfast, consisting of red her-
rings and onions, with a copious accompaniment
of early purl—a mixture of warmed gin and beer
—he repaired to the shop of the piece-broker,
where his presence excited no small surprise.

" Your servant, sir," said he ; " I understand you have had your house robbed since I
was here last ; and that you have chosen to say,
just because I made all your fastenings so secure that it was impossible for any one to break
into your shop, that you think I have some
hand in the business ; now I have only got this
to say, I am a poor lad, 'tis true, but I am not
going to have my character taken away. Touch
my honour, touch my life ; my reputation's my

* Flash house.

bread; and unless there's a public apology immediately made to me in the " Daily Post," for the defamation so unjustly heaped on me, why, my attorney shall bring an action against you for libel, that's all. People are not going to have their lives sworn away for nothing. My integrity is well known ; I could be trusted with thousands ; and if you injure my credit, you'll have to pay swinging damages for it, I can tell you that." The poor piece-broker was electrified at this audacity ; he could not deny the fact of Jack's having made the fastenings of the shop extra secure ; and had nothing more to bring against him than the circumstance that had been communicated by Mr. Wood, of some fustian having been found in his (Jack's) box. The ruinous consequences of an action for false imprisonment flashed across him, and he was on the point (being naturally a very timid man) of expressing his conviction of Jack's innocence, and begging pardon for his suspicions, when Mr. Wood suddenly entered, apparently greatly inflamed with choler, his face looking as crumpled and as red as a pickling cabbage. He started at seeing Jack ; the rubicundity of his visage assumed a purple hue.

" Tog — fillain — thief !" said he, seizing Jack by the throat, " put I have caught you, Saint Tavid pe plesset."

"What have you got to say against me?"
said Jack, who had for a moment been thrown
off his guard, but instantly recovered his effron-
tery, "What are you collaring me for?"

"Passion of hur heart, hear this!" roared
Mr. Wood; "are you not my apprentice, look
you? have you not proke into my garrets, look
you, like a thief in the night? have you not
roppet me, look you?"

"No!" said Jack, sternly; "so take your
fingers from my throat, or it may be worse for
you."

"Not roppet me!" spluttered out the Welshman, almost strangling with rising rage, "not
roppet me! Got's poty, have you not proken open
your pox, and taken away honest Mr. Pain's
fustian, pesites going off with your own pistols,
which I had left there, for they are wilful ploot-
thirsty weapons—mercies on hur, and often times
kill a poty pefore he is aware of it—not like
your gentlemanly peaceful swords, that never
kill any poty, put when you want them to to it,
which was the reason hur tid not choose to mettle
with your fire-arms, look you—To you not call
all that ropperies and treasons?"

"No, I. don't," said Jack, impudently;
"surely a man has a right to do what he likes
with his own! I only took what belonged to
myself—the fustian was my own, and so were

the pops,—and now what have you got to say to that, old mousetrap?"

"Mousetrap! Oh! Saint Winifret, and all the eleven thousand virgins, tit ever any one hear the like of this?—here is plasphemies and sacrileges and setitions, look you."

"We had better let him go, neighbour," whispered Mr. Bains to the exasperated Welshman, "we may get into trouble; you see what a desperate young dog he is, and we have no evidence."

What might have been the effect of this advice to Mr. Wood we are not able to say, for just at this moment Mr. Daniel Nibblo, the constable in whose hands the warrant for Jack's apprehension had been placed, entered the shop for the purpose of making some inquiries as to his haunts.

Mr. Nibblo was a short thickset man, with a flat hard-looking face, in the middle of which was placed a rather large nose, carbuncled with a profusion of grog blossoms; his eyes were small, but piercing, and seemed to lie in wait in his head ready to spring out on any one he wanted; his frame was bony and sinewy: he was dressed in a plain brown coat with stiff skirts, and waistcoat and breeches to match; high shoes with large silver buckles; a round bob-wig and cocked-hat: he bore in his hand a cudgel with a knob at the top

of it, of about the diameter of a two-penny loaf.
He had commenced life as a quitam attorney, but
becoming broken down by malpractices, had
sunk into a bailiff's follower, from which situation
his ferret like qualities and wolfish ferocity had
raised him to the rank of constable; to use his
own words, he had left the civil for the criminal
service. He was particularly fond of interlarding
his discourse with a variety of dog-latin law
phrases, which he rendered still more mongrel
by invariably, through ignorance, misapplying
and mispronouncing; they served, he said, to
give a weight to his conversation, and produced
a wholesome awe in the multitude. His quick
and practised glance informed him at once of all
that was passing; and in a moment he had released Jack from the gripe of Mr. Wood, and to
his great surprise and terror had accommodated
him with a pair of ruffles to his wristbands, as he
termed it, by very securely handcuffing him.

Jack began to repent of his gratuitous bold-
ness; and both Mr. Wood and Mr. Bains commenced explanations, which were abruptly cut
short by the myrmidon of justice.

"It is all very well, gentlemen," exclaimed
this worthy; " but you must permit me to say,
ex officio, the affair is now in the hands of justice
— it is too late for you to withdraw — the law
must take its course — I am responsible to the

public. Were I to release this daring offender, as you seem to wish, I should be compounding felony, liable to be caught in *fragrante delictoe*, and that is an enormity which shall never be winked at by me."

After much conversation, during which Jack vehemently protested his innocence, asserting that the fustian which had been seen by Mr. Wood in his box, and which he had that morning sold to a member of the Jewish persuasion, in order to enable him to purchase a new chest of tools, had been given to him the week before by his mother, the inflexible Mr. Nibblo consented that Jack should accompany him and Mr. Bains to Mrs. Sheppard's in Spitalfields, in order to ascertain from her whether the suspicious fustian had been given by her to Jack, or not — Jack having declared the Hebrew unknown to whom he had disposed of it. Mr. Wood, whose really good heart had been much moved at seeing Jack in the custody of the officer, expressed his readiness, if Jack could really prove his innocence, and would promise amendment for the future, to take him back again into his employment, and pass over what had occurred.

It was with a beating heart Jack repaired with the constable and Mr. Bains to the house of his mother ; he had not visited her for some months, and felt he had no right, from his neglect, to expect a very cordial reception. She was at home when they entered her shop, and, though surprised to see him accompanied by two strangers, immediately ran to embrace him.

" My dear, dear Jack!" she exclaimed, how is it that I have not seen you so many months? — what has occasioned your absence — and why are you here now?"

" Heyday!" cried Mr. Nibblo, " how is this, young fellow?—Why you said just now you saw your mother only last week—and here, she says, she has not seen you for some months: this is what we call in the courts *nulle testificandumb!*"

Mrs. Sheppard stood motionless; the words of the constable, particularly his dog-latin, to which she attached some dreadful meaning, together with a glance at the handcuffs, which she now saw for the first time, perfectly petrified her.

" Gracious heavens!" she exclaimed, what does all this mean? My poor, poor boy?"

" Nothing, mother!" cried Jack, eagerly, anxious to put her on her guard, " the gentlemen only want you to confirm that it is true you really did give me.that piece of fustian which you brought me last week to make a working-jacket and trowsers of, because somebody says I stole it from this here gentleman, when you know you gave——"

" Silence, silence!" angrily roared Mr. Nibblo,

" here's contempt of court, prisoner — why, you are putting the words into the witness's mouth: — take care, ma'am, take care, or you may make yourself *party cepts crimini* in this affair — you both stand on very ticklish ground : all I want to know, and I speak *quod warranto,* is, whether you did *bonâ fide* give this youth a piece of cloth called fustian — to wit, last week, *anno domino* in the present year ; — now remember, ma'am, you are on your adjudicator, so take time to consider."

The poor woman became dreadfully pale. Jack fixed a keen and anxious glance upon her: she trembled — she hesitated : there was a moment's silence — the constable looked sternly judicial — poor Mr. Bains looked more like a culprit than a prosecutor. Mrs. Sheppard met her son's meaning glance. True love never wholly departs with the object that possessed it : the affection felt for the father revives in his widow with double force and purity as she gazes on their offspring : she sees the father's image in the son; and even when nature has not blessed their mutual passion with this sacred succour in deprivation, faithful memory will still invest inanimate objects with the thoughts and feelings of other days. The vacant chair, the favourite book, the accustomed room, will all recall, as they are gazed upon, images of the departed loved

I I

one — will all awaken emotions of tenderness
that may seem to have been dead in the heart
for years, but which their vision, as by a magic
spell, recalls at once into life and action. So it
was with Mrs. Sheppard: she forgot, as she
wistfully looked upon Jack, all his neglect and
wilfulness; she remembered only his present
peril, saw only the tenderly cherished son of
the father she had loved with so ardent and sincere a passion; and at all hazards — ay, even to
the peril of her soul, such is the love of a mother — determined to screen and save him.

" Yes," she exclaimed, with an effort of desperation, " he has spoken the truth — I did give
him the fustian — it was last week. When I
spoke of his long absence, do you not know
that to a fond mother a week appears an age —
a day a year?"

Mr. Bains looked convinced — not so Mr.
Nibblo.

" Hum!" cried that sceptical person, incre-
dulously; " not being a mother, ma'am, I cannot say any thing about days being years; all I
can say is, any year that has only four-and-
twenty hours in it must certainly be an *anus
mirabilis*, as a certain learned Gent. of my
acquaintance used to say. But now to speak
de facto, my good woman — recollect you are
upon your *asseveranter*, your *allocater*, as I said

before; if you really did give the fustian in question to the prisoner in custody, you can have no objection to state from whom you got it yourself."

Oh, no, no," said the trembling woman, exchanging anxious glances with her son, " it was from a — a — weaver."

" Ha! and his locality ? " said Mr. Nibblo; " you must state that; in what bailliwick ? where is his *vennue?*"

" Sir ? " said Mrs. Sheppard.

" I mean, where does he live ? my good madam," answered Mr. Nibblo, with a forensic air.

" In — in Spitalfields, sir," faltered Mrs. Sheppard.

" Umph! Spitalfields is a wide place, ma'am," returned the constable; " perhaps you can favour us by saying what street, what number ? "

Jack was in a torture of suspense. " I — I do not quite recollect," said the perplexed and agonised woman.

" Umph! You don't exactly recollect ! — very good — just what I thought," drily returned the man of warrants; " then perhaps, ma'am, you'll be so good as to accompany Mr. Bains, the prosecutor, and refresh your memory by pointing out to him the identical house of the aforesaid weaver, that he may ascertain the truth in *propria personæ;* and I, in the mean time,

will remain in *custodiam* here with the prisoner.
You can permit your man to step out for a pot of
ale, and let me have whatever you have in the
cupboard, I am not particular. I have departed
from the strict duty of my office, in allowing
your son this indulgence; he ought to have
been committed at once; the sessions are just
on, and——"

"You shall have all you require, sir," said
Mrs. Sheppard, gratefully; "there is a bottle
of wine, which I had stored up for the birthday of — of —" here looking at her son, she
burst into tears, in which she was accompanied,
from at least one eye, by Mr. Bains, who was at
that moment seized with a sudden desire to
blow his nose, which he did with great vehemence, wisking his handkerchief about in a singularly loose manner.

"Forgive me, sir," said the poor widow, at
length recovering herself; "but my heart is so
full. There is a small case bottle of spirits;
here is bread, butter, cheese, and you shall
speedily be supplied with some ham, and beef,
and ale: only name what you want, sir—you
are welcome to all we have; and I thank you
for your kindness to my poor Jack."

"What you have named will be quite sufficient, my good woman," answered Mr. Nibblo,
complacently; "you need not get any thing
else; I can manage with them."

The viands were produced, and Mrs. Sheppard, with a lingering step, departed to point out the weaver from whom she had bought the fustian to Mr. Bains. To describe the streets they went down, the turnings they came up, the many unsatisfactory inquiries that were made, would unnecessarily occupy the reader's time; suffice it, Mrs. Sheppard walked poor Mr. Bains nearly off his legs, who, beginning to be heartily tired of the business, and finding that whenever they left off they were just as wise as when they had first begun, compassionately told the widow he was quite satisfied, and had no doubt she knew the street and house, if she could only recollect them; and moreover, that there was the weaver she mentioned, if they could only find him; that he would make it all right with Mr. Nibblo, and was sorry he had caused her any annoyance. He then, with some difficulty, forced a dram on the poor woman, to recruit her exhausted spirits, and with no difficulty at all persuaded himself to follow her example. Returning to her home, they found Mr. Nibblo very contentedly emptying the bottle of wine, with the assistance of Jack, whom he had graciously permitted to bear him company; the ale and spirits had been discussed some time previously.

" It's all right, Mr. Nibblo," said the considerate Mr. Bains.

" Oh, it's all right," answered the constable, " is it ? "

" Yes, the street is there," said Mr. Bains ; " the weaver does live in the house — I am quite satisfied."

" Oh, what you've seen him then ? "

" Why — not exactly," hesitated Mr. Bains ; " he was not at home, as it were ; but it's all right."

" Very well ; then I have nothing else to do but to take this young gentleman's *habeas corpus* to St. Giles's roundhouse, lock him up there for the night, and to-morrow morning convey him before Mr. Justice Parry, who no doubt, as it's *all right*, will declare it a case of *nolle prosequi*, and give him his *committimus* and discharge him immediately."

There was an irony in the tone with which these words were delivered by the constable, an air of malicious satisfaction in his manner, that did not escape the quick apprehension of Mrs. Sheppard. Woman is ever more ready in the understanding the language of looks than man ; she has a more present prescience of the meaning unconsciously conveyed by tone and gesture, than has the proud lord of the creation who claims such an intellectual supremacy over her : — she saw at once Jack's fate was sealed, that her falsehood was known, that she had become the suborner and accomplice of crime, had borne false witness and forfeited her fair name, only to end in her own detection, and render her son's guilt still more black — she gave a piercing shriek as the constable rose to convey her son to prison, and sunk senseless on the floor. Jack felt no inclination to stay and witness further the remorse and agony that had been his work.

" Let us go," he cried, " to the roundhouse. God bless you, mother," and he imprinted a kiss on her cold and senseless cheek. " You will take care of her, ma'am," said he to a neighbour the foreman had summoned to her assistance; " tell her to keep up her spirits, that I will soon see her again, and that there will be no occasion to trouble herself any further about this plaguy fustian; and now, sir, if you are for a walk to St. Giles's," addressing the constable, " I'm your man — so on with you."

" After you, sir; or you may give me your arm, which you like—any thing to make things agreeable — verdict, guilty," muttered the constable aside — " *nemine contradicente*."

With these words he grasped Jack's arm, and, followed by the stultified Mr. Bains, made his way from the widow's house in Spitalfields to the roundhouse in St. Giles's.

CHAPTER THE FIFTEENTH.

JACK A PRISON-BREAKER.

ESCAPE FROM ST. GILES'S ROUNDHOUSE. — THE LOST ONE FOUND. — LOVE IN A COTTAGE.

On arriving at St. Giles's roundhouse, Mr. Bains having quitted them at St. Clement's Church, not very much satisfied with the day's adventures, to report progress to Mr. Wood, the authoritative rap of Mr. Nibblo soon caused the door of that edifice to be unbarred by Jack's old acquaintance, Mr. Hannibal Guffin. The parochial functionary started as he saw our hero, and stared, as the saying is, with all his eyes.

"Your servant, Mr. Guffin," said Mr. Nibblo. "These comes greeting," delivering the warrant and Jack into the beadle's hands; "yes, know all men by these presents," he continued — "but, lord bless me, how you stare! have you ever seen this young hell-bird before?"

"Why, I don't exactly know," equivocated the beadle, wisely conjecturing that he had nothing to boast of in his acquaintance with him.

"I think we *have* met," said Jack.

"Well, I have a something in my head that

almost convinces me that I have seen you before," observed the beadle.

Ay, ay," returned Jack, " that's safe; you need not cudgel your brains any further at present."

" Oh! well, if you are old acquaintances," said Nibblo, " no occasion for any other introduction. You can tuck him up comfortably for the night, can't you, Guffin? — and to-morrow morning I'll come and procure him an audience with Justice Parry — you'll see what the charge is — a small affair of fustian — just enter it in your books, and then I'll say bye-bye to you; — but stop, I must not forget my ruffles."

Here he was about to remove the handcuffs from Jack, when he was restrained by the beadle's exclaiming, with a look of great alarm —

" For Heaven's sake, what are you about? — why, you surely would not let this young hang-dog loose upon me, would you?"

" Why not?" inquired Mr. Nibblo; " you can easily give him a rap on the head if he's obstroperous, can't you?"

" Ah! but two may play at that," said Mr. Guffin, with much feeling; " no, no, safe bind, safe find; we had better let him remain as he is. I'll be answerable for your handcuffs; and, what's more, if you'll only be so good as to give me a hand up with him to the top room,

and help me to fasten him in for the night,
there is a jug of water there, and it's quite light
—I'll——"

"Well what, Mr. Guffin?" asked Nibblo.

"Why, I'll stand a dram of the best—ay,
two for that matter."

"Agreed," cried Nibblo.   "Now, young
fellow, tumble up; here's a writ of *fieri facias*
against you; you must go under the screw."

"I am afraid you are putting yourself to a
great deal of very unnecessary trouble and expense, Mr. Guffin," cried Jack, significantly.
"Do any of your lodgers ever bolt the moon?"

"Why, I don't know," growled out Mr.
Guffin; "but there'll be a moon out presently,
so you can try, if you like."

"Why, that's true, so I can; there *will* be
one out, as you say.   I should advise you, Mr.
Nibblo, as a friend, to take a deposit for your
handcuffs."

"I'm not afraid," laughed Nibblo; "you
won't swallow them."

"Why, not exactly," said Jack.   "Pray,
Mr. Guffin, hadn't you a young woman here in
your custody, some time ago? She took French
leave, I understand; have you seen any thing
of her lately?"

"No," growled Guffin, who didn't like these
inquiries of Jack.

" Then I have," replied the other; " she
sent her love to you; and said that the *three*
gentlemen who came and took her away forgot
to pay you for her lodging; and that, if you
would give me the particulars of it, I was to
settle it with you."

" Go to the devil with you!" said the beadle,
surlily; " do you think I carry my accounts in
my head?"

" If you'll just take the trouble to search
your nob for the score — dot and go one, eh,
Mr. Guffin?"

The beadle writhed with stifled rage.

" Come, come, my chick!" said Nibblo, who
began to be impatient for his drams, let's have
no more of this chaff; walk your chalks to your
sky-parlour. I'll give you a leg up."

Jack was here conducted to the top room of
the roundhouse, (which consisted of two stories,)
Mr. Guffin considering he would be the most
out of the way there; and after securely lock-
ing and bolting him in, the pair of congenial
worthies retraced their steps down stairs again.
No sooner was he left alone than Jack took a survey of his lodging. It was a square room; and
by the light which was admitted through a small
loop-hole, with an iron grating not large enough
to admit of any one forcing their bodies through
it, he perceived the only furniture of the room

was an old feather-bed, with a dirty blanket on
a crazy truckle, and a high-backed leather-bot-
tomed chair, on which there was a jug with
some water. Sitting down on the bed, he began
to muse on the events of the day, his present
prospects, and what was likely to be his future
fate. The image of his beloved Bess recurred to
his mind, with all her bridal beauty; he soon
lost all thoughts of himself in speculating on
what might be *her* hapless destiny. At that
very moment she might be falling a victim to
the lawless violence — the brutal lust, of her
hateful persecutor, the soldier, and he not there
to save or die for her. The idea was agony.
" And what restrains me ?" said he : " what
hinders that I should scour the earth to seek
and succour her ? — These senseless walls. Ah !"
he continued in a tone of triumph and contempt, as a thought suddenly flashed across his
brain — " Ah ! shall I then suffer my free will
to be controlled by a few bars and bricks ? I,
that have life and action ? shall animate spirit
yield up the mastery to the mute resistance of
these inanimate walls ? No ! the sense, the being
that made them what they are, were shamed
for ever, could they not un-make them. About
it then. — Yes ! up, Jack, up ! the day shall be
your own !"

Jack's heart bounded at the idea : every sinew

seemed to brace itself for the attempt: he was all animation, all buoyancy; his energies, his senses, all hurried to his aid; one eagle glance below, above, around the room, and his resolution was taken — his plan was laid. It would have been easy for him to have removed a plank of the flooring, and penetrated through the cieling to the room below, but he did not know who might be its tenant. The walls were massive: to have made an aperture in them would have occupied too much time; the roof presented the best point of attack. Although hands were made before tools, Jack knew that, for his work, they were but of small use without them. To disengage one of his very slender hands from the handcuffs was, though a very painful, not a very difficult task; all his limbs and joints were singularly flexible and pliant. Unfortunately, on searching his pockets, he found nothing to aid his purpose but an old razor; but with this he set to work. His first step was, with this razor, to cut a stretcher, or bar, from the back of the chair, one end of which he formed into a sharp point; then drawing the feather-bed into the middle of the room, and placing it so that it might receive, without noise, all that might fall from the cieling, he mounted the chair and commenced operations. With the sharp point of the bar he soon managed to unloose a considerable quantity of the lime and mortar; he then dislodged several of the laths, and began to remove the tiles by poking at them with his bar. He had made, in this manner, a very formidable orifice, when, unfortunately, one of the tiles rolling off the roof, which was rather slanting, fell on the head of a worthy clergyman, who was at that moment passing the front of the watchhouse, in deep meditation on some spiritual observations for his next Sunday's sermon. However this gentleman might have wished his thoughts to have been assisted by inspiration from above, that which was afforded by the falling of the tile was by no means agreeable to him. Turning sharply round, and looking up, in the confusion of his ideas, occasioned by the concussion of his cranium, he began to bellow out " fire, murder, and robbery."

This alarm was distinctly heard by Jack, who was aware that, to avoid immediate detection, he had not a minute to lose. Making a plunge through the aperture he had effected to the rafters, he, with a sort of harlequin's leap, gained the roof—not, however, without removing a great quantity of tiles and rubbish in so doing. It was nine o'clock in the evening: the cries of the reverend clergyman, who happened to be Mr. Topping, the rector of St. Giles's, soon brought a great mob around him; a thousand questions were asked in a breath.

Jack Sheppard's remarkable escape from St Giles's Round House

" What is it ? — Where is it ? — Who is it ? inquired different individuals.

" Murder! fire! thieves!" answered the reverend gentleman ; " the prisoners are escaping."

" Where? where?" demanded a myriad of voices.

Jack saw that, to effect his escape, he must create a diversion. Mr. Guffin, the beadle, had now joined the group outside. Mustering all his strength, Jack, holding on by the coping-stone, pulled up a great part of the roof, and immediately precipitated it down on the heads of the astonished and affrighted mob below; then sliding down a considerable way, by a leaden pipe affixed to the back part of the building, he cautiously dropped into the neighbouring churchyard, and making his way over the church-wall on one side, while Mr. Guffin had proceeded up stairs to the scene of his late captivity, joined the mob, most of whom were half blinded with the dust, by a circuitous route, and greatly added to their mystification, and his own diversion, by hallooing out — " There he goes — I see him — that's his head behind the chimney — no, it's only a tom-cat — Ah! there he is, escaping down that street — stop him, stop him!"

The mob immediately gave chase at full speed, and while they made their way down one street, he, very safely and coolly, walked off down another.

Jack's first object, on thus regaining his liberty, was to seek the sanctum sanctorum of Mr. Hind, which, to avoid observation, he reached by a back way: he found that notable publican and singer very desperately engaged in chanting the well-known canticle of " Mad Tom," roaring with much wildness, as he issued from his cellar, —

> " Forth from my dark and dismal cell,
>   Or from the black abyss of hell,
>   Mad Tom is come."

" Dear me, Mr. Hind," said our hero, much surprised by this singular greeting, " how wild you look; is any thing the matter? has any thing happened?"

" Matter! matter enough," gloomily answered Mr. Hind; " a great deal too much has happened;" here he resumed his song—

> " Fears and cares oppress my soul."

" What! haven't you heard the news, youngster? Your pal is lumbered."

" Who? Blueskin?" quickly asked Jack.

" Yes, Blueskin," said Mr. Hind, with a sigh; for in Blueskin he had lost one of his best and most constant customers; " he was nibbled this afternoon, upon old Blackerby's warrant, and is now in rumbo." *   Here again he began singing —

> " 'Come, Vulcan, with tools and with tackle,
>   And knock off my troublesome shackle.'

But that's past praying for, I fear; however, he made a very pretty wrestle for it when he was taken—didn't surrender until he had got a very handsome crack on the sconce. There's one comfort, Mr. Wild's gone to him with the doctor;" and here again he hummed—

> " 'To see if he can cure his distemper'd brain.'

There must have been some plaguy nosing † somewhere; somebody's been giving tongue.

> ' Hark! I hear Actæon's hounds.'

But what the devil!" he exclaimed, suddenly breaking from his subject, " how is it I see you here? why, I thought you had been laid up in lavender by Dan Nibblo? Old Wood said you were."

" And Old Wood said right," said Jack, who was very sorry to hear of his friend's misfortune. " But having and keeping are two very different things. Help me to take off this other ruffle," said he, alluding to the handcuffs; " I had

---

* Newgate.   † Giving information.

only time to disengage myself from one : they belong to old Nibblo ; but I shall make a present of them to Mr. Wild. "

Hind released him from the ornament.

" Blueskin being taken, I must make myself scarce, I suppose," said Jack ; " no doubt the cry is up — the hounds are out."

" Yes," said Mr. Hind, singing with a very ill grace —

> " Ringwood, Rockwood, Jowler, Bowman,
> All the chase do follow."

Jack waited to hear no more, took a hasty leave of Mr. Hind, crossed the water, and soon arrived at the Mint. Obtaining admission into the late lodging of his friend Blueskin, he packed up the articles he had left there in the morning, loaded the pistols he had bought with Mr. Wild's money, and depositing them in his bosom, set out to seek his fortune wherever chance might lead him.

Hurrying along he knew not whither, Jack, soon after quitting the Mint, and darting down some obscure and ill-tenanted streets, found himself in the middle of St. George's Fields. These fields, now covered with rows of well-built houses, and intersected with broad and secure roads, were, at that time, the dissolute haunts of the very re-fuse of the metropolis. Considered as the property of the public, they were freely used for the erection of booths, and as the standing place of ca-ravans, shows of wild beasts, &c. in their progress to and from the country fairs. Their stunted herb-age was the common pasturage of costermongers' donkeys, higlers' worn-out mares, and other des-titute animals : they were unfenced, untended, and only divided from each other by some stagnant ditches, with here and there a straggling tree, partaking, by its blight and dismemberment, of the general desolation of the spot. The only house of entertainment that skirted them was a low pot-house, known by the name of " The Dog and Duck," the resort of minor thieves and hedge prostitutes, who congregated there in great numbers nightly, spending their ill-gotten gains in obscene revelry, singing, dancing, drinking, and fighting, for the diversions commonly ended in a general brawl : they were usually joined by a few bloods upon town, who came there to un-bend, as they called it ; in other words, to gratify a vulgar taste and an innate love of blackguardism with impunity. In after days this house became a very notorious house of entertainment : the gardens were fitted up as tea-gardens — an orchestra was erected for concerts, and it was, sixty years since, the principal scene of the ex-ploits of the Toms and Jerrys of that day. The ostensible reason with many for visiting this place was to drink of the waters of a certain mineral spring, which were said to cure every disorder, but, in reality, to indulge in waters of a much stronger description, that were more frequently the cause of every disorder.

The site of this resort of infamy was part of the ground on which the present New Bedlam is erected, as is evident from a stone that is seen, on which is carved the figure of a dog holding a duck in his mouth, inserted in one of the walls of that institution by the proprietor of the original premises, the late Mr. Hedger, the father of the present chairman of the Surrey Sessions, as a grateful memorial of a fabric from which he had derived the greater part of his fortune. Strange retribution, that the place which had once been the scene of riot and disgrace, should now re-echo only to the ravings of madness and despair!

On Sundays, St. George's fields were frequented by a select variety of bird-catchers, boxers, dog-fanciers, badger-drawers, bull-baiters, football-players, and itinerants of every description.

As Jack unconsciously made his dreary and dirty way over them, he chanced to pass " The Dog and Duck." The sounds of riot attracted his attention; he heard music, both vocal and instrumental, and, feeling his mouth parched by excitement, in addition to being extremely tired with the exercise and exertion he had gone through during the last few hours, he stepped in to procure at once some rest and some refreshment. Calling for some liquor, an ill-looking tapster showed him into a large room at the back of the house, in which, sitting on benches at various small tables in the middle of the room, were assembled together, drinking, smoking, and carousing in every possible manner, from eighty to one hundred persons of both sexes.

Taking his seat on a back bench, which was affixed to the wall, and ran regularly round the room, all the moveable seats and tables being occupied, Jack was some minutes ere he discovered that immediately before him, though with his back towards him, there was sitting on a bench, in company with another person, at one of the tables, no less a character than Mr. Jonathan Wild. Jack's attention was first attracted by the mention of Mr. Wild's name in a conversation that was going on between the two.

"How is it, Mr. Wild," said Jonathan's companion, who, it appeared, was one Mr. Shickery, a pettyfogging Fleet attorney, or sixpenny lawyer, as they were called, who procured straw bail for insolvent tradesmen, and was Old Bailey solicitor to some of the more thriving pickpockets, engaging witnesses for them when wanted, and having an extensive practice in similar lines of respectability,—" How is it, sir, that I meet you here—beating up for recruits, eh?"

" You have hit it, Mr. Shickery," returned the great man; " some of my best troops have just been clapped under hatches. Splitting has been the order of the day among them. Bob Wilkinson, who was nabbed and sent to the Whit by Justice Hewitt, for being concerned in making cold meat of Peter Martin, the Chelsea pensioner, and some other little jobs, has peached Milksop, Lincoln, and Lock: Lock has been laid hold of by Justice Blackerby, and has sneezed from a larger nose than t'other; and to-day, my boy Blueskin has been collared, and he has informed against Bill Blewitt, Dick Oakey, Jack Junks, or Levie, as we call him, and Matt Flood, besides others, of a round dozen of speaks in which they have been concerned. Bob Wilkinson must ride the three-legged mare, for I never pardon murder: there's two or three others must mount the nubbing cheat too; as for the rest, as they don't quite weigh their weight yet, I must manage to get them off— now this will thin my ranks a little, so, as I must keep up my troops to the full complement, I 've come here to see who I can enlist."

" I believe you can't come to a better place," returned Mr. Shickery.

" Why, no," said Jonathan, " I generally get

some volunteers here; I have had most of my best men from this country, Mr. Shickery, — there was Will Maggot came from here."

"Oh, what the spice Toby Cheesemonger?" said Mr. Shickery.

"The same," returned Jonathan. "I need not tell you, Mr. Shickery," he continued, "that the Mint is the place where tradesmen, who have lived a little too fast, generally retire to when the game begins to get up: they usually bring a few broad pieces with them, and, as long as the coin lasts live like fighting cocks; but when the gelt's gone, and it gets low-water mark with them, then's my time—they are glad to do any thing then."

"By the bye, speaking of Will Maggot, Mr. Wild, would it be impertinent to ask what is become of that blade?"

"Oh, the scoundrel!" replied Mr. Wild, "you know what I did for that rogue, Mr. Shickery, or if you don't I'll tell you: finding he could not get bread to his cheese by his business, the dog came over here; as he was an active clean-limbed young fellow, I administered to his necessities, and finally concluded by proposing the road to him as an honourable way of raising the wind: I furnished him with dog's meat * and ammunition†; in short, from being a rotten

* A horse.   † Pistols.

cheesemonger, I made a complete gentleman of
the snaffle * of him, contenting myself with only
taking four fifths in the pound of his gains."

" And very liberal too," said Mr. Shickery, who
did not usually leave his clients quite so much.

" So I thought," said Wild; " but see the
ingratitude of man, Mr. Shickery.   After I had
put bread in his mouth the villain became dis-
contented, and deserted : for a long time I could
obtain no trace of him ; but one day, a gentleman
coming to my office to inquire after some tatlers
that had been fobbed on the Oxford Road, by a
single bridle cull, and not being able to find, on
referring to my books (for you know I'm very
particular, Mr. Shickery, in noting down my orders), that any gentleman under my command had
been on that road for at least three weeks before,
a suspicion crossed my mind that it must be my
cheesemonger.   A few inquiries satisfied me I
was right; so, arming myself at all points, off I
set to Oxford in search of him.   I peeped into
all the stables on the road, examined the horses,
drank with the ostlers and chamberlains, and
inquired what company frequented their house;
but without success, till, within a short distance
of Oxford, I met with the Oxford stage, the
coachman of which told me that they had just
been stopped and robbed by a single toby man,

* Highwayman.

not a quarter of a mile from the spot, and bade me be upon my guard. From the description he gave me I had no doubt it was my gentleman, so I clapped spurs to my horse and gallopped in the direction Cochy had pointed out. On arriving at the scene of action that had been, I halted like an experienced general, and fell to considering what a man of any discipline would do after such an incident in order to puzzle and beguile his pursuers, in case any hue and cry should be raised to take him: looking around me, I presently found a bye-lane on my left hand, and rightly considered that my cheesemonger, being a man of some conduct, must have struck down that lane after he had finished his adventure. Accordingly, I took the same course, doubled my speed, and, after a short gallop, came in sight of a man in a great coat, well mounted. I judged I had now come to the end of my inquiry: I therefore slackened my pace that I might prepare for battle. My gentleman hearing the tread of a horse looked back, but, seeing only one man, did not think that it bore the appearance of a pursuit, and therefore never moved a step the faster. I must tell you I was at such a distance that he could not recognize my sweet phiz — I was as thickly stuck around with pistols as the man in the almanack is with darts, already cocked and primed, but hid from observation by my riding coat. As I approached nearer to him, however, Will cast another look back, and immediately twigged who was his touter *, upon which, without more ado, he faces about manfully enough, and, guessing my business, boldly bade me stand off, for that he had done with me. I, however, hadn't done with him ; still I thought the fox's was my game, so I set to wheedling him, told him I meant no harm, that I was there by chance, and begged we might be better friends than ever we had been. I had my hand all this time on a pistol, but it being under my coat my man of cheese could not perceive it ; so I kept on wheedling and wheedling, and drawing closer and closer, till, at length, arriving within a distance where I had a sure and fair aim, I suddenly drew it forth, let fly at him full in the face, and then, rapidly drawing my hanger, with one blow felled him to his horse's feet, where he lay weltering in his gore.

" Having obtained this signal victory over my valiant knight of the butter tub, you may be sure I was not long in looking after my plunder. Rifling his pockets, I found fifty odd guineas there together with some movables of value, of which having taken livery and seisin, according to the law of arms, I went to the next town, leading the horse of the slain as a trophy of my prowess.

* A person on the watch.

Inquiring for the first justice of the peace, I surrendered myself, telling his worship I had killed a highwayman, and giving a direction where I had left the body, his worship sent and had it conveyed to the town hall, when it was known by some stage-coachmen and others to be the carcase of the *mitey* highwayman that had infested the roads for some time past. Having signified to his worship that I was Jonathan Wild, the famous thief-taker, I was released on my own recognizances, and returned to town loaded with my plunder — and that's the way I 'll serve all such scoundrels that would desert from their allegiance, and rob me of my just revenues."

" Quite right, Mr. Wild," returned Mr. Shickery — " quite right." Jack's ear eagerly drank in this recital: he plainly saw, by the cool manner in which Jonathan narrated this exploit, that he was a man of too much determination to be wantonly trifled with. Jonathan had ordered in a fresh flask of gin — the royal liquor, as it was then called ; and, while over this he and his worthy friend Mr. Shickery were arranging the plan of a little bit of perjury, against the ensuing sessions, a nymph from one of the neighbouring lanes volunteered a *pas seul* to the company, which she performed with rather a scantier quantity of drapery than is allowed even at the Italian Opera House. It is needless to say, it produced thunders of applause, and a very considerable shower of browns.

At this moment Jonathan's attention was attracted by the entrance of a gentleman at the lower end of the room, who strutted down, dressed in the very height of the fashion—a laced cocked-hat, a peruke which fell all in ringlets round his neck, a brocaded waistcoat, a laced coat, with large moulded metal buttons, bearing on their surface the device of an anchor, and a great profusion of mock jewellery, consisting of chains, brooches, and rings. He held a gilt-headed ebony cane in his hand, and wore a pair of false mustachios, to give him a foreign and *distingué* appearance.

" Ah, ah!" said Jonathan, as he fixed his eye upon him, " there is one of my men, Mr. Shickery; the fellow little thinks I am here; he is the very chap I wanted to meet."

" What, that fine gentleman?" said Mr. Shickery; " why, he seems quite a beau."

" Ay, ay, thanks to the tailor," answered Jonathan; " that blade is one of my *spruce prigs,* as I call them. I shall show you some sport with him, in a minute or two: he has been keeping out of my way for some time; he must give an account of himself. I picked him up in a booth at Southwark fair. The cull was one of your Grub-street scribblers, and gained a wretched living by cutting down old plays, and making drolls of them. The drolls of ' Hero and Leander,' and the ' Siege of Troy,' performed at Kit Bullock's booth at Bartholomew fair, were among his productions. The fellow was fond of aping the gentleman, and thrusting himself among his betters; of course, his literary talents did not furnish him sufficient to enable him to do this without assistance; so, scraping an acquaintance with him, as he was acting the gallant in one of the boxes of the booth, I enlisted him into my corps. As he was not exactly fitted to become one of my dragoons——"

" Your dragoons!" interrupted Mr. Shickery; " what are they, Mr. Wild?"

" Why, they are the second division of my troops. My *cavalry*, or toby men, that only take the road on horseback, are the first. My dragoons are gentlemen that serve both on horse and foot—bold, manly fellows, that I generally send forth doubly armed; they either take the air on the wide common, well mounted, and nobly attack the stage-coach, in the face of open day, or else lie in ambuscade on foot, or wait *perdue* in some dry ditch to surprise the heedless traveller. I count these among my best men, because they have two strings to their bow. Then there's my *mill-ken coves*, or *cracksmen*, gentlemen that speak to a case, and are not afraid to break open houses. I've got a young fellow of this class just coming out : he promises to be a rare one; his name's Jack Sheppard; he'll be a great man or hanged before he's one-and-twenty, or my name a'n't Jonathan Wild." Jack modestly drew back at this flattering mention of himself. Mr. Wild continued — " My fourth division, the spruce prigs, of which this fellow is one, are a class of gentry of some address and behaviour. I reserve them to send to court on birth-nights; also to balls, ridottos, plays, and assemblies, for which purpose I furnish them, as you see by that pattern, with laced coats, brocaded waistcoats, fine perriwigs; and sometimes provide them with handsome equipages, such as chariots, chairs, footmen in liveries, a *valet-de-chambre* — the servants being all thieves like their masters. That fellow, Jacky Planksty, as he's called from his love of a Dance — he's fond of cutting a caper, and, but for his chicken heart, might soon dance upon nothing, — is an adroit hand enough. At the last instalment at Windsor, the dog had the address to possess himself of the Duchess of Marlborough's diamond buckle : she applied to me for its recovery, but only offering twenty guineas, I frankly told her the thing was im-- possible : — ' Why, madam,' said I, ' it cost the gentleman who took it forty for his coach, and other expenses, to Windsor.' You shall see now how I'll frighten him. He some time ago, with some other rogues like himself (for there's a society of them), robbed and greatly disfigured a *French* gentleman, and never gave me any share of the profits, for which I'll now bring him to book." With these words Jonathan made his way to where the beau was standing, and tapping him on the shoulder, presently re- turned with him, he looking very pale and con- fused. Making him sit down, Jonathan, with many menaces, began to question him where he had passed the last two months.

The beau, in a very great fright, begged Jonathan to forgive him, urging he'd been in gaol in Lincolnshire, where he went to entrap a lady of fortune ; but that, miscarrying in his de- sign, he had spoke with a silver tankard and some spoons, for which he was committed ; " how- ever," he said, " I managed so well with Nimble Dick, who appeared as my servant, that nothing was found upon me — so the pimps discharged me on my trial for want of evidence ; but," con- tinued he, " I am now on a capital lay, Mr. Wild, if you'll only let me go, I am sure of getting a gold watch, and, upon my honour, I'll bring you

some money to-morrow, besides standing a bottle
to-night, with the money I have got from
Mr. Pinkethman for a new droll 'Pyramus and
Thisbe.'"

What the result of this intercession might have
been Jack was not suffered to know, for just then
a quarrel having taken place between a sailor and
a drunken blood, who had seduced a black lady,
the exclusive possession of whose charms had
been guaranteed for sundry broad pieces paid by
the tar, a general fight soon became the consequence — the lights were all put out — the
tables overturned — the fidler's head broken —
the glasses smashed, and a scene of confusion
created which beggars all description ; and in
the midst of which Jack managed, undetected by
Mr. Wild, to vacate the premises, and make good
his retreat.

It was now fast approaching to midnight :
the sky, which had all the evening looked lurid
and unsettled, now became overcast with large
masses of black clouds; the atmosphere, which had
been particularly heavy and oppressive, changed its
temperature, and became dankly chill. A sullen
silence brooded all around. Jack, seeing that a
storm was fast approaching, pushed his way
briskly onwards to procure a shelter for the night.
Quitting St. George's Fields, and crossing a spot
called the Mall, a much frequented rural walk at

that time, he entered upon some marshes forming part of Lower Lambeth; they were lonely and disagreeable, little frequented by day, and still less by night: the progress across them was rendered more difficult by a quantity of plashy pools and clumps of dwarf osiers.

It was whilst traversing this desolate route that a low gust of wind arose; the stars were obscured from sight by the hurrying masses of dark cloud; and the moon had sunk in the heavens: it now became so intensely dark that Jack could not distinguish his path, but blindly made his way along with the greatest difficulty. The gust of wind we have mentioned gradually died away in a series of low moans and fitful sobbings. The silence became still more ominous; some large drops of rain then fell, at distant intervals, with a force and plash that caused an indistinct terror from being of rare occurrence. The elements were in this uncertain state when, all at once, there was a vivid flash of lightning, which completely lit up the whole scene, making the darkness more terrible, by making it perfectly visible. It was instantly followed by a report, as from a cannon, which was caused by the falling of a thunderbolt; this seemed to be the signal for a general conflict of the elements. A storm arose, such as is but seldom experienced in favoured England.

It will be remembered that the month was August. The storm was one that might be called a harvest storm. It is remarkable, but true, that the genius of the tempest usually rages more violently in summer than even in winter. The rain began to descend in torrents, falling literally in sheets of water; the wind blew a perfect hurricane; and, between every pause, flashes of blue forked lightning, and rebellowing claps of thunder, loud and long-continued, seemed to awaken, to assert their supremacy.

Jack was quickly drenched to the skin, but he stoutly pushed onwards, till, emerging from the marshes, he found himself near the antiquated Manor House, Vauxhall. The Gardens, which were at that season a place of great entertainment and resort, had been closed for some hours, the performances invariably ending by eight o'clock. He looked round in vain for some place of safety and shelter, and heartily wished himself in Mr. Wood's little back garret again.

The storm did not at all abate its rigour, nor did he slacken his pace; he pushed on till the appearance of a cluster of nine noble elms, now bending and shrieking in the blast, informed him he was in the little sylvan spot which, from their vicinity to it, bore then, as it still does now, the name of "Nine Elms." There was no public-house

there in those days: two or three gentlemens'
seats, and about the same number of rude cottages, all closely barred up, seeming, from their
stillness and absence of any sort of light, as if
they were the mansions of the dead, formed its
only residences.

Hurrying down the little lane that runs
through it, and crossing an intermixture of
fields and market gardens, Jack now found himself on a wide common, which from its conti-
guity to the Thames, that then burst upon his
view, roaring and writhing in the storm like a
lashed monster, he immediately knew to be that
of Battersea.

" Surely this common must lead to some human habitation," he exclaimed ; " at all events,
I have no alternative but to cross it." Again
the tempest raged with redoubled wildness, and
again he increased his speed, when he was
stopped by suddenly encountering a party of six
or eight gaunt-looking men, whose approach he
had not, in the darkness, observed.

" Halloo, youngster!" cried out one of them,
in a harsh loud voice ; " what are you doing
out at this hour? I must take the liberty of
searching you, my kinchin cove ; you can be
after no good."

Here he began to address a few words to his
companions in the Romanee tongue, which Jack

partially understood, expressing his conviction that, as he was so wet, the best thing they could do would be to strip Jack to the skin, and accommodate him with a lodging in a neighbouring ditch.

From their pattering Romanee, Jack immediately knew they were gipsies, ; and as any attempts at resistance against such odds in number and strength would have been the height of madness, as also would have been any appeal to their compassion, he bethought himself of an expedient which, as it ultimately proved, completely served his turn.

" What, brother Romaners !" he exclaimed, " why, you surely wouldn't go to harm a ben cove* like me in the darkmans†, would you?— see here, my dimber dambers, I am one of yourselves, free of every common from Romeville to Lesser Egypt — I bear the seal of Pharaoh, my hearts," holding his wrist out to let them ascertain by the glare of the lightning that he was speaking the truth; " and I charge you in the name of Queen Zara, and under pain of the curse of the Red Sea, to let me pass unmolested, and afford me aid and succour, by telling me where I may procure a shelter from the storm."

" Ah, a Romanee brother ! under what chief were you naturalized ?"

* Good fellow.   † Night.

" Duke Martin, the black," returned Jack, boldly.

" Ah! the Earl of Hungary," replied the gipsy," we must let the cull pass free, brothers — the gipsy must not break faith — a true Romaner always respects the seal. Pass on, boy; keep by the bank; never mind the biting cutting blast from the river, nor the chilling dashings of the spray, and a short quarter of a mile hence, upon the common, you will find a house where, if it's shelter you are seeking, you may chance obtain it. It is rather a queerish place, certainly, but any port in a storm, as the shipmen say. It is called the Red House, not for its colour, for age has made it black enough for that matter, but because it was the last place in which Ikey Samuels, the Jew pedlar, was seen alive when he was returning from Chertsey fair with the produce of his wares; he was found in a ditch a short distance from the house, with his throat cut and his pockets turned out, the morning after he had put up there. Old Luke Royster, the landlord, swore that he knew nothing about it; that the poor sheeny had left his house the night before in safety, and as there was no evidence, why, the matter dropped. If Luke should ride rusty, and refuse to let you in, you can give him the pass word, " Corn in Egypt," and that will gain you admittance whoever may be there;

perhaps there may be some knights of the post there — their pops have been heard about these quarters lately. If you should fall into any of their hands, you have only to show them the seal, that will be sufficient — thought may go free then. And now, ben darkmans to you, son of the tribe."

" Ben darkmans to you, my Romanee coves," said Jack, "and thank ye, brothers— zounds, it comes down faster than ever, we've staid pattering here too long," and away he dashed again.

" A pretty chick, that," said a gipsy, as he and his companions resumed their walk to town.

The two parties were soon out of sight of each other.

The stunted willows that skirted the common nearest the river moaned and bent to the blast as Jack made his way under them. He was not long in arriving at the house to which he had been directed by the gipsies. It was a rude, uncouth structure, the work of different periods, built entirely with wood. It may be proper to mention here, that though standing nearly on the same site, this was not the Red House that is now so much the resort of our cockney and other shots. It has long been swept away, and the present structure erected in its place, with its frontage of glaring red, expressly to give a colour to the former's questionable name — " The Red House." Pigeons are still plucked in the modern structure, as in the old one ; but the shooting practised, though perhaps not less sanguinary, is of a more allowable and innocent description.

Lights were visible through the crevices of some of the crazy boards, for the house was closely shut up, and between the gusts of the storm Jack heard a murmur of voices within. He knocked long and loud at the door, but no one answered ; for some time he continued his application, and at length a gruff voice within was heard, demanding —

" Who 's there ? — What do you want ? "

" I 'm a traveller," answered Jack, his teeth chattering with cold. " I want shelter and refreshment."

" Then you can't have them," answered the voice ; " we are all gone to bed."

Drenched and shivering as he was, Jack thought it would be folly to stand on further parley, so he resolved to give the pass-word at once.

" What, won't you let me in ? " he exclaimed ; " You need not be afraid — ' *I have corn in Egypt.*' You 'll let me in now, I suppose."

" Oh ! that 's another matter," resumed the voice ; " wait a minute, and I 'll open the door."

Some bolts were withdrawn, the chain unfast-
ened, a rusty lock turned, and Jack was once
more under cover.

"Come in," said Mr. Royster, for it was the
worthy landlord himself. "You must be quick,
and let me give you what you want at once, for
I've a private party in the ale-room—some
gem'men that are met there on particular business, and wouldn't like to be disturbed. You
won't want to stay here till the morning, will
you?"

"I have no other resource," said Jack; "I
am completely worn out with walking, and you
hear the storm is raging as furiously as ever.
You may give me a shake down any where
—I'm not at all particular."

"I am sure I don't know where I can put
you," answered the host, looking somewhat perplexed. "Stop! now I think on it, there is
the little lumber room, at the top of the house;
it stands on the flats, where the gem'men goes
up to take views of the beautiful prospects, and
smoke their pipes in the fine weather—my ob-
servatory, as I calls it. You must hold hard on
by the floor, if the wind should happen to carry
your nest away, which I shouldn't at all
wonder at, for it's a gimcrack place."

"It will do capitally," said Jack, "I'll warrant me. Now then, just give me a hunk of

bread and cheese, and a double dram of strong waters to keep out the cold, and I don't care how soon you show me to my straw."

" Step this way, then," said Mr. Royster; " you shall be accommodated in a breath; but if you had not had that pass from Romanee, the devil a bit you'd have got in here, I can tell you that."

Taking Jack into a little side bar, Mr. Royster soon produced a loaf, and part of a Dutch cheese, with a curious globular-shaped bottle, formed of thick black glass, filled with Hollands of extraordinary strength. Jack fell to immediately, and worked away in such right good earnest, as very soon nearly to clear all before him.

Loud and imperious cries of " Landlord—landlord — Luke Royster!" issuing from the ale parlour, Mr. Royster hurried Jack up some crazy stairs to the lumber room he had spoken of at the top of the house. It was a wretched shed, which seemed scarcely able to hold itself together: there was a small window at one side, formed by a bull's-eye pane of glass, to admit the daylight, and a door in the front leading out to the roof of the general building, which was flat, and afforded to occasional guests and visitors convenient prospects of the surrounding country. As Jack afterwards discovered, access was obtained to this roof from the bowling-green and skittle-ground at the back of the house, by means of a small wooden spiral staircase, which, but for being accommodated with a hand-rail, would have seemed very much like a ladder. In this select retreat, amid a profusion of old baskets, broken chairs, and other lumber, there was, fortunately for our hero, a truss of straw and two or three bundles of hay. Bidding Jack not to be surprised if he was disturbed by any noise in the night, Mr. Royster, shaking down the straw and arranging the bundles of hay, so as to form a sort of bed, wished Jack good-night, and returned down stairs to attend on his particular guests in the ale parlour. He was no sooner gone than Jack threw himself down on the straw, and, fatigued as he was, despite the tumult of the tempest, immediately fell into a sound sleep, in which we will for the present chapter leave him.

CHAPTER THE SIXTEENTH.

JACK A BENEDICT.

THE PRIZE REGAINED.—RURAL FELICITY.—THE ASPIC
'MONGST THE FLOWERS.

How long Jack slept he knew not: he was awakened by a sense of restlessness, which is not unusual after great fatigue, when we start after a short slumber, feeling as if we were even too tired to sleep. He rolled from one side of his humble couch to the other, turned about and about, and endeavoured, in vain, to re-compose himself to rest; there was a thrilling of weariness in every limb, amounting almost to pain, that effectually prevented him. The storm had completely died away — the wind was hushed, as were the pealings of the thunder and the peltings of the rain — he could distinctly hear the voices of the guests below, intermingled every now and then with loud guffaws of laughter, announcing they were still engaged in their revelries.

Finding sleep impracticable, Jack arose and shook himself: his limbs were a little stiff from his exertions and the drenching he had experienced; his clothes, however, from the heat of his body, had completely dried on his back, and the glow, occasioned by the copious drams of strong Hollands that he had taken, seemed to offer a guarantee against any evil consequences. A bright flood of light streaming through the pane of glass we have before mentioned, induced Jack to unfasten the door of his cabin that opened on the roof of the general building.

A change, as if wrought by enchantment, presented itself on his doing this : the clouds, having discharged themselves of their stormy elements, had left the sky perfectly clear and serene : the moon had again risen, and, as if to re-assert her empire in the heavens after the late conflict, beamed with even a broader, fairer refulgence than usual, pouring a rich galaxy of silvery pearls upon the living waters of the Thames, which derived additional brilliancy from their ever-changing and sparkling motion. The common itself was bathed in liquid light, from the reflection of the moon on its dank verdure—all was calm and pellucid beauty.

Jack, who afterwards proved himself a bit of a poet, though perhaps not of the very first order, could not help being struck with the splendour of the scene : — his glance wandered across the Thames. On the opposite bank to the left, stood the noble gardens and sacred halls of Chelsea Hospital, founded by a luxurious monarch, at the instance of the fine, free-hearted Nell Gwynne.

As Jack viewed this honoured retreat of the veteran brave, he could not help thinking how much superior was that queen of frail ones to the many frail queens, of which history records such sad and degrading memorials. He had remained gazing for some time, lost in various reflections, when he was aroused from his reverie by the distant splash of oars, and, looking forward, distinctly saw a boat making its way from that part of the opposite shore towards the right, then known by the name of the Five Fields, Chelsea, a place notorious for having been the scene of frequent robberies and murders. Rowing directly towards him, he observed it more minutely. A tall female, closely muffled up, stood in the stern of the boat, seemingly attending to another female figure, which, enveloped in white, appeared to be crouching down at her feet. Three or four men, in the uniform of foot-soldiers, were seated in the other part of the boat not occupied by the rowers. As they neared towards a parcel of rude stones, which had been fixed in the water as a sort of landing-place, nearest that part of the bank which led to the Red House, Jack, not willing to be regarded as a spy, concealed himself behind some boarding supporting the lower part by a high flag-staff erected on the flats, for the purpose of colours being hoisted on the occasion of rowing-matches, &c.

It was not long before the party gained the shore, and began to hail the place of their destination, as it turned out to be.

" Ahoy! Ahoy, there! Red House — landlord — Master Royster — Luke — bear a hand — make her fast there, Charley! Now come — look sharp there — are you going to keep us here for ever?"

The door of the Red House was immediately opened, and Mr. Royster appeared, bearing a light, followed by a gentlemanly-looking portly person in black, and some others.

" Why, what the devil has detained you, friends, till this time?" inquired Mr. Royster.

" Why, the storm to be sure," answered a voice from the boat; " who the plague would have thought of crossing the water in such a hurly-burley as we have had? But come, lend us a hand."

The party now began to issue from the boat, the tall muffled female supporting the one we have noticed as being enveloped in a white mantle, whose deep sobbings were perfectly audible. The soldiers followed; Jack thought he recognised the face of one of them, but in the confused light, occasioned by the flickering of the candle borne by Royster, and the gleams of the moon, he could not, at the moment, recollect where he had seen it. Making their way to the house the door was soon closed upon them, and Jack returned to his shed, in some surprise at the scene he had just witnessed. He could not conceive what could be the purpose of a visit at such an hour. A thousand strange conjectures stole across his mind: he felt a secret prescience that some strange adventure was about to occur in which his interference might be required; and, without any fear for the consequences, his first step was to look at his pistols, the product of Mr. Wild's gratuity. On examining them, he found the priming had sustained no injury from his drenching : he therefore cocked them ready for action. There was a great murmur of voices below; he distinctly heard much hurrying of footsteps backwards and forwards, and slamming of doors; but nothing occurred particularly to command his notice till he heard a door open at the back of the house leading into the yard, and immediately beneath distinguished a low muttering of voices, one of which sounded strangely familiar to him: its hollow tones could not possibly be mistaken for any other than those of Zara, the gipsy queen, the mysterious person who seemed to exercise so strange an influence over the destinies of his lost bride, poor Bess.

Greatly excited, and resolved, at all hazards, to gratify his curiosity, Jack immediately stole out of the door of his fragile nest, and, stretching himself full length on the flat roof at that

part that commanded a view of the back of
the premises, the moon then shining in all her
lambent majesty, discovered to him two persons
engaged in close and earnest conversation; he
immediately recognised in one the well-known
figure of Zara, now divested of the mantle that
had shrouded her, for it was she whom he had
seen in the boat.   The other, a male, was a portly
but somewhat shorter person, dressed in black,
and bearing the air of a respectable attorney, or
some other professional character; he appeared
to have been speaking with some apprehension,
for Zara was endeavouring to assure him.

" Make your mind easy, Squire," said the
sibyl, " I have noted well the planets — the
wench's die is cast. From the conjunction at her
birth disgrace and guilt were threatened her: I
read a felon's fate within her horoscope; that I
this night have snatched her from; the baleful
influence of adverse stars may be averted if we
foresee it timely : the camp and the canteen,
and not the lofty hall and gay assembly, as in
thy solitude thou'st feared, shall be her portion. I
snatched her at her birth from rank and fortune,
moved by an artful villain — that bold, bad
man ——"

" Hush! mention not his name," shudderingly
interrupted her companion, " it chills my blood
to hear it."

" I have no pleasure in mentioning it," bitterly answered the gipsy; " but, as I said, I snatched her at her birth from rank and fortune : it was a wicked deed, yet not mine all the guilt, and I have made some expiation. I snatch her now from infamy and crime, the prison and the scaffold; and though the lot to which I have consigned her is humble, it is honest—what would'st thou more, Squire, to calm thy fears? Hast thou not seen her wedded with thine own eyes scarce twelve hours since, and to the soldier, Rupert Lyon. Is he not now with her, surrounded by his comrades? Will not their nuptials here be consummated?—Can she escape?—for shame— for shame."

" Well, well—I will be satisfied," said her companion, who did not, however, appear over and above convinced with her arguments. " You have kept faith with me—done all that you promised. You say the soldier departs to-morrow with his regiment?"

" Ay, for America," cried Zara, exultingly.

" And bears her with him?"

" Thanks to his officer's permission : your gold, Squire, purchased it; fear not, she'll ne'er return! I am to join them in the morning to see their embarkation, and give the dower to Rupert you promised with his bride. I'd not stay now. Poor Bess!—the wench is squeamish; her bridal night may be a rough one. Where do you go from hence, Squire,—to Edgware?"

"No, no, not there; never have I visited it since that fatal night. I shall return to Hampstead."

"I 'll see you on the road. There is a ferry just below; the boatman knows me, and will get up to take us over: a back gate here leads to a path directly in our line; we need not go back to the house to say farewell. Luke Royster has my orders, and morning's dawn will see me here again. Come, Squire, cheer up—this way. Why, what a heavy step!"

"My heart is heavier than my steps, good Zara," said her companion, in a tone of much deep sadness. "I know not how it is, but though that which has passed within these few hours makes me secure for ever, I could fain wish that it had never passed. That terrible storm! it seemed to wake in reprobation. The very elements recoiled at what was doing. Heaven grant we do not fatally repent it!"

"Faint heart!" indignantly sneered Zara. "Why, Squire, I deemed you more a man. You will think otherwise to-morrow. Rouse up! this way—this way!"

She drew him almost unconsciously after her; their echoing footsteps died away in the distance, and Jack, who had listened with an intensity almost painful, to every word that had fallen from them, withdrew again to his shed, his senses in a perfect whirl of astonishment, indignation, and alarm. A thousand plans presented themselves to him for the rescue of his beloved Bess from the power of her ravisher— for that it was she and the soldier, that had accompanied Zara in the boat, and were then below, there could be no doubt. Ere he had time, however, to resolve upon any thing, a loud shriek which reached his ear, and which he instantly recognised as the voice of his bride, determined him. Drawing forth his pistols, and rushing out of the room with the fury of a hunted tiger, he with one bound dashed down the stairs, and bursting into the ale parlour, from whence the cry proceeded, saw his beloved Bess struggling in the rude embraces of the ruffian Rupert. He instantly discharged his pistol. The villain let go his hold, but Bess was immediately seized by his companions; the discharge of a second pistol soon however set the poor girl at liberty again. With a shriek of joy she flew towards him. Holding her with one hand, and seizing the poker with the other, Jack made his way towards the door, which in the confusion of his sudden appearance, and the consternation excited by the fire-arms, he gained ere they had power to intercept him. Upsetting a table, the better to cover his retreat, and extinguishing the candles, which happened to be upon it, in their fall, leaving the room in total darkness, he locked the door on the outside, and rushing out at the front, made his way, with Bess in his arms, to the little stone jetty, or landing-place, where he had seen the boat moored that brought the party there. Safely depositing his fair burden within it, he unloosed it from its fastenings, hastily seized an oar, and pushing it from the bank was soon in the middle of the river. The tide was favourable, and with but little exertion they rapidly drifted down towards Putney.

They had floated completely out of reach when they saw the party they had left emerging from the house, and witnessed the rage and disappointment manifested at their escape. By the lights hurrying to and fro it was plain the baffled party was searching for the boat, which they had evidently missed. There being now no immediate danger of being overtaken, Jack had time, as they floated silently down the stream, to devote a few moments to his beloved. We will pass over the tender endearments they exchanged on thus unexpectedly regaining possession of each other; nothing is so rapturous in reality, and so mawkish in detail, as the caresses of lovers. Love is a wholly selfish feeling, not to be participated in, or calculated to excite any sympathy except when unsuccessful, by any but the parties personally concerned. Bess's history was soon told. She had been hurried from place to place, she knew not whither; this, however, she did know — that, in spite of her intreaties, her prayers, her tears, the haughty Zara, urged by a stranger she had never seen till that time, had but a few hours before caused her to be united, almost through violence, to the hateful soldier, by the aid of a Fleet parson; that then she had been conveyed to a canteen in the neighbourhood of Chelsea, where the soldier had remained drinking with some of his boisterous companions, till the subsiding of the storm allowed the whole party to cross the Thames to the Red House, from whence Jack had so providentially rescued her.

Jack's relation, in turn, was suited to circumstances. His search for her, and his being forced to seek shelter in the Red House, accounted for every thing. Holding a council of war, Jack prudently considered the enemy's first step would be to cross the water in search of them; he therefore wisely determined, in order that they might take nothing by their motion, not to cross the water at all, but to keep close in shore, on the Surrey side. After floating down the river some time, and passing the ferry at Chelsea Reach, he saw a very convenient creek, running considerably into the bank, into which he found he could run his boat, and by means of the sedge, the high flags and rushes, and the over-hanging osiers, remain perfectly concealed.   In this creek, then, he moored his little bark, and waited the progress of events, that he might better shape his future course.   They had not continued there long, when the sound of voices along the bank, in the distance, and the glaring of lights, announced that their pursuers were advancing in the direction towards them.

"Lie close, Bess," whispered Jack; "doff your bonnet, lass, that your white ribbons may not discover us, and nestle to me, love — closer, closer, dear."

Bess required no second bidding.

"Ah! they stop at the ferry," cried Jack, ex-ultingly, "just as I thought; they want to cross, and have come here for a boat.   Ah! that splash-ing of oars — 'tis the ferry-boat returning in the very nick — hark, they hail it."

"Ahoy — ahoy, there, ferryman — quick — quick! you are out early, old man!"

"Surely you can have had no passengers at this hour?" inquired one amongst the party, whom Bess recognised, by the voice, to be the soldier.

"Ay, but I have though," returned the ferry-man; "I have just taken a couple over; plague on them for rousing me out of my night-cap in this manner, though they paid well : if they were for any love passage, which I should hardly think they were, I wish they had stopped till it was fairly morning."

" 'Tis they," ejaculated the soldier, eagerly ; " that jade, Bess, and the scoundrel that took her off, and obliged me with a bullet in the fleshy part of my shoulder — he must be a very devil incarnate — that fellow, no doubt, has cut the boat adrift, and come here to gain time."

" He's got seventeen shillings to pay for broken glass and china," growled out Luke Royster, " if ever I catch him, I can tell him that. Do you know which way they took after you landed them, boatman ?"

" Oh, yes ! they took the King's Road, and, I dare say, are at Knightsbridge by this time. I heard them talk of making their way to Hampstead."

" They must get into town first," returned the soldier ; " we may overtake them in the Five Fields."

" Ay, ay, and knock his brains out if you choose, there's nobody to prevent us there— it's a nice place that," muttered Mr. Royster.

" We must follow them instantly, boatmen," cried the soldier, " so tack about—now, my lads, jump on board, we have not a moment to lose— over's the word."

"I shall require double fare such an unseasonable hour as this."

"We'll not quarrel about the money, boatman," answered the soldier, "you shall have treble fare, only take us over quickly."

"That's another thing," said the boatman, feathering his oars; "now then, my masters, just dress the boat a bit to keep her steady, and you shall fly."

The old ferryman was almost as good as his word—he half performed a miracle; in three minutes the whole party were nearly across the river.

"Nothing can be more plummy than this, Bess," said Jack, in high spirits, as he saw them depart; "they are on a wrong scent: it's the old hag, Zara, and the mysterious cove that was with her, that the old fellow carried over; they are safe to follow them to town; and, while they are gone, now's our time. I've, in my hurry, left my luggage behind me at that infernal Red House, and, if I mistake not, so have you, lass. Now, it won't do exactly for us to commence matrimony without a rag to our backs, or a stiver in our pockets, so I shall just take the liberty, while the party are engaged in their wild-goose chase, and the worthy landlord is absent, to return to the crib we've just left, and help myself to my own. We never could have a better opportunity. There can only be the slavey in charge of the premises (for, you see, they have got the tapster with them), and, no doubt, she's asleep fast enough, though if she shouldn't be, or should happen to wake, I can soon manage her. You lie close here, and in twenty minutes I'll return with our little property, and something else to make us comfortable into the bargain."

" Dear Jack," cried Bess, who half trembled at the risk he was about to run, " be cautious for my sake, dearest."

" Never fear, wench!" cried Jack; " but let me feed my bull-dogs before I go," coolly beginning to re-load his pistols. " There, now all's right, so off I go." With a hearty kiss, Jack departed, and once more made his way to the Red House.

All was perfectly quiet as he approached it; there was no light visible, no sound audible. Entering the garden through the gate at the back, which the gipsy had left open, he crossed the bowling-green and skittle-ground, and softly ascended the spiral staircase we have before noticed, which ran up by the side of the house, and led to the flats on the roof. He found the door of the lumber-room was, as he had left it, open to his purpose; he immediately entered and secured his bundle, from which he took a dark lantern, which he illumined with his friend Blueskin's phosphorus box, and began cautiously to descend the stairs in the interior of the house.

Making his way without any interruption to the little ale parlour, the locality of the late conflict, and which presented a sad scene of confusion, he soon secured Bess's little bundle, and also took possession of the soldier's side-arms, consisting of his bayonet, cartouche-box, &c., which had been incautiously left there, well aware that their loss would subject the back of the son of Mars, on the following day, to an exemplary scratching of the Cat at the halberts. From the ale parlour Jack proceeded to the bar, where he found the maid-servant, sitting in an arm-chair, in a most blissful state of somnolency, and making such a noise with her own nose, as effectually to prevent her being disturbed by any other noise less violent.

In the bar Jack helped himself to several "inconsiderable trifles," particularly the loose coin in Mr. Royster's till, amounting to about three pounds, in silver, copper, and gold, a very fine knuckle of ham, a choice bag of biscuits, a bottle of ale, and another of curious old brandy, all of which he carefully stowed in his capacious pockets. He was then about departing, when all at once his eye rested upon the well-known wallet of Zara, which was deposited on one of the shelves of the bar, as it would appear, for greater safety. Jack remembered the few words that had dropped from the gipsy in the garden, respecting Bess's portion.

" There can be no harm in my taking this," he thought ; " 'twill only be my right—what I 'm entitled to by law, by virtue of my wife—so, with your leave," he exclaimed, and immediately pocketed it, to bear company with the other property. Leaving the bar, and softly opening, and carefully closing after him the back door, he was, in five minutes more, safe in the arms of Bess.

Their mutual joy at the result of the expedition may be easily imagined, especially when, on examining the wallet, they found it contained, along with a variety of other articles, twenty guineas in gold, the fortune intended to have been given with Bess to the soldier.

" As he is not at his post, I must be his substitute," cried Jack, pocketing the cash ; " but now, Bess, for a little refreshment ; you must needs stand in want of some, and, to confess the truth, so do I, and then we'll about ship and away."

Making a hasty, but extremely relishing repast off the ham and biscuits, which they washed down with the ale, and a small portion of the brandy to keep the cold off their stomachs, Jack committed the soldier's accoutrements to the custody of Old Father Thames, to whom also he confided the care of the boat, which he sent adrift without oars or rudder, and then, taking Bess under his arm, pushed on in the direction of Richmond, stopping to rest some time in the ruins of an old mill which they passed in their progress through Kew.   As they now took their time, it was broad day when they arrived at Richmond, and they found no difficulty in procuring some breakfast at the " Three Pigeons," a small public-house in a bye street, in that side the town nearest the river : here, the place appearing private and convenient, they resolved to put up and spend a few days of their honey-moon. To avoid discovery, they kept themselves to themselves as much as possible, content with their own company, and wishing nothing else.

Who shall tell their delightful evening walks in the park, and on the hill of that beautiful town, so completely justifying, by its rich mound and sheeny splendour, both its ancient and modern appellation.   In Richmond, then, did the lovers continue some time — " the world forgetting, by the world forgot," till a visible diminution in their little treasury warned Jack it was time to look out for squalls, and he beat about him to find if he could not procure some honest employment in his own trade of a carpenter, and provide a lodging which should be at once more economical and comfortable than that afforded by "The Three Pigeons." Love and a cottage occurred to them both — to Bess poetically, to Jack practically. She only saw, in the perspective, roses and eglantine, sunshine and smiling cherubs, the cooing dove, the gurgling brook, the shepherd's pipe, innocence and happiness. Jack thought of the savoury rasher on the coals, the barrel of ale, brown bread, and a pipe at evening with a neighbour, some noisy urchins, plenty and content. Both were equally satisfied with the prospect. Not deeming it exactly prudent to settle on that side the Thames, Jack crossed the water, and accidentally falling in with a master carpenter in the little town of Fulham, to whom he represented he had served his time with a person in Smithfield, he was engaged by him as a journeyman.

A very neat cottage, situated in the midst of gardens, happening just then to be unoccupied in the pleasant neighbouring village of Parson's Green, Jack, under the name of Edgworth, immediately became its tenant. Although, instead of doves, it was only visited by some chirping sparrows, and a dirty puddle ran by the side of it instead of a purling brook, Bess managed to be satisfied with it. Jack's expectations being more realisable, he was, of course, satisfied. How long their unmixed happiness might have continued, if it had not been for a circumstance which shortly afterwards occurred, it might have been hard to say: but, alas! " the course of true love never did run smooth ; " and love in a cottage— except it happen to be a cottage *ornée*—was never known to continue unalloyed for more than a month, and that month the honey one, at least as far as our experience has permitted us to ascertain. An event soon occurred that blighted all their hopes, marred all their joys, and o'erturned all their plans: but it is of too much importance in this history not to form the subject of a separate chapter. We shall therefore leave our unsuspecting lovers to enjoy their last meal of bread and cheese and kisses, in the uncloyed felicity of their rural retreat, and screw up our courage to the narration of the many stirring and exciting incidents that will rapidly follow.

CHAPTER THE SEVENTEENTH.

LOVE LAUGHS AT LOCKSMITHS.

A NEW FOE WITH AN OLD FACE. — CAPTURE OF EDG-
WORTH BESS. — JACK'S ASTONISHING ESCAPE FROM
THE NEW PRISON.

ON the day of the untoward occurrence to which we have alluded in our last chapter, Jack had, early in the morning, left his beloved Bess, and repaired, according to custom, to the shop of his new master, Mr. Timbs, for so that gentleman was called. He found Mr. Timbs in unusual good spirits.

" We shall have a visiter, Edgworth," said he; " a brother chip—yes, my old fellow-apprentice, whom I have not seen for these twenty years, and whom I had quite lost sight of. Having, through a friend, heard of my settling in this town, he has written me a letter, signifying his intention of coming and spending the day with me, to talk over old times, and be once more boys again, as we used to be—rather old boys, to be sure; but no matter for that, it's no consequence how old every other part may be, if the heart be young. My limbs may be fifty, but my heart's only fifteen; therefore I'm resolved to be merry, and enjoy myself to-day, if I never do again; and you, Edgworth, shall enjoy yourself too. Yes, yes! my old friend and fellow-apprentice knows how to value a good workman, and will not refuse to take a glass with you, though he was never any great things of a workman himself. Poor fellow! we are not all gifted alike. Therefore you will hold yourself in readiness, Mr. Edgworth."

Jack expressed his willingness and gratitude. Mr. Timbs left him finishing some little jobs whilst he went to the stage office to wait his old fellow-apprentice's arrival.

Merrily whistling away in the lightness of his heart, and sending the shavings flying in all directions, Jack thought no more of this intimation till it was called to remembrance by the brisk re-entrance of Mr. Timbs, exclaiming with much glee —

" This way, my dear Owen, this way — here we are, all snug and comfortable—this is an unexpected pleasure, 'faith !"

"Owen!" said Jack, the name strangely tingling in his ears, "why, surely it can't be——"

Ere he could finish the doubt it was at once removed—his old master, Mr. Wood, stood before him.

"Mercys of Got! who is this, look you?" screamed out the astonished Welshman, on seeing Jack.

" My journeyman, Edgworth," answered the good-natured Mr. Timbs, " and a very clever fellow he is too, I can assure you."

" He is one very great rascal! look you, Roger Timbs," roared the ancient Briton. " Journeyman! he is my apprentice, look you — and what nonsense is this you talk apout? — Etgworth! — Etgworth! — the villain's name is Sheppart, though Got help me, he has peen more of the wolf than the sheppart; put hur will have justice — to not let him go, he is one rogue, one runaway; he has proken into houses, proken out of prisons, look you — help, help, goot peoples, in Got's name, in the King's name," *seizing Jack's collar*, " hur charges you all to aid and assist, look you."

Mr. Timbs was petrified by this sudden movement of his friend, and so, to confess the truth, was Jack; but the enraged Cambrian's outcry, having collected together a considerable number of spectators, our hero was soon secured; and, on Mr. Wood's information of his being one of the most notorious villains breathing, was conveyed to the Fulham Cage, which just then happened to be empty. The constable of Fulham, having some parish business which required his attendance before their worships at Westminster, was on the very point of setting out for town,

therefore, after a somewhat wordy recapitulation
by Mr. Wood of Jack's various offences, it was
settled the constable should convey him to London
at once; Mr. Wood declaring, " he should not
pe aple to eat a pit till he hat seen the fillain
hanged." Jack was, of course, allowed no time
to take leave of poor Bess, who did not discover
what had taken place till some hours afterwards,
when, almost heart-broken, she determined to
follow and search him out.

Arriving in London, it being too late to take
Jack before the chamberlain that day, he was
conveyed to the house of Mr. Justice Newton,
who, after a short enquiry, committed him to
St. Ann's roundhouse, preparatory to a further
examination in the evening. How poor Bess got
to town, and by what means she traced Jack out,
it is not exactly necessary to detail. It will
be remembered that she had only been united
to the object of her choice and love a few
short months, that she was eighteen, was a
woman! What wonder then that she arrived at
St. Ann's roundhouse nearly as soon as Jack
himself? It so happened, that Mr. Hannibal
Guffin, the parish functionary of St. Giles's, was
passing St. Ann's " Donjon Keep" at the very
moment the constable of Fulham was conveying
Jack to its custody, and recognising his former
prisoner, he stept in to renew his acquaintance

with him, and put his brother authority, the keeper of St. Ann's, upon his guard.

Jack recognised him in the most courteous manner as he saw him enter, affectionately inquiring after his health, and hoping he had sustained no cold the last evening they had met from the thorough draught which had been admitted through the roof of the judicial domicile.

" By the by, Mr. Guffins," said Jack, " you don't happen to have the bill for the repairs of the building in your pocket, have you ? I should be sorry to put the parish to any expence ; and as I was the cause of making them necessary, I should be most happy to hand over the cash."

Mr. Guffin grinned, on what has been figuratively termed the wrong side of the mouth, at this bantering of Jack, and not caring to answer him, proceeded to relate to his cotemporary in office the manner in which Jack had withdrawn himself from his society when introduced by Mr. Niblo — hinting at the necessity of not trusting him out of sight, and the propriety of supplying certain ornaments to his person in the way of chains, &c. It was while engaged on this interesting topic, that poor Bess made her appearance : she was, by far, too beautiful for any one that had once seen her to forget her. Mr. Guffin instantly knew her again.

" Ah, ah, madam!" said he; " what, I've caught you once more, have I? You don't get away this time! Lay hold of her, Mr. Clinch," addressing the St. Ann's worthy; " don't let her escape; she's a desperate offender."

Poor Bess gave a scream of alarm, and Jack, aroused to a pitch of madness as he saw her rudely seized by the Fulham constable and the *par nobile fratrum*, Messrs. Clinch and Guffin, caught up a quart pewter measure, and instantly commenced a vigorous symphony on the heads of the congenial trio, and, but for the intervention of two or three of those ancient and super-annuated persons, the watch, who had accompanied Jack and the constable from Justice Newton's, would very likely have got clear off a second time with his beloved; as it was, Jack was overpowered by numbers, and was obliged to yield to the persuasion of the weighty arguments furnished by their long staves. Bess was taken into custody as an accomplice, and was furthermore detained on the former charge of being concerned in the robbery of the plate composing the memorable May-day garland; also, with having escaped from the roundhouse. She in vain protested her innocence, and that she had only come to see her dear husband, for so she called Jack. The guardians of the peace had been too much damaged, and were too much incensed, to listen to any thing.

All the manacles and fetters in the place were then routed out to secure so daring and desperate an offender as Jack, and he was speedily decorated with a complete set of double irons, including fetlocks, hand-cuffs, &c. This was the first time Jack had ever been in chains, and they did not sit so easy on him as they did on many after occasions. He was then plunged, with Bess, into a strong dungeon at the back of the buildings. Bess had, however, picked up, unperceived, the spike of a halbert that had been broken off in the scuffle, with which Jack speedily disengaged himself from his *insignia*, as he termed the darbies, and then proceeded to perforate the wall of the cell. What might have occurred if the sagacious Mr. Clinch had not happened to be listening at the door at the time, by which means the point of the instrument was very near opening a communication with his brains, through a hole in his skull, it is impossible to say. The astonishment at seeing him free from his chains may be imagined.

It was now deemed dangerous to tarry any longer, and accordingly the whole *posse comitatus*, it drawing towards evening, proceeded, in much awful state, to the mansion of the Justice. Here they found Mr. Wood, Mr. Bains, and

David Lloyd, the milkman (who had heard of the capture of Bess), and Mr. Niblo, awaiting them.

The various charges were gone into. Mr. Wood's was heard the first; but after much spluttering, it appearing to the worthy justice that Jack, being then an inmate in the house, had only entered his bed-room at night through the window instead of the door, and that the property he had carried away had been only brought there by himself, and was the greater part his own, the charge of house-breaking and robbery in this case was dismissed, for, as the worthy magistrate remarked, there was no law to punish a man for robbing himself; and though it was to have been wished Jack had entered his bed-room by the more usual means of access afforded by the door, yet his coming in by the window could not be constituted into burglary, seeing that he was then authorised in the use and possession of the premises; that as for his " showing his indentures a fair pair of heels," that was a subject of consideration for the chamberlain, and not for him, Justice Newton.

The choleric Welshman was much displeased with this decision, and was spluttering forth some most incoherent remonstrances, when Jack requested some one would do him the favour to hand him the tongs, that he might lay hold of the mouse's tail that was then sticking in Mr. Wood's throat, and would inevitably choke him if not pulled out.

Mr. Bains's charge was more successful, as was also that of David Lloyd against poor Bess; and when to these was added Mr. Guffin's evidence of Jack's daring rescue of Bess, and his own subsequent escape from St. Giles's round-house, and Mr. Clinch's testimony of his violence and hardihood in that of St. Ann, the worthy justice felt no hesitation in issuing his warrant for the direct committal of the two prisoners, for trial, to the New Prison, Clerkenwell; his wig having been perfectly raised from his head with astonishment at Jack's audacity and fearlessness.

It was late in the evening when the lovers arrived at the gate of the New Prison, to which place they were conveyed under a strong escort. In the absence of Captain Geary, the governor, they were received by the head turnkey, Mr. Shackle, who, in consequence of Jack's character having been sent along with him by Justice Newton, resolved to accommodate his two prisoners, whom he considered man and wife, with a lodging in the strongest part of the prison, called, from that circumstance, the Newgate Ward; in addition to which he furnished Jack with a pair of double links and heavy bazils of

about fifty pounds weight. Tired out with the
events of the day, Jack and Bess, on being
locked in till the next morning, threw themselves down on their straw bed, and without
deigning to taste of the little loaf of coarse
brown bread and jug of water that had been
provided and left for them, endeavoured to seek
forgetfulness of their sorrows in sleep. Jack,
who never took any thing very much to heart,
was soon buried in a profound slumber, and
Bess very shortly after sobbed herself into a
short repose. The next day, the news of Jack's
committal having been made public, numbers of
persons, who had heard of his rescue of Bess,
his daring escape from St. Giles's roundhouse,
his violent attack on the authorities of St. Ann's,
and his near evasion from their custody, came
to see him. He was all life and spirits, dancing,
singing, joking; he made a great mock of always
carrying his own music with him wherever he
went, and asked several of his visiters if they
wanted to purchase any old iron, telling them
he had just set up in the marine store line; that
he had a stock on hand, which he was willing to
dispose of, and would leave at the house of any
person who might be inclined to purchase it.

Mr. Shackle, the head turnkey, was particularly tickled by Jack's sallies, declaring that he
was a comical dog, and would be sure to make a

great noise in the world in time; he did not
fail, however, to keep a very sharp look out
upon him, narrowly watching every person that
approached him, and suffering no conversation
to pass that he was not privy to. Amongst
other persons who came, as they said, to gratify
their curiosity, Jack perceived one he thought
he knew; he was, however, very much surprised at the individual sedulously keeping at a
very respectable distance from him, and avoiding all communication with him. It must be
Black Martin, he thought; there can be no
mistake in those swarthy features; yet, why
does he not recognise me? Ah! that glance of
intelligence between him and Bess. There's
something in the wind! Let me draw off
Shackle's attention. Here he began to tell the
gaoler a droll story, suited to his peculiar taste,
which he had heard recounted by Blueskin,
during the recital of which Bess found an
opportunity of exchanging a shake of the hand
with Black Martin — for it was he. Jack waited
with the utmost impatience for the departure of
the visiters. No sooner were their backs turned,
under the convoy of Mr. Shackle, who attended
upon them to let them out, than he rushed
eagerly towards Bess——

"Now, lass," he exclaimed, "I saw Black

Martin — what lay have you been upon ? —
there's corn in Egypt — is there not ?"

" There is, Jack," exclaimed Bess, delight-
edly, at the same time displaying a small file, a
couple of gimlets, and a chisel.

" Bravo!" cried Jack; " by the Lord we'll have
a merry evening of it: 'twill be the last one we
shall pass here, so we may as well enjoy ourselves, girl. Hide the implements — put them
in your bosom, with them, hope, confidence, and
courage, we can't have a better chest of tools —
yes, 'tis Whit-Sunday, I think; it shall be a
holiday for us.   Hush! here Skackle returns."

" Well, Mr. Shackle," Jack continued, gaily,
as the gaoler re-entered, " really I begin to find
these lodgings of yours exceedingly snug and
comfortable — no rent nor taxes to pay, no fear
of fire — so well waited upon too — secured against
thieves — such attention — then such an airy situation, so well guarded — really, if one could
only now and then be favoured with the company
of such a pleasant fellow as yourself to a bowl of
punch, I would not tell my name to put up at
any other tavern."

" Why, as to that, Jack," returned Mr. Shackle,
" we are new acquaintances as yet, not but what
we shall be old friends enough by and by, I dare
say. You seem a pleasant rogue enough, and it's
my foible to be seduced by good company ; there-

fore when a lad of spirit, as you seem to be, is willing to spend his money like a gentleman, and wishes to bestow a bowl on me, I am not the man to refuse him such an indulgence; therefore, if you have a broad piece you do not exactly know what to do with, give it to me, and as soon as I've supplied all the other inmates, that do us the honour to put up here, with their bread and water, and locked them up comfortably for the night, I'll order in a double crown bowl of the best, and we'll see if we can't do honour to it. Your good lady, here, can doubtlessly assist us; we shall have plenty of time before the governor goes his last rounds."

" Admirably arranged," cried Jack, in high spirits; " my Bess shall lip you out some of her primest chants, she warbles like a nightingale."

" That's your sort," said Mr. Shackle; " I'll be back in the turning of a key."

" And you shall find us in the right key," laughed Jack; " Bess sings none the worse for a few bars accompaniment, I tell you that."

" No, no; caged birds often carol the sweetest," replied Shackle, departing to perform his promise.

" For heaven's sake, Jack, what is it you mean to do?" asked Bess, as the sound of the turnkey's footsteps died away in the distance "

"Do!" cried Jack; "I mean to do this fellow Shackle, and undo the doors of our prison ?"

"With so many bolts and bars, and with those fetters ?"

"Psha! love laughs at locksmiths," said Jack; "Venus was always more than a match for Vulcan; I tell you, wench, we shall change our lodgings to-night, I am going to bolt the moon."

The explanation of this very enigmatical piece of intelligence was cut short by the re-entrance of Mr. Shackle, who had performed his office of chamberlain to the various guests under his care with more dispatch than usual.

"Well, Jack, my fine fellow," said he, "here I am, and Scraggs will not be long before he brings us the punch."

"Take a seat, Mr. Shackle," said Jack, arranging one of the bundles of straw that had helped to form his bed, for the room was totally devoid of furniture; "make yourself quite at home; excuse my being in déshabille — I have not had time to change my things yet," shaking his fetters.

"Oh, certainly," said Shackle; "there's nothing like being free and easy, all the world over."

"You are right," returned Jack, tastefully arranging the remainder of the straw, part to serve as a table, and the other part as a sofa, for himself and Bess, "free and easy *is* the word, certainly."

Here Scraggs entered with the punch, which, to do Shackle justice, it must be confessed was composed of the best materials. After Scraggs, at Jack's instance, had tossed off a full glass by way of hansel, drinking to their better acquaintance, the party sat down to enjoy themselves, Jack observing he had no doubt they *should* be better acquainted before long. As we have observed, Jack was in high spirits; he did every thing he could to make himself agreeable, cracked a thousand jokes, and told a number of capital stories, which, having a turn for low comedy, he did with much humour; he also sung a great number of flash and other songs, which he had heard at Mr. Hind's free and easy's, to the turn-key's great delight. One of these, which pleased him more particularly than any of the others, was the following, which Jack sung with a rustic simplicity, both of look and manner, that would almost have made a by-stander swear that he had never been within fifty miles of the metropolis in his life, but had spent all his days in village alehouses, and his nights in thickets and preserves.

The Poacher's Song.

1.

" All among the green leaves,
    'T is there our craft we ply,
In the pleasant season of the year,
    When there are none to spy;
And to the ale-house after,
    With store of game we creep,
Where we with song and laughter
    Our merry counsel keep.

Chorus.

All among the green leaves, &c.

2.

" All among the green leaves,
    'T is there we win our gold;
We set our snares, for pheasants, hares,
    By law still uncontroll'd,
In the pleasant season of the year,
    A very merry gang,
The squire may stare, the parson swear,
    And the magistrate go hang.

All among the green leaves, &c.

3.

" All among the green leaves,
        'T is there we have our home ;
    And when the moon is shining boys,
        How fearlessly we roam !
    The keepers may be watching us,
        But not a jot care we ;
    For we are merry poachers,
        And we 'll merry poachers be.

        All among the green leaves, &c."

Mr. Shackle having expressed a desire to be favoured with a copy of this song, Jack grasped his hand with much warmth of friendship, and energetically assured him, that before the next four and twenty hours were over his head, he himself would furnish him with *a copy* of it. In addition to these pleasantries, Jack, with every fresh glass, proposed some choice toast ; but as most of these toasts, according to the taste of the times, had a double meaning, and as we are not exactly sure which meaning our readers might choose to take, we must be excused from re-peating any one of them here. Bess, in her turn, was by no means backward in contributing, as the saying is, to the harmony and conviviality of the evening ; she sang a variety of gipsy songs in a singularly wild and beautiful manner. Among these were several that were traditionally supposed to have been handed down by the tribe in their original emigration from the east, when forsaking the doctrines of Bramah, and driven without *caste* from their own burning plains, they reached Egypt, and, dispersing themselves throughout Europe, became the wandering race they are. One of these, describing the life of that portion of them that sought refuge on the Indian ocean, and led a piratical life, sailing from isle to isle, ran thus : —

Song of the Sea-Gipsies.

1.

" From isle to isle o'er the Southern sea,
    We merry gipsies roam;
After the sun still sailing free,
    The ocean our bounding home.
Ever we live on the dancing wave,
    Our tent the spreading sail;
No land can claim us as its slave,
    Our freedom's in the gale.

    Sea-gipsies we, from year to year,
        One livelong summer prove;
    Sailing from all that's bleak and drear,
        To welcome joy and love.

2.

" And ever as o'er the waves we rove,
    The wandering sea bark's fate
We read in the stars that shine above,
    What calms, what tempests wait !
Under a rock, the storm we mock,
    And fearless brave the breeze ;
And all that 's stray on our ocean way,
    By right of prize we seize.

        Sea-gipsies we, from year to year,
            One livelong summer prove ;
        Sailing from all that 's bleak and drear,
            To welcome joy and love."

Mr. Shackle was so charmed by this last chant, that, with Jack's permission, he could not avoid expressing his admiration by gallantly impressing a kiss on the lips of the fair songstress. The bowl being now drained, and it approaching near the time for the governor and his officers to make their last round of the prison for the night, the head turnkey left them, not, however, before he had assured them he had found in their society much pleasure, and heartily wished they might often pay him a visit, when he would endeavour to make every thing comfortable for them short of letting them go, but that he was too fond of their company for that. Jack assured him he should never want him to do that, and, with much interchange of good wishes, they parted.

Hastily disposing the straw in its usual order, they lay down to await the governor's coming: it was not long before the prison bell sounded the hour of ten, and the distant noise of bolts, locks, and bars fastening and unfastening announced his approach. Whether any circumstance had aroused his suspicion or not, he was very particular in examining Jack's irons, the grating that formed the window of his cell, and the fastenings of the door. Jack assured him that every thing was quite right, and expressed his gratitude at the kind care he evinced in their behalf, fearing he should never have it in his power to re-pay him as he ought. The governor bade him keep his irony to himself, and retired, as Jack said, rather grumpily. No sooner was he gone, and out of hearing, than Jack, bidding Bess join him in the old duet of " Beggars and Ballad Singers," purposely made such a noise as to attract the attention of one of the watchmen outside of the prison, who immediately repaired to the governor, just then returned from his rounds, and disposing himself to the enjoyment of a hot chicken and a night-cap of mulled Madeira, choicely spiced. To him he reported what was going on. Heartily cursing the interruption, and growling at every step

he went, the governor once more repaired to
Jack's cell, where he found Jack and Bess exer-
cising their lungs with such good will, as almost
to stun him.   Again examining Jack's irons and
the apartment very carefully, and finding all was
right, the governor ventured to remonstrate with
Jack on his want of good manners in raising
such a disturbance when they were all going to
rest.

"Lord love your heart, Captain!" said Jack,
"why, you wouldn't be so werry cruel as to
wish us to be here without enjoying ourselves,
would you? We didn't come here for good
manners, you know; did we, Bess?" and here
again they both began singing——

"There's a difference between a beggar and a queen,
    And I'll tell you the reason why;
A queen she cannot swagger, and get drunk like a
        beggar,
    Nor be half so happy as I."

"Besides," continued Jack, "it's Whit-Sunday, you know, governor, and every body
takes a little pleasure then: it's a poor heart
wot never rejoices." There was no answering
this; so the governor only shrugged up his
shoulders, and departed, leaving Jack and Bess
to sing till they were tired, when, as he sagaci-
ously said, he had no doubt they would leave off.

No sooner was he fairly gone the second time than Jack, still singing as before, took the file, and commenced, in good earnest, releasing himself from his irons. He worked away with such right good will, that in rather less than half an hour he had completely divested himself of those somewhat troublesome ornaments to his person, and throwing them down in the straw, he, in the joy of his heart, again began singing, adapting his words to his situation——

"I am a wild and a rambling boy,
   My lodging 's in the isle of Troy;
A rambling boy as all shall see,
For I 'll soon be at liber-tee."

Following up his successful operations, Jack now made a hole in the wall, by which he ascended to the grated aperture above, forming the window of the cell. Here, with incredible labour, he managed to take out, first, a large oaken bar, above nine inches thick, then one of the iron bars, lustily singing all the time——

"I wish I was a little fly,
   In my love's bossum all for to lie," &c.

Having accomplished the removal of these impediments, he now looked out, but found his ardour somewhat damped on discovering that they had to descend a height of at least four-and-

Jock Sketch Pinxit.

twenty feet before they could reach the ground; but difficulties only served to increase Jack's resolution. Immediately descending into his cell, he took the sheet and blanket which had been furnished them, and tying them together, fastened one end of the blanket round Bess's waist, who expressed her willingness to brave every danger for the sake of her dear Jack. With these he managed to raise her up to the window, then passing her through the cavity he had effected by the removal of the bars, cautiously commenced lowering her outside, into the yard below.

" Steady, lass, steady!" he exclaimed, as she swayed from side to side.

" Hush, Jack, or we are lost!" suddenly whispered Bess, seeing a watchman turn round the corner. Jack paused, Bess remaining suspended mid way in the air. At length the watchman's voice, calling " Half past eleven, all safe!" dying away in the distance, convinced them he had departed, and Jack completed Bess's landing. He then fastened his end of the sheet to the remaining bars of the window, and soon let himself down, humming, as he went, ——

" Now all the world shall plainly see,
    Jack Sheppard is at liber-tee."

But what was his disappointment when, arrived

at the bottom himself, he found he had only got out of one prison into another; or, to use his own expressive words, "out of the frying-pan into the fire?"

"Why, it 's wheel within wheel here, wench!" said he. "Confound me if we haven't let ourselves down into the yard of Clerkenwell Bridewell. I recollect, now, it joins the prison. What 's to be done? I should like to know! We are worse off than ever, girl! That wall 's between twenty and thirty feet high, at least. How the devil are we to manage to get to the top of it? We must either scale, or climb it."

"I 'm sure I don't know," said the confiding Bess. "I 'll do any thing, dearest, you tell me, to get out of this horrid place."

"Well, well, girl; we 'll never say die till we 're dead, at all events," said Jack; "let me see," he continued, reconnoitring, and making a circuit of the yard. "Ah! I have it; here 's the great gate; we can manage it capitally."

We have said Black Martin had, along with the other tools, given Bess two gimblets; fixing these in the door at proper distances, Jack made them serve as steps, and by their help, and the assistance afforded by the locks and bolts of the gate, he managed to ascend to the top of the wall; once reaching this, the sheet and blanket soon enabled him to raise Bess to the same situation. Forcing off some spikes of the *chevaux-de-frisse*, and fastening the blanket and sheet to it, as he had before done to the bars of his window, as the clock of Clerkenwell Church ushered in the morning of Whit-Monday, May the 25th, 1719, they had both safely gained the outside of the Bridewell, and were once more at liberty.

CHAPTER THE EIGHTEENTH.

JACK IN BUSINESS.

PARTNERSHIP WITH BLUESKIN. — JONATHAN WILD'S LEVEE.—JACK'S WAREHOUSE AT THE HORSEFERRY.

IT was a fine clear moonlight morning, when Jack and Bess took their departure from the New Prison, one of those mild balmy mornings that peculiarly belong to May, which exist in an atmosphere of their own, make a world of their own, have thoughts and feelings wholly belonging to themselves, a delightful calm, a refreshing vigour, a juvenility and inspiration, which thousands pass through the world, and depart from it, without ever having once, except by accident, become acquainted with, restrained by those formidable giants, sloth and custom. Thrice happy are the birds, the flowers, the breezes, and the much be-pitied portion of the labouring classes, whose avocations force them out by day-break, that they enjoy the purest portion of nature's existence.

Jack felt new life as he inhaled the odours of awakening morn. If such young hearts as his own, and that of his beloved Bess, could have grown younger, this was the scene, the hour in which they would have done so. One moment for counsel and Jack's course was decided.

"Witsun Eve!" exclaimed Jack, "there will have been late revellers at Hind's : early as the hour is, the odds are they will not yet have retired — we shall get admittance there — the Hundreds of Drury is our port then, girl — ay, to Wych Street, to Wych Street."

London, that mighty heart of England, was now lulled into temporary repose : its riotous pulses were awhile stilled — its arteries slumbered gently, calmly. Jack and Bess made their way through the silent and almost deserted streets without any interruption. Jack felt a twitch, whether of his mind or body he did not stay to ascertain, as he passed the familiar and tranquil dwelling of his old master, Mr. Wood, where he had spent so many happy, because guiltless, hours. A low murmur of voices, and some glimmerings of light between the shutters, soon showed Jack he had been right in his conjectures : he gave the well-known signal, the door was soon opened, and Mr. Hind stood before them.

"What! Jack — Jack Sheppard, my rum cull ! and your doxy too ! You here at this time of the morning!" and here he began singing according to his usual custom —

> " To-morrow is St. Valentine's day,
>   All in the morn be time,
>   And I maid at your window
>   To be your Valentine."

But what the devil! I thought you were in Clerkenwell quod, ken; but come in — here's plenty that will be glad enough to see you — gad! this will be a rare surprise — walk in, young madam," addressing Bess, and here he resumed singing as he fastened the door —

> " Then up he rose and donn'd his clothes,
>   And oped the chamber door;
>   Let in a maid, that out a maid
>   Never departed more."

Proceeding to the little back parlour, with which the reader is acquainted of old, Jack was at once astonished and delighted at finding there his old pal and school-fellow, Blueskin, Mr. Jonathan Wild, Black Martin, and several other respectable gentlemen, including Mr. Wild's satellites, Mr. Quilt Arnold, Esquire, and the patriarch.

" Done you all, by Pharaoh!" roared out Black Martin, exultingly, as he saw Jack enter, " I was certain he would be here."

" A bite by G—!" said Blueskin, " what a sap I was not to bar the bubble!"

" No bubble at all," returned Black Martin, "I merely conveyed my old acquaintance Bess there,

two or three tools in the Quod Ken, and I was
certain, with their assistance, the night wouldn't
pass over without Jack being at liberty, and I
naturally thought this would be the first place
he would come to. I have fairly won my wager
— glasses round — so bring them in, Joe — they
can never come in a better moment."

> " I am gone, sir, but anon, sir,
>   I 'll be with you in a trice —"

sung Mr. Hind, disappearing.

It is almost needless to say that the reception
of Jack and Bess was of the most cordial and
enthusiastic nature; the recognition of Blueskin,
in particular, was more than usually hearty and
joyous. Black Martin's winnings being brought
in by Mr. Hind, Jack recounted the details of
his escape, much to the astonishment and commendation of all present. The encomiums bestowed by Mr. Wild were indeed most flattering,
as were those of his two satellites, Mr. Quilt
Arnold, Esquire, and the patriarch: the latter
declared, upon " his conschance, that he should
not have thought so much of Jack's getting away
by himself, but that hish bringing Besh with him
exceeded any thing in the way of escape he ever
remembered in all hish prishen experiensh."

In answer to some surprise expressed by Jack
at Blueskin's liberation from Newgate, that gen-

tleman informed him that, giving some evidence which led to the conviction of Oakey, Levee, and Flood, he had not only expected his pardon, but had also claimed part of the reward offered by government; but this the Court had refused on the ground of his not being a voluntary witness, also on account of the desperate resistance he had made when he was taken, and had ordered him to be sent to the Compter, where, in default of his consenting to be transported for seven years, he was to find security for his good behaviour before he could be discharged; that Mr. Wild had acted like a father to him, had paid for the cure of the wound in his head, which he received when he was apprehended, and had allowed him a small sum weekly to furnish him his little comforts, for which he vowed eternal gratitude, declaring he would lay down his life any time to serve Mr. Wild.

Here Mr. Quilt Arnold, Esquire, hemmed very significantly, and the patriarch indulged in a long grin of sardonic commendation. Mr. Wild coolly remarked that he might one day put him to the proof, while Mr. Hind nearly choked himself in emptying his glass of brandy and water, part of it going the wrong way.

Blueskin resumed: — he had been fortunate enough to procure two of that class of respectables, known as poor, frozen-out, gardeners, to come forward in his behalf, who, by representing themselves to the Court as eminent market horticulturists, were allowed by Sir John Fryer to become security for his good behaviour for seven years.

" So you sees, Mister Blake, you musht pe a very goot poy," remarked the patriarch, " it wash a very goot joke when old Vigsby axed you how long it vould pe pefore you cumd afore the Court again, old Hapeas Corpus, the keeper of Voot Street, answering three sessions — I says two — ha, ha, ha !"

All the company laughed amazingly at this sally of the Hebrew ; and the clear blue daylight beginning to steal into the room over the shutters, making the yellow flare of the mutton fats, as Blueskin termed the candles, look extremely unhealthy and disagreeable, a proposition was made for a general move. It was settled that, as no doubt a hot pursuit would be set on foot when Jack's escape with Bess should be discovered in the morning, that Blueskin should provide them, *pro tempore*, with a secure lodging in the Mint until Jack's future operations should be finally determined on : the company therefore broke up, Mr. Wild remarking, he supposed he should see Jack soon, and Mr. Hind closing the door on the whole party while humming the beginning of the fine old Bacchanalian —

" When Bibo thought fit from the world to retreat," &c.

Shaking hands with the usual parting benedic-
tions, the party disappeared to different quarters
with a celerity very remarkable, vanishing like
so many evil spirits at the first crowing of the
cock — Mr. Wild and his satellites one way, Black
Martin and his associates another, and Blueskin,
Jack, and Bess to the Strand ferry, where making
free with a boat, they helped themselves to a
cast across the Thames to the opposite bankside.
The pure morning air from the river was quite
refreshing and invigorating, after the heated and
fatiguing atmosphere of Mr. Hind's back parlour,
impregnated as it was with the fumes of brandy
and tobacco, and the effluvia from the rancid fat
of his tallows. They gained the sanctuary of the
Mint long before any of its denizens were stirring,
but Blueskin being an old inhabitant soon procured them admission through its closed and
guarded entrances, knocking up an intimate,
the proprietor of a select lodging-house in this
sacred retreat, especially devoted to the accommodation of " single men and their wives," as the
Portsmouth landladies are accustomed to signify
during war time. Jack and Bess entered on the
occupation of a remarkably airy garret, upon
very easy terms.

Promising to see them about noon, to breakfast,
for it was now fairly morning, Blueskin left them,
and, worn out with the bustle of the last twenty-

four hours, the lovers threw themselves into each other's arms, and were soon locked in a profound and reviving slumber.

It was quite the middle of the day before they were waked by Blueskin, when a cabinet council was held over a beefsteak, rendered *piquante* by some choice onions, and washed down by two or three mugs of strong porter, which that azure-hued worthy Blueskin, whom Jack styled on this occasion " a heavenly-faced fellow," had provided for their breakfast. It argues no disrelish, on the part of Blake, when we remark, he looked blue at this compliment.

" You are in for it now, Jack," said he ; " it's no fault of yours, but you can't be honest if you would ; you must live, and so must pretty Bess here : the only thing you have got to endeavour now, since the world will make you a thief, is to be a good one."

" I will, I will !" cried Jack, emphatically, taking heart by emptying three parts of the contents of one of the mugs we have alluded to.

" You must not go rashly to work," said the prudent Mr. Blake, observing Jack's determination : " situated as you are now, you will require some protection — only Jonathan Wild can render you secure. By the bye, to-night he

greeting, ushered them, by the back stairs, to
some upper apartment. Jack could not help
feeling some expectation and curiosity. At
length the Patriarch came to say that the leevy
was opened, and that he might follow him up-
stairs, and take his turn to be presented.

Jack immediately obeyed the summons. The
Patriarch conducted him to a spacious back
room on the first floor, at the door of which, inside, stood Blueskin, in his office of first knob-
stick in waiting : he was rather ludicrously attired : he wore a counsellor's old gown over
his own clothes; was strongly armed with two
or three brace of pistols and a hanger; and had
on his head a bag wig and cocked hat : he held
a sort of official wand in his right hand.

As Jonathan happened to be very particularly
engaged at the moment Jack entered, he had
time to look about, and survey at his leisure the
singular scene which presented itself. At the
back of the room, which was crowded with
Jonathan's subjects, sat that great man himself,
in a large arm-chair, before a table, on which
were various articles of booty, writing materials,
pistols, proclamations, &c.; behind him stood
his gentleman-usher, Mr. Quilt Arnold, *Esquire;*
and around the room, on either side, were congregated his numerous followers, divided into
their several classes. To the right were his

cavalry, or high toby men before mentioned—
gentlemen who took the air by moonlight, well
mounted and armed. They were dashing-look-
ing fellows, with cocked hats, laced coats, and
formidable weapons; and bore, most of them,
watches, pocket-books, portmanteaus, and other
articles of plunder. On the other side were the
dragoons, also before noticed—gentlemen who
served occasionally on horse or foot: their
plunder was much of the same description.
There were then the mill-kens, or housebreakers, — ruffianly-looking fellows, — few of
them without some parcels of plate, silver candle-
sticks, tea-pots, and the like. Near them were
some fellows in the attire of gipsies and countrymen, who attended to make their different reports from the various fairs they had lately
visited. Some nymphs of the *pavé* next attracted Jack's attention; these mostly had
handkerchiefs, snuff-boxes, and other light articles. In addition to them, there were the
spruce prigs, and other minor thieves, who
might be classed as sharp-shooters; and a whole
battalion of young recruits, consisting of boys
from ten to fifteen years old.

Jonathan was consulting with Mr. Tutenague, a very dexterous artist whom he kept constantly in his pay, respecting the re-setting of
some diamonds in a necklace that one of his

ladies had picked up at a masquerade a night or
two previously, with some other alterations necessary to be effected in some similar articles of
jewellery just brought in. They were interrupted
by a rough-looking fellow, in a naval dress, having very much the appearance of a smuggler,
who was announced by Blueskin as Captain
Roger Johnson.

"You are welcome, Captain," said Jonathan;
"what news of my good sloop 'The Hawk?'
and how do our friends at Ostend?"

"All's well, Governor," said Roger; "I
duly landed your last cargo, and saw it safely
deposited in the warehouses of your factor, Dick
Norman: he has sent you advices from Bruges
and Ghent respecting the watches and the goldsmith's notes I took him in our last voyage; I
shipped in a cargo of Hollands previously to my
return: 'The Hawk' is now laying safely off
the mouth of the river; and I mean, wind and
tide permitting, to run my cargo this very
night."

"Bravo!" exclaimed Jonathan, rubbing his
hands with satisfaction; "if ever I should have
a squadron, Roger, I'll appoint you its admiral;
I must have a private conference with you, by
and bye. Mr. Tutenague, you have my full instructions touching the removal of the crests, and
substitution of the ciphers on that family plate.

Gentlemen of the road,"—addressing the toby-
men,—" you have had my full directions as to
your several courses, and I have fully accounted
with you for the product of your last excursions.
Ladies,"—addressing the nymphs,—" I have always peculiar satisfaction in receiving any thing
from your hands—convinced that no one can
regret parting with their property to such
charmers."

It may be mentioned that Jonathan was a
devoted admirer of the sex, and was then living
with his fifth wife.

" As for you, gentlemen,"—addressing the gipsies, and those in the garb of countrymen,—
" your next place of destination must be Barnet
Fair, whither I shall accompany you myself: my
presence will inspire confidence in the multitude; they will not imagine there can be any
danger where I am, and will therefore fall the
easier victims. You, Tom Dunn, may tell Bernard Tuckey, when you see him, that I will
afford him a secure asylum in my own house.
I will suffer no one to be hanged who keeps
his faith with me, and fairly accounts for his
plunder. Rob the world as you will,—you
shall do it with impunity,—but you must not
rob me; that is death without benefit of clergy.
You know I strictly keep my faith with you.
When did Jonathan Wild ever forfeit his word?"

" Never, never!" exclaimed the whole assembly simultaneously.

" You are right, my children," returned Jonathan; " when hundreds of pounds' reward has been offered for many of you, and you have put yourselves in my power, on my giving my word for your safety, did I ever betray you?"

" No, no!" exclaimed one and all; " no, never!"

" I have saved many of you, when the halter was fairly round your necks; have kept prosecutors out of the way, suborned witnesses, and supplied evidence. Whenever I have let the law take its course, and furnished the knubbing cheat with another victim, I have been urged to it by treachery and disobedience. It was necessary to my power — to your safety, — was inevitable for the existence aud welfare of the paternal government under which you have so long flourished."

" Hear! hear! hear!" was re-echoed round the room.

" You all acknowledge me your king, then, rogues?" exclaimed Jonathan.

" We do! we do!" was the general answer.

" You will obey my laws?"

Every one bowed in token of homage, and a universal shout was raised of " Long live Jonathan Wild!"

" Enough, enough, my children ; I am satisfied," returned Jonathan, with an air of fatherly
dignity ; — " but stay," — his eagle eye fixing
upon Jack, — " methinks I see one here you
must all be acquainted with — a new comrade." ·

Here Blueskin announced our hero with all
due formality. At the name of Jack Sheppard,
every eye was fixed upon him : the news of his
daring exploits in St. Giles's roundhouse, and his
wonderful escape from the New Prison, had been
bruited abroad, and he was regarded with singular
interest and curiosity ; all the young prigs, in
particular, looked upon him with much admiration. A regular introduction to all Jonathan's
subjects here took place ; the sign of fellowship
was given ; Jack ·received a lieutenant's commission among Jonathan's dragoons, with permission to leave for the cavalry whenever so inclined.
His name was formerly entered in Jonathan's
army list, — for so was the book called in which the
different gangs were registered, — and a particular
district and company were about to be allotted
to him, when Jack, gratefully acknowledging the
favour that had been shown him, requested permission to serve for a time as an engineer, — in
other words, as a house-breaker, — his genius
having a decided bias for laying siege to and
storming the fortresses of his Majesty George the
First's lieges : his request was most graciously

complied with ; and the different parties present, having regularly given in their reports, and deposited their various articles of plunder with Jonathan, who dispatched them to his several warehouses, were allowed, after they had received their pay, being about one fourth the value the booty they had brought, and had their further orders delivered to them, to kiss hands and leave the presence.

Jack could not help being struck with admiration at the statesman-like manner in which Jonathan conducted all these transactions. His subjects, while they appeared to place the most unbounded confidence in him, evidently feared him ; indeed there was an air of cool determination discernible in the midst of all his bland assurances of protection, while they *continued to deserve it*, that was well calculated to keep them true to their allegiance. The apartment in which he received them was also evidently fitted up for effect : in addition to the portraits of Captain John Hind, Mull'd Sack, and other eminent characters of the same class that decorated the walls, there was the last dying speech of Jack Hall ; two or three bills offering large rewards for the apprehension of criminals at that time actually in Jonathan's employ ; there was also more than one brace of pistols, some handcuffs, and other objects of a like nature, adapted to en- force respect; nor were occasional glimpses wanted of Jonathan's sceptre, his silver-headed constable's staff. When the room was cleared of all but the great man, Jack, and Blueskin, —

" You see, my son," said the monarch, " the manner in which I conduct my government. I receive you regularly into my service with much satisfaction, anticipating in you a valuable auxiliary. You desire to begin business as cracksman : 'tis well ; follow me to my magazine — my armoury — and select your own tools."

Here Jonathan conducted Jack, down stairs, into an extensive apartment under ground, on the walls of which were arranged, in regular order, a large quantity of picklocks, files, saws, crowbars for forcing doors and windows, centrebits, knives, bludgeons, and almost every other article used in the exercise of the predatory profession.

These Jonathan made no scruple of showing to casual visiters, asserting he had taken them from the different desperadoes he had secured in the course of his vocation ; but his real motive in collecting them together was for the purpose of furnishing his subjects, whenever they might require or stand in need of their assistance ; for he was too good a general ever to send his men on any expedition without their being properly armed.

After much judicious advice from Jonathan

Y Y

on the subject of Jack's future operations, the latter took his leave, and returned, with Blueskin, to Bess.

On the following day Jack engaged a cottage, at the suggestion of Blueskin, in the neighbourhood of Camberwell, which appeared to be admirably adapted for his views. It was situated in a bye place, called Higglers' Green, on one side of the high road, at the bottom of a long narrow lane, called Windmill Lane, but better known by its more common appellation of Cut-throat Lane, from its having formerly been the scene of a murder, and other atrocities. Higglers' Green was a sort of muddy common, on which had been erected some eight or ten rude cottages, detached from each other, and in different situations, but most of them having communications, by means of back gardens and other contrivances. A low-roofed beer-house was situated in the centre of these dwellings, in which the few neighbours usually met for the purposes of riot and debauchery. Several cross paths, much unfrequented, and difficult of access, led from this little community to Lambeth, Kennington, and other adjacent parts, and afforded means of escape, if necessary. The inhabitants of the cottages were all persons of desperate character; and as no one could approach the spot without being perceived at a great distance, and there were always plenty of fierce dogs about to give the alarm, it formed a very secure place of retreat.

After domiciling himself here, Jack next, in conjunction with Blueskin, looked out for a place in which to deposit any plunder they might in future acquire; after some search, they found an old stable, situated by the water-side, near the Horseferry Road, Westminster. It had possibly been used originally for the accommodation of cattle repairing to the ferry, but had now fallen into neglect. As there was a ready passage across the river from this spot to Lambeth on the one hand, while Town was easily and privately reached through many of the bye-streets in the neighbourhood of the Abbey, Almonry, and other portions of Westminster, it appeared to be highly eligible for their purpose. Possession of it was soon secured, and thus provided and established, it was agreed that on the following day Jack and Blueskin should regularly commence business.

CHAPTER THE NINETEENTH.

THE PROGRESS OF BURGLARY.

A CRACKSMAN'S LIFE. — JONATHAN WILD'S CORRE-
SPONDENCE. — JACK AS GOOD AS HIS MASTER.

THE first exploit Jack and Blueskin committed
in partnership together was at the house of
Mr. Carter, a mathematical instrument maker,
near St. Clement's Church, with whose nephew
and apprentice, Anthony Lamb, Blueskin had
managed to scrape an acquaintance at one of the
free-and-easies of the Black Lion. A very
wealthy master tailor by trade, one Mr. Barton,
happening to be a lodger in Mr. Carter's house,
Lamb was easily persuaded to give Jack and
Blueskin admittance in the middle of the night
for the purpose of paying him a visit. Lamb
was too conscientious to be concerned in any
robbery of his uncle and master; but, as he said,
a tailor was nobody : he would not rob any man
living, but the ninth part of one was quite a different thing. Accordingly, repairing to Mr.
Hind's, Jack and Blueskin remained there drinking till the clock struck two, when, being well
armed, and provided with all the necessary implements for their design, they cautiously made

their way to Mr. Carter's house: here, giving a
signal, which had been previously agreed upon,
the door was softly opened by their confederate,
Lamb. Pulling off their shoes, and leaving the
street door a little ajar, for the more easily effecting their retreat, Lamb conducted them to Mr.
Barton's chamber, and then slunk off to his
garret. The door of this room being locked,
Jack, with a dexterity perfectly marvellous,
forced it without giving the slightest alarm, and
then leaving Blueskin, who had a pistol ready
cocked in his hand, on guard outside, with orders
to fire if there should be any resistance, he lit a
small dark lantern, and stepped silently into the
apartment. The poor tailor, little dreaming of
what was about to occur, was locked in a profound and pleasant slumber.

Jack lost no time in going to work: drawers
were opened, cupboards forced, and boxes ransacked, with a celerity and silence absolutely
magical. Once only was he disturbed in his operations — the tailor had nearly awakened himself
by his own snoring; but changing his position
by turning round to the wall, for his face had
before been towards Jack, he was soon faster
than ever: this gave Jack an opportunity of
making still shorter work of it. Searching the
trunks and drawers, he discovered a variety of
clothes made and unmade, which he dexterously

packed up in two large parcels, and placed them
in charge of Blueskin ; he then picked the lock
of an iron chest fixed in the wall, from which
he took a number of Goldsmith's notes, guineas,
broad pieces, bonds, and other securities, to the
amount of more than two hundred pounds : this
done, he put the tailor's rings, which were lying
upon the wash-hand stand, upon his own fingers,
gently drew the watch from under the pillow
pressed by the unconscious sleeper's head, and,
helping himself to a glass of ratifia from a private
case bottle, which he found by the bed-side,
darkened his lantern, bowed politely to the sleeping *sneider*, and rejoined Blueskin without any
interruption.

As had been settled, they stole down stairs
with their booty, leaving the street-door open
behind them, Anthony Lamb remaining in his
garret, feeling all the time as innocent as if he
had actually been the quadruped whose name he
bore.   It was not long before a neighbour of
Mr. Carter, getting up earlier than usual, to
request the attendance of an ancient priestess of
Lucina, at the pressing instance of his good
lady, then in the condition " all ladies wish to
be who love their lords," finding the mathematical instrument maker's door open, and no
one stirring in the house, suspected that something was wrong, and instantly gave the alarm.

This awakened the poor tailor, who jumped out of bed in the greatest consternation, and soon found, by breaking his shins over his trunks, &c., that lay scattered about his room, what sort of visiters they were that had favoured him with their company.

The first step of Mr. Carter and his lodger was to run up to the garret of Anthony, to whom their suspicions were immediately directed by his known practice of keeping late hours, and frequenting houses of ill repute. They found Anthony apparently buried in a deep slumber. After much shaking and calling, he gave a loud yawn, and stretching forth one arm, by which he almost put out the tailor's eye, suffered himself to be made acquainted with what had happened. They were, however, not to be deceived; a few close questions soon confused him; they charged him, point-blank, with being concerned in the robbery; and, on the entrance of a constable to take him into custody, he cried *peccavi*, and avowed his willingness to confess all.

Jack and Blueskin meanwhile hurried along the Strand with their booty. Passing through Parliament Street, they soon reached Westminster Abbey. As they stole by it, the deep shade of that venerable and sacred edifice—its dark masses seeming to frown upon them in the

bright moonlight — cast a temporary gloom over
Jack's mind that he would willingly have avoided.
Shadows have oftentimes more of apprehension
in them than realities; there was reprehension
to Jack's conscience in that of the holy building.
Passing the princely hall of the Red King, and
the irregular buildings of the House of Com-
mons, then lone and silent, as if they formed
part of a city of the dead, they made their way
to their stable, on the overhanging bank of the
river adjoining the ferry. The waters seemed
to sob mournfully and reproachfully as the
rising tide bore them against the bank.

Jack essayed a little merriment to drown
their influence.

" A glorious booty, Blueskin," said he.

" Booty!" answered Blueskin; " nonsense —
only a little cabbage! Where did you say you
would meet poor Tony to-morrow night, Jack?"

" At the music-house, among the *bona robas*,"
answered Jack.

" You should have fixed Newgate, poor devil,
if you really wanted to meet him," laughed
Blueskin; " for he'll be sure to be there."

" I fear so," said Jack. " You didn't let him
know where we hang out, did you?"

" Not quite such a flat as that," returned
Blueskin. " Ha, ha, ha! poor Lamb is a lost

mutton. Well, he won't be the first lamb that's been sacrificed by his *Sheppard.*"

Here both the parties indulged in a hearty fit of laughter. Concealing their booty in the loft, among some hay placed there for the purpose, they locked up their warehouse, and soon got a lift from an early boatman to Lambeth, from whence they made their way over the fields to Higglers' Green, where Bess was anxiously awaiting their arrival.

As Blueskin had foretold, Lamb, on being taken before a magistrate, made a full confession, but was unable, from not knowing, to state where his accomplices were to be found. He was, of course, committed to Newgate, and being tried at the next sessions, through the kind intercession of his master and the good nature of the suffering tailor, who pitied his youth, escaped the heavier penalty of the law, and was only rewarded with transportation.

The clothes, jewelry, bonds, &c. of Mr. Barton, all but the actual money, were duly forwarded to Jonathan, who as duly accounted for and made his market of them.

The partners' next robbery was in the house of Mrs. Cook, a linen-draper in Clare Market, which they broke open and robbed of property to the amount of sixty pounds. Poor Bess was innocently made an accomplice in this robbery,

Jack having requested her to be in waiting in the neighbouring street, and consigning to her custody a portion of the valuable linen, silks, satins, and laces, which belonged to their booty. Jack then robbed in succession the house of a Mr. Phillips in Drury Lane, where he ransacked the stock of Mrs. Kenrick, who rented the shop, and also the mansion of Mr. Charles in Mayfair, which he became acquainted with through a Mr. Panton, a master-carpenter, who had employed him for a short time as journeyman, not knowing him, and had sent him to execute some repairs there. This mansion, which was situated in the Piccadilly end of Mayfair, he broke open, and took from it a quantity of silver spoons and forks; six gold rings, one set with a stone; four suits of apparel, a considerable quantity of linen, and seven pounds ten shillings in money.

It was very soon, as he said, all " Charley over the Water" with the money; but the other articles, after being first deposited in the stable, found their way to Mr. Wild, and were disposed of accordingly. Numerous other burglaries and robberies rapidly succeeded these; but to recount all Jack's daring and successful depredations would fill a volume : he did not always get clear off, however, but was successively made the inmate of every roundhouse within the bills of mortality, from which he as successively escaped.

London was alarmed, and Westminster waxed pale : locks, bolts, and bars were at a premium ; and the Fleet parsons found their business more than doubled by the number of single young women, who became afraid to sleep alone through fear of the redoubtable Jack Sheppard : his acquaintance was courted, so great grew his fame, by every prig and scamp throughout the metropolis. King of the key, lord of the lock, and baron of the bolt and bar, locksmiths and ironmongers were, under his reign, in the ascendant.

During this period he lived with Bess happily enough. Though unconscious of any participation in them, she was the cause of more than one half his depredations : to his ardent love for her, his wish to furnish her with every comfort and every luxury she might desire, must be attributed at least one half of his robberies.

Living in a sort of fairy world of her own, enveloped as she was in love and felicity, knowing no privation, having no want ungratified, she troubled herself little as to the means by which her happiness was procured ; her whole soul was centered in Jack ; her faith was firm in his affections ; he was her idol, her all : her confiding trust in him was that of the noble Arabian courser for its chief. " The lightning of the desert " would as soon have thought of scrutinising the means of its beloved master, from

whose hands its daily meals were received, as
she Jack's.

Jack's life rolled onwards regularly enough.
When not engaged with Blueskin in the Mint,
planning fresh projects of plunder, he would
pass the day in the little beer-house we have
before mentioned, at Higglers' Green, with
some of his neighbours: these consisted of two
or three bankrupt traders, that had run away
from their bail, an outlawed attorney, some
dealers in contraband goods, under the semblance of costermongers, a couple of smashers,
or utterers of counterfeit coin, and three or four
other persons who, having no ostensible mode
of getting their living, we must charitably set
down as living upon their wits, that being a
general description, affording a sufficiently wide
latitude to the imagination. Here the hours were
spent in drinking, smoking, playing of cards and
dominoes, arguing, singing, spelling over an old
" Daily Post," or listlessly gazing upon the mingled groups of ragged children and donkies,
mongrel curs, grunting pigs, and noisy cocks
and hens, that idly sported and foraged over the
withered patch of common on which this little
community was established, the women meanwhile were engaged in cooking and washing, or
leaning over their palings gossiping with each
other. The scattered ash-heaps by the side of

the miserable cottages, the dirty pools of water running before the doors, the neglected gardens, with their few stalks of cabbages, straggling sunflowers running to seed, broken palings, and the stunted dried-up herbage of the common itself, with its wild thistles here and there, and the few remains of almost leafless hedges, gave the whole a barren, squalid, comfortless, and dissolute appearance. Yet, amidst all this contamination Bess lived unsoiled; she mingled not with her neighbours; Jack was all in all to her. She found sufficient employment for her time in attending to their humble dwelling, which, within that circle of poverty and shift, was a model of neatness and comfort. When evening had set in, Jack would sometimes take her, arrayed in her best costume, through a sequestered path across the fields, to " The Fountain Gardens," at Lambeth, a well-known place of entertainment at that time—the precursor of Vauxhall. Here there was not much fear of detection, the gardens being only frequented by a certain class, and no gaoler or constable caring to visit them, except upon positive information, and then not unaccompanied.

Here they were usually entertained with a song, recounting how a certain swain, named Damon, was conducted by an antediluvian personage, called Cupid, into a pleasant grove, where a certain nymph, 'yclept Chloe, was most conveniently lying asleep on a bank of roses, fanned by some obliging zephyrs — the time being always May — when, after many tender sighs, and an appropriate blush or two, the intervention of another old-fashioned deity, called Hymen, generally ended the business, amid the cooing of doves, the murmuring of brooks, and the warblings of nightingales, to the infinite satisfaction of all parties. Cakes and ale, and a general dance, were also among the attractions of this place, and a cool refreshing walk home in the moonlight, Bess leaning upon Jack's arm, and interchanging tender endearments with him, wound up the day pleasantly enough.

Thus passed away nearly a twelvemonth, when one afternoon, turning over some old things which had been condemned as lumber, Jack stumbled on the wallet of the gipsy Zara, which he had taken from the Red House, in which, as we have before mentioned, was a packet of somewhat dirty letters. Idleness, that often engages in employment which industry had never undertaken — or curiosity, or some other motive, led Jack to unfold one of these scrawls and examine it. Though no great scholar he could read aptly enough : the name of Jonathan Wild, subscribed to the letter, instantly insured its attentive pe-

rusal; to his great surprise he found it ran as
follows: —

" Cripplegate, Feb. 20, 1702.

" QUEEN OF MY HEART,

" THOUGH I have resigned the cares of sovereignty I shared with you, to which your love
and favour raised me, despite my being alien to
your blood and stranger to your race, the in-
terests of the tribe are still as dear to me as
ever.   I know full well, my Zara, that though
king consort, I am but your subject; and though
you've vowed before the patrico to honour and
obey me, your will should still be law to me;
but the Squire, love, is imperative: 'tis not
sufficient that the husband's blood yet stains his
sword, and that the mother has miserably perished without the knowledge of her father's will
— the child is still remaining: this he would have
removed.   Black Martin, with a chosen few I
can depend upon, will be with you at nightfall
near the Witch Elm upon the Edgworth road:
the nurse must be inveigled from the cottage;
during her absence some of the gang must fire
it — it will be thought the infant perished in the
flames — I like not murder.   By these means,
while we save life and soul, we shall retain a hold
on our employer's gratitude; 'twill be a certain
income to us.   No doubt the woollen-draper has

some clue, should we e'er need it, not that I think the Squire will prove ungrateful; but we'll make sure.

> " Believe me thine, my queen,
>
>   " JONATHAN WILD."

This letter was directed to Queen Zara, the encampment, Hornsey. Several other letters of a similar nature, all of them written by Jonathan, when holding the rank of king of the gipsies, accompanied this : they were all addressed to Zara, and chiefly related to the affairs of the tribe; then came a paper written in a delicate Italian hand : the writing, apparently much blotted with tears, seemed to be part of a letter; what remained of it ran thus : —

" Oh, my father! could you see your once-loved Elizabeth now, surely you would not longer retain your anger. As my little innocent Bess smiles on me, and reminds me of her ill-fated sire, the hapless victim of my cruel cousin, the thought will rise to me, that my fault—if fault it was—has been too terribly avenged. These lines may never reach you, my dear father. I feel that I am dying—why should I live? The world is now a blank to me, for it was centred in my Arthur. Could I obtain your pardon, or, failing that, your promising protection to my child, I could yield life in peace. Should I fail, while yet I live, to reach you, to implore your blessing, there is a packet at the draper Kneebone's—that generous man to whom I owe so much—he's sworn he'll but deliver it to one who bears the signet-ring, so long an heir-loom in our family. I have described it to him. You may go safely there, my father. I have not compromised the honour of our house—no, he knows nothing, though in possession of the documents, that will efface the stain unjustly cast upon my fame, prove my child's rights, my Arthur's claims to our alliance. Farewell, my father! The pen is faltering in my hand—the light is fading from my eyes. These blinding tears—I may—I can no more. Bless—but if thou canst not—wilt not—oh! do not curse thy poor Elizabeth—smile one day kindly on her child, her pretty Bess.— Farewell—farewell, my father!"

Though not exactly one of the melting mood, Jack felt somewhat touched at these lines: a suspicion instantly darted across his mind that the pretty Bess alluded to in them, and the child mentioned in Jonathan Wild's correspondence, respecting whom there appeared so much mystery, must be one and the same—and that one no other than the partner of his fortunes, his own beloved Bess: if so, it was plain some treachery had been played her. Rights were withheld from her, perhaps fortune, title. He remembered the mysterious conversation of the gipsy and the stranger in the garden of the Red House, on the memorable night when he had rescued Bess from the power of the soldier, and he determined not to rest till he had fathomed the whole mystery, and seen full justice done to her.

His first step was to question Bess herself touching all she knew of her early history: he did not think proper to make her acquainted with what he had discovered, or hint to her his suspicions, intending to surprise her, when he had reduced doubt to a certainty, and perhaps restored her to rank and fortune. A thousand bright visions of the future crossed his mind: possessed of wealth, and blessed with the love of Bess, he pictured his retirement from the hazardous life he then led to some other land, where, safe from the fears of detection, and freed from the necessity of plunder, he might forget his past misdeeds, or at least, by future good, make expiation for them.

Bess could tell but little: her earliest remembrance was wandering with the gang from place to place, while but a child. She knew no mother—had called no one father. Zara had brought her up, but more in fear than love; she had been shown some trinkets—had worn them, as belonging to her, upon high days and holidays. All the tribe called her Bess, and some few Edgworth Bess; but why she knew not, except that she'd once been told she came from Edgworth; that they were sometimes visited by Jonathan, of whom all the gang appeared to stand in awe. She had heard Jonathan had once been king of the gipsies*, by virtue of his marriage with Queen Zara, who had herself chosen him from all others, and publicly announced her choice to a general council of the whole tribe; but that though a provision had been made for him by the gang, as king-consort, and he had been allowed his own separate kettle and household, he had thought proper to abdicate, and had been divorced from Zara, at her

---

* The notorious Charles Hitchen the city marshal, Jonathan's prototype in villainy, and precursor in his trade of discovering stolen goods, in a pamphlet entitled " The Regulator, or a Discovery of Thieves and Thief-takers, &c." before mentioned, published expressly to expose Jonathan Wild, has the following passage : —

" When king of the gipsies, Jonathan Wild executed the hidden and dark part of a stroller to all intents and purposes, until in Holborn, by order of the justice, his skittish and baboonish majesty was set in the stocks for the same."

Jonathan Wild in his pamphlet, in answer to this, giving an account of himself and the city marshal, does not deny this assertion of his having been king of the gipsies, but contents himself with remarking, " That he need not mention Hitchen having been nearer the pillory than ever a certain person was to the stocks."

own request, probably from her tawny majesty
having found their union was not likely to be
blessed with any progeny.   Bess further stated
that Wild was wont to notice her, and give her
presents, calling her his bank; and once had
said, she was a mine of wealth to him.   That
Jonathan and Zara—who was of a very violent
temper — had some time since broken their
friendship with each other, she understood,
about herself, but knew not the particulars;
that a strange gentleman, the one who saw her
wedded to the soldier, was brought to her by
Zara, and seemed much moved at seeing her,
exhibiting extreme alarm and anguish;   that
Zara had suddenly shown the greatest desire to
get her married to the soldier, Rupert Lion,
whom she had introduced to her; but of the
cause of all these circumstances she was perfectly ignorant.   This was the sum of Bess's
knowledge; it certainly was not much, but it
served to confirm Jack's suspicions.

Jonathan Wild was the first party he made up
his mind to apply to : as Jonathan derived more
profits from his labours than from any other of
the gang, he thought he would not refuse to
give him the necessary information for restoring
Bess to her rights, whatever they might be.
From Zara, even had he known where to find
her, he did not expect much.   Having once de-

cided on any thing, Jack was never very long in commencing proceedings.

Towards night, taking a bye-path which led him to Walworth, he made his way to the Mint, where he was joined by his friend Blueskin, who, on learning he was going to Jonathan Wild, volunteered to accompany him. On their way to the Old Bailey, Jack made Blueskin briefly acquainted with the errand that took him to the great man. Blueskin promised to stand by him back and edge. Requesting a private audience with Jonathan, through his gentleman usher, Mr. Quilt Arnold, *Esquire*, while Blueskin remained outside, Jack entered at once upon the business.

" I believe, governor," said he, " you'll allow that you havn't any gentleman under your command that works better for you than I do; I have cracked, known and unknown, no less than forty-three kens within the last six months; and you know what a very low per centage I have been contented with upon my booty."

" I have never denied your merits, Jack," patronizingly said Jonathan, " nor shall you want my protection whenever it may be necessary. To do you justice, you are as clean a workman as any in town, and mill a crib with a neatness and expedition that does you the greatest credit. What do you require of me — any preferment ?—Even to furnishing you with the best nag on the road—"

"It a'n't that, governor," interrupted Jack, "I want no reward of that kind; the long and the short of it is, little Edgeworth Bess is now Mrs. Sheppard."

"What! pretty Edgworth Bess?" exclaimed Jonathan, "I wish you joy, Jack. Ah! you young chaps are nothing without a mistress. I am always delighted when I find any one of my clever fellows fond of the ladies — it shows they have a spirit; I never mind their having a dell, nay, nor two, for that matter, provided they don't trust them too far, for I have a failing that way myself, Jack. Do you want me to put her on my books? I have a vacancy among my court and opera ladies, now poor Sally Salisbury's gone — can she cut a pocket in a side-box, or take a watch at the drawing-room?—I will provide her with a chair and liveries if she can: the jade will become a hoop and stomacher as well as the best."

"You are right in that respect, governor," said Jack, "though you are rather on a wrong scent with the other: the fact is, if I'm informed rightly, she need not want a chair or liveries of any body, but can have one of her own, if she only had her rights; now you are just the man that know how she can obtain them, and won't refuse one of your best men the necessary information."

Jonathan started ; a heavy cloud immediately settled on his brow. Jack, however, continued—

" What's Bess's is mine, governor, and what's mine is my own ; so I only ask for my own, and, connected as we are, I don't well see how you can refuse me. — I'll slum you the best ken there is in London next week, and charge nothing for the booty, if you'll only whiddle *—so now come and let us know all about it."

Jonathan had, by this time, resumed his usual composure, and answered Jack in rather an under but very determined tone.

" Hark ye, Jack, where you have got your information from I neither know nor care : it is evident you can know but little or you would not apply to me. I will deal openly with you. You are a good workman, a very good workman, and an honour to your profession, and I would do any thing in the way of business to serve you or your doxy, but good will must have its bounds where honour is concerned. You know, while faith is kept with me, I never forfeit my word : 'tis true the wench has some rights, but what they are is my secret, and you must obtain them from some other quarter than me. I am faithfully and honourably paid for keeping it, and as

* Confess.

long as I continue to be so, will not betray my
employer to you, if there was not another rogue
left unhung in England."

"And this is your determination, is it?" coolly
asked Jack."

"It is," said Wild, rather sternly, at the same
time giving a stamp with his foot, which immediately brought in his satellite, Mr. Quilt Arnold,
Esquire.   A glance of communication passed
between them, and the minion instantly took a
position behind his master.   Jack took no notice
of his entrance, but continued his conversation.

"Since that's your determination, now hear
mine, governor: the cove that wouldn't act
jannock by his fancy girl, and be steel to the
back bone in support of her rights, is a rank
cur, and that's a title which shall never be borne
by Jack Sheppard.   'Tis true you are a very
great man, and I, perhaps (glancing at his own
somewhat slight figure), am rather a little one;
but if you were ten times greater than you are —
if you were twenty Jonathan Wilds, and I only
half Jack Sheppard, I'd not suffer you, or any
other man living, to do the wrong thing to my
mort, and so I tell you plainly."

"Dog!" cried Wild, furiously, at the same
time firmly gripping a bludgeon he happened to
have in his hand, "this to me — do you forget
that you are talking to your master?"

"You have not trapp'd me yet," said Sheppard.

" No, I do not," returned Sheppard, putting his hand in his breeches pocket, " nor should you forget that you are talking to Jack, and Jack's as good as his master any day."

" Ah, defied!" roared Jonathan ; " seize him, Quilt."

The latter made the necessary movement—

" I won't trouble you," said Jack, knocking him down with the butt-end of a pistol, which he drew from his breeches-pocket, and which was one of the brace he had purchased with Jonathan's first money. Jonathan immediately raised his bludgeon to fell Jack to the earth.

" You have not trapped me yet," coolly remarked Jack, observing his intention, at the same time most retributively clapping the mouth of the pistol to Jonathan's head. At this moment Blueskin, who had apprehended some mischief, and who had been alarmed by the fall of Quilt Arnold, rushed in with another pistol, which he also presented at Jonathan, while, with a bludgeon in the other hand, he again prostrated Quilt Arnold, who was attempting to rise, clapping his foot upon his body to keep him down.

" Villain!" said Jonathan, gnashing his teeth with baffled rage, " you shall hang for this, if there's not another rogue left unhung in England;" his favourite expression.

"Another word, Jonathan," said Jack, "and I'll blow your brains out. Drop that bludgeon; not a word of alarm, for your life."

The thief-taker was for once taken by surprise, and stood aghast.

"Gag and bind that hound, Quilt Arnold, Blueskin, while I take care of his master."

Mr. Quilt Arnold, Esquire, was immediately accommodated by having his own neckcloth thrust half down his throat, and so secured as to prevent his uttering the slightest exclamation: his arms and feet were then firmly bound with his own garters, which happened fortunately, according to the fashion of the day, to be very substantial ones. Jonathan was next waited upon; searching his pockets, a strong pair of handcuffs, and a regular iron gag, made in the shape of a pear, which he usually carried about him, were soon found, and were directly devoted to his own especial service. A little investigation round the room soon discovered two or three strong ropes; with these Blueskin adroitly bound the Jupiter Tonans, Jonathan, and his satellite, back to back, in which enviable situation they left them, and departed, persuading the patriarch (who had remained down below, and knew nothing of what had been going on) to accompany them a little way on the road, when they promised they would treat him with a glass; observing that his master and Mr. Quilt Arnold, Esquire, were in close consultation with each other, and would not wish to be disturbed for some time. Thus did Jack Sheppard quarrel with Jonathan Wild.

CHAPTER THE TWENTIETH.

HOUSEBREAKING FOR LOVE.

A VISIT TO MR. KNEEBONE.—TURN LOVE OUT OF THE
DOOR AND HE'LL COME IN AT THE WINDOW. —
SYMPTOMS OF YELLOW STOCKINGS.

TAKING the patriarch to a house where they
were not likely to be directly sought for, in the
event of Jonathan's suddenly getting free, the
partners soon made that believing Hebrew very
drunk, when they left him plunged in a deep
slumber, which promised to last some time; they
then held a consultation as to the course they
were to pursue; it was decided that Jack
should immediately leave Higgler's Green, Jonathan being aware of his " whereabout " there,
and they well knew what they had to expect
from him.   To this place they therefore repaired
at once, and packing up what few articles there
was that were moveable, and selling the rest for
a small sum to the proprietor of the beer house,
the moneyed man of the community, to Bess's
great astonishment they cut over the fields to
Lambeth that very same night, and crossing the
ferry by the palace, soon gained their stable,
with which retreat they had not made any one

acquainted, not even their employer, Wild. Here it was settled they should pass the night, and that Blueskin should, the next morning, search for a lodging in the adjacent neighbourhood of Tothill Fields, where there were many haunts in which they could securely conceal themselves. A very few words of explanation sufficed to satisfy Bess for their sudden removal.

The night had set in dark and stormily, but they crept up to their little loft, which, as before stated, was well stored with hay, for the better concealing their booty. The convenient Blueskin, who, to do him justice, was an excellent caterer, having procured a capital country-made pork pie of ample dimensions from a dairyman near Palace Yard, with a couple of bottles of ale, and another of usquebaugh, for so whisky was at that time called, as the wind howled over the river and rocked their fragile retreat to its foundation, and the waters moaned beneath them, and beat against the base of the building, they nestled themselves warmly and cosily among the hay, and enjoyed their humble repast with a relish and content that might have been envied by kings.

The angry blast and pattering hail-storm, though dreary enough to the benighted wanderer, often sound not unpleasantly to the ears of those who can listen to them at ease, beneath the shelter of some snug, secure, and protecting roof. Chatting, joking, laughing, the time passed away, and the chimes of the Abbey had long proclaimed the departure of midnight ere Bess warbled both Jack and Blueskin to sleep with one of her gipsy ballads.

On the following morning Blueskin got them a lodging in a part of Tothill-fields, inhabited almost wholly by dog-fanciers, rat-catchers, and other dealers in animals, most of them persons with very liberal ideas of morality : here, all the dogs lost, stolen, or strayed, throughout the metropolis, were sure to be heard of, on a proper application being made.   Held sacred by constables and others, it formed a very fit place for our hero's concealment.   Blueskin betook himself to his mother's residence in Rosemary Lane, after agreeing with Jack that in future they should carry on business solely on their own account, without the intervention of any agent.

No sooner had Blueskin left them, and they had settled themselves as well as they could in their new residence, than Jack's thoughts again returned to the hope of discovering Bess's family, and restoring her to her rights.   It was plain that from Jonathan Wild there was nothing to hope ; he, therefore, determined to visit Mr. Kneebone, and endeavour to procure the packet, mentioned in the paper, written by the unfortunate lady that had, no doubt, been the mother of his beloved.

He had not seen this gentleman since he had quitted the service of Mr. Wood, and knew not how he should be received. He felt conscious he had acted ungratefully by him, and hesitated at the thoughts of facing him; but his love for Bess, his anxiety for her welfare, made him brave all. It was not until the dusk of the evening on the following day that he ventured out, for he well knew a strict search would be set on foot for him by Jonathan. Using all possible caution, he at length reached the dwelling of the single-hearted, generous woollen-draper.

His first step was to see Mrs. Partington. That worthy woman's instant impression, on seeing him, was, that she beheld an apparition: accordingly she screamed, sunk into a chair, and was about to go into a fit, when Jack begged her, for God's sake, not to expose him to danger, by alarming the neighbourhood, but to compose herself, and listen to him; that he was no ghost, but really and *bonâ fide* Jack Sheppard. This seemed to frighten her still more.

" Are you sure, Jack," said the good woman, " that you 've not come here to break us all open, and rifle us, and that you don't mean to commit a burglary on poor dear Mr. Kneebone, and cut the throat of the whole house? for you know what a terrible desperado you are. Dear me, you fairly make my back open and shut. Whenever I even think of you, I feel all goose-flesh. I'm all of a creep, and don't know whether I'm standing on my head or my heels."

Jack assured her the house was perfectly safe, and every body in it, as far as he was concerned; that he had been forced, by bad treatment, to do what he had done; but that he was about to repent, and leave off his wicked course of life.

" Lord send it, Jack!" said the good woman; " it is never too late; and I'll give you my own great family Bible, with pleasure."

As this was a large folio volume, nearly as big as a side of bacon, Jack felt it would be a very troublesome companion to return home with, and therefore declined accepting it, till a better opportunity should present itself.

" I have merely come," said he, " to ask a few questions of my early benefactor and kind friend, to whom I have behaved so ill — tell him how penitent I am."

" But are you sure, Jack, you are not come to steal any of the plate?" asked the simple-minded dame; " are you sure you've got no house-breaking tools in your pocket? — Mercy on me, what is that?"

" Only a snuff-box," said Jack.

" Dear me, I thought it was a crow-bar!

then you've not come to commit a highway robbery?"

" No, upon my word and say so."

" Well, I will believe you," returned Mrs. Partington, who never thought that any one could
falsify such a solemn asseveration as that; "follow me up stairs to the parlour, and remain outside the door till you hear me cough, when you
may come in."

Jack did as he was desired.

At the first intimation that he was in the
house, the worthy woollen-draper was violently
excited.

" What! that scoundrel, Jack Sheppard,
here?" he exclaimed, " send for a constable,
Mrs. Partington — reach me my blunderbuss —
I'll hang him — I'll shoot him — I'll — I'll —"

." You'll pardon him, sir," said Mrs. Partington, persuasively: " the poor lad has been led
astray by bad company ; ' evil communications,'
you know, sir — he has returned like the pro-
digal son."

" And you want me to be killed as the fatted
calf!" exclaimed the incensed Mr. Kneebone.
" No, no, Mrs. Partington, let him take himself
off directly, while you go for the constable,
and I ascertain that my blunderbuss is properly
loaded — I 'll not see him, I tell you."

Jack did not think it necessary to wait Mrs. Partington's signal any longer; he therefore crept in.

"Indeed you wrong me, sir!" he exclaimed, "I have been a great sinner, but I would not harm you; I implore you but to satisfy me on one point. You have a sacred charge, a packet — left you years ago; I cannot produce the signet ring that should be presented by the person claiming it, but, I conjure you, let me see it — indeed you'll do no wrong: I implore you to let me have it — it vitally affects the fortunes of one of the truest, fondest, best—one with whose destiny my fate is indissolubly bound."

Feeling, which much oftener takes away the powers of expression than it bestows them, had, for once, made Jack eloquent; and he was proceeding, in a strain of forcible and glowing language, to urge compliance with his request, when the sudden rising of Mr. Kneebone, in the height of indignation to which this monstrous proposition, as he thought, had carried him, as suddenly stopped him.

"Rascal!—Villain!—this is beyond all—get out of my house—get out of my sight, or I shall do you a mischief—I shall murder you, I shall! —Give you another person's property indeed! —Where is my blunderbuss? — where's the poker?—Why don't you go for a constable,

Mrs. Partington? — Here, help, help, neighbours ! — Seize the villain !"

Finding the alarm really about to be given, and that there was no chance of Mr. Kneebone's listening to reason, Jack now thought it prudent to make off.

Jack returned to Bess with a heavy heart. He now felt, more forcibly than ever, the propriety of the resolution he had adopted not to make her acquainted with his suspicions and views till he had, one way or the other, satisfied himself what would be the result. By awakening no hopes he could cause no disappointment: accounting for his absence in the ordinary way, he held a consultation with himself what was best to be done — his last hope had failed him. As with Jonathan, it was now clear he had nothing to expect by fair means from Mr. Kneebone ; that worthy man's prejudices being too strong to admit of his listening to reason, he determined to ask the advice of Blueskin, who usually saw every thing in a very clear, straight-forward way. Towards evening, that trusty pal returned from Rosemary Lane to look out for squalls, as he said—in other words, to plan some fresh robberies. Taking him to an adjoining skittle-ground, Jack, between the pauses of the pins, unbosomed himself, finishing by asking what, in such a situation, was to be done.

3 c 2

" What !" quoth Blueskin, laying down the
wood he was at that moment about to handle,
" Is it possible you can ask such a question,
Jack ? Well, that is a good one — why, man, if
you can't get the papers by fair means, you must
get them by foul — if he won't give them to you,
you must help yourself to them."

" What do you mean ?" said Jack.

" Why I mean, if you can't get them any other
way, you must steal them."

" What ! crack the ken ?"

" Identically !"

" Joe, Joe," said Jack, transported with the
idea, which had not occurred to him before,
" you must certainly be inspired — I'll do it this
very night."

" Ay, ay, the sooner the better," laughed
Blueskin, " and I'll accompany you."

" But mark me," said Jack, seriously, " Mr.
Kneebone was the friend of my boyhood—was my
earliest benefactor : his property must be held
sacred : — though, for my dear Bess's sake, I will
break open his house and steal from it that which
is her's by right, I would not take the value of a
farthing from him to save me from the hangman :
this must be a speak for love, Blueskin — you
must content yourself with nix my doll for your
share of the booty."

" Ay, ay," again laughed Blueskin, " we'll see all about that — only let us get in."

" You promise me, then ? "

" Nothing so sure," returned Blueskin—" that is, over the left."

This last mental reservation of course was not meant for Jack's knowledge.

" It's decided on, then," said our hero; " Blueskin, you're a true friend. Bess shall get us some beafsteaks and onions for supper: we'll then have a pipe and a bowl of rum slim, and by the time we've finished, it will be time for us to go to work."

" Agreed," cried Blueskin, " nothing can be better arranged, my lad."

It was between one and two o'clock on a fine July morning when they set out to Mr. Kneebone's.

" Acquainted with every hole and corner of the house, the only assistance I shall require of you, Blueskin," said Jack, " is to remain outside, and watch that I am not surprised; I shall enter the ken from the back — we shall be less liable to observation that way."

" You have only to command, captain," said Blueskin, who had every reliance on Jack's superior skill in these matters, " and you'll find your faithful lieutenant Blueskin ready to fall into the ranks and obey orders."

Arriving at the spot, no one being in sight, Jack placed Blueskin as centinel, and, getting over the back wall of Mr. Kneebone's house, commenced cutting through a strong wooden bar that was placed over the cellar; it was speedily removed, so strong was his wrist, and so adroit was he in the application of his tools: he had then to shoot back the bolts of the cellar door, and force the lock; this he effected as noiselessly as expeditiously. From the cellar he stealthily made his way up stairs to the well-remembered bedroom of Mr. Kneebone: here his heart sunk within him. He remembered the many happy hours he had passed within the house, the many acts of kindness he'd received from Mr. Kneebone; and the thought that he was there, a confirmed burglar, to commit an act of robbery, smote him with painful consciousness. He listened at the keyhole with death-like breathlessness — not a murmur was to be heard — all was awfully silent: he softly turned the handle of the door; it opened to his touch — Mr. Kneebone, unsuspecting and relying, had not even locked it. He entered the room — the massive damask curtains, thickly quilted, that depended from the huge four-post bedstead in which the good man slept, were closely drawn around him, and he lay reposing in a species of living tomb; only his equal and tranquil breathing proclaimed the existence of any other being than Jack within the apartment. Cautiously lighting up his dark lantern by means of his phosphorus box, Jack let the light become visible only by the most imperceptible degrees : a sudden glare might have awakened the sleeper ; but Jack well knew that, when accustomed to it, the eye will repose as undisturbedly in the broadest light as in the deepest gloom. The experiment was successful : no symptoms evinced themselves of the sleeper's consciousness of any change.

There was a small escrutoire which usually stood on a table in this room, in which Jack knew Mr. Kneebone was accustomed to deposit his money and other valuables : in this Jack naturally thought he should find the precious packet of which he had come in quest. He found the escrutoire in its accustomed place : as he approached towards it he suddenly paused, alarmed by a noise he thought he heard below, as if of some one moving. He knew there was only Mr. Kneebone and Mrs. Partington in the house. —Could he by any chance have disturbed that good woman ?—He thought not : besides he recollected she slept in an upper apartment, and the sounds proceeded from below : he had however known her at times to sleep in a small turn-up bedstead in the front kitchen — she might have got up to procure something : he thought he would suspend operations for a while till she had retired again. He listened, but not hearing any further noise, all continuing profoundly still, he made up his mind it must have been fancy, and again turned toward the escrutoire.

It stood on the accustomed table which was placed against the wainscot between two windows, in the front of the room that looked into the street. His first care was to see that the curtains of these windows were drawn, that the unusual circumstance of a light being seen there at that early hour might not attract the attention of the watchman. As he raised the lantern for that purpose the light fell full upon a portrait which was hung directly over the escrutoire—he started—it was the portrait of his mother!

Although apparently taken in her girlish years, he could not be deceived in it. Who is there that, passing with her his earliest years, has ever wholly forgotten his mother? The love of our manhood may be effaced from our memory by time and absence: the features that have haunted us night and day may become no longer familiar to us; but the love of our childhood, pure filial love, remains true through every change, and accompanies us even to our graves: though long severed from us by the tomb, the maternal face is one of those that still smiles kindly on us as eternity opens upon our vision, robbing even death of its sting, and mortality of its victory.

She was dressed in a robe of simple white; a rose was in her bosom : the colours had become mellowed by time, and it bore the appearance of gently fading; the fresh hue of the complexion had also deadened; the features had a wan and saddened air with them, heightened by the raven jet of her hair; the eye, which rather declined downwards than otherwise, appeared fixed on some object; and the painter had so contrived it that, from whatever point you looked at the picture, you could not help imagining that object to be yourself. As Jack met its glance, he fancied it regarded him with a look of melancholy reproach : he remained riveted to the spot for some moments, unable to turn his eyes from it. There is strange power in the eye — a world of hidden intelligence, that has only to be sought for with earnestness to be instantly discovered. The strange fascination ascribed to the orb of vision, by which the deadly reptile transfixes its victim, is not wholly fabled : the lion's strength has been known to quail beneath the steady gaze of the surprised traveller.

Mimic as it was, Jack stood spell-bound and irresolute before that mournful glance. Ashamed of his weakness, he at length, by a desperate

3 D

effort, wrested his attention from it. He turned to the escrutoire; the picklock trembled in his hand; still he saw his mother's restraining look. He shut his eyes — in vain; it was still there; it seemed to warn him. A world of fond remembrances flashed across him — her constant tenderness, her virtuous counsels. Again, in desperation, he essayed the escrutoire, prompted by his love for Bess; and again, as if urged by some supernatural influence, was his attention attracted to the picture: the picklock fell from his hand. Fearing the noise it made might arouse the sleeper, he hastily extinguished the light, and resolved to abandon his intention. Cautiously hurrying from the room, he stood outside some moments to recover himself.

To account for the unexpected appearance of Mrs. Sheppard's portrait in Mr. Kneebone's bedroom, it must be remembered that, as we have before stated, she had been the early and only love of that gentleman. This memorial of his affection might at one time have caused pain, and added bitterness to disappointment in its contemplation; but it not unfrequently happens that objects, the display of which gives at first the keenest anguish, become, by the intervention of time, the most precious and treasured: that very anguish subsiding by degrees into a softened melancholy, from which are often drawn feelings of calm and chastened tenderness that almost amount to pleasure.

Removed from the immediate influence of his mother's memory, which had so unexpectedly arrested his purpose, Jack became more collected, and began to retrace his steps down stairs: while doing this, it occurred to him that adjoining the shop, at the back, there was a small room, which was used by Mr. Kneebone as a sort of counting-house, in which to keep his books, bonds, and other valuable papers — there being a strong cupboard in the room, where they could be securely placed. " Perhaps," said he, " I may not wholly lose my labour yet; " for he felt ashamed to return without having at least made an effort to accomplish his undertaking. " I should prove a traitor to my love, did I not make another attempt; but, then, my mother's portrait. Ah! it was just so she used to look at me, when my boyish wilfulness, my youthful waywardness, would excite a moment's anger in her bosom. Anger! no, no! it was not anger — 'twas sorrow." Jack had never read Shakspeare, and knew not how strongly Nature was asserting the truth of that immortal bard.

" But, then, my poor Bess! Why," he continued, " may not the precious packet have been deposited, along with Mr. Kneebone's other papers of importance, in this room;—it were disgrace to depart before having ascertained this.

Repairing to the room, he was astonished to find the door of it wide open. This appeared to him to be an act of supererogatory carelessness, for which he could not account. The cupboard in question was also open, and the books appeared to be lying about in some confusion. He had no time, however, to waste in conjecture. After a minute search among a large bundle of papers, tied with red tape, and marked " Private," he at last found the precious packet. It was simply directed " To my Father."

He was about to raise it to his lips, when he distinctly heard the heavy steps of some one in the shop. Again hastily extinguishing the light, he remained in stifled apprehension: placing himself so that he could not be perceived, yet could perceive all, he directed his attention towards the shop. The fanlight over the door in the passage, the only means by which the light from without could be admitted, was so obscured by dust and filth that the beams of the moon could hardly make their way through it. It was, indeed, " darkness visible ;" but, in this gloom, Jack distinctly saw a tall dark figure slowly leave the shop, and vanish down the stairs which he had so recently ascended.

Could it be some supernatural being, intent to warn him? He had heard of apparitions and ghosts, and his thoughts immediately recurred to his very small and doubtful knowledge on that subject. The first serious reflections we turn towards the shadowy beings of another world are always very far from satisfactory. Bold as Jack was — and he was always ready, to use his own words, " to face either man or devil" — he felt he dared not, after what he had seen, descend into the cellar. There appeared to him no sense in following a preternatural appearance, for such he felt assured it was: he therefore made his way through the shop-door into the street, taking heed, however, to fasten it carefully behind him, intending to replace the bar over the cellar, that his benefactor might not be a loser any further by his visit. Stealing round to the back of the premises, he found Blueskin, as he had left him, on guard.

" Ah, Blueskin!" he exclaimed, " how glad I am that I am once safely out of that house! Do not laugh at me — but Heaven has set its finger against my entering there. I have had supernatural warnings: the semblance of my mother — yes, her pictured form — has frowned in reprobation; but that's not all — I've seen an apparition!" Blueskin laughed. " Do not ridicule me," continued Jack; " 'twas in the shop. If e'er I saw one bearing mortal form, 'twas there I beheld it; a figure somewhat taller than yourself, and stouter."

The mirth of Blueskin here became downright obstreperous. " I beg your pardon, Jack," said he, becoming at last somewhat more rational, " but I really never could have thought you would have been such a precious muns; however, we won't talk about that *now*. Come along, my boy; let's be off as fast as we can; there may be danger in remaining here another moment. I'm glad you're come. You've got the fakement, I hope?"

" I have," said Jack.

" That's all right, then; this way."

Here he began to hurry Jack along at a very quick rate: Jack mechanically followed him. At length Blueskin stopped, apparently out of breath, and quite exhausted.

" For Heaven's sake! Blueskin," said Jack, who had now completely aroused himself from his late gloomy mood, " what is the matter with you? Why, you appear to have grown twice as lusty as you were, all of a sudden; surely you have not got more than one coat on?"

" One coat! my prince of pals," cried Blueskin, — " why, I've got fifty on: look here my trump," — throwing open his waistcoat, and disclosing an immense quantity of superfine cloth closely rolled round his body — " one hundred yards at least."

" Good heavens!" said Jack, " surely you haven't been robbing Mr. Kneebone—my gene- rous patron, my kind, my constant friend?"

" Indeed, but I have," returned Blueskin. " What would you have thought of me, if I'd visited your friend and patron, as you call him, and had not been a customer: this cloth will fetch us twelve shillings a yard at the least, and Will Field's just the fence that will buy it of us."

" What, then, the apparition in the shop——"

" Was me," said Blueskin, laughing heartily : " I little thought I was putting you in such a fright. It struck me, instead of cooling my heels outside, that, while you were employed above, I might do a little business below."

" Then it was you who forced open the locks of the counting-house and cupboard?"

" To be sure it was, my boy," said Blueskin, in great glee; " but I didn't find much there; only a parcel of musty old books and papers. I'd a devilish sight better luck in the kitchen: see here — how very foolish it is of people to leave their silver spoons about!" Here he showed a quantity of plate. " I took a snack of cold beef and a mug of ale, that they mightn't say I

was proud, and stood upon ceremony. There's
one thing I'm bound to own, and that is, that
their mustard's capital ; — well, I do think mustard eats better from a silver gilt spoon, in a pot
to match. I admired the pattern of our friend
the draper's so much, that I brought them away
with me."

Jack groaned with vexation ; this was what he
had neither contemplated nor expected : he felt
hurt and mortified at the thought that his kind
benefactor should suppose him guilty of such
baseness and ingratitude, and he well knew the
first suspicions would be directed to himself ; —
but the deed was done, and it was useless to say
any thing further : he therefore contented himself with a salvo that it had been done without
his knowledge, and against his wish.

Reaching their stable without any interruption,
the partners safely deposited their booty there.
While, with the precious packet, Jack repaired
to Bess, Blueskin returned to Rosemary Lane,
where he expected he should find his friend,
Will Field, whom he had mentioned to Jack as
being likely to purchase the cloth and plate ;
they having no Jonathan Wild to apply to
now.

"Be careful," said Jack, "and mind who
you trust : you know Jonathan has set his dogs
at our heels ; and, though they are at fault at

present, if once he gets on the scent, he'll never rest till he's hunted down his game."

"The pursuit has certainly been hot about the Mint," returned Blueskin; "but there's no fear of Will Field,—he's one of the right sort."

"Well, well; of course, you know best, Blueskin," replied Jack: "I only gave you the caution. Good by, lad!"

"Good by!" said Blueskin; "I shall just get to the Lane as the Sheenies are turning out." They parted.

Jack's first step, on reaching his lodging, was to examine the important packet. It was some time before he could find an opportunity of doing this unobserved. Breaking the seal with a trembling hand, after unfolding a number of blank envelopes, he came to two enclosures: one was a certificate of marriage, dated April, 1701, between Arthur Montalbert and Elizabeth Smith; the other was a register of the baptism of Elizabeth, the infant daughter of Arthur and Elizabeth Montalbert, and was dated January, 1702. Not a line of any kind accompanied these documents, and Jack found himself nearly as far off as ever. 'Twas true he had discovered the family names of the unfortunate pair, and possessed the means of substantiating the legitimacy of his beloved Bess; for he was now more than

3 E

ever convinced that she was the infant daughter mentioned in the register. But what likelihood was there that this would ever be necessary? How was he to trace out the families of either of the ill-fated couple? Smith was so common a name, and Montalbert had a foreign sound with it. Jack fell into deep reverie, in which he remained till his reflections were disturbed by the sudden entrance of Bess. Hastily concealing the papers, with some confusion, Jack made an excuse for visiting the room of one of their fellow lodgers. Bess started; a deep crimson overspread her face, which gave place to a death-like paleness.

" You were reading something," she faltered; " may not your Bess be made acquainted with it?"

" It was a letter from Blueskin," Jack replied, with some hesitation, " upon business, with which you had better remain unacquainted."

" And was the letter you were reading yesterday from Blueskin, too?" anxiously inquired Bess, fixing on him an earnest gaze.

" Yes, yes," Jack replied, rather pettishly, not relishing this catechising.

" I did not know that Blueskin wrote so delicate and beautiful a hand as that appeared to be, from the slight glimpse I caught of it," returned

Bess, in a tone of mingled irony, reproach, and sadness.

Jack hurried from the room, to avoid reply. As he closed the door, the deep sobbings of Bess announced that she had yielded to a burst of grief, for which he hardly knew how to account.

" Foolish wench!" he muttered; " surely she can't be jealous: these women are all so unreasonable. Well, well; her satisfaction will be all the greater when she finds out what really is the case, and how groundless and unjust her suspicions are." Jack little knew that there is less danger in an infant's playing with a naked sword, than in a lover trifling with a woman's jealousy.

CHAPTER THE TWENTY-FIRST.

JACK IN NEWGATE.

THE RECEIVER WORSE THAN THE THIEF. — THE BITERS BIT. — JACK'S CAPTURE.

On the following morning, Blueskin again visited Jack : he was accompanied by a stranger, whom he introduced as his friend Will Field, — a clumsy set fellow, with a loose shuffling gait, a bony countenance, and hooked nose, and whose clothes hung upon him much in the fashion of an old coat on a scarecrow. Bess was evidently displeased with his appearance; though she returned his salute with civility, she instinctively shrank from him; in truth, there was a wiliness of look about him, which, though it might have passed with the multitude as an indication of cleverness, would, to a physiognomist, have borne the appearance of deceit and cunning. Jack welcomed him cordially.

" You are not to expect, Jack," said Blueskin, " to find, in my friend Field, here, a practical workman like ourselves; all men have not nerves alike, nor abilities either, I may say. Will is rather diffident of his own powers, as far as working for himself goes; but a better touter, whenever a customer's wanted for any swag, there is not to be found in all Romeville. There isn't a Lock, or Fence, from Paddington to White-chapel, that he don't do business with; and I should like to see the Case that he's not free of. I've been telling him of our little expedition the other night, and he says he knows a cull that's in want of just such a bale of cloth as we've spoken to; therefore the sooner we let him see the goods the better."

I'll use you well, Joe, you may depend upon it," said Mr. Field, "if it's only because I know your mother; though I say it myself, you'll find me as honest a factor, and as prompt in payment, ay, even as Jonathan Wild himself."

" Then we'll take you to the lumber ken at once," said Blueskin; " of course, we are all on honour."

" Oh, yes; honour, certainly," replied Mr. Field, warmly; " don't I know your mother?"

" Well, this way then," said Blueskin.

The trio repaired to the stable, into which Field, with some caution, was admitted: he expressed great satisfaction at the sight of the cloth, and said that he would certainly take it off Blueskin's hands, if it was only because he knew his mother. Having measured it, and ascertained the weight of the plate, Field, with many expressions of goodwill, took his leave, announcing his intention of returning the next morning with the money, which, he said, would be about eighty pounds, at least. He had, previously to this, advised them to be very cautious not to suffer themselves to be seen about the stable any more than they could possibly help, that they might not excite suspicion, as he knew Jonathan's satellites, the Patriarch, and Mr. Quilt Arnold, *Esquire,* were searching for them in all quarters, and he shouldn't like any thing to happen to Blueskin, because he knew his mother.

In the afternoon, Blueskin having an engagement with a young lady of his acquaintance, whom he had promised to treat with a bowl of wine, and a sight of the horse-riding at the Three Hats, Islington, Jack determined, in order still further to prosecute his inquiries for the restoration of Bess to her rights, to ferret out the gipsies, and try what he could learn from them on the subject. With some trouble, he discovered that a portion of them were encamped in a lane between Highgate and Holloway: thither he determined to repair.

It was a lovely summer's afternoon when he set forth. Crossing St. James's Park, he made his way through the broad road of Tottenham Court, stopping to refresh himself at that well-known baiting-house, the " Adam and Eve ; " when, crossing the fields on which now are built portions of St. Pancras, and Camden and Kentish Towns, avoiding the high road, he made his way, in the shade of the pleasant hedgerows, towards Highgate. The birds were singing above and around him; daisies sprang beneath his feet; the sun shone with a genial warmth, tempered by the balmy breezes that wantoned gently across his path. Highgate Hill at length appeared in sight. Leisurely climbing its steep acclivity (it had no tunnel then), and arriving at its summit, Jack rewarded himself for his toils with a cool tankard at the first house of entertainment that presented itself.—Declining the proffered honour of being sworn on the Horns, he then, by dint of repeated inquiries, made his way through a number of small shady lanes, or bridle roads, till at length he came to one, embowered among the trees, in a retired spot between Highgate and Holloway. Impassable to vehicles of every kind, and having scarcely room, in some places, for even a horseman to pass,—to say nothing of the overhanging branches which crossed each other from the old trees fringing the high banks on either side, which rendered the traveller's keeping his saddle a matter of much uncertainty,—this lane was but rarely traversed.

The curling blue smoke, ascending from the wood fire over which was suspended, as usual, the general stock-pot, served, as on former occasions, to conduct Jack to the gipsy camp; though even had this banner been wanting, he would have been at no loss — the sharp nose of Fox detecting his approach at a considerable distance. The welcoming bark of this sagacious cur was soon followed by the hearty gratulations of all the tribe. A thousand inquiries were made after the health and condition of Bess; also, whether there were any signs of "Hans in kelder" yet, &c. Queen Zara was fortunately absent; therefore, after restoring his strength with a leg of a barn-door rooster from the stock-pot, and some other little trifles, which he washed down with some draughts of the crystal stream diluted with the gipsy brewage prepared from a receipt peculiar and only known to the gang, — and which was neither wine, beer, nor spirit, but an agreeable and exhilarating drink, or cordial compound, partaking of the qualities of all three,— he found plenty of opportunities for satisfying his purpose.

His first application was to the Prime Minister and Field Marshal, Black Martin, who had always manifested much friendship for him. This illustrious person perfectly recollected the circumstances which had led to Bess's introduction into the gang.

" It was in the little town of Edgeworth," he

said, " that we set fire to the cottage of the old woman and bore away the child, then an infant, who, from that circumstance, was afterwards called Edgeworth Bess, and who is now your autem mort, ben cove, Jack. Jonathan Wild, who was then king consort, planned the whole affair. What his reasons were, I could never learn ; 'tis certain they were not plunder : the owner of the cottage was a poor woman, who had formerly been servant in some great family, and had taken in the child to nurse ; we had a difficult matter to enveigle her out. When she returned at midnight, and found the cottage reduced to ashes, as she supposed through her negligence in leaving it, and understood from the neighbours that the child had perished in the flames (for such was the general supposition), she lost her wits, I'm told, and has been crazed ever since. Our queen brought up the kid herself ; but who the kid really belonged to, and for what purpose she was kidnapped, has always been a mystery. If Poll Maggot was here now, Mahogany Poll, as her husband, poor Will Maggot, the spiced toby cheesemonger, used to call her — if she was here now, she might let you know a little more about it ; but she sets off with the lady's maid that's going to smuggle her this evening into a house of a person of quality in St. James's, where she's to tell the fortunes of all the female part of the family; that she can easily do, for she's wormed all their secrets out beforehand from Mrs. Abigail, who was sent here expressly to take her. I expect she'll make a good night's work of it; she'll be sure to pick up a few odd spoons and trinkets, and perhaps a watch or two; and they'll never dare say a word of the matter when it's discovered, lest they should be blamed for their own carelessness and credulity; besides which, no doubt the jade will be well paid."

" I must visit Edgeworth," said Jack, involuntarily, his attention not having been at all attracted by these last remarks of Black Martin,— " Yes, I must visit Edgeworth — I must see this poor mad creature, if she be still alive; I must learn what family she lived with — it will afford a clue; but who shall I get to accompany me, and search her out for me? — who is there that can recognise her?"

" Why, the very mort we are talking about," replied the Egyptian chief. " I'll tell you what I'll do, lad: where's your tent, that is, your ken? — Where do you hang out? Just give me the office, and I'll send the slut to you the day after to-morrow; she shall go with you to the very spot."

" You will!" said Jack, gratefully grasping the vagrant minister's hand; " do that, and I'll

honour and bless you for ever; but secrecy —
Bess must not know a single syllable of what's
going on—she has no suspicion."

"Leave a gipsy alone," laughingly observed
Black Martin; "Mahogany Moll will be as close
as an oyster; nay, better than that, for when
secrecy's the word, the jade wouldn't even open
to the knife."

"Capital! Capital!" said Jack, in ecstasy;" I
may depend, then?"

"You may, you may; leave it all to the
cook."

They rejoined the gang — the glass and toast
went round, seasoned meanwhiles with laugh
and joke and song, and it was not till the moon
was riding high in the heavens, plaiting the
foliage with her silvery light, that Jack took his
farewell, and retraced his steps homewards.

The lane was partially in gloom, owing to the
thickness of the overhanging branches, and there
was a deep stillness in the air, only broken by
the occasional hum of some insect, and the soft
ripplings of a neighbouring brook; but when he
emerged at the top of the lane into an open
meadow, the flood of splendid light, in which he
seemed all at once to be completely bathed, as it
were, had its effect even on his every-day nature.
It was a delicious walk home through those fields,
so calm, so dreamy, so fresh, and Jack was almost

sorry when, arriving at length at St. James's Park, one of the obscure streets near the Abbey brought him into the neighbourhood of his own retreat. As he turned into Tothill-fields, the contrast betwixt its close muggy oppressive atmosphere, almost fetid with the rank odours of the number of animals pent up as if in another but less saving ark, and the mild reviving breath of nature that he had inhaled from field and flower during his walk home, struck him most forcibly; the presence of innocence in the one resort, and the feeling of guilt in the other, could not be mistaken. The abiding place of each was strongly marked out by their attributes — Jack's heart was softened, and he felt almost saddened at the silent lesson that was read him.

" Well, well!" he mentally ejaculated; " let me but restore Bess to her rights, let me but gain the means to seek some other country, and live beyond the reach and fear of want, and I will forswear my present course of life, and become honest. I could have wished to have done something for men to remember me by — there is no labour I would not undergo, no privation I would not endure, could I but achieve some deed that might render my name celebrated, and get me talked of hereafter. Yes, I feel that I am not without ambition, but I have shut out to myself all the paths of honourable enterprise. —

What can I do to make my memory renowned? — Who, when I am gone, will cast a thought upon Jack Sheppard — the low-born burglar? —'tis madness thinking of its possibility."

Poor Jack! how little did he imagine that his adventures were to occupy the attention of succeeding generations; that he was to figure on every stage, the favourite hero of the play and the pantomime; that the novelist and romance writer would embalm his fame in their pages, and that the more than usual brevity of his mortal career would be compensated by a length of immortality in fiction, far exceeding that of many of the greatest warriors, statesmen, and other worthies of his age.

Jack found Bess sitting up for him; she was thoughtful and pensive, but she essayed to look cheerful, and to receive him with her wonted welcome: he saw she had been weeping, but he forbore to inquire the cause, rightly attributing it to his absence; he contented himself with evincing more than his usual tenderness towards her. They arose the following morning with their accustomed good humour. Jack spoke of a little excursion of pleasure to which he intended to treat Bess in the afternoon—a visit to Sadler's Wells, then a very favourite place of amusement: her countenance regained its gaiety; she became once more all smiles, and returned Jack's kisses, when he left her, after breakfast, to accompany Blueskin, according to their appointment with Field, with a fervour and sincerity that assured him of her continued and ardent devotion.

Jack found Blueskin waiting for him at the public-house where it was settled they were to meet. Taking a morning draught, and playing a game of skittles, they amused the time till the approach of the hour of their appointment with Field, who was to join them at the stable. To the stable then they repaired.

"Halloo, Jack!" said Blueskin, who was the first to reach the door, "what's in the wind here?—a screw loose, by all that's damnable! Why, here's the jigger * open; surely we couldn't have forgotten to have locked it after us yesterday. No! here's somebody been playing booty.—Why, the Case has been cracked!"

Jack rushed forward; the door had indeed been broken open.

"It must have been that infernal fellow that knew your mother, Blueskin," said Jack. "I thought, all along, there was something cross about the scoundrel; pray Heaven he mayn't have turned snitch! Let us look if the swag is safe."

* Door.

Quick as thought they ascended to the loft; the hay was there, but, as Blueskin remarked, "the cloth and plate had danced the hays, and vanished."

"Damnation! I'll chive* that villain Field," said Blueskin. "Rob a pal! it's death, without benefit of clergy. The world will very soon come to an end now, and the sooner the better; for who'd wish to live in it? When there's no honour left among thieves, it will be in vain to look for it any where else. But come, Jack, the sooner we cut our stick, and leave this place, the better; we can't be off too quickly. I've always heard the receiver was worse than the thief; and now, dam'me, I know it. Rob a pal!—A fellow that nursed me when I was a child!"

"Yes, he said he knew your mother, Joe," said Jack, with a bitter sneer; "that made him, I suppose, make so free with our property; if you can't take a liberty with your friends, who can you do it with?—But let's be off—this way."

Opening the outer door to quit the stable, to their utter surprise they encountered Jonathan Wild's satellite, Mr. Quilt Arnold, *Esquire*, who was apparently in attendance there to receive them.

* Knife him — cut his throat.

"Good morning, gentlemen," said that worthy, bowing with ironical politeness; "Mr. Field's compliments, and he's sorry he cannot have the pleasure of waiting upon you this morning, touching that little affair of the broadcloth, but he sent me instead, in hopes I shall do as well."

"Trapped, by G —," roared Blueskin, at the same instant felling Mr. Quilt Arnold to the earth. "To the loft, Jack — the river; it's our only chance of escape; no doubt, the fellow has got plenty of his companions at hand."

To the loft they accordingly flew like lightning, and opening a little door that looked upon the river, were about to precipitate themselves below, when they were stopped by the apparition of the Patriarch, who was waiting, in a boat, with a couple of constables, immediately beneath.

"How do you do, my dears," said the Israelite, with a grin. "You can jump down; dere's no danger; ve'll take care of you; those that are porn to be hanged, will never be drown'd, you know."

Muttering execrations, they retraced their steps, on the chance that Quilt Arnold might be alone, but no sooner had they re-descended, when they were met by a body of constables, as well as Quilt Arnold, who had by this time regained his legs, and was brandishing a huge hanger. Blueskin instantly drew out a pen-knife, the only thing in the shape of an instrument of offence he had about him, and swore he would stab the first man that should stop him.

" Then I 'm the first man," said Quilt, boldly; " and Mr. Jonathan Wild is not far behind me; and if you don't instantly drop that knife, I 'll chop your arm off."

At the formidable name of Jonathan Wild, the weapon instantly fell from Blueskin's hand, and both he and Jack were instantly secured. Jonathan then made his appearance.

" Snug hiding place, this!" he exclaimed; " I am sorry to disturb you, but business is business, you know. Where are the bracelets, Quilt? we mustn't be less polite then they were to us the last time we had the pleasure of meeting — psha! those ruffles are a mile too large; don't you know that Jack has the power of distending the muscles of the wrist? You must hand him number one, those we use for the young prigs."

" I'll take care of number one, governor," said the satellite, with great glee, thrusting Jack's wrists into a very small pair of handcuffs.

A whistle from Jonathan here brought the patriarch to add to their number, who very officiously waited upon Blueskin. When the partners were both firmly secured, Jonathan gave the word—to the Strand ; and the whole party proceeded to make their way there.

Jack preserved a sullen silence, while Blueskin gave a vent to his feelings in a variety of inward execrations. As they passed through the streets, Jonathan leading the way, followed by Quilt Arnold, the patriarch, and the two prisoners, and a whole posse of constables bringing up the rear, the report that the renowned Jack Sheppard was taken arrested every one's steps, and so great was the crowd that gathered round to catch a glimpse of so dexterous and daring an offender, that it was with the utmost difficulty that they could force their way along. Jack would have taken advantage of this concourse, and attempted a rescue, but receiving the solemn assurance of the patriarch, that on the slightest movement indicative of such a design he would immediately shoot him through the head, Jack thought it prudent to forego such a resolution. Whether purposely or by accident, in going down the Strand, Jonathan took them past Mr. Kneebone's house.

" There's the ken," said he, pointing to it with malicious satisfaction.

" I beg you wouldn't mention it, Mr. Wild," said Blueskin, who now, for the first time since his capture, found his tongue. " I know very well I'm a box of cold meat*, I'm quite sure of that; all I care for is the bone-pickers † getting hold of me — I should not like to be made an atomy of at Surgeon's Hall, that I must say."

" Make your mind easy, Joe," blandly answered Jonathan ; " don't be afraid of the ivory-turners having any thing to do with you — I'll take care to prevent that, for I'll provide you with a wooden surtout ‡ myself."

" The devil thank you and your surtout," muttered Blueskin to himself.

Jack did not dare raise his eyes to the house, fearing to encounter the reproachful glances of his early benefactor, and the good-natured Mrs. Partington ; he however passed it with a bold and determined step. Reaching Fetter Lane, Jonathan conveyed his prisoners to the house of Justice Blackerby, to undergo an examination, for the purpose of getting them committed at once to Newgate.

As Jack had conjectured, the first witness that appeared against them was the acquaintance of Blueskin's mother, the infamous Field. He deposed, that having become acquainted with Blueskin, he had been as good as a stepfather to him.

" I think you said stepfather," fiercely growled

---

* A dead man. † Surgeons. ‡ Coffin.

Blueskin, who, if he could at that moment have turned his eye into a boarding pike, would most assuredly have run it through Mr. Field's body; " I think you said stepfather !"

Field resumed : having known Blueskin's mother, he had, out of respect to her, consented to become an accomplice in the robbery of Mr. Kneebone's house. Here Jonathan groaned with conscientious horror, and Jack lifted up his hands and eyes, while Blueskin contented himself with doubling his fist, and shaking it very earnestly at the witness. Field continued —he had certainly assisted in stealing the cloth.

" He tells no lie there, at all events," said Blueskin, " though it was not exactly from Mr. Kneebone."   As a proof of what he affirmed, he could, he said, produce a part of the cloth himself.

" He could produce the whole, if he chose," said Blueskin, unconsciously committing himself. " Damn me, if I'll ever have any thing to do with any scoundrel who knows my mother again !"

On Field's testimony, who was admitted King's evidence, Jonathan Wild giving bail for his appearance at the sessions, Jack and Blueskin were fully committed on the capital charge, and a warrant was instantly made out for their immediate removal to Newgate. Arriving at the Old Bailey, Jonathan had the prisoners con-

veyed to his own house, while he sent over to Newgate to prepare for their reception. Introducing them into his armoury for greater security, and being left alone with them, he thus addressed Jack : —

" You seem down on your luck, Jack! I thought you had been a braver man; every one to his trade; this is but what you must have expected; you know I'm a man to be trusted; whatever I say I mean, and religiously observe. I told you, Jack Sheppard, I'd hang you, and I'll keep my word."

Jack smiled contemptuously. " You'll not hang me yet, Jonathan," he exclaimed; " I told you I'd make you restore my poor girl to her rights before I'd done with you, and I'll keep *my* word."

Jonathan gave a scornful laugh. At this moment a third prisoner was brought in by one of Jonathan's minor runners.

" Ah, ah! what, is it you, Simon Jacobs?" cried Jonathan, with evident satisfaction; " why, it never rains but it pours! But it's a pity the patriarch hadn't the pleasure of taking you — set a Jew to catch a Jew, you know."

" Yesh, and a thief to catch a thief, Mishter Vild," said the discomfited Hebrew, gnashing his teeth.

Jonathan grinned awry. " You see what it is

not to act fairly," said he; "but you needn't be very much afraid—I don't think you'll bring forty pounds this time. I wish this mad fool," pointing to Blueskin, "was in your case; I shall endeavour to bring you off as a single felon. As for you, Joe," he continued, addressing Blueskin, "your attachment to this rash cull, Sheppard, leaves me no alternative. You must die; but you shall not be anatomised; and I will send you a good book or two."

"Damn his good books," muttered Joe, between his teeth; "he's a charitable church-warden, he is. We shall see who will die first."

Mr. Quilt Arnold, Esquire, now came in to announce that every thing was prepared for their reception at the Royal Hotel, for so he facetiously termed Newgate; and that the keepers would be most happy to have the honour of being introduced to them. To Newgate then they went. They were met at the door by Mr. Austin, the head gaoler, who was attended on the occasion by his two under-turnkeys, Messrs. Langley and Revel; the trio welcomed their two visiters most warmly. Being conducted into the lodge, the usual process of ironing took place. Jack's fame necessarily rendered this a task of much circumspection. The heaviest fetlocks, bazils, and handcuffs the prison could furnish, were produced and fitted upon Jack, who manifested the utmost indifference.

" There," said Mr. Austin, after conveying Jack to a strong dungeon, in which he was stapled to the floor by a chain, fastened with a massive padlock, and communicating with his irons, sufficiently long to give him the range of the cell; " there, Jack, if you can get away from this place, why I give you leave, that's all."

" I'll take you at your word, my nibbs," said Jack, with a laugh; " but won't you let me have my pal with me?"

" No, no! too good a judge for that," said Mr. Austin; " visiters of your distinction should always be accommodated with a private room — Mr. Blake's apartment is at the other end of the building."

" I think now, Jack," said Wild, coolly, as Mr. Revel brought in some straw and a blanket, with a pitcher of water and a brown Tommy, as the prisoners were accustomed to call the Newgate loaves; " I think you've got all you want, and are quite comfortable, so I'll leave you."

" Oh yes! Mr. Wild," said Revel; " I promised Jack the first time he visited us, that if ever he came to stop here I'd take care of him, and so I will—he'll be as snug as a bug in a rug here; but we must leave him now, I've got to attend Mr. Blueskin — good by for the present, Jack; see you again by and by."

"Don't put yourself out of the way," said Jack, "any time will do — good day. Mr. Wild, I'll give you a call the very first opportunity, depend on it."

"When you can, I've no doubt you will," dryly returned Jonathan, "and I shall expect to see you, but not till then. Now, Mr. Austin, I'm at your service. As Jack has not intimated his intention of paying his footing here, I must lay down the entrance money for him, I suppose."

"Which shall be expended in a half-guinea bowl of punch to drink his good health in — Jack ain't used to the place yet; we shall, I dare say, be very good friends when he once is."

With these words Mr. Austin, his official Revel, and Wild departed, closing the ponderous door on our hero, and putting into effect all its massive machinery of locks, bolts, and bars. Thus was Jack, for the first time, at that height of a felon's notoriety, a prisoner in Newgate.

CHAPTER THE TWENTY-SECOND.

JACK IN NEWGATE.

JACK'S CONDEMNATION.—POLL MAGGOT.—THE ESCAPE FROM THE LODGE.

THE first thing Jack did, after the departure of the gaolers and Wild, was to examine, very minutely, the state of his new lodging; the result was not very satisfactory: the walls were all of massive stone; there was no light but that which was admitted through a strong iron grating over the door, which door opened into a passage that led to the interior of the prison, where some of the turnkeys were always sure to be found: his irons, though strong and heavy, he did not take much into account.

" I must trust to chance and opportunity," he exclaimed; " Rome wasn't built in a day — there's plenty of time for me to concert some plan of escape between this and the arrival of the dead warrant. That infernal villain, Field — he did provide us with a customer for our goods, certainly — himself, the scoundrel! Poor Bess! — What will be her distress when she hears of my capture? Her fears will magnify the danger

3 H

a hundred fold. Then how shall I manage to send her the intelligence? — Plaguy unlucky, too, that this should have happened just at this time ; had I but had an opportunity of seeing the gipsy Maggot, and visiting Edgworth with her, Fate might have done its worst ; I might, perhaps, have procured intelligence, through Mahogany Poll, to have enabled my insuring Bess's future welfare — my own I should not have cared about."

He was interrupted in his reflections by the re-entrance of Mr. Revel, a rubicund-looking gentleman who not unaptly illustrated his name, both in person and nature. Mr. Revel was fond of enjoyment ; he loved a cheerful glass, and had a very pretty wife, though she was ultimately carried off by one of his prisoners — whether from love or revenge is not known. He was fond of a joke, and delighted in a good song and a funny story.

" Well, Captain Sheppard," said he, coming in and shutting the door, " I thought we should have the distinction of entertaining you at last. You won't find Newgate such very bad quarters, if you'll only take to it kindly."

" I desire nothing better," returned Jack ; " is there any thing to be had here ?"

" Every thing but liberty," returned Mr. Revel ; " that is, if you've only plenty of money. I dare say you didn't come here without being properly breeched — trust you for that."

" You may take your oath of it," said Jack, laughingly, at the same time chinking some broad pieces which he happened luckily to have in his pocket.

" That's your sort," said Mr. Revel, " it's no use coming empty-handed here; we like gentlemen that do the handsome thing."

" I know it, my trump," said Jack; " and as a proof of it — what will you take to drink, Mr. Revel? — only give it a name."

" Only *you* give it a name, Captain," said Mr. Revel; " you can have any thing; for my own part, I am not at all particular, if it's only wine or punch; to be sure I do give the preference to punch, but I can put up with wine."

" Punch, then, by all means," said Jack; " a crown bowl to begin with. Here's a broad-piece; you can give my compliments to the other gentlemen of the key, and tell them to drink the change out of it to our better acquaintance."

" Bravo!" cried Revel, in high glee; " well, if I have a failing, it's being fond of the company of a fellow of spirit."

The punch was duly procured, and Jack was so droll over it, and ingratiated himself so much with Mr. Revel by his convivial qualities, that the social turnkey readily undertook to get a note conveyed for him to his good lady, Mrs. Sheppard—for so Jack thought proper to style Bess. In this note Jack informed Bess of what had happened, making, however, as light of it as possible; and, as she was liable to be apprehended on the charge of being concerned in the robbery of the plate of the May-day garland, as also for breaking out of the New Prison, he advised her to await the arrival of Poll Maggot, and only to visit the prison in company with her; desiring that Poll, the better to avert suspicion from Bess, might pass herself off as his wife. In the course of the next day this note was answered in person — both Bess and Poll came to visit him. Liberally feeing the turnkeys, greater indulgence was extended to them than to visiters in general; they were allowed to remain longer with Jack than was usual with one in his situation.

Bess did not appear to be at all pleased at Mahogany Poll's passing for Jack's wife, though the first burst of her grief in witnessing the sad condition in which Jack was placed restrained her from giving vent to the full force of her misgivings. It may be remarked, that though somewhat matronly, Poll Maggot was uncommonly comely, and might have awakened feelings of jealousy in a heart much less devoted than that of poor Bess. Comforting her as well as he could, Jack devised a thousand plans of escape; but the sessions drew near without any thing being decided on.

In the meantime Poll Maggot had contrived to have a private interview with Jack, and expressed her readiness and willingness to afford him all the assistance in her power to enable him to obtain the much-desired information respecting Bess; although, as she said, Bess should not show her tantrums to her in the way she did.

This made Jack wish, more than ever, to gain his liberty. His love of Bess was even stronger than his love of life; but still no practicable means of escape presented itself.

At last the day fixed for Jack's trial arrived, and, with his accomplice Blueskin, he was placed at the bar. He had employed no counsel, for he knew it was useless. Jonathan Wild was to have been one of the witnesses against them, but this was prevented by a circumstance which is too memorable to be passed over, and which might have saved the hangman some future trouble. Just before the trial, Wild desired to speak with Blueskin in the bail-dock, and while they were there, in order that his testimony might not operate to the injury of Jack, Blueskin suddenly pulled out a clasped penknife, and drew it across Jonathan's throat; but the knife being somewhat blunt, the wound, though it effectually prevented Wild appearing as a witness on the trial, and was of a very dangerous character, did not prove mortal, or the triple tree at Tyburn would have lost one of its most distinguished ornaments. Bitterly did Blueskin regret that he had not provided a knife sharp enough to have cut off his former patron's head at once.

" I shall deserve to be hanged," he said, " if it's only for that."

The testimony of Mr. Kneebone, and the perjury of Field, were however sufficient to make out a case against both the prisoners. The jury found them guilty without retiring, and sentence of death was immediately passed upon them. Jack would have heard it with unconcern, but a piercing shriek from the gallery, which went to his very heart, for a moment unmanned him. It was Bess — she had fainted in the arms of Poll Maggot, and was carried, in a senseless state, out of the court.

The two principal witnesses had each excited strong, but very different emotions in the bosoms of the prisoners; the sight of Mr. Kneebone, although conscious he had been no party to the robbery intentionally, gave Jack the keenest reproach; he turned his eyes away from the mild testimony of his revered benefactor, who gave his evidence with a reluctance which fully evinced his sorrow.

Jack's stifled feelings almost choked him, and he would gladly, at that moment, have escaped by death the anguish of a contrition which he felt was unavailing.

Blueskin's sensitiveness was no less aroused by the appearance of Field, although he exhibited it in a very different way : he gnashed his teeth, and threatened him with every variety of violent gesture ; in fact, it was with the utmost difficulty he was restrained from jumping over the bar, and throttling him in open court, while at the mention by the villain of a knowledge of Blueskin's mother, he became absolutely raving.

Immediately after their return to prison they were placed in the condemned hold. Hundreds of people of all ranks flocked daily to gratify their curiosity with the sight of the renowned house and prison breaker, and the emolument of the keepers, who exacted a liberal gratuity from every visiter before they would afford them the gratification so much desired, was more considerable than ever had been known even in the days of Claude Du Vall himself.

Jack passed a merry time of it ; he had been visited by nearly all his old acquaintance, including

Mr. Wood, his fellow apprentice Griffith Thomas, and even worthy Mr. Kneebone and Mrs. Partington. The honest Welshman freely forgave Jack, and treated him to a can of ale, though, as he said, he was a sad tog. To Mr. Kneebone Jack made a full confession, and implored his pardon; his kind benefactor was affected to tears. He could give Jack no information respecting Bess's parents, further than that they had lodged in his house; they came as strangers; the lady had borne an infant girl during their residence with him; he had been present at the christening of it, and thought it possible, from a particular mark about its person, that though grown up to womanhood, he might still recognise her. The young couple had staid with him till the tragical death of the gentleman, who had fallen, it was alleged, in a duel at Rosamond's pond, compelled the lady to leave him and retire into the country; previously to doing this she had placed in his hands the packet, to obtain which Jack had forfeited his life. Mr. Kneebone had never seen the unfortunate lady or her infant since that time; he fervently bestowed his blessing on Jack, and offered up his prayers to Heaven that the pardon of the Father of all good might be added to his, and that Jack might obtain that grace hereafter which he could not expect on earth. Jack was deeply moved; f a truly contrite heart could obtain re-

mission for past offences, such was his at that
moment. As for Mrs. Partington, she sobbed
and prayed by turns; and the necessity of con-
soling her somewhat restored Mr. Kneebone to
composure.

At the earnest entreaty of Bess, whose agonized
feelings were all this time wrought up to the
highest pitch, heightened, as they were, by jealous misgivings of Poll, whose attentions were no
less constant and anxious than her own, Jack had
petitioned to have his sentence of death com-
muted to transportation; but he had been too
daring and notorious an offender to allow of this
grace being extended to him by the government.
The Court was at this time resident at Windsor,
which caused a delay in signing the dead warrants
for the execution of the various malefactors, that
was rather unusual. Taking advantage of this
delay, Bess had provided Jack with some watch-
spring saws, which no one knew better how to
use than himself; but still nothing had been
decided upon. At length the arrival of the dead
warrant for the execution of two of the prisoners
put Jack seriously upon his mettle. It was followed, on Monday the 30th of August, by the
warrant for his own execution on the Friday following. He now plainly saw there was not a
moment to be lost, he therefore roused himself
for action; he was doubly urged — the attempt

to effect his liberty was at once for love and life. To break out of the condemned hold was impossible on many accounts, and he looked out for some other means: his fertile brain was not long in suggesting a plan, which, though bold in the extreme, appeared both practicable and easy.

In the lodge of Old Newgate, it may be proper to remark, there was a hatch with large iron spikes, which hatch communicated with a dark passage, which conducted, up a few steps to the condemned hold. Through this passage it was customary to allow prisoners under sentence of death to pass from the condemned hold and speak to their friends inside the lodge, through the hatch. During the bustle incidental to the knocking off the irons of the two unfortunate prisoners who had been ordered for execution previously to the arrival of his own dead warrant, Jack managed, unobserved, to saw through a great part of one of these spikes; and on the evening of the day before that fixed for his own death, after the visiters had nearly all departed, Bess and Poll, as had been previously concerted, came, as they said, to take their last farewell of him. Revell and Langley, the two turnkeys on duty, were relaxing themselves, after the fatigues of the day, in a little recess close to the entrance of the lodge, with a game at " All Fours." In this recess, every one who came in or went out of the lodge must necessarily pass them ; they therefore deemed themselves secure. In addition to this precaution, the lodge was attended by a demi-official servant of the prison, known by the name of Shuffling Sawney. This nondescript, for it would really have been difficult to have defined him truly,. was a mixture of rogue and fool, sharper and natural ; he had formerly been confined in Newgate for some petty larceny, when he had made himself so useful in cleaning out the wards, waiting on the turnkeys, and doing all the little odd jobs of the gaol, that when the term of his imprisonment expired, he was, at his own earnest request, still allowed to remain an inmate.

" I have no home but Newgate," he whined; " and if you turn me out, what is to become of me?—it is so natural to me!—Ain't you my fathers?"

" Well, well!" said Mr Austin, moved, and, perhaps, a little flattered by the reluctance Sawney evinced to leave them. " As, perhaps, we may make you useful in whipping the juvenile offenders, ironing the capital ones, attending to the pillory, running on the prisoners' errands, and waiting upon us, why, I think, we may manage to let you remain a hanger-on ; but, mind, all will depend on your good behaviour ; if you show the least compassion or indulgence to any one, or are guilty of the slightest disobedience to our orders, however hard they may seem, that instant out you go: so you know your doom, Sawney."

Sawney was too cunning to subject himself to the punishment of being turned out of Newgate, and was therefore very guarded in his behaviour before any of the authorities of the prison.   His predominant passion was a love of secret mischief, not unusual with those coming under the denomination of naturals or idiots; this itching for mischief he would practise alike on friend and foe, if he could but do it with impunity; to get any one into a dilemma was his delight.   As may be surmised from his *sobriquet*, he was from the north country, and was shrewdly suspected to have formerly belonged to the Tolbooth in " Auld Reekie."   Jack had become a favourite with him, from the liberality with which he paid him for the various little offices he performed for him.

On this eventful evening, as we have said, Sawney was in attendance in the lodge, lurking and shambling about, as was usual with him. He saw Poll and Bess enter; they were closely muffled up in large hoods and scarfs, and appeared, from holding their handkerchiefs to their eyes, to be weeping bitterly; he fixed an oblique

glance upon them with an expression of much sinister significance. To relieve themselves from his unusual scrutiny, they gave him a broad piece; he turned it over, and chuckled with malignant satisfaction; he saw at once there was something on foot; and the idea that the very men—his employers, his patrons—to whom he owed the means of shelter and subsistence, might get into trouble, gave him a feeling of much inward satisfaction. Placing himself at the back of Revell's chair, as if to watch the progress of the game, he stood immediately between the turnkeys, and Jack and his companions, a position which enabled him to observe, askance, what both parties were doing.

Jack's first step was to complete the sawing off the spike; this he did, favoured by the affected sobbing of Bess and Poll, and his own loud expressions of consolation to them.

" You'll lose your Jack, Governor, if you don't mind," malignantly drawled out Sawney to Revell, with marked emphasis, observing the movement, as that functionary was putting his knave in jeopardy, to secure him one point of the game; " the queen will take it."

Poll had by this time removed the spike, and Jack, with the assistance of the faithful Blueskin on the one side the hatch, and the two women on the other, was forcing his slender form through the narrow aperture he'd made.

"Well; all fours is a fine game," said Sawney, dryly, observing the movement; "a very fine game. Ah! the deuce—that's low, Mr. Revell."

Jack was here muffling his irons with a towel, brought for the purpose, and disguising himself in a similar hood and scarf as that worn by Bess.

"Farewell, dear Jack!" sobbed Bess, as if taking leave of him; "I must tear myself away."

"That's high, Mr. Revell," said Sawney, as Langley laid down the ace. "I'll let you out directly, ma'am; this way."

With his handkerchief to his eyes, Jack passed the two turnkeys, made his way, with a profusion of sobs, through the lodge door, and was the next moment in the street, closely followed by Bess. Sawney returned.

"Having lost your Jack, Mr. Revell," said he, pointedly, "there's the game; you and Mr. Langley are quits."

"Well, I'll play you another game, just to see who is conqueror," said Mr. Revell, "and then we'll lock up for the night."

"But not before you have let me out," said Poll, advancing.

"Halloo!" said Mr. Revell, surprised; "why, I thought the two women were gone!"

" And so did I," said Sawney, maliciously;
" let us see that this is really a woman!"

He was proceeding to an inspection rather
more close than necessary, when a smart slap
on the face from the gipsy, by arousing the risi-
bility of the keepers, permitted her departure.
A very few moments after, and the escape of
Jack was discovered. The consternation and
surprise of the gaolers must be conceived: in
the first burst of their rage, they accused
Sawney of aiding and abetting; but he artfully
exculpated himself by reminding them of the
caution he had given Revell, that he would lose
his Jack if he did not mind. The mixture of
stupidity and simplicity he assumed succeeded;
and he was allowed to join in the general pursuit, which was immediately set on foot in all
quarters. Gloating over the angry reproaches
of the indignant Mr. Austin, and enjoying the
downcast looks and mortified air of Revell and
Langley, Sawney's participation in the search
was confined to directing his steps to a neighbouring Geneva shop, where he regaled himself
with a part of the broad piece Bess had given
him.

CHAPTER THE TWENTY-THIRD.

JACK A FUGITIVE.

JACK'S WANDERINGS. — VISIT TO EDGWORTH. — JACK'S RECAPTURE.

THE first thing Jack and Bess did, on leaving Newgate, was to get into a hackney-coach, and drive past Jonathan Wild's house to the Black-friars stairs, where they took water to Lambeth, and put up at the " White Horse," an obscure public-house, only frequented by watermen and fishermen, in an alley by the bank-side, where they felt themselves quite secure. Jack easily found an opportunity of getting rid of his irons.

In the mean time the news of his escape was bruited forth in all directions. That he should have effected it before the very keepers' own eyes, was an act so daring and dexterous, that all London was astounded. It had been Jack's intention, had he been detected in passing through the lodge, to have seized upon some of the weapons that hung over the chimney-piece, and have fought his way to liberty. Moving about with Bess from place to place, for it was in a ceaseless change of quarters that he ensured security, Jack at length found the pursuit so hot, that, by the advice of a friend named Page, the son of a respectable tradesman in Clare Market, with whom he had become acquainted while he was an apprentice to Mr. Wood, he left Bess with his mother in Spitalfields, and withdrew for a time to the quiet little village of Warnden, in Northamptonshire, where Page had some relations, and where it was not likely, from its distance from town, and the want of regular communication at that period, that Jack's name and exploits had ever been heard of. This journey they effected pleasantly enough on foot, resting themselves, during the heat of the day, at the different hedge alehouses by the road-side, and only travelling in the cool of the evening and the fore part of the morning; the nights they usually passed in some outhouse, or under some hayrick belonging to the different gentlemen's mansions on their road; there being much less suspicion, and much more charity, then than there is now. In this way they reached Warnden.

Page's relations were small farmers —honest simple people—who owned the land they lived on, the culture of which supplied them with every necessary of life, while its surplus produce furnished them with the few luxuries such unsophisticated natures required for the entertainment of casual visiters. Their farm was neat and compact; its thickly thatched roof and substantial walls presented the very image of comfort. All around proclaimed plenty; a well-stored granary, orchard, kitchen-garden, piggery, poultry-yard, a range of beehives, with stacks of fodder for cattle, a small river running at the back, well stored with fish, a rabbit-warren, not a mile distant, and plenty of game in a neighbouring wood, to be had for the shooting, on an understanding with the keepers, effectually shut out all fears of starvation.

The worthy people received their kinsman, Page, and his acquaintance, Jack, with a hearty welcome: the best they had was at their command; in fact, it was one scene of eating and drinking while they staid there. The first thing in the morning there was home-made brown bread, buttermilk and clouted cream from their own dairy, broiled fish and game, new-laid eggs, bacon of their own curing, and strong humming ale of their own brewing — these served for breakfast. Then a walk over the ploughed fields, or a turn at fishing and shooting, brought dinner time, with its substantial geese, joints of pork, capons, puddings, and a variety of vegetables, doubly delicious from being fresh gathered from the garden. In the afternoon, a bottle of home-made wine would be produced, with fruits just gathered from the orchard, some preserves, and

a spiced cake of the good dame's own making.
At night, a cold rook pie, some toasted mush-
rooms, cheese, nuts, and cider, with a tumbler
of spirits, would complete the day's entertainment; and they would retire to rest in the snug
little tent bedsteads, with their white furniture
and clean home-spun sheets, fragrant with lavender, to awaken the next morning to renewed
enjoyment.

At first the various noises incidental to rural
life, the thousand twitterings of the birds at early
morning, the crowing, cackling, gobbling, quack-
ing, grunting, and lowing, of the poultry and
cattle, with the eternal cawing from a hard-by
rookery, sounded rather strangely to Jack's ears;
but he soon got used to them. Page had given
a satisfactory reason for their staying some days
at the farm; the good unconscious people were
easily satisfied, they never dreamt of guile.

It was the beginning of September, the most
beautiful of the autumnal months, and here Jack
might have revelled in unmixed enjoyment; but
after the novelty of the first few days had passed,
the very serenity and comfort he experienced
began to cloy upon his sense — his thoughts
yearned to Bess, and the recovery of her fortunes.
What wonder, then, that, after sojourning there
about ten days, during which he thought the
eagerness of pursuit after him must somewhat

have abated, he should bid his kind entertainers
farewell, leave this scene of calm and pure de-
lights, and once more retrace his steps to town.
As ill-luck would have it, no sooner had he arrived in the metropolis than, in crossing through
Holborn, he passed a milk-cellar to which, only
a few days before, Jack's old acquaintance, David
Lloyd, the Welshman, from whom the May-day
plate had been stolen, had removed; Lloyd happened to be looking up at the time, and catching
a glimpse of Jack, with all the sudden choler of
his countrymen, he immediately began to give
the alarm for the purpose of having him secured.
Jack's only chance was immediately to take the
door off its hinges and throw it down upon the
pans of milk; in the confusion which this created,
he made good his retreat.

Arriving at the Cock and Pie, public house,
where they refreshed themselves, they sent for
Bess, and as they well knew David Lloyd would
make no secret of their being in London, they
determined to set off for Finchley. Jack chose
this retreat for two or three reasons : in the first
place, it was out of the way; and in the next place
he could make his way from it by some unfrequented cross roads to the gipsy encampment
at Highgate. Jack did not find Bess in such
good spirits at his return as he expected; she
was thoughtful and pensive; there was evidently

something on her mind; she did not appear to be at all satisfied at Jack's account of his absence; for the first time she pressed him to make their union legal; he could take her, she said, to the Fleet, where their marriage could be privately and securely performed. Jack desired nothing better than this, but the moment had not arrived; he satisfied her as well as he could. The next morning, without acquainting her with his intentions, he made his way to the gipsy encampment, where, as he expected, he found Poll Maggot. Zara had not yet returned. The gang welcomed him with their usual warmth, but he did not stay long to partake of their hospitality; his object was Edgeworth, now called Edgeware, as we before noticed, and to this quiet neat little town he at once repaired, accompanied by Poll.

Poll's first step was to seek out the poor house, a clean, though humble dwelling, situated on a green; here she enquired if crazy Sally was alive. An old woman, who was sitting basking in the sun, was pointed out to her as being the object of her search. Rather small of stature, and withered in her appearance, the precision with which her dress was arranged, the taste and good order displayed in it, would not have led any one to suspect the slightest aberration of intellect in its wearer, had not a lurking wildness in her eye, and the anxious haggard look that

overspread her features, betrayed too evidently a
mind ill at ease.

" Let me speak to her," said Poll to Jack ;
" I know how to draw her out: you must be
well acquainted with the tantrums of these
mad creatures if you want to get any thing out
of them. Good morning, mother," she exclaimed, advancing towards the poor maniac ;
" cross the gypsy's hand with a bit of silver, and
I 'll read you your fortune."

" Ah! a gipsy," exclaimed the bewildered
woman, a gleam of recollection suddenly darting
across her brain, and lighting up her eyes with
anger. " Begone, wretch !"

" Nay, but listen to me," said Poll, sooth-
ingly.

" Listen to you ! I did listen to you, listened
but too well for my peace," said the maniac, with
a shudder. " Had I never listened to you, never
left my home, never deserted the sacred charge
entrusted to me, I might not now be the lost
crazed thing I am ; but my brain was scorched
up with the fire that laid my cot in ashes, and
destroyed the precious babe I swore to cherish.
Her family have perished with her. No one to
claim their wealth, to bear their honours. I was
her murderer !—I that first lisped within her
grandsire's halls. An alien now, foe to her race,
possesses them ! Tell me my fortune ! — have

you not told it me ? — ruin, degradation, madness, want. Away witch, away."

" Nay, nay," said Poll, " 'twas not your fault, 'twas accident."

" Thou liest! the villain Pargiter, the wily lawyer, the distant kinsman of the babe, 'twas he suborned you — he was her mother's enemy, her father's murderer — well may he revel in his proud manor house, 'tis with their wealth — had the old Baronet repented sooner — the proud Sir Tracy ——"

" Sir Tracy *Smith!*" eagerly exclaimed Jack, recollecting that Smith was one of the names in the marriage certificate.

" Ay, Sir Tracy Smith," sharply returned the maniac, " the father of my young, my beautiful, my much wronged, much loved mistress ; the grandsire of the murdered babe. That manor house of Frognall, it was his. Though now a viper warms him by its hearths, there is not one fairer to be found 'mongst all the pleasant dwelling places in those sweet shades of Hampstead, my native home."

" Mark you that, Jack," whispered Poll, who had all the shrewdness and quickness of the gipsy tribe in extracting information from the most unguarded word, the most trifling circumstance. " You hear, Sir Tracy Smith, of Frognall Manor House, Hampstead, your Bess's grandfather ; a distant kinsman, the lawyer, Pargiter, is in possession of her rights, is living in her halls. There is but one thing more, and I 'll soon fish that out. You said the old man's was a late repentance, mother." Here she addressed the maniac in a distinct but low voice.

" Too late ! too late !" shrieked the maniac. " He made a will — he left his pardon and his wealth, his lands, his houses, when they were in the grave, ha ! ha ! ha ! The villain has it in his keeping ; he dreams not that I know it — but I do — ha ! ha ! ha !"

The wild shrieking laugh of the phrensied woman, here brought some of the inmates of the poor house to her side.

" You must away, strangers," said they, rather angrily, to Jack and his companion ; " you have aroused her mood, it may be dangerous your staying, leave us to manage with her."

With these words they hurried their unhappy charge into the house.

" We have got all we want," said Poll, exultingly, " and may depart satisfied ; there's a will you find, the villain has it."

" But how are we to get possession of it ?" said Jack.

" Psha ! where there's a *will* there's a way," laughed the gipsy, " and Jack Sheppard is not the Ben Cove to be long without any thing he wants, when once he knows where it is to be obtained."

Jack became thoughtful; they repaired to the little public-house of the Eight Bells, where Jack liberally refreshed Mrs. Maggot for her services.

"I must go to town to-night," he exclaimed, a sudden thought occurring to him. You will return to the camp, Poll, and the next time we meet I trust you will find Bess a lady, and Jack on the eve of securing freedom and safety for life, when he will show that he can be grateful to those to whose good services he will have been mainly indebted for blessings so unlooked for."

"Say no more, dimber Jack," said Poll, "I only hope all may turn out as you wish; it is not often that I practise my art for myself, or any of those belonging to me; I left it off when the cards deceived me respecting the fate of my autem ben cove, poor Will Maggot. They said he would not perish by the hands of justice; perhaps he did not — yet that villain Jonathan! 'twas by his hand he fell — but no more of this, for once I'll cast a figure."

Here she drew various configurations with a piece of chalk on the table, and after casting them up backwards and forwards, tracing and retracing them several times, with rather a puzzled air, she bade Jack go forth and prosper.

" You will succeed in your enterprise," she said, " and yet there is a something behind ; but as it is past my art to reveal it, we will hope for the best."

They parted, the gipsy for Highgate, and Jack for London. He determined, whatever might be the hazard, before deciding on any thing else, to see Jonathan Wild that very evening, and make him one last proposition. Repairing to Fleet Market, he made his way, about ten at night, up Break-neck Stairs, and through Green Arbour Court, to the back of Jonathan's house in the Old Bailey.   Acquainted with a secret entrance that would conduct him to Jonathan's study, he waited till the whole house appeared to have retired to rest. He knew Jonathan delighted in bold measures, and would take no advantage of any confidence that was placed in his honour. Ascertaining by a light in the study window that Jonathan was there, he softly crept up the stairs, as softly turned the handle of the door, and in a moment the redoubtable housebreaker and indo-mitable thieftaker stood before each other.   Jo-nathan started, and grasped a pistol.   Jack coolly held one ready cocked in his hand, his finger on the trigger.

" I come on business, Jonathan," he ex-claimed; " I am under your roof, and throw myself on your good faith."

" I have never forfeited it yet, Jack," said Jonathan, surprised, but firmly, " say what you have to say, you are safe within these walls; the price of your blood is within my pocket, I leave it to others to see judgment done on you."

" Well then, Jonathan," returned Jack, " I have discovered the secret of Bess's parentage, I know the villain who has her property; help me to restore her to her rights, and name your own reward."

" Hark you, Jack," said Jonathan: " since we last met, things have changed; circumstances have rendered it expedient for me to make myself heir to the property; I possess the means, and you know Jonathan Wild too well to suppose that, when he is certain of the whole, he would forego his security for the chance of obtaining a half."

" This is your fixed resolution?" said Jack.

" It is," answered Jonathan, calmly.

" Very well, then I know what to do," said Jack, with a determined air. " What law do you give me, Jonathan, from the time I leave your house?"

" Half an hour," said Jonathan.

" I have your word?" said Jack.

" You have," replied Jonathan, " which I never yet broke to a thief, though I may have done so to an honest man."

" I believe it," replied Jack ; " farewell, Jonathan."

" Farewell, Jack Sheppard," said the thief-taker.

Jack left the house the same way he had entered, perfectly unmolested by Jonathan, and began, through many circuitous turnings and windings, to retrace his steps back to Finchley, having settled in his own mind, after he had seen Bess, to repair to Hampstead, and pay a visit to Mr. Pargiter at the manor-house Frognall. Unfortunately for Jack, no sooner had he departed in the morning, than Bess, conjecturing his visit was to Poll Maggot, and stung by jealousy, resolved to follow and watch him ; but Jack, by turning down a by cross-road, in a contrary direction to that which she thought he would have taken, unconsciously eluded all her endeavours to track him ; she blindly rushed onwards, scarcely knowing whither she went or what she was doing. The frequent interviews of Jack with Poll Maggot, respecting which he had observed such mystery, his wish that she should appear as his wife at the prison, her joint anxiety to effect Jack's escape, his absence in the country, and evasion of Bess's request to legalise her union with him by marriage,—all convinced the poor girl that in Poll she had a favoured rival, who would, ere long, wholly deprive her of Jack's affections. She had almost unwittingly made her way to town, when fatigue forced her to stop, and she became aware of the hopelessness of her attempt to overtake him. She turned to retrace her steps; at this moment she was observed by the unlucky milkman, David Lloyd, who was passing at the opposite side of the way; he instantly recognised her as the principal in the robbery of his plate, and as the reputed mistress of Sheppard, and burning with revenge for the late destruction of all his pans of milk, and for a pair of broken shins into the bargain, no less than for his former loss, he determined to follow her at a distance, and dodge her to her hiding place.

" Where the female is," said he, " there will the dog fox be found."

The Welsh, with all their choler, are at times patient and persevering; he tracked her footsteps to Jack's retreat at Finchley, saw her safely housed, and was returning late home, when he again caught a glimpse of Jack on his road, though unperceived by him. This confirmed him, and, with a glad heart, he hastened to town to give the necessary information for Jack's seizure in the morning.

Bess's reception of Jack was any thing but cordial, and he could not avoid rallying her.

" What! pouting, Bess ?" he exclaimed; " in

the sulks?—this is not right. What have I done, that I should be received with such black looks?"

"Ah, Jack," said she, "that you must best know. I only know that you have withdrawn your confidence from me, that you have secrets, and surely that is enough for one whose passion is as ardent and sincere as mine; 'tis plain that you no longer love me; you have taken another into your companionship—that odious Poll Maggot; you scarcely think it necessary to conceal it. Have you not passed her off as your wife? —Then your fortnight's absence—your refusal to wed me!—Ah! Jack, Jack, you cannot deceive me!"

Jack could not avoid a smile at the unfounded nature of her suspicions.

"Do not treat me with derision," she continued; "that I cannot bear—have you not secret meetings with her?"

"Suppose I should say I had, Bess," said Jack, good-naturedly, "it does not follow that there is any petticoat treason in it."

"Have you not been with her to-day?" inquired Bess, with much bitter anguish.

"May be I have, and may be I haven't," answered Jack, laughingly.—"Hark ye, lass, get this *Maggot* out of your head as soon as you can, make your mind easy, and give me one of your sweet smiles again, and I promise you, on the honour of a cracksman, that before four and twenty hours have passed over my head, you shall know all."

" There is a secret, then?" eagerly asked Bess.

" Well, then, there is," said Jack.

" And one in which she is concerned?"

" I'll not deny that neither," said Jack; " but come, put me a rasher on the coals, and get me a draught of something good to wash it down with, and let's forget all this till to-morrow.— I tell you Bess, girl, there's bright days in store for you yet; you have linked your fate with a burglar, a condemned one, but you might have done worse, wench—Jack will make you a lady still."

" No, no! no more plunder, no more crime; let us fly to some other country, far from the cruel men that seek your life, far from this treacherous Poll Maggot." Here again poor Bess sobbed deeply, though her manner was more subdued. " Let us live in obscurity, in innocence; I will work my fingers to the bone for you, dear Jack, if you will only remain the same true fond heart that first I knew you."

She sunk into his arms in a paroxysm of tender emotion. Jack kissed the tears from her cheeks, and ere they had retired to rest, managed, by sundry endearments and assurances, somewhat

to recompose her.   In the morning, Page called
upon Jack early, pursuant to appointment, to
accompany him to an acquaintance with whom
they had some business; their way lay across
Finchley Common. Sauntering along, closely en·
gaged in conversation on their future operations,
they had proceeded a considerable distance before
Jack's quick and restless eye discovered any thing
to excite suspicion; but all at once, at the very
extremity of the common, before the door of a
small alehouse at the outskirts, bearing the sign
of the Fox and Hounds, the unusual appearance
of a coach and four, with several persons both
mounted and on foot, convinced him they were
betrayed.

   " We are trapped, Will," said he, fiercely ;
" the blood-hounds have got scent of us — by
hell, there's that villain Austin !—Ah ! he sees
us—he comes followed by the whole pack. —
Turn about, lad, into the footpath, their horses
cannot follow us there —fool ! that I should have
left my pistols behind me — fly, fly, we must not
be taken to-day — to-morrow, and I would care
not to lose my liberty — quick, quick !"

   Like lightning they darted into a by footpath, but Austin and the rest pressed hard upon
them. Jack being lighter and more active than
Page, soon outstripped him ; and while Page
fell into the keeper's hands, he had made his

way into a farmer's stable by the road side, where he concealed himself under some straw. Page made no resistance, and was immediately secured; the search then became general for Jack, who might have got off but for a little girl espying one of his feet under the straw. The keepers on this discovery immediately threw themselves on him, and though he struggled violently, yet, overpowered by numbers, he was at last forced to yield, and once more became their prisoner; binding him hand and foot, they placed him in the coach, on the box of which was David Lloyd the milkman. Austin and Revell took their seats on each side of him, while Langley faced him with a brace of loaded pistols, ready to blow out his brains at the least attempt at escape. The party then formed themselves into a procession; first proceeded a body of mounted constables, strongly armed; then followed the coach and four, with numerous persons on the box, roof, and behind, waving their hats in token of victory, these, it must be premised, were persons mostly connected with the gaol; the rear was brought up by other mounted and strongly armed con-stables, with a numerous body of persons on foot, mostly attracted by curiosity, though some few were so from sympathy. In this state they proceeded to London, the whole having rather the appearance of the triumphal *entrée* of some

great conqueror, than the capture of a common
housebreaker. It was two o'clock in the afternoon ere they reached Newgate, so much was
their way impeded by the crowds of persons the
news of Jack's capture had congregated together.

Jack made an attempt to spring out of the
keeper's arms as they were conveying him into the
lodge, but they were too quick for him, and immediately conducted him to a strong room in the
very centre of the prison, known by the name of
the Castle, remote from all the other prisoners,
where he was hand-cuffed, loaded with double
irons, and fastened with an enormous padlock to
a heavy staple in the floor; and here the keepers
for that time left him, it may reasonably be presumed, plunged into the most hopeless despair;
but such was not the case, as will be seen in the
following chapter.

CHAPTER THE LAST.

JACK'S DEATH.

JACK'S WONDERFUL ESCAPE FROM THE CASTLE-ROOM. — ROBBERY OF MR. PARGITER. — THE PREDICTION FULFILLED.

IF Jack had been an object of curiosity before his escape from Newgate, his fame was now increased tenfold — hundreds flocked to see him; lords, ladies, authors, and artists, who, pitying the sad condition to which he was reduced, and admiring the good humour with which he bore his fate, and the pleasantry and readiness with which he detailed his various exploits, gave him considerable sums of money; and many would even have furnished him with tools for his deliverance, which he would have liked much better, but they were too closely watched; the money however enabled him, in some measure, to solace his sufferings. Bess had flown to him on the first news of his capture, as also had Poll, but the keepers, profiting by experience, refused them admittance. Jack was not at all daunted, difficulties only served to increase his ardour; his thoughts were wholly bent on devising plans for another escape; he had set his soul on visiting the lawyer, Pargiter, and effecting Bess's restoration to her rights; in addition to this, there was an innate love of notoriety; his biography had been printed, and his portrait published in all shapes; to break a second time out of Newgate, while it gratified his love and saved his life, would crown his fame—would be an act worthy of his genius. It was something very like a noble ambition that fired him; he felt there was nothing he dared not attempt, could not accomplish.

The proper opportunity at length presented itself; on Wednesday, October the 14th, the sessions were to begin at the Old Bailey, when Jack knew that the keepers would have so much to do in attending the court that it would leave them but little leisure to visit him; he therefore thought this the proper period for his purpose. Accordingly next day, about two in the afternoon, when Mr. Austin, attended by Langley and Shuffling Sawney, brought Jack his dinner, and giving it to him asked if he wanted any thing more, saying, if he did he must speak then, as he could not visit him again till next morning, Jack replied in the negative. The keepers then, as usual, very carefully examined his hand-cuffs, feet-locks, and other irons, and finding them secure, left him. No sooner were they gone than Jack set to work. He first, with great pain and exertion, worked off his handcuffs, and then, with a crooked nail, which he fortunately found upon the floor, opened the great padlock that fastened his chain to the staple. He next twisted asunder a small link of the chain between his legs, and drawing up his feetlocks as high as he could, made them fast with his garters, so as to prevent their clinking. He then commenced attempting to get up the chimney, but he had not advanced far ere his progress was arrested by a large iron bar placed across the inside of it; this caused him to descend, and set to work on the outside. With a piece of his broken chain he speedily picked out some mortar, and removing a small stone or two about six feet from the ground, got out the iron bar, which proved to be an inch square, and nearly a yard long, and was ultimately of great service to him; he soon made so large a breach that he effected a passage into a room above, called the Red Room. In this room he found another and much larger nail, which also turned out to be a very useful implement to him. The door of this room had not been opened for seven years; but in less than seven minutes, such was the undaunted resolution, and almost super-human exertion of Jack, that he had wrenched off the lock, and got into the entry leading to the chapel of the prison, which happened to be adjoining. Here he found a door bolted on the other side; but Jack defied stop, and set toil at nought ; to break a hole through the wall, and force the bolt back, was the work of a moment. Arrived inside of the chapel, while the big drops of perspiration fastly coursed one another down his brows, the awful silence and solemn gloom of the sacred place cast a momentary chill upon his energies. Sinner as he was, he involuntarily sank upon his knees, implored heaven's pardon for the offences he had committed, expressed his deep repentance, and prayed for strength and fortitude to enable him to accomplish his escape, that he might live to sin no more. He arose confirmed in spirit, and ready to oppose every obstacle that might present itself. His communion with Heaven had been rude and brief, but it had yielded him confidence and solace.

Passing through the chapel door, he broke off one of the iron spikes, which he kept for future use, and then made his way through an entry between the chapel and the lower leads. The door of this entry was very strong, and was fastened by a ponderous lock of unusual security. In addition to this the night had now set in, and he was forced to work in the dark ; but all these impediments proved trifles to Jack's perseverance and determination. In half an hour, by the help of the great nail we have mentioned, the chapel spike, and the iron bar, he forced off the box of the lock and got open the door ; this led to another door still more difficult, for it was not only locked, but firmly barred and bolted. For a moment his heart sank, and his spirits failed him ; but the thoughts of a shameful death at Tyburn, and Bess and poverty on one side, and on the other of Bess a lady, and he in ease and safety, renowned, admired, again recruited his flagging energies ; he paused a few moments for breath and renewed strength, then desperately setting to work again, he wrenched the formidable fillet from the main post of the door, the box and staples came off with it, and the door flew open.

It was now eight o'clock, and there was no other obstruction to Jack's proceedings, for he had only another door to open, which, being bolted on the inside, was unclosed without difficulty.

As he placed his foot on the lower leads, with what a refreshing freedom did the breath of Heaven, from which he had been so long shut out, play o'er his throbbing temples ; what a bracing energy, a soothing calm did it administer to his exhausted resolution, his spent and toil-worn faculties ; he stood for a few moments to inhale its influence, the felon's heart was softened, his spirit was rebuked spite of his bravado. He bent in reverence, almost unknowingly, yet still he owned Heaven's providence, and as he bent, breathed forth a brief "thank God! thank God!" Recovering himself, he now mounted a wall and got upon the upper leads of the prison; there was no moon, but the stars shone brightly; he looked on the broad expanse before him, there was a softened hum dying around him, as if the mighty city was settling itself into repose; he longed to commit himself to the protection of its thousand retreats, and his consideration naturally turned to the way by which he could descend with the greatest safety. After a careful inspection, he found the most convenient place on which he could alight would be the roof of a turner's house adjoining the prison, but the depth was too great to admit of his making a descent without something by which he could let himself down; he therefore retraced his steps to his old abode, the Castle-room, having some difficulty in making his way over the heaps of rubbish he had created by his operations. Procuring the blanket with which he had been used to cover himself he returned, and making it fast to the wall with the spike he had taken out of the chapel, he slid gently down on the turner's leads just as St. Sepulchre's clock was striking nine. It happened that the door of the turner's garret was open, through this he stole softly down two pair of stairs, when he heard some persons talking in one of the rooms. His irons

by chance clinking, a female voice exclaimed,
"Good Heavens! what noise is that?" — when
a man answered, " Perhaps the dog or cat."

Somewhat alarmed, Jack, who was now completely worn out, retreated again to the garret,
where he reposed himself for upwards of two
hours; after which he crept down once more to
the first floor where the company were, and
there heard a gentleman taking leave, and saw
the maid light him down stairs. As soon as the
maid returned to the company, he resolved to
brave all hazards and depart. In stealing down
the remaining flight of stairs, he stumbled against
the parlour door; however, instantly recovering
himself, he got into the street undisturbed.

By this time it was past twelve o'clock. Boldly passing the watch-house of St. Sepulchre, he
bid the watchman good morning; then making
his way down Snow Hill and through Holborn,
he turned into Gray's Inn Lane, from whence he
went across the lonely fields on which now stand
great part of Lamb's Conduit Street, Russell and
Brunswick Squares, into the highway of Tottenham Court; in the fields on the other side of
which, now forming the sites of Charlotte Street
and Fitzroy Square, then a very out of the way
and very lonely place, he found a deserted ruined
building that had formerly been used as a cow-
house, in which he took shelter and slept soundly

3 N

for three hours. Having his fetters still on, his legs were necessarily greatly bruised and swelled, and he dreaded the approach of daylight lest he should be discovered. Examining the state of his pockets, he found he had nearly fifty shillings about him ; but he knew no one to whom he could send for assistance.

At seven in the morning it began to rain hard, and continued to do so all day, so that no person appeared in the fields ; and during this melancholy day he would, to use his own words, have given his right hand for ' a hammer, a chisel, and a punch.' Night coming on, and being pressed by hunger, he ventured to a little chandler's shop in Tottenham Court Road, where he got a supply of bread and cheese, small beer, and some other necessaries, hiding his irons with his long great coat. He asked the woman of the shop for a hammer ; but she had no such thing ; on which he retired again to the cow-house, where he slept that night and remained all the next day.

He would immediately have sought Bess, but he knew not where to find her ; independently of which, he was certain a strict watch would be kept wherever she might happen to be residing.

At night he went again to the chandler's shop, supplied himself with more provisions, and again returned to his hiding-place. At six the next morning, which was Sunday, he began to beat the basils of his fetters with a large stone, in order to bring them to an oval form to slip his heels through. In the afternoon, the master of the cow-house by chance visiting the place, and seeing his irons, said, "For God's sake, who are you?"

Jack said that he was an unfortunate young fellow, who having had a love child sworn to him, and not being able to give security to the parish for its support, had been sent to Bridewell, from whence he had just made his escape, and implored him, for Heaven's sake, not to betray him.

The owner of the shed, who was a married man, and of an easy good-natured disposition, said, that if that was all, he did not see that there was much harm in it; but that he didn't care how soon he was gone, for he didn't much like his looks: he then went away. It was well for him that he did so, for Jack had resolved to make a desperate resistance rather than be taken.

Soon after his departure, a man in the garb of a mechanic crossing the fields, Jack called to him, and repeating the story of the love child, offered him twenty shillings to procure him a smith's hammer and a punch. The poor man, tempted by the reward, complied with his wishes, and assisted him in getting rid of his irons: by five in the evening he was once again unfettered.

Night coming on, Jack tied an old handkerchief round his head, tore his woollen cap in several places, and made a number of rents in his coat and stockings, so as to give him the appearance of being a beggar; in this disguise he sallied forth. To describe his various wanderings would fill a volume, and our limits are becoming but too circumscribed. Every where his exploits formed the subject of general conversation; some reviled him, and expressed their wish that they could retake him, but the major part pitied and admired him. He reposed that night in a beggar's lodging house, or night cellar, in St. Giles's, and slept soundly and sweetly on a wretched pallet, that would at other times have defied all rest.

The next day, Monday, he ventured, towards evening, to the Haymarket, and joined a crowd that were surrounding two ballad-singers, who were most lugubriously chanting forth a metrical narrative of his adventures and escapes. In one of these persons, to his great surprise, he recognised the vocal Mr. Hind, the landlord of the Black Lion. He had been turned out of his house, which had been shut up by order of the justices, and being deserted by Wild, was now in the greatest misery and destitution. To this person Jack resolved to disclose himself. Making him a private signal, Hind soon disengaged himself from his companion and the crowd, and privately joining Jack, they made their way into an obscure public house in Rupert Street, the land-lady of which Jack had heard express herself in a friendly manner towards him, as he had casually taken a draught there in the morning.

Conferring together, Jack learnt that Jonathan Wild had been indefatigable in his search after him; as also, but with different views, had been Bess, who was at that time living in the old lodgings in Tothill Fields. Jack saw plainly, that, for his own safety, the sooner he could get out of the kingdom the better: he was glad he had learnt where to find Bess.

Hind rented a wretched garret in Newport Street, the occupation of which he freely offered. Jack's mind was soon made up. His first step was to procure some decent clothing, and send for his mother; he could not resolve on quitting England without taking a last farewell of her; he therefore despatched Hind to Spitalfields in search of her, appointing to join them at a public house in Maypole Alley, in the neighbourhood of Clare Market, the landlord of which he knew was friendly to him.

" That meeting over," said he, " I shall have to speak to a ken at Hampstead to-night—one in which Jonathan is interested; and to-morrow, in company with the girl I love best, I shall quit England for ever."

" What, pretty Bess, eh ?"

" No, no! she must know nothing of this as yet."

" Oh, oh! I'm mum; sly dog!" said Hind.

" Yes, Jonathan Wild," continued Jack, " by that time I shall be in a way to clear off all old scores with you."

" I am delighted to hear that," said Mr. Hind, essaying to sing, but breaking down in the attempt; " Jonathan is the most ungrateful of villains, and will die like a dog."

They parted; and while Hind repaired to Spitalfields, Jack, having the key of the garret, took a turn down Monmouth Street to look after some clothes. Passing a shop where there was only a young woman sitting, he thought this a favourable opportunity; accordingly, jumping over the hatch and blowing out the candle, he so frightened the girl that she immediately fainted, and he had leisure to help himself to whatever he wanted, with which he made clear off before she recovered.

Changing his things in Hind's garret, he now repaired to the place of meeting. His appearance was so completely metamorphosed, that few would have recognised him. He had not long to wait for the arrival of his mother — the heart-broken woman was too anxious to see him, to delay a moment : their meeting was a touching one — almost too much even for the sensibility of Mr. Hind, who was obliged to have recourse to frequent libations of brandy to keep his spirits at all up.

Mrs. Sheppard embraced her son a hundred times; but her joy at beholding him safe was more than counterbalanced by her fears for his danger; she conjured him, as he valued her life, as well as his own, not to lose a moment in getting out of the reach of pursuit.

" Quit this fatal country," she exclaimed, " dear Jack! Quit the evil courses, the wretched associates, that have brought disgrace and ruin on you. My prayers, my blessings, shall attend you. You need not go without resources; here are the hard-earned savings of long years — my little all, put by for your poor sister's marriage portion, — but 'tis better thus; take it — take it, and Heaven protect and prosper you."

She placed a pocket-book within his hand; an affectionate struggle between them followed, but Jack could in no way be induced to touch a penny of it.

" He could do well without it," he said; " he did not want it — he soon should be in a situation to succour her."

With many tears and last fond looks the poor woman at length tore herself away; and it now getting somewhat late, Jack parted from Hind, agreeing to meet him at his lodgings on the following morning.

Leaving Hind, Jack set about procuring the various articles for his expedition; these consisted of the usual house-breaking tools, a brace of pistols and ammunition, a stout hanger, a few yards of cord, and a dark lantern. To obtain all these was a matter of no difficulty in the dissolute environs of Clare Market, which were, at that time, the head-quarters of every species of villany. He pushed briskly forward to the gipsy encampment at Highgate, to procure the co-operation of the faithful Poll Maggot. The gang had retired to rest, but the barking of Fox soon aroused them. Poll sprang from her tent, and expressed her willingness to accompany him.

" Zara is absent on some of her night wanderings," she said; " we cannot, therefore, have a better opportunity."

It was near twelve o'clock, when, reaching the top of Hampstead Hill, they were about turning down the little lane leading to Frognall, where the mansion occupied by the villain Pargiter was situated; the moon shone brightly—all was calm —most of the inhabitants of Hamptead had retired to rest; only a twinkling taper here and there in some lattice casement announced the presence of man. As they turned to go down the lane, Poll suddenly disappeared, and a tall gaunt figure crossed Jack's path and barred his steps; he started — it was the well remembered form of the gipsy Zara. She fixed on him a piercing glance; a cloud at this moment passed over the moon, and threw them both partially into shade.

" And it indeed is thou!" she exclaimed — " can nothing withstand the decrees of destiny? Will not the watchful eye, the stone wall, the bolt, the bar, the lock, the chain, the gyve, restrain the victim doomed by fate from rushing on his ruin? No, no! who shall hope it? — This I foresaw when light first dawned upon thee; but where is *she*, the partner of thy destiny? Ah! why is she not here to do her work? But she will not be long — there is her natal planet, Venus, fair as of wont, yet surely shining paler, sadder; and there is Saturn, baneful as ever. — Fly, fly, be warned while yet 'tis time — enter not the house — be warned, be warned, I say."

" Away, hag!" cried Jack, angry at the interruption, and accounting for her presence by the near neighbourhood of the spot to the encampment of the tribe, " away with your mummeries; I am not to be fooled by them — off to your tent, I say — dare to dog my steps, or be a spy upon my actions, and, by hell, I'll brain you, witch."

Here he fiercely presented a pistol to her head; the gipsy flinched not.

" Slave of fate, he rushes on his doom; the warning is in vain, rash fool! but destiny is all powerful."

Uttering these words in a sad and solemn tone, she strode slowly away, and soon was lost in an adjoining thicket.

Jack was a little unsettled by this encounter, but Poll rejoining him (she had fled unobserved on catching a glimpse of Zara), he soon regained his determination : he found the Manor-house — an old but noble building; leaving Poll on guard at the door, he set to work. We have no space to detail the skill by which he gained admittance, and penetrated into the very bed-room of the lawyer Pargiter, the treacherous kinsman of poor Bess, whom he forced, at the muzzle of the pistol, to deliver up all the papers requisite to substantiate her rights; her grandfather's will, and a series of letters fully corroborating her identity, tracing her from her birth in the house of Mr. Kneebone to her abstraction from the cottage of Crazy Sally, her residence with the gipsy tribe — in short, every circumstance that was necessary to satisfy the most sceptical.

Strongly binding and gagging the villain, Jack now felt no hesitation in helping himself to whatever was in the house he thought might suit his purpose; he dressed himself like a gentleman in a ruffled shirt and a genteel suit of black, put on a light tye-wig of several guineas value, clapped a silver-hilted sword by his side, slipped his fingers into some valuable rings, put a gold family watch in his fob, and, in addition to the precious documents, lined his pockets with some odd rouleus of broad pieces, which he happened to discover in an old escritoire.

" It will be all in the family," he exclaimed, taking down the lawyer's dressed cocked hat; and now, looking more like a lord or duke than any thing else, and having got all he wanted, he prepared to depart. So skilfully had his operations been conducted, that he had not disturbed even a single domestic. He found Poll Maggot as he had left her, at the door on guard.

" Well, my ben cove," said she, " all plummy ?"

" Nothing can be better, my lass," answered Jack, gallantly imprinting, in the joy of his heart, a warm kiss upon her ripe lips.

" Ah, traitor!" shrieked a piercing voice, " I can doubt no longer — seize him — 'tis he — tear him from her — Tyburn, rather than with her!"

'Twas Bess; and ere Jack had time to recover from his surprise, he was seized by Quilt Arnold, the Patriarch, and a strong body of constables, who rushed forward, headed by his implacable enemy, Jonathan Wild himself.

" Bess, Bess!" said Jack, sadly, who saw at

once all that had occurred, " your fatal jealousy
has destroyed us both — and that at the moment,
too, when I had secured your rights, and had
obtained for you the means of rank and fortune."

" Yes, the prediction is fulfilled," said Zara,
mournfully, as she emerged from some trees by
the road side; " Heiress of Sir Tracy, riches
and rank have come too late. I fain would have
averted this, but it could not be — the stars will
work their destiny."

Our narrative draws to a close — Why should
we seek to linger over the unavailing remorse and
despair of the luckless Bess? — Why should we
dwell on the brutalising details of Jack's execution
at Tyburn, which soon after followed this, his last
capture? Jack did not die till he had secured Bess
the possession of her ample fortune and estates,
all which she would willingly have resigned to
have bought him but one hour of added life.
Every effort that could be made to procure his
pardon or escape was tried, but unavailingly.
Jack's fame had become too notorious.

To account for Bess's luckless appearance with
Jonathan Wild at the very moment when Jack
had effected all, it may be necessary to state that
it was the unconscious work of Jack's old acquaintance, Hind. When Jack parted with him,
his intellects had become somewhat muddled
with repeated bumpers of brandy, which, as we

have stated, he had taken to keep up his spirits; the fresh air, instead of restoring him, only added to the effect of the liquor. It was in this glorious state that he happened, unfortunately, to meet with poor Bess, to whom he could not avoid communicating that he had seen Jack — had just parted with him. Fired with jealousy, the sharpness of woman's wit soon drew from him the further intelligence that Jack would, the next day, leave the country in company with a favoured female, who, she had no doubt, was Poll Maggot.

In answer to her eager inquiries where she could find Jack, Mr. Hind cunningly told her that was a secret; that Jack was going that night to crack the ken of an acquaintance of Jonathan Wild's at Hampstead, which would make the fortunes of him and his doxy; he knew no more.

Distracted, mad, scarce knowing what she did, and heedless of all consequences, so she but gratified her revenge, for such she mistakingly supposed her excess of love, Bess hurried from Hind to the residence of Jonathan Wild. He was alone. Almost incoherent with passion, she related to him the story of her wrongs, her ill-requited love; she told him she would put him in possession of a secret that would preserve the property of one of his friends, if he would pledge himself to tear Jack from the arms of her rival. She did not wish his death, though she would rather see him hanged a hundred times than know him the property of another. Sad wretch! how falsely did she read her own heart. She knew, she said, Jonathan could get him transported, which would be bliss to her if it but tore him from Poll. Wild readily promised every thing. When she mentioned the house of one in whom he was interested at Hampstead as her only clue, Jonathan was at no loss to divine, from Jack's late discovery and conversation, that he meditated a visit to Pargiter. Assembling his forces, thither they accordingly instantly repaired. The fatal result has been stated.

On Monday, the 16th of November, the day of Jack's execution, he made one last attempt for life and liberty; it was more on Bess's account than his own. Having obtained a penknife, it was his design in his way along Holborn to have cut the ropes that bound him, and have sprung among the mob, most of whom he knew were favourable to him, and to have darted down Little Turnstile, where his escort could not pursue him; but the plan was discovered, and, after a desperate resistance, the knife was taken from him, and he was secured.

A mourning coach, which contained the ill-fated victim of unfounded jealousy, followed the sad procession. Jack's remains were deposited,

the evening of his execution, in a humble grave, under the protection of a regiment of guards, whose presence the excitement of the multitude had rendered necessary, in the church-yard of St. Martin's-in-the-Fields; but they were not destined to remain there long.

In a retired part of Edgeworth church-yard, there is a beautiful monument of white marble, overhung by a venerable yew. On one side of this are inscribed the initials J. S., with the date, November 16. 1724. On the other side, E. S., and the date of February 20. in the year following; a brief three months! In this tomb repose the ashes of the renowned house and prison breaker, Jack Sheppard, and those of his unfortunate partner in love, the ill-fated Bess.

Of the other personages of this narrative, it may be sufficient to say, the faithful Blueskin perished a few days before his friend, and Jonathan Wild's career did not continue more than a few months afterwards: he had lived by treachery, he died midst execrations, and his bones now moulder in a doctor's surgery at Windsor, unblessed, even with a grave. Such is the end of crime.

APPENDIX.

ABSTRACT of The Life and Actions of JOHN SHEPPARD, *written by himself during his confinement; delivered to Mr. Applebee on the day of his Execution.*

JACK states that he was born at Stepney, 1702, of poor but honest parents, who settled in Spitalfields, and that he was sent to school to a Mr. Garret, in Bishopsgate Street. His father, a carpenter, dying, Mr. Kneebone, the woollen-draper, took charge of him, and got him apprenticed to Owen Wood, a carpenter, in Wych Street, where he became acquainted with Edgworth Bess, and through his master's carelessness fell into bad courses, frequenting the Black Lion, a flash-house in Drury Lane.

His first robbery was at the Rummer Tavern, Charing Cross; he then robbed Mr. Bains, got taken to St. Giles's Round-house, from which he broke out, and joining with Blueskin, robbed Mr. Barton; being committed, with Edgworth Bess, to the New Prison, he effected his escape with her by scaling the walls of the Clerkenwell Bridewell. This escape, he thinks, has been over estimated. He details his taking a stable at the Horseferry, Westminster, for a warehouse; describes his robbery of his benefactor, Mr. Kneebone, and relates the manner he was betrayed to Jonathan Wild by Field, the receiver; he narrates his condemnation through the perjury of Field, and speaks of the villany of Jonathan. He describes his extraordinary escapes from the Lodge and Castle-room in Newgate, and dwells upon his various wanderings; but as they are fully traced out in the novel, it would only be needless repetition to notice them further. He speaks disparagingly of Blueskin's courage, and says, only his cutting Jonathan Wild's throat could have made him so considerable. He censures the treachery of Edgworth Bess, and professes great contrition; but it is easy to perceive, such a thing as repentance was very far from his thoughts, and that, had he obtained the opportunity, he would have continued his career with even greater daring and diligence than before.

Of the genuineness of this confession there can be no doubt; our Abstract is from a rare copy in the British Museum, obtained through the courtesy of the Directors.

THE END.

www.ingramcontent.com/pod-product-compliance
Lightning Source LLC
Chambersburg PA
CBHW080944020726
47505CB00009B/2132